The Rain Men Series

Control the Weather – Control the World

Operation Seeding

Global Chaos

May Day Cometh

By

Michael J Andrisano Sr.

Table of Contents

Dedication

To my Wife and Family. To those who love to read and find themselves on an adventure.

Acknowledgment

To my Wife Mary and all her support over the years, it has been your ride as the driver. Thanks, Love.

About the Author

Michael is an award-winning author. Author of the Harold and Megan Adventure series. Harold the High Knight and Princess Megan – The Return – The Warlock – and soon to be released The Scottish Moors.

With two more in the Rain Man Series. Global Chaos: Control the Weather - Control the World, and a third book in the series - May Day Cometh.

Christianity, Karma, and Reincarnation: Book One in the God Our Father Series. Book two - The Story of a Boy and His Best Friend God. Outskirts Press published both.

An Argument for a Cure. Published by CSN Books, it is an award-winning book.

It rained in the spring of 1949 from lower Virginia to the Alabama Gulf Coast. Those who had heard the sirens were still alive. Those who fled the floodwaters born from once slow-flowing creeks were saved. Those who paid it no mind were now lost, or maybe alone on this night, praying to stay alive.

Rain, Rain, Go Away, Come Again Another Day

Josh sat in the Civil Defense's headquarters and had no idea as to what he would do next. Sitting there, he watched through his swollen and darkened eyes as the Red Cross volunteers continued to work around the clock, bringing in food and water. Things right now were insane to him and to all those who sat around him, staring blankly at the bare floor. They were wondering what life would be like when it all came to an end. It had been raining—torrential, miserable, cold, wet rain for the last four months. It seemed as though the rain would never end. He had already lost his house, his crops in the fields, and his livestock. He watched it all wash away one day, right before he was rescued. His mother and father are still listed as "Among the Missing." No one could figure out why God was punishing everyone.

Not more than a hundred miles north, four men were sitting in a comfortable office discussing how effective they had been in making it rain. With smiles visible on everyone's faces, they raised their glasses and toasted with a twenty-year-old scotch whisky. After the toast was made and the last drop drained from their glasses, one man turned to the others and spoke, "Gentlemen, I am so glad you have come to see the value of my needs. After this lovely rainy episode, I must surely get the full support of both the Senate and the Congress in making my promises come true."

A small-statured man, a senator from Tennessee, whose teeth were stained yellow from years of smoking his father's crops, said, "Yes, sir, we will have subsidies for the farmer, and it will start with the tobacco industry, by God, it will, and I have only to thank you, gentleman."

"My pleasure, Senator. It was our first real test, gentleman, and it has surpassed our greatest expectations, I would say." The speaker was the president and CEO of H.T. Wetco, a growing company, who had discovered a way to ensure that cloud seeding could be done with the right delivery system. One of their scientists, a young man named Beach, had made the discovery, and now they could take this all the way to the bank. This was what made the day so special and brought smiles to the faces of everyone in the room.

A Four-Star General sitting in the chair next to the window, taking all of this in, now stood and said, "If I may have your undivided attention, gentlemen. I have a question to ask. Currently, it has been raining cats and dogs for months. We have achieved our goal, and, of course, the military will buy the sole rights to this. But my question still needs to be asked, which is exactly how do we get it to stop?"

"Not a problem, General. Rest assured that we have already put that into motion as we sit here. It'll all be over in a few days. Next time they see rain, it will be when God provides it." This came from H.T. Wetco's chief operating officer, Ted Hammond.

After everything was said and done, and when the celebration came to an end, sitting alone in the same room they had just used for the celebration, General Margate turned and looked at Bob Thurston, the real head of H.T. Wetco, and said, "You know as well as I do, Bob, that what I am about to say cannot leave this room."

Turning to his left and looking directly at the General, Bob Thurston could almost read his mind. He knew what the General was on the verge of saying, and he wholeheartedly agreed with him. And as bad as others may think of this, he knew it was the only way to keep a secret as a secret.

The General, sensing this, said. "I can send a couple of good men down there to take care of it, and you take care of this on your end as well. We cannot afford ever to ruin a good thing now, can we, Bob?"

"No, you're right, General," said Thurston. "And I have a way of making that change as well."

They are both smiling now. Bob Thurston and General Margate loaded their glasses one more time. Hell, there was no sense in letting good scotch go to waste.

It Begins

Darkness was settling in over Gatlinburg, Tennessee. On cool nights like this, when the mists come undulating down off of the Smokey Mountains, you can't see ten feet in front of you.

"Maybe driving so fast wasn't the best thing to do," thought Boris. But running out of gas wasn't an option either. Right now, they needed gas, or the whole mission would be lost, and that was unacceptable. So, driving fast on this winding, dark road that disappears on every turn had to be done, and so far, Alex was handling this car like the expert he always claimed to be. The dusty old roads, you'd have thought someone would have taken the time to pave some of these back roads by now. After all, it is 1949.

However, the dirt and trailing dust cloud that the car created continued to follow them along the winding, often narrow, and bumpy path. It seemed like an eternity before they would see any sign of life. Then, going around another one of these endless blind corners, maybe salvation was at hand, for there was light in the middle of a field. After drawing closer, they could see it was a general store, and most of the places around sold gas. It looked abandoned, sitting there alone out in the middle of nowhere.

Shaking his head, Boris saw that not only weren't the roads paved, but by the shabby looks of most places they'd seen, maybe in this entire state, there was not a bucket of paint for sale. It looked as if everything around here was in dire need of some paint.

As the car pulled into the lane leading to the store, Boris continued in his silent personal lament on the unsightliness of the state. Especially this sad-looking place someone had the nerve to call a store. Even in darkness, one could see that the clapboards were gray and in disrepair.

Outside, a single stuttering clear bulb fought valiantly to remain lit above the gas pump. Its light was almost lost to the moths and bugs struggling with each other for the right to die against the burning glass. The only other light spilled out of an open front door, fighting back a darkness that seemed to paint the entire area black. No light, however, would ever escape from the dirty brown windows that appeared to have grown out of the sides of this shanty, like dark stains on an already-dirty shirt.

As the car pulled next to the pump, they both felt a sense of relief, knowing that they might yet make it to their destination that night, which eased the anxiety they had felt over the last few miles. Alex had forgotten to fill it right to the brim before they left Memphis. Boris now thought of all the things that could possibly go wrong, and one of them was running out of gas. He would take care of this "problem" later. As far as he was concerned, Alex was a waste. He was certain he could have done the job on his own. But right now, he needed to fix one problem at a time: first get gas, then directions, and then move on. He had a job to do that night, and not even Alex would get in his way.

Stepping out of the car and walking around to the driver's side, Boris said, "Fill it up. I'll go in and pay."

`As soon as Boris was clear of the door, Alex stepped out and started to stretch an aching back as he called out, "See if they have any candy, will you? I can use something sweet right now. So, get me a Coke, too."

Alex Brandt had just been recruited by a mutual friend to come to this flea-bitten state to help with a "special" job. Although he had no idea who Boris was, seeing how it had all happened so quickly, he readily agreed. He had been sought out, recruited, and well-paid solely to help eliminate someone who posed a potential threat to the country. It seems as if a certain person now living in Tennessee was a communist leader living here in secret. Alex knew this needed to be handled before this leader could influence the people in the area that the American government was ignorant of their needs and that Communism was the way of the future.

So, signing on for this job was easy, especially after seeing what had happened in Europe at the end of the war with those damn Russians. He had even killed a few Russians "accidentally" because of the way they tried to rape and kill innocent Germans at the time of war. Killing Communists and Germans during the war was easy for him. Now, this lousy bastard living in Tennessee, of all places, will become just another number to his list. Suddenly, his thoughts were shattered as a shot rang out, breaking the soft hum of the fluorescent lights that had been present.

The night cries of the crickets went silent as well, and the air became full of electricity as Alex's nerves wanted to burst through his skin. He knew immediately that the sudden lack of noise just served to enhance his awareness of his surroundings. Alex killed people for a living now, and that was why he was here tonight in this backward place. Quickly crouching down, he scanned the area for any signs of someone who would come running to the shanty to see what had just happened. Then, just as suddenly as it had started, it ended. He could hear the chirping once more of field crickets, and the eerie hum once again filled his ears.

"Alex! Alex!" Boris whispered loudly, "Get in here now!"

Getting up from his spot behind the car, Alex walked to the front steps leading up into the shanty, and in two short leaps, he was at the front door. Peering inside, a smile crossed his face, followed by a chuckle. Dead on the floor was a man about forty years old, as if he were fast asleep. A pool of blood was now forming around his still body. The blood seemed to be extremely bright red, brighter than normal, he thought. Then, it dawned on him that it seemed brighter against this ugly, dirt floor.

Laughing out loud, Alex said, "What the hell, man? Why'd ya shoot the guy?"

Giving Alex a stern look, Boris replied, "I had to look at a map to see where the hell we are! I had to find out if we were anywhere close to where we had to be. Damn it all, it turns out we're miles away from our target! We missed our turn about three miles back." Now pointing at the man lying there, he continued, "The jackass here said the sign must be down again. So, after he told me the way to go, I had to make sure this hillbilly didn't remember me asking for directions. Besides, he had no change for my twenty, and all I had was my twenties. Take the soda, get me one as well, and grab some food. I'll drive the car now, so hurry up, and let's get the hell out of here."

Turning, Boris walked out the front door, leaving it wide open, as light once again spilled across wooden steps leading to the dirt at its bottom, showing the warped gray-stained wooden steps that would need repairs soon before they collapsed, as would the rest of this pile of scrap wood, he thought.

Finding the house had been easy enough once they saw the dirt road that led off the main road. Boris couldn't wait to get out of this state. Turning off the lights and the car's engine to slow it down, the car crawled to a stop in the driveway that led down to the cabin.

Creeping up to the side of the cabin, Boris couldn't hear any noise coming from inside. It was now three-thirty in the morning, and the job, for all intents and purposes, should have been done long ago. But that idiot had missed a turn, and they almost had run out of gas. So here he was at this ungodly hour, looking for a way in before the Senator would wake up to take his nightly piss.

The window slid open easily as Boris stepped over the sill and leaped into the room. Closing the window, Boris walked over to the front door and opened it for Alex. Silently in the darkness, Boris and Alex crept down the hall. What should not happen now is to knock something off one of the many tables that lined the hall. Locating the back bedroom on the first floor, they each knew that it was the critical time for what they came to do, and it had to be done quickly and quietly by opening the door, walking to the sides of the bed, doing the job in unison, and then getting the hell out of there.

As planned, they were barefoot as they quietly crept to the bed. Alex to the left side and Boris to the right, already in their hands, was a tool of their trade: a choking wire made of steel. It looked like a piece of barbed wire wrapped between hard rubber handles. As the spikes would go into their fleshy throats, only a gargle would escape, never giving one a chance to yell out and warn the other. Stopping in their places, they nodded to each other and then pressed the coated bracelets straight down. With each man weighing over two hundred pounds, both men easily used their body weight to help provide extra leverage and pressure.

Silently, they killed the Senator and his unfortunate girlfriend. The young woman, now lying there, dying under the pressure applied to her neck, was in shock as she stared up at a smiling Alex. "She couldn't have been older than twenty-five. Wow, what a beauty," he thought. Then, just as fast, his thoughts turned to the fun he had missed out on by killing her so quickly, thinking maybe next time he should look first.

Boris had already made up his mind as to what would happen next.

As Alex walked by him to get their shoes, Boris reached out and, wrapping his left arm around Alex's neck, put the dagger deep into his side. Turning and twisting the blade, it went right up and into the heart. That was when Boris made a slashing move. It was a move to make sure that when Alex hit the floor, he would be dead.

As if on cue, Alex slumped and fell to the floor, thinking he should have known better. Next, Boris would lay the naked bodies out so that when they were found charred, it would look as if they had a great time together before the fire had taken their lives. He never knew that dead people could weigh so damn much. Oh, he had his share of killing people, but Boris couldn't remember having to set them up as puppets. "This was like work," he thought.

Boris knew that there wasn't much time left before daybreak would rise over these hills. With local people moving about, someone was bound to spot the fire, even if the cabin was set well back on yet another dirt road in these woods. Pouring pine pitch around the bedroom, throughout the hall, and back into the kitchen, Boris lit the candles and threw them into the bedroom.

"Goodbye, Alex. Have a great time in hell." With that said, a chuckling yet exhausted Boris walked out the front door.

The drive back to Washington, DC, would be long, but if he got a room somewhere outside Memphis, he should be well rested when he goes to get the rest of his cash.

1953: The Korean Decision

Major General Margate, Admiral Haines, and Air Force Lieutenant General Folsom all sat comfortably in the coziness of the warm officers' café, overlooking the airfield in Osan, Korea, as the project known as "Hailstorm" was in its final preparation.

H.T. Wetco's improvement on the delivery system of their Seeding project will be used in combat today. As they continued to sit and look down, each knew the importance of the cargo now being loaded into the B-29 that stood ready to take flight. Its mission was top secret and commissioned by no other than the United States President himself.

Truman, seemingly, was showing a lot more guts since his last edict to drop a bomb. However, this was a crucial mission in the war. If this worked as professed, it would become a weapon of great importance to the American troops on the ground who fought for every inch of foreign turf in these newly formed police actions. Now that the Chinese have entered the war on the North's side, this weapon could become a stabilizer. Especially with the damn Russians, who seemingly controlled the air at first, but were now in a complete rout with the fight the F-86 Sabre was bringing to the MiG 15s. With that type of air support, this should be a walk in the park for the big B-29 Super fortress that was now gunning down the runway to take flight like a giant albatross taking wings early in the dawning of a crisp new day.

General Margate, turning to his company, began, "Gentlemen, it's awfully hard to travel in the winter, up north, when conditions are normal. If this newly functional means of making it snow works, then for every mile they advance on our troops, it'll cost them dearly. And we will have enough time to make our positions a helluva lot stronger. It would seem that the tactics are slowly evolving into trench warfare, and in this place, it means a very harsh winter for anyone not prepared for it. And very soon, it will become a lot harder for anyone who is not ready. I'm predicting an early snow that will close many of the mountain passes, or that's at least what we are hoping for."

"Well, General, exactly how does this newly designed weapon work?" asked Admiral Haines. Haines was not a part of the upper echelon in Washington, not a member of the Joint Chiefs of Staff, as was Generals Margate and Folsom, both here today to witness the event. Folsom was to report directly to Washington, and then to the President, after the early snow began to fall and stick to the ground.

It was September in Korea, and soon, in this region, the snow would prevail anyway, and that would slow all ground troops from gaining any ground in this war. The B-29 that had just departed belonged to the men of the Twenty-Second Bombardment Wing, once stationed in Okinawa to fight this war. Just recently, they had been reassigned back to England for a much-needed rest. Just long enough to pick up better B-47s until the B-52 bombers would become available to the Air Force. Unknowingly to them, if this project were to work today with great success, their future would be tied to this secret for years to come.

"Well, Admiral, let us say that if we needed to make it rain or snow to prevent an army from engaging our troops in combat, we could have that capability after today's test. Imagine what strength we would have on the battlefield. We could clear skies for our air forces, we could create fog for our ships, and certainly, if we knew the weather in advance, we could prepare to help our ground troops a lot easier, quicker, and without delay," finished General Folsom.

"Now let me get this straight. I'm here to watch it snow at the hands of what is inside that massive airplane that just took off seconds ago," said Admiral Haines.

General Margate nodded at Folsom, who began. "Admiral, we need your field support. You're in charge of naval operations here in the Pacific Rim, and we need you to validate the entire event, if necessary, in the future. All we ask is that when we get the go-ahead on this project, you support us one hundred percent. Personally, I don't care how I kill the bastards. Should a truck overturn or a tank or, damn it, have all of them fall into a ravine on the way to fight my boys, I don't care. Whatever I have to do to make it easier for our men, I'll do. And this development surely has the potential to make some men hopefully lose the will to fight, for it is so damn cold. Or, hell, with any real luck, they'll freeze to death somewhere out there. If I can trap their logistical support in heavy snow while I bomb the blazes out of 'em, who cares? Surely not me," finished the General as he summoned a young waiter to pour him more coffee.

"You know, Admiral, he's right. Whatever we have to do to make it better for our side, I am ready to forego any idea that there isn't some kind of righteousness in this whole affair," added Margate.

"Hell, if we could drown them all in the rain, why not? And if my boys can drop a bomb into the clouds and make it snow, then so be it. Lives, Admiral, American lives are at stake here, and that's why Tru. I mean, the President made this decision. Hell, he bombed the shit out of the Japanese to prevent a lot of losses of American and Allied lives. With so many damn Chinese out there, what the hell are a few less going to hurt the world?"

With that, Admiral Haines smiled at them both and pointed down to his cup to summon the waiter again. He said, "Fill it up, son. I think it's gonna be a long day and even longer night."

Vietnam, 1969

Retired Army General Margate sat sipping a cold glass of water as he sat comfortably outside the Majestic Hotel in Saigon on Dong Khoi Street, waiting for his friend Bob Thurston, CEO of H.T. Wetco, to arrive downstairs. Rattling the ice around in his glass, he couldn't help but notice two things taking place here. The first was the number of good-looking young women walking around with ear-to-ear smiles. He'll have to do something about that a little later in the week, he thought. Second was the amount of activity going on here in a city that was often considered a deadly place. A city where, every often, an explosion could be heard, or sporadic gunshots would ring out in the middle of the day.

Yet, that stopped nothing in the day-to-day activities of those who made a living from war. The place was bustling with Americans, Russians, and people from all over the world who seemed to have gathered in these areas. These are seemingly magnificent places to somewhere one could walk along the edge of death, just out of reach but close enough on some days to smell the stench and see the misery that it brings. But here, sitting in this oversized wicker-styled chair, Margate was just as comfortable as if he were sitting on the front porch of a hotel in New England. This place could have passed for any number of grand hotels in America, located somewhere near a military post.

There were hawkers of weapons, news, and information, as well as governments dressed in white or light blue, with vertical, darker blue-striped seersucker suits. Some are dressed in bright yellow leisure suits, while others wear loafers without socks, light brown khaki shorts, sneakers, and madras-colored shirts unbuttoned at the collar. It was as if this was a weekend trip to a hotel spa instead of a war zone in the middle of Asia, as they pretended to know important people, dropping names as if they actually meant something.

"Deep in thought, are you, or can I interrupt?" asked Bob Thurston, friend-confidant and newly formed partner of a country club outside of Washington, DC.

"No, sit and relax. Have a scotch. I was waiting for you before I could enjoy one myself," said Margate.

"So, when do we meet with General Scott?" asked Bob.

"He's on his way over here now. I assume that would be him pulling up now." Waving a hand in the air and standing up to get the attention of the man in the white suit exiting a sleek town car. The man looked up, waved back, smiled, and bent over to talk to the driver. After several seconds, the car pulled away, and the man turned and walked up the stairs with another younger man in town. This one had been standing at the side of the stairs leading to the upper porch deck and had been out of sight of both Bob and Margate.

As the two men approached the table, Margate stood and extended his right hand. First, shaking the older gentleman's extended hand, he said, "Glen, it's great to see you again."

"You too, General, it's been, what, two years now?" replied Major General Glen Scott.

Then, extending his hand again and shaking the other's hand, he said, "Mr. Dobbes, how are you? It's great to see you, as well, sir." Pointing to two empty seats, he said, "Please, gentlemen, sit, and we can get some refreshments and some food when we get hungry."

Everyone knew each other. General Scott headed up a secret covert operation called EnMod, short for Environmental Modification, for the U.S. Army Strategic Defense Systems. Mr. Dobbes was his CIA counterpart; his sole purpose in life was not only how the EnMod group affected countries at war with the United States, but also in the Cold War. The ability to make life miserable for one's foes by making it rain or snow or by creating a drought excited a lot of people back in Washington.

Now, everyone at the table was also acutely aware of the fact that the U.S. Senate now had a Bill before it that, if passed, would add another 150 million dollars into the coffers, legally. Seeing how right now their budget was unlimited, thanks to the CIA, this was both good and bad news.

Should this knowledge ever see the light of day, it would be possible that another company or two would decide to get in on the action that, so far, was reserved only for Bob Thurston's company, H.T. Wetco. But right now, they were here to view the end results of having had it rain for another fifty days past the monsoon season. Troops on both sides were unable to do anything other than try to find relief from the pouring rain. However, the Ho Chi Minh Trail was littered with bodies buried under mudslides, which was the reason for this celebration.

Much like the snow in Korea, which found hundreds of dead Chinese buried under avalanches and snowdrifts, death also came to Americans, but frozen from being ill-equipped. Also, the ensuing mudslides during the thaw claimed hundreds of lives, as well. "But, what the hell?" thought Thurston. "After all, they're only Chinese. Who could possibly miss one?"

But Vietnam was just as bad. The "tunnels" where the Cong lived, ate, and hid flooded as massive rains took the lives of those who were too weak or injured or too slow to move. Thurston was feeling great about his product, and he couldn't afford the U.S. Senate to get involved, that's for sure.

"So, was the final outcome tallied?" asked Bob. "Would love to know some kind of a final figure of how many we sent to see Buddha." "So far, Intelligence has put the figure around eighty-seven hundred, not counting civilians," replied Mr. Dobbes. "Really?" quipped Margate with a smile on his face. "Great number. Imagine the dollar savings of nine thousand rounds of ammunition or mortars not spent on killing the little bastards."

"Now, now, General. They do have a lot of value and are peaceniks at heart, according to some of these Hollywood starlets," chimed in Scott, with a smile playing across his face.

"Look, I couldn't care less about these places: Korea, Vietnam, Cambodia, Laos, China, Russia, wherever else we have been," said Bob. "Right now, all I care about is where we go next and if the Senate is going to approve the Bill?"

Almost as one, everyone seated turned to look at Mr. Dobbes, waiting for his response. One thing about the CIA right now is that it was the running arm of the U.S. Government's covert and secret war department. And make no mistake about it, they had a hand in everything.

"I have it on good authority that by next year, it'll get approval," said Mr. Dobbes. "I can see that about 170 million dollars will be put into your coffers by the end of next year. This will also mean that we will have business in Africa and South America. We need to do some things differently in the years to come, gentlemen. When the U.N. gets wind of this, well, believe me, the other countries will be screaming for our heads. It probably means within two years, we go "black" to leave no footprints. There is no way we can afford to lose control of this program. Screw what the world thinks. This program is just too damn important for us," he finished, waving over to a boy standing by to wait for their table, a table that was well-secluded and well out of range for anyone to hear what was said.

Earlier, Mr. Dobbes had the area "swept clean," and he and several of his men made sure that it stayed that way. Even now, his men made up a third of the people out on the veranda, sipping some kind of beverage on this hot day. Power, he loved it almost as much as Bob did. However, even he had to admit Bob was a one-of-a-kind maniac to power, money, and that damn company of his.

Reagan

Bob Thurston slammed his fist hard on the table, shaking it to the point of knocking over a clear water container and several glasses. The mess was everywhere immediately, prompting Pete Winslow to get up rapidly to wipe some water off his trousers. "I don't give a rat's ass about what the man thinks. I was out fighting communists when he was making damn movies with a monkey!" yelled Bob once again. "Meeting adjourned, except for you, Pete. I want you to stay. I need to get something straight in my head right now, and I need to talk to you about it."

Leaving the room was Todd Thurston, grandson of Bob and future heir to the throne. Along with him leaving was Dr. Joseph Fineman, the chief of operations, and Doug Peele, the company's treasurer, who had just informed Bob, in an otherwise easy Monday morning meeting, about a rumor he had heard from some friends on Capitol Hill. One said the United States' current president, Ronald Reagan, was considering starting a High-frequency Active Aurora Research Program (HAARP). Although this was not a major consequence, the project would be managed by a joint U.S. Air Force and Navy committee, with funding provided from the Department of Defense's budget.

Doug's internal memo was given privately and stated, "The heart of the program will be in the development of a unique ionosphere heating capability and to conduct pioneering experiments required to adequately assess the potential for exploiting ionosphere enhancement technology for DOD purposes."

When Bob first saw the memo, he was not concerned until he found out that it suggested under a new follow-up discussion held with their scientists that this would be used to 'heat the ionosphere, and future advances would be to manipulate and control the weather and climate, including the destructive use of ocean waves, creating tsunamis. This technology could also be used for the melting or the destabilizing of the polar ice caps, intentional ozone depletion, triggering earthquakes, and control of the human brain by utilizing the earth's energy fields.' Bob had had enough when he slammed his balled fist onto the table and dismissed everyone but Pete Winslow.

"Pete, I have to ask you a very important question, son. I need to know your allegiance. Is it to Margate or me," said Thurston, standing directly over Pete as his eyes seemed to bore a hole in him.

"Why, to you, sir," replied Pete. "General Margate does not need my services, and I have always thought of you and this company as my home these past four years. The military has no real place for me, why I gave it up to come to work for the General and now you, sir."

"Pete, I need to send a message to someone very high up, very high up. Let's say the top man. Do you have anyone we can trust to do a job like that, send a message, and when all hell breaks loose, and it will, mind you, he can handle it? Or we can make it all go away?" said Bob in a very calm tone so that only he and Pete now knew what was being said this day, this moment.

Looking up at Bob, Pete replied in a quiet voice. "Sure, sir, I don't see this as a problem, at least one that we can't make go away, concerning all parties, of course."

"Of course," said Bob. "Here is our dilemma, Pete; I need this "ac- tor" to get a message. I need him to see that he is not invincible and that there are controlling forces that must remain in control. We can't have some dumb-ass private controlling the weather from someplace in the bowels of a government building in Hoppog, Virginia. Hell, I - we have been doing this country's dirty work for fifty years, and now we're to step aside. Hell no, I say, hell no!" lamented Bob. Then, in a very low voice, he said, "I want this to be nothing that anyone, not anyone, can bring back to my doorstep, understood?"

Looking at Bob, Pete now knew that he had to make the biggest life decision. This was not something that one took on and survived, at least not for long, they didn't. But he wanted this badly. He wanted so much to be a part of something this big. Something this powerful!

So, without any further thought, he said, "Consider it done, Mr. Thurston."

"No, Pete, call me Bob, and when it's done, take our jet to any place in the world. Stay a while and have a good time, and make sure you don't spend a dime of your own having fun," said a smiling Bob Thurston as he walked away.

Pete knew of a young man whom he had working for him on and off, doing little odds and ends. "A real whack job," thought Pete, but useful nonetheless. He could plead insane after he did it, with the promise that the company would make sure that he would be a free man later. Pete flew to Los Angeles that very night and a meeting was set up to ensure his potential prize knew what would be in store for him.

Associated Press published the following on March 31, 1981:

The family of the man charged with trying to assassinate President Reagan is acquainted with the family of Vice President George Bush and had made large contributions to his political campaign . . . Scott

Hinckley, brother of John W. Hinckley, Jr., was to have dined tonight in Denver at the home of Neil Bush, one of the Vice President's sons . . . The *Houston Post* said it could not reach Scott Hinckley, vice president of his father's Denver-based firm, Vanderbilt Energy Corporation, for comment.

Bob woke to the morning paper and read about the incident in Washington and smiled as he called into the office on his speaker phone,

"Gene, please get me a nice breakfast this morning. I feel like having a couple of eggs, some nice buttered toast, and my usual coffee. Oh yes, and get something for yourself so I don't eat alone. I would like to celebrate by having a nice relaxing morning, so cancel everything until this afternoon. I don't want to take the smile off of my face just yet."

Star Wars

On March 23, 1983, President Ronald Reagan called upon "the scientific community in our country, those who gave us nuclear weapons, to turn their great talents now to the cause of mankind and world peace, to give us the means of rendering these nuclear weapons impotent and obsolete."

This quest was officially named the Strategic Defense Initiative (SDI). The press dubbed it *Star Wars.*

Unbeknownst to Bob and his engineers at H.T. Wetco, the Department of Defense will begin construction on the HAARP-IRI in earnest in 1990. It will become a field of antennas living on the ground in Southeastern Alaska.

In August 2002, The Russian State Duma, or Congress, expressed major concern about HAARP by filing complaints at the United Nations and the U.S. State Department.

The State Duma's International Affairs and the Defense committees will issue a joint report that will say, "Under the High-Frequency Active Auroral Research Program (HAARP), the USA is creating new integral geophysical weapons that may influence the near-Earth medium with high-frequency radio waves. The significance of this qualitative leap could be compared to the transition from cold steel to firearms or conventional weapons to nuclear weapons. This new type of weapon differs from previous types in that the near-Earth medium becomes an object of direct influence and its component at once."

BusinessWeek will also report, "China's future will see at least 35,000 people engaged in weather management, and it will spend upwards of $40 million a year on alleviating droughts or stemming hail that would damage crops." Droughts have ravaged Downwind of China, North Korea for over a decade.

China will make it rain in Beijing to clear the air for foreign visitors and remove pollutants, showing the world how clean Beijing is without its usual daily smog.

Bob sat back and read more news concerning what he always thought of as an excuse by Reagan to silently get America back to work. Secretly increasing government spending with more secretive government work. "Oh well, "he thought. "At least my product is still being used. Not only by this government but by governments around the world. Who the hell can afford radio equipment? Most poor countries can't afford to feed their hungry people."

Bob had no pity, far from it, and he knew his company was behind what China and Russia were doing to their neighbors with rain, and he couldn't care less. Now that the backward camel jockeys had a lot of oil money despite being great-paying customers, he reflected on himself. Retired now, he often reflected on how it was and could have been if he still had the only product available in the world. But in a sense, he did. After all, didn't Todd just receive a 200-million-dollar payment for their company's Global Impact Heat and Restoration of Climate Exchanges project?

Whatever the hell that meant! Smiling, Bob sat back and waited for his only appointment for today before he could get to the club and kick back a few with his best friend, General Margate. Speaking over the intercom, he asked Gene if the Senator (what's his name?) was still on for today.

Grandpa Frank, the Rainmaker

"Claire! Claire!" yelled Frank. "Where are you?"

"Right here, Frank, relax. I'm right next to the bed, sitting here reading quietly. What's the matter?"

"Nothing, I just didn't hear you, is all. How long did I fall asleep this time?"

"Not too long. I'd say you slept for a good hour or so. Do you feel any better now?" asked Claire.

Frank and Claire had just celebrated their fifty-fifth wedding anniversary last year. "Too long with the same woman," Frank declared that day. "I should have had twenty by now." Then, looking at Claire, his wife for these many years, he just smiled and said, "But none of them would have been my Claire, and without her, we wouldn't be here right now celebrating this day, would we? Over the years, many women looked at me with that look in their eyes, but none excited me as your grandmother did. None of them, well, maybe one did, but I never looked back."

Now, everyone was laughing at Grandpa Frank, as everyone knew that his love for his wife always had been the focus of his life. Every day, it seemed Grandpa Frank would catch someone and have to listen to him talk about the secret to a long marriage.

Laughingly, he would say, "You have to ignore your wife, let her talk your ears off, and get what she wants and have it her way, or let her at least think that was happening and then do it your way. Never get caught, mind you, because then the argument would begin. Well, let her win that, and then get back to your business. Eventually, you get too old to argue, and she just complains about you having it all your way, and then after a while, it's back to all smiles and grandchildren and more smiles. After all, you both have been down too many miles together, and there's no turning back at that point."

On that anniversary day, everyone brought gifts, and the weather was fine, with a bright Virginia sun shining down on them. As the heat seemed to turn up as the day wore on and the humidity grew heavier, Grandpa Frank suddenly fell out of his chair. It wasn't as if anyone was around him watching over him and crowding him; only little Campbell and Michael were there, his great-grandchildren, sitting on the ground in front of him playing. Perhaps that was also an accident, considering the twins were only two years old. Grandpa did like the fact that they never cried around him. So, their father, Peter, would leave the kids by him to keep them quiet. But now Michael was crying because Grandpa Frank was lying beside him and not moving.

"Frank, are you okay?" asked Claire once again.

"Yes, dear, just thinking about the day it all happened so suddenly. I'm watching the children, and then I don't remember anything but waking up in my bed. Then, being told that I had just come in from the hospital after having suffered a stroke. I can't talk that well anymore, and I'm as blind as a bat. Claire, I tell you, I sometimes wish I were dead. Not being able to see your face anymore or the children's. I lie here and wonder what happened. How could this have happened to me? I exercised all those years; we ate well, I never smoked, had an easy job. I was a scientist and knew what was going on in the heavens by Jesus. I made it rain when no one else could. I wasn't some Indian dancing in the fields or a man with a tambourine screaming to God. I was the one who made it rain, by God, and now

I'm lying here in bed, blind, and can't remember a damn thing about it. Frustrated? You bet I am. I wish I were dead!"

"Stop it, Frank! Or, by God, I'll leave and go to Susan's. No more of that silly death talk. You scare me with that nonsense. Do you hear me, Frank? I won't tolerate it. Everything is going to be fine. Dr. Sabian said that you will likely regain your sight. You suffered a stroke, and you went into a coma, but you're alive, and that's what counts. Quit thinking of only yourself and think of me just this once. Think of the kids and all those who love you. This talk of self-pity is not you, Frank, and I won't stand for it. Do I make myself clear to you?" Claire seldom raised her voice at Frank, but she had to make it clear to Frank that living is worth it, no matter what the facts were.

Only the living could make changes. The dead didn't have a reason to. Frank smiled to himself, not knowing if Claire was watching. Claire would understand his smile after all. No one on the planet knew Frank as she did. So, lying there in comfort and not wanting to make himself an ass again, Frank once more drifted off to sleep. Only this time, a deep sleep found him snoring, to Claire's dissatisfaction, but one that said Frank was getting some much-needed rest as the doctor had ordered. So, for now, Claire would gladly put up with his snoring.

Dreaming, Frank found himself back in time, alone, and the only one to admit that what he was proposing was science, real science, not that damn science fiction stuff that Aubry Adleson was proposing. His was real science; it was. But Adleson had the whole group convinced that he wasn't right for the job to begin with, all because Frank was new to the company and younger than that old fart. But damn it, I was right; if I was anything here, I was right that it would work by God! After all, I had researched this and done my homework for almost the past two years. So, what if I was new to this section of the company? They would not have sent me to this research side and told me to head up this project if they didn't think I could handle it.

This afternoon's meeting was going to be a full-on confrontation. I need the ten thousand dollars in seed money. This would be costly for the company, but I will acquire it and put it at the forefront of new discoveries. Hell, I'm not God, but I run a close second. I can make it rain. I'll make more rain than God if I have to just prove that Adleson is wrong.

The head of the Department of Science and the rest of the company's big shots would attend the meeting that afternoon. Everyone wanted to know exactly how this could work, and he knew they all wanted to say they were there when the first decision to proceed with this project was made.

Later, if Frank were to win any science prize for his discovery, that would be a big feather in his cap. That would really aggravate Adleson. But right now, he needed total acceptance of his science. Then, any accolades from anyone but Adleson might be welcomed. But this was a project beyond the normal. Ultimately, if they understood and came to believe in this project, the world would be better off. He would alter weather patterns and jet streams, causing climate changes worldwide. All from the greatness of his science, no longer would there be droughts anywhere in the world.

Only five years had passed since the United States had dropped the big bombs on Japan. But in doing so, it had saved the lives of a lot of young American and Allied men. Those young men are alive today thanks to a hard decision that President Truman made. Difficult, yes! Yet, the right decision was so desperately needed in those dark, desperate years. But this bomb would be different if you could call it that. This is one for peace and prosperity, one that will help millions of people stop going hungry. His bomb was going to make it rain. "I'm going to seed the clouds and make those clouds give up their soul." Frank thought.

"Right here in the United States, we were suffering from drought. In our Midwestern states, farms, and industry were dying from the lack of rain and water for crops. It all faded to dust bowls, as it had years earlier. In many countries worldwide, people were starving due to prolonged droughts. Droughts that make people beggars, droughts bad enough to have starved little children until they died from malnutrition, no, my work is for peace and prosperity. Soon, the world would know my name."

So, going into this meeting was easy. Frank was certain that his method would work. Sure, the end results would be exactly as he claimed. A miracle from man's science and a gift to mankind, and Frank was the delivery boy. Opening a side door, Frank looked in and saw that everyone was waiting patiently in anticipation of his entry and his first and final explanation of his project.

Clearing his voice for effect and looking around as he stood by the door, he felt naked, framed against the starkness of the green colors on the wall and the glare from the fluorescent lamps burning in the hanging fixtures. Frank, with all eyes on him, started for the podium. As he journeyed forward, looking at some of the people in the room, he couldn't help but notice most of his colleagues, fellow scientists, who watched him make the journey with smiles and well wishes plastered over their faces.

They all knew that this would be great for the company. For most here, it also meant more government work in their future. Some of the old timers, though, stared at him with blank expressions on their faces, like vultures waiting for him to fall flat on his ass. As Frank came closer to the front, he could not help but notice that there were more military officers than scientists sitting where his team should be. He knew the military wanted in on this now that the war was finally over and the world seemed to be settling down.

This would also create a great propaganda message for the United States. Especially in the Middle Eastern areas and the North African regions where those countries were war-ravaged, and more often than not, water was scarce. As Frank finally finished his triumphant walk, he reached the front of the room, and a hush fell over the sixty or so people gathered, all to hear him talk about exactly what he had to say about his project.

"Operation Seeding."

Again, clearing his throat and ensuring he would get everyone's attention, Frank nodded to no one in particular to let them know that he was ready to begin. He looked out at the first couple of rows. Staring at him were all of the presidents and vice presidents of the company, past and present. Frank knew he had to start immediately before they could become restless; he needed to ensure his control. Frank would need to make this go off right. The company needed this project to be funded, and the project needed to be acclaimed, as it should be. Now, with all eyes on him, he knew everyone would listen to every word he said that day. Later, there would be time for questions and plenty of skeptical ones for sure. He was certain of that. Right now, he was in charge; he was "The Man".

He was going to change the world as everyone knew it, and with that running through his head, Frank began.

"Good afternoon, gentlemen. I am going to pass out a brochure and a small booklet concerning the project, 'Project Code Name Is Operation Seeding.' You all know the company policy states that no one leaves the auditorium with company documents undeclared for public scrutiny. They will be collected at the end of this presentation, and please remember, hand them back in without any notes written on them."

You could hear a couple of giggles coming from the back. "They are the property of this company and cannot be made public until the company relinquishes these findings to the general public. Oh, by the way, our bosses are here today sitting upfront, so if you have any complaints, please see them at the end of the program." Frank added that in retaliation for the clowns who snickered in the back. With that said and a large smile, he leaned to the side of the podium to acknowledge those officers in attendance. For that, he received a few laughs and many smiles.

"Now, along with the brochures and booklets, we will be watching a movie clip of what has occurred in the lab and our field trial. Our one and only test flight in the field will, without a doubt, make some disbelievers into believers." Now moving to the center of the room was Don Jennings, who was both a friend and a colleague of Frank's, to help with running the projection machine. "I would ask that you please hold off any questions until we review the information now being handed out to you and after the movie itself. Thank you."

Don Jennings and a few team members started handing out the booklets. Then, backing off and asking that the lights be turned off,

Frank continued talking in the darkened room with the whirling sound of the projector starting to rise above his voice level.

"Gentlemen, we all know that 'seeding' clouds have been something that has been a hit-or-miss situation since the end of the war. Up until now, various degrees and differences in opinions have caused "seeding" to become almost a nonissue, under the belief that it is uncontrollable and unsafe. The use of NFPA 704 rating of Blue 2, silver oxide, can cause temporary incapacitation or result in a possible residual injury from making chloroform, especially with intense or continued exposure.

Past accidents have been harmful to people living below the seeded cloud cover. To prevent these accidents, I felt we could look into a better delivery system to expose the clouds with a concentration of dry ice or frozen carbon dioxide in a more sustained and influential pattern. Due to the expansion of liquid propane into a gas, our experiments led us to also produce ice crystals at warmer temperatures than those produced by silver iodide. Hygroscopic materials, such as salt, will allow us more effective control. If you will, a more precise downpour of the water we all seek. My experiments have led me to findings that prove we can also use honey, glycerin, ethanol, concentrated methane, iodine, methamphetamine, or sulfuric acid. These deliquescent materials or substances are mostly salts. These salts have a strong affinity for moisture and will absorb relatively large amounts of water.

Thus, if the atmosphere of water is exposed, it forms a liquid solution, meaning these liquescent salts create rain. After careful evaluation and additional testing, I have added these solutions to include calcium, magnesium, and zinc chloride.

So, I cannot only make it rain but make it rain acid, the kind you don't want falling on your land or crops. I can alter the rain that falls in any area and make it so that the composite materials in the ground, trees and plants, and basic substances, such as food crops, can become too detrimental for anyone to eat or use. Although I understand that this was and is not the purpose of my work on this project, it comes from the outgrowth of my experiments. The sole purpose of this project has always been to make rain and only good, clean, cold rain to feed these crops.

Where Mother Nature may have failed you, I won't. If you would be kind enough to go to the next booklet, you will see the testing results of compound mixing. Because of these results, the amount of a particular material or compound can be and is affected by the ambient moisture in it. So, it will now be considered as the coefficient of hygroscopic expansion CHE, which I will also refer to now as CME, the coefficient of moisture expansion, or the coefficient of hygroscopic contraction known as CHC. You must now understand that the differences between the two terms are a matter of sign convention. Or, just a difference in point of view to whether this indifference can be found in the moisture that leads to contraction or expansion."

Suddenly rising to his feet was the company's chief operations officer, Ted Hammond. All heads turned, eyes focused on the figure walking toward the podium. Frank was now signaling for attention, asking for the lights to be turned back on. This, of course, caused an immediate transient blindness of everyone.

Hammond said, "Excuse me, Doctor. Are you saying we can make it rain whenever and wherever we want? We can make it rain poison if we care to?" Hammond sounded frightened at this point.

Frank was surprised. His first thought was, there goes the question-and-answer period.

Getting back to reality, he looked at his boss and said, "Yes, sir, Mr. Hammond."

Hammond now turned and walked over to the company's CEO, Bob Thurston, leaning forward, quietly exchanging a few words. Again, Hammond faced Frank and said, "Please wait a moment while I discuss something with Mr. Thurston."

After what seemed like a long private discussion between the two of them, Mr. Hammond turned to the audience and said, "Would all of you please leave? Also, Mr. Adleson, would you please ensure that no one leaves with any of the information we have handed out? Gentlemen, please leave all materials on your seats. Thank you. Now, please wait outside, and we will let you know when our meeting will be reopened. Thank you so much, and I would ask that Generals Jackson and Margate please wait here. Frank, you stay as well. We have further questions to ask you."

With that, the place started to clear out as quickly as if the fire alarm had sounded. Everyone began exiting as if the last one to leave would lose their job. This project would become a non-issue and would be turned over to the military, but whatever was to take place in that meeting, every person was glad they were not in there.

Alone now, the five of them sat waiting for Hammond to speak.

"Gentlemen, I think we have a problem. I can see that this project could become a Pandora's Box. For shit's sake, Frank, why the hell didn't you come to us first before you decided to put on this dog-and-pony show of yours? Damn it, this is sensitive material here, and your telling the world that you can make it rain is one thing.

Frank, you must have known the damage that sharing could cause, such as acid or liquid fire, besides water. It's just irresponsible, damn it! I spent the best years of my life fighting Nazis and all of the foolishness they wanted to bring into this world. Now someone in my company is capable of this bullshit!" Mr. Hammond's voice was at an octave; anyone outside in the hallway would hear.

That tone, if not the message, was reason enough for everyone eavesdropping to escape from there as fast as their legs could carry them away. A loud and angry Ted Hammond was something that all employees in this company feared.

Hammond turned and, facing Bob Thurston, asked, "Bob, are you aware of this and the project's scope? Did you sanction this?"

Standing up and facing Hammond, Bob said, "Now listen, Ted, no one is going to make it rain acid on anyone, not on my watch. However, this company can use the money that it could bring in. When did we become so uppity here? Sure, Frank may have been wrong in exposing this to everyone, but it's done now. And we can still reap the benefits of it. Even if the rest of the world can never know exactly what it is we have here."

"Wait a minute, Bob. Why would you involve us in this conversation unless you had something in it for us? Exactly what are you thinking here?" asked General Margate.

General Jackson began to speak and slowly relinquished the floor to hear the answer General Margate would receive.

"We can share this information with our military, at a cost, of course, but share it. After all, we have a significant amount of money invested in this, and you have a substantial amount of money to spend. That is why you're here today, isn't it, gentlemen? Besides, Margate, you owe me. We did serve together, and what we have been through together is the reason why I brought you in here today to specifically help you get another star," Bob finished, looking at General Jackson.

"Let's not go there, you two, enough said," said General Jackson, a longtime personal friend of both of them. "Just how much are we to pay for this information? And, of course, we have to verify it as well and have it tested and working to our complete satisfaction."

"Oh," said Ted Hammond, "I think we can reach a fair market price."

"I do have one question for you, Frank. How soon can we begin testing and developing a rocket or launching vehicle for this, and how long before it could be operational? Exactly how far along is your process? And please don't tell me it's still all theory," said General Jackson.

"Frank, wake up, dear. You're talking in your sleep and groaning about something from the war. What's the matter?" asked Claire to her now trembling husband. Frank was lying there one minute peacefully asleep, now wide awake and feeling cold.

Clara and Justin

Clara and Justin had been getting to know each other over the last two years. Justin knew he loved her, and by looking into her eyes, he could almost see she felt the same, or at least he thought she did. Justin knew, however, that no matter how he felt, he wouldn't be the first to say anything, especially now. Clara was just as much an FBI agent as he was now that graduation day had finally arrived. The only thing they didn't know was where they were to be posted, which was anyone's guess. Maybe with a little luck, they would both be assigned to the New York office where most of the action was. After all, why become an agent if you didn't want to walk into the flames of hell, right?

"Justin Beach."

Someone had just called out his name, and coming out of his stupor, he remembered he was sitting in the main hall, and it was graduation day. A kick to his shins also reminded him to get on the move. Sitting next to Clara for these past two years, he found that he knew her kick as if it had been happening to him all his life.

"Move, silly, get up there," whispered Clara. She was Clara Beach and next in line to receive her diploma, and Clara couldn't wait. In this graduating class, twenty women were present, and she was graduating in the top three, and it felt great. She was proud of her effort in her training and classwork. She had earned this. Finally, her day of reckoning had arrived, and Clara wouldn't daydream this away. She sat listening to every word, drinking it all in. Right out of college after receiving her master's degree in sociology, she headed straight to the academy. She realized that this didn't give her much time for a personal life, and up until this point, she still felt it was all worth it.

"Clara Beach."

Almost leaping out of her seat, Clara was a walking smile down the aisle, knowing she was just seconds from achieving her second goal in life, becoming an FBI agent. Both her mother and father were in attendance today to see her graduate. However, what would have made the day even more special would have been if Grandpa Frank and Grandma Claire had also been there. Clara could never get the image of Grandpa Frank, at that anniversary party, lying there as if he were dead. Little Michael was crying from the weight of his body, pinning him to the floor. It had been a stroke. Clara knew he was okay and resting at home now. The first thing she would do when she got her things together here was to go back home to spend time with the one man in her life who supported her every move. It always had been her grandfather.

He always stood behind her and would tell her parents that she "needs to become who she is, not what you want her to be. What could you two want of her? Do you think she would like to become a stuffy attorney or an accountant sitting in some office? Commuting daily, marrying some guy named Snook, and having forty kids. Let the child become an FBI agent, as long as she doesn't arrest one of us in the family." Then, laughing, Grandpa would hug her and say, "Go ahead, Clara, become who you want to become, and I'll handle the Indians."

"So today, Grandpa, this is for you," she thought with tears in her eyes.

After the ceremony, Justin came over to Clara, who was standing with her mom and dad, and said that his folks had already returned to their hotel. His mom wasn't feeling well. The heat seemed to be getting to her, but she wanted to ensure that Justin asked Clara and her parents to join them for dinner at the hotel later that night. He was not to accept no for an answer. They had all met on many occasions since Clara and Justin first came to the academy. Almost immediately, they became friends, especially sharing the same last name.

"Tell your mother thank you, Justin, but tonight is going to find us on the road home before the night gets too far," said Marian, Clara's mother.

Just then, Clare spoke up as she turned to her mother and said, "Well, not so fast, Mom; I still have the celebration and cake at the main building with all the graduates. Then, by the time that's over, I still would need to shower and change. So, I may not be finished until, say, six-thirty or so. Why don't we all go out and have a final dinner around here? Then we can get to bed early and leave for home in the morning. I want to get there early so I can visit Grandpa for the rest of the day."

Turning to face her husband, Marian said, "What do you think, Edward?"

Edward was Clara's father, and if he said they would stay, they would stay, especially since no one else would volunteer to do any of the driving. The driving part of any trip was always left up to her dad to handle. When Clara and her brothers received their licenses, there were just too many arguments on the right way to drive to suit everyone. Of course, this was the real reason why her dad acquired the job for life, whether he wanted it or not.

"Okay, I agree with Clara," Dad said. "Maybe we should stay the night and leave in the morning. The two or three hours of driving will be easier for me then. Especially after a good night's sleep, you are going to let me sleep, right, Mare?" Turning and smiling at her mom, it was as if they couldn't wait to be alone.

Her mom smiled and said, "You know, Ed, sometimes you're like a spoiled little boy, and sometimes I just need to ignore you."

With that, Marion turned and gave a quick hug to Clara and then to Justin. Then she turned and, grabbing her husband's arm, said, "Let's go, Ed; suddenly, I'm tired as well."

With that, they all departed and returned to the main parking lot, where Justin and Clara would head to the main building to continue the celebration and maybe pick up their assignments. That's the part that had them both a little squirrelly, the not knowing where they would be heading. After spending two years together almost day and night, not knowing left an uneasy feeling that they both shared concerning their departure. They both would have two weeks away before their assignments began. Hopefully, Justin would get what he wanted in New York, and Clara would move on to Los Angeles, where she always wanted to work.

Turning and heading back to her dorm, Clara thought about why she and Justin had yet to become exclusive. She knew they were in some sort of unspoken relationship, but she wanted more. And she was growing more confused every day. Although she wanted to give Justin some room, she also hoped there would be some chance for them to be together as a couple sometime in the future. But who knew what to think about a possible long-distance relationship if that is how it will turn out?

Tonight, they would find out their field assignments after two years of working together while becoming best friends. However, they both shared feelings for each other, knowing they might be separated. Would it all come to an end? Is that what was bothering her? After all of the good and bad times they shared here, Clara didn't want it to come to an end. She believed he was the reason why she had made it through the academy's grueling physical testing and emotional strain. She counted on Justin to be there, always encouraging her, and she came to depend on him. He always managed to give her one more reason to go on for one more grueling day. He helped her to find that level of comfort she had never found around another man.

They had known that the bureau frowned on their agents fraternizing together while in the academy. Because of that one-time chance, a romantic relationship could someday compromise both agents out in the field. But that nagging question continued in her mind. Did she love Justin, or did she just miss him, knowing he might have to leave her? Walking down the hall and upon entering the cafeteria, she could see Justin standing with Brad Berk. Now, pasting a false smile on her face, she continued walking right up to the two men. As far as Clara was concerned, Brad had to be the class bigot. He had been hitting on her since their first day at the academy. His arrogance completely turned her off. It wasn't until they were in a hand-to-hand combat class that she finally had the chance to show Brad that she was more than just a female. Brad's father, uncle, and grandfather had been FBI since Hoover. This meant that Brad thought it was an all-boys club. Brad believed membership should belong only to those whose families have served for generations. He didn't care for newcomers, hence his title of the class bigot. Stepping up and grabbing Justin's arm, she said, "Hi, Brad, congratulations!"

"Clara, I was just telling Justin that you and I have been assigned to the same place. Can you believe that?" said Brad.

"Oh, really," she replied, "And how did you know that already?" Now, turning and looking into Justin's smiling face, she needed some sort of confirmation. Not getting any, she asked, "Justin, is this true? You know where I'm going?"

Although feeling somewhat relieved as she would finally know her fate, Clara waited for one of them to speak up. Quickly becoming somewhat disappointed over the fact that Brad and she would be starting their careers in the same city, and who knows where Justin was heading, dampened Clara's mood even more.

"I must have pissed someone off", she thought, of all the rotten luck to be getting stuck with this guy. Not wanting to seem upset, she turned once more and, looking up at Justin, asked.

"Justin, have you found out yet where you're going?"

Smiling at her and knowing she was waiting for his answer was killing her. He said, "Yes, all three of us were assigned to the same field office. I couldn't let this guy be alone with you now, could I?"

Clara squeezed his arm a little harder, saying to herself, "Thank you, God."

Then Justin turned and, smiling at her because he felt her squeeze, said, "I haven't actually seen the assignments yet. It seems Berky boy here has some inside information on where we're headed."

Brad laughed, knowing he had done what he wanted to do. Scare Clara by having her think he could arrange to have her and him assigned to a separate post away from Justin, giving him another chance at her. Laughing out loud now, he slapped Justin on the shoulder.

Looking at Clara, he smiled and said, "See you guys later. I have to go and talk to new Agent McCalister to see if she would like to celebrate today over a nice bottle of champagne I have in my room." Turning with that smile affixed to his face, he bid them goodbye and walked away.

"Damn, I don't like that guy," said Justin. "Why are we being punished by being assigned to the same field office? We must have pissed someone off."

Clara smiled. "Come on, big shot, let's go get some cake and find out exactly where we're headed."

Luke Weeks

Like all basement storage areas, the lighting was dim, and the familiar stench of rotting cardboard boxes accompanied it. It permeated the air with a matching intensity to the heat that always existed in these dark places. Luke was in a good mood no matter what the circumstances might be. After all, he was finally out of the mailroom and assigned to his own desk. Now, the world was laid out in front of him. He could do anything that he ever wanted. Someday, everything he ever wanted would be his, and why not? Hasn't he been the one working so hard for everything he ever had since he was a boy? He worked his way through college to get his degree, saving every penny, not taking any time for himself, with only one goal in mind: to get ahead, and now he was on his way. Everyone in Lewisburg thought he was crazy for taking this job in Washington, DC, especially when it entailed working for a one-term senator named Pillow.

Hell, the name was funny enough, let alone the fact that the man he is replacing as interim senator was found smothered underneath five pounds of cocaine. Anyone who wanted the seat would have been given it if they had half a brain. So, a dentist named Pillow decides to buy the office, and Luke follows him to Washington.

Everyone thought what a waste of time for such a hardworking, smart farm boy who was now headed into a dead-end career. Even the few friends Luke had were concerned. Everyone thought that Pillow was an idiot, but Luke knew better. At first, he thought maybe they had been right, seeing how he was stuck in the mail section of the senator's task force. His job was answering letters and writing back to children who had written a question to their senator. Mainly, they wrote because they would receive a letter addressed to them from Washington, DC. In the right frame, it always looked nice on the living room wall.

Mostly, Luke would find himself apologizing for the senator not being able to make some fundraiser or dinner for a local yokel back home. As if that's all the man had to do, run back to Lewisburg whenever someone drops his name. Even some old widow wanted to know if he was ever returning to work on her teeth, crazy old lady. No one respected the man, and it was up to Luke to make it happen. Luke had done his job well here. He worked more closely with the senator because he had done so well in responding to all those letters and making excuses for him. So, the senator began to take notice. Now Luke had been reassigned to the "spin team," which got him a new office in the basement.

Today, he was in the dungeon of the Capitol building below the Senate chambers. Luke had to verify some information pertaining to an old senator from Tennessee who did some work on crop dusting or watering nonsense that led to the possible poisoning of the tobacco fields in his home state. This led to significant crop destruction and the tobacco industry's first of many payments from the government, known as subsidy payments. The senator also ensured the government would raise more taxes on raw, uncut tobacco and cigarette sales.

What Senator Pillow had to do with all of this was not yet known to him. His boss, Mable Gardner, needed the information to assist the senator with work assigned to him by a committee on which he was not even seated. However, the senator's decision was clear to all. "Get the information so I can look good enough for an assignment to a viable working committee. Get me all the information on the subsidy payments to an industry that was never losing ground in America, the tobacco industry, and I needed it yesterday!" shouted the senator.

But to Luke, who didn't care what his assignment was, it was only a matter of time before he would move up even farther into the senator's main group of advisors. Maybe even one day, it would be Luke, the senator of Pennsylvania, and someone else would be walking down these same deserted, dark, smelly corridors looking for something that happened years ago but had found new life. Until then, he would do whatever it would take to make him the senator's number-one man. Luke could see his goal coming more into focus, and anyone and everything was fair game.

Tully and Jeff

Tully stood perfectly still. As much as she wanted to scream, she suppressed not only the actual scream but also the fear of what her scream could bring to her. She was scared, and she knew she had to calm herself down, suppress her desire to look straight down, kick out, or at least scream at the top of her lungs. Tully knew that the large black water moccasin crawling across her right foot would soon move on as long as she remained calm. How she had not seen the snake was beyond her, as careful as she was out here in the wild. Yet, occasionally, she made a mental mistake that led to such encounters. Tully also recognized that, over the years of her working in the field, she had experienced harmful or potentially deadly encounters as part of her job. It was the feelings, however, after these incidents, that often hurt her more.

More often than not, she would experience a huge burst of adrenaline coursing through her system during this kind of excitement. It would wreak havoc on her for days. The shakes would often be almost unbearable after one of these episodes. Once they had become so bad, she trembled uncontrollably until she finally fell asleep. Her first brush with such a gross sense of fear had her quivering so much that she couldn't stop crying afterward, almost to the point of hyperventilation. It happened in the jungles of Brazil. The meeting was with a jaguar. A big male who wanted her as his next meal. The jaguar had crept into their camp and tore at her tent in the middle of the blackest nights three years ago. Tully was mesmerized, locked in place, unable to move or breathe. She watched the animal defiantly stand its ground as the men in the camp tried to fight it off. But before it did slink slowly back into the forest, their eyes met, and

Tully was glued to its stare. Those blood-red eyes bespoke a thousand words. She was food, and it was hungry, but by the grace of God, it finally turned and slowly walked back into the dense underbrush of the local jungle.

That's when the quaking began. She suddenly had no control over her own muscles or bowel movements. It wasn't until hours later, when her terror subsided, that she fell asleep in Jeff's arms. Snakes are her life as a paid member of the Herpetological Education and Research Facility, out of St. Louis, Missouri, with degrees in biochemistry and herpetology. With Jeff's degree in herpetology and biomechanics, they made a great team.

Tully and Jeff had just returned from the snake-infested fields of the Punjab region in India to study the king cobras. In the Punjab region, humans and snakes coexist in the working fields, and contrary to opinion, most of the time, the snakes leave the people alone. On the rare occasions where they come into contact, the humans are usually killed at least seventy-five percent of the time. These statistics were the reason a joint study was initiated to eradicate or capture these deadly snakes.

The water moccasin was starting to notice her tension, and she knew she had to regain her thoughts to calm herself down before it attacked. Suddenly, the snake was at eye level as she jumped backward. Looking up, she saw Jeff's smiling face as he swung the snake in the air. She sighed in relief, knowing she was out of danger, at least for the moment.

Thank God for Jeff. He was Jeff Osburne, her husband, and co-leader here on this exploration for a zoo in Philadelphia. The zoo needed more water snakes for a new reptilian exhibit opening in May.

Jeff was also a graduate of Penn State, located in State College, where the two of them met their first year and had been together ever since. Traveling the world looking for exotic snakes. Their work came from public or private zoos to large corporate research grants from private industries with which they had contracts. Together, they gathered information, although lately, field studies regarding rising global temperatures have mainly been done. They hadn't been able to correlate global warming with the loss of any species they continued to study. That was what had brought them to the jungles in Brazil. Everyone was screaming about global warming, and they just could not find any real evidence to support it.

FBI Team Leader

"Damn it!" John swore. The hammer hurt when it smashed into his already aching fingers, and today was no different than the last time he decided he would try to work outside in the yard. Every time his wife, Beth, yelled out his name, he managed to strike something other than the nail. Why can't she just quit being so loud, he thought. There she was again, complaining some more.

"John! Come on! Let that go right now. We have to get to Lucy's game on time. I don't want to be late again. Why do you insist on always making us late?" Beth must have asked that same question to her husband for what must have been the umpteenth time since they had been married.

Looking up at his wife, John shook his head and said, "Beth, you always make me miss the nails when you're yelling. I can't think straight now. The fingers on my left hand look like chopped meat. Please get me two more bandages, and I'll clean up out here. I just want to wrap up the power tools, so if one of those little Indians from next door gets into our yard, he won't cut himself up too badly."

Turning around to wrap up his drill and power saw, he smiled, knowing Beth had to be steaming. Sending her on a last-minute errand for the bandages and remarking about her best friend's kids always got her goat. Oh well, such is life. With so many things to do around the house, John sometimes didn't know where to start. It seemed as if every time Beth watched a home improvement show, he had another project to do. With so many little things that get in his way of completing any project, the whole summer would be spent out back with his hammer and nails. Shrugging his shoulders, John continued to wrap up the cord. Turning at the sound of Beth's approach, John smiled as he gazed up into her face. Beth had her hand stretched forward.

"Here, take these, and let's get going. Cathy and Mark are probably there by now, and it's your daughter's game. Don't you ever have any sense of time? Why must we always be late?" Beth said, then almost pleadingly sighed, "Now, *John, let's go.*"

"Beth, did you remember to bring water and snacks for the kids? It's going to be another hot one today," said John. Now sitting comfortably in the front seat of Beth's new blue minivan with the air-conditioning blowing on his sweaty face, John couldn't help but think that this new van was a little overboard, even for Beth. With the folding seats, video attachments, a backup camera, and many other pricy gadgets, John wondered when automobiles had become so complex.

"Ya know, Beth. I was just thinking about the cost of this minivan and how things are changing so much. By the time our children are grandparents, what exactly will this world be like? Haven't you ever thought about those issues?" asked a bemused John.

"Not when I'm with my husband and traveling down the road going to our daughter's ball game. No, there's a time and a place for that, John, and this is neither the time nor the place," Beth said.

Lucy had made the traveling All-Star Little League baseball team and would be playing her first game today. Lucy was John and Beth's only child. Lucy was not the son John had hoped for, but she was turning out to be quite a tomboy. To know her, you immediately loved her. Not only could Lucy hit a baseball as well as any boy. But she had a wicked curveball. All the boys found it hard to hit, especially when delivered by a tall girl with long flaming-red hair flaring out from under her ball cap. Now, that look worked alongside a thousand freckles and a smile that would warm your heart.

John Bloso worked for the FBI and was stationed in Washington, DC. Too often than not, he was too busy to get to Lucy's games, and when he did manage it, he was the happiest man in the world at that moment. Sitting back and making himself as comfortable as possible on the bleacher seats, he could only smile as he watched his only child reach the pitcher's mound, bring her left arm back, and let her famous curveball fly.

Tomorrow was a busy office day. The new recruits would show up, but today, right now, he was there to watch his daughter.

Washington, DC

"All right, everyone, settle down!" yelled Senior Division Chief Ricker. "Let's get started, shall we? First, I would like to congratulate all of our new agents. Welcome to the club. I'm Operations Supervisor Jack Ricker. Either you guys know someone, or you're doing penance. I don't care what it is because now you belong to me. We here in Washington are the best and brightest. At least, we like to think so. After we assign you to a team in a specific division, you are to familiarize yourself as quickly as possible. You will be questioned daily on current situations outside of your team functions. I expect everyone here to meet the qualification requirements on time. If you have problems, bring them to me. If I can't solve them, then it goes to senior leader agent John Bloso."

The first month went by so fast that Clara didn't have a chance to even think about her relationship with Justin. She was so busy with cases ranging from counterfeiters to locating the nearest deli when she was sent out for coffee. Seems some things never change, and one of those things was being a grunt when you're the new kid on the block. It made her day on the rare occasions that Brad was asked to fetch her coffee, and she made the most of it by ordering the most ridiculously complex coffee on the menu.

Her visit home after graduation was short and seemed like ages ago. Grandpa Frank insisted on getting her diploma blown up, and suddenly, his living room turned into her own museum display. It was heartbreaking to leave behind all the people that she loved so much, but this was new and exciting, and what she had longed to do all her life. Finally becoming a field agent with the FBI, Clara was certain she had found her calling.

Coming out of her revelry, she couldn't help but feel someone watching her. She felt eyes behind her. Turning, she noticed a man who seemed to be in the deli every time she was, and he was staring at her. He was sort of creeping her out. He now leaned against the deli counter, pretending to peruse the meats in the case, knowing she had caught him staring. Once again, glancing in her direction while twirling a set of keys in one hand, he acknowledged her with a big grin on his face. Clara walked over to him and asked, "Excuse me, do I know you?"

"I apologize. I didn't think that you noticed me, actually. I really don't mean any disrespect. Just that it seems as if every time I'm in here, well, so are you. Do you work around here?" asked the young man.

"Yes, as a matter of fact, I do. As you know, I sometimes come here for lunch," replied Clara.

Leaning towards her conspiratorially, he said, "FBI, right? I'm impressed. Being a female agent has to be tough."

"Not too bad. How did you know?" questioned Clara.

"One day, you went into your pocket for some money, and I couldn't help but notice a gun on your belt and a badge on the side. If I didn't see the badge, I was going to dial 911 on you."

Smiling now, the young man held out his hand and said, "Luke, Luke Weeks. I work for Senator Pillow from Pennsylvania. We just arrived this year and you must have heard about our old senator on the news. Seems he had a bit of a drug problem, and he was found dead one day in his office."

"Yes, I do remember hearing about that," Clara said, shaking hands with Luke.

He reached into his coat pocket, pulled out a business card, and handed it to Clara. "My card. If you're ever in the area, let me know, and maybe we can grab lunch. On me, of course."

Taken aback, Clara said, "Maybe, I guess, if I ever have the time." Luke was attractive and well-built, and who knows when having a contact in a senate office could come in handy one day. "Sure, maybe I could make an appointment to get there one day. You can walk me around the senate building, and I can see what it's like," Clara responded.

"Great, I'll look forward to hearing from you. Oh, by the way, I never did get your name," Luke said.

Laughing now and going into her handbag, Clara pulled out her card and handed it to Luke, saying, "Clara. Clara Beach."

Getting back to the office, Clara thought that maybe this was a test of some sort, so she decided to tell her immediate boss. After all, one can never be too careful, even if the guy did work for a senator, as he claimed. Luke came on as someone sincere, and he dressed very nicely and was well-mannered, it seemed. But something in his eyes said differently, and she couldn't put a finger on it, but it was something. Maybe she shouldn't say a word about the encounter. But having these thoughts about it did mean something. So, better safe than sorry, she would tell Justin as soon as she found him. It seemed as if she had nothing but work and more work piled on every day, and if she didn't look busy enough, then there was even more work asked of her. It's what she wanted, but sometimes not at all what she expected it to be. She had been a field agent for six months now, and she thought maybe the workload would slow down, but in Washington, DC, it was as if nothing did, or maybe the people and their problems just never took a break.

Senator Pillow from Pennsylvania

Luke could not understand why Mable was being such a jerk about those papers. He had been down in that damn dungeon every day this past month.

I thought it was going to be different working directly with Pillow. I guess it would be if that idiot Mable would get her facts straight. One minute, I needed to locate papers regarding tobacco, and now I have to find something about projects and people who can make it rain.

Mable had instructed Luke to go downstairs to the archives and research two men, Hammond and Thurston, who run a company contracted by the US government.

"So, what," thought Luke. "So are a lot of other companies. What's the big deal?"

He was also looking for the names of two generals, Margate and Jackson. It seemed that both Jackson and Hammond had been dead for a long time. All this switching, digging, and shuffling papers around made no sense to Luke. For God's sake, most of the papers were completely marked out in black ink because of their classified content. He was only allowed to read the papers due to the new national security laws and the Freedom of Information Act, which granted Luke access to the papers.

But what good is that if they're all blacked out? What could the senator possibly get out of this crap? The woman who worked at the front desk in the Archives moved exceptionally slowly, and it was driving him crazy. Everyone found them to be true bureaucratic pains in the asses, as most of them were. All seemingly overweight, overbearing, snobby librarians. He wanted to scream, "Just give me all of the files, not just a few, and hurry! I really don't want to be stuck in this dungeon all day again!" Instead, he had to wait for the papers, read them, and make notes every day. Some files he would make copies of, then return them all, as he was forced to waste more time. This was driving him insane.

Luckily, he passed the time thinking about his new find. Clara from the FBI. Clara was a fine-looking woman. He couldn't help but think of her in bed. She would be good. Afterward, he would become too busy with his work for the senator to be bothered with her. Too many pressing issues to handle, just not enough time in the day, he would tell her. Just like all the other women he met in Washington. Yes, Washington was turning out to be far better than Luke thought it would be.

Mable Gardner was no fool. She knew that her boss was a sneak and a liar. If he wasn't telling lies to his family, especially to his wife, then he was lying to his constituents. Senator Pillow was definitely embracing his new position as a senator select; he liked the power and the money. She knew that the senator, who was once a meek dentist, had some secret deal in the works, one that could ensure him a seat on a committee. Normally, junior senators, especially those who were appointed to fill a seat, couldn't get spots on the committees. They were reserved for senior senators. Mable knew that he was up to something because, lately, he was acting more like the snake he was fast becoming. He had Luke in the Archives Department every day, even though she had given the senator everything that was found regarding the tobacco fiasco. Now, he insisted that he needed more; he was like a dog on the trail of a bone. Senator Pillow was especially concerned with a company called H.T. Wetco, one of the largest

Department of Defense contractors. She would find out what he was up to; after all, she was his chief of staff, and if she was going to stay in Washington, DC, long after this ass wipe was back cleaning teeth in Pennsylvania, she needed to carve a little piece from the pie for herself.

"Senator Pillow to see you, sir," said Gene. Gene Bishop had been with H.T. Wetco for most of her seventy-three years. She was a young girl when Mr. Thurston first laid eyes on her and asked her to become his personal secretary. However, in today's ever-present need to be politically correct, she would be classified as his personal assistant. Reflecting on all the years spent here, Bob and Gene did have their intimate time together, one which had led to a promise of marriage right after his divorce. But that never came, and what the hell? He was now an old man ten years her senior, and it no longer seemed important to either of them. Bob's wife, Marla, had passed away some fifteen years earlier from breast cancer, and now there just wasn't any need for her to marry the old man, she thought. They had been in love so many years ago. Gene was still smiling at the thoughts of her and Bob in their youth as she closed the door behind this brash young senator from Pennsylvania.

"Good day, sir," said Senator Pillow to Bob Thurston, former CEO and COO of H.T. Wetco, who was now a non-working functionary. Under his direction, the company made millions in defense department sales. Now, the company is doing triple that number under the helm of his grandson, Todd Thurston. Since Todd has come aboard, the shares at H.T. Wetco have increased tenfold. They had gone from eking out an existence of a hundred million in sales a year to the US government and some foreign governments to clearing two billion dollars this year alone. Bob was smug, and rightly so, as he had been a part of this company since its inception at the end of the Second World War. He and Ted Hammond worked tirelessly to make this company one of the biggest in the nation in government sales. The war was good and bad for Bob and Ted.

As officers, they met and worked with some of the best the war produced. At the end of the war, this gave their clients respect, which helped them bring their company into the new world order. But Ted Hammond had different ideas and a direction he needed to take, and he sold his shares back to Bob. Death seemed to stalk and find Ted right after that departure. No one knows for sure, but Bob never again mentioned Ted's name, especially when amongst old friends.

"Yes, Senator, how are you? Won't you come in and take up some time of an old man? Some days, it's great to sit here listening to my own thoughts as I win all of the arguments. Other days are spent reviewing speeches Todd is preparing for the shareholders. Not many of my counterparts and old friends are alive anymore, and not much someone my age can get into trouble doing. So, what can I do for you, sir? Seems you've come a long way just to talk to an old man. I don't suppose things in Washington have quieted down so much that you have a lot of time on your hands," said a smiling, warm Bob Thurston. Sitting back down, he turned and motioned to a chair across from his for the senator to sit in.

Taking the seat and quickly looking around the office, Pillow saw that it was bleak. Aside from some old photographs taken immediately after the war and some he had seen from the war, nothing else stood out. Taking a chance, he used this information and spoke.

"Mr. Thurston, it is my pleasure to be meeting you today. Taking the time to see someone like me is very gracious of you. I really don't mean to take up much of your time, but I need some advice, and I think you're the only one who can help me."

"Please, Senator, go ahead and let's see how much truth there is to that statement. At my age, there's usually not much help I can give anyone anymore. As I mentioned earlier, my grandson handles all the responsibilities related to the company. I think they call me a figurehead." said a laughing Thurston. "After all," now sitting back in his chair to add some authority, "I still don't know if you mean me or the company now, do I, sir." Not looking away from Pillow, he said in a different tone of voice, "Go ahead and let's see how I can help you."

Seizing the chance to make his first impression a lasting one and get his point across immediately, Pillow began to speak quietly as he stared directly into Thurston's eyes.

"Well, as you must already know, sir, I was, let's say, selected to this position as senator. In less than twenty-four months, I have to run for this office in an election process that might not bring me back to Washington. But I may have some reasons why your company will help me. I will need some personal funds and some election campaign funds as well. I think that your company will be more than willing to make those contributions."

Bob Thurston was taken aback. He was at an age where he was more pleasing and accommodating than he had ever been in his working lifetime concerning business dealings. Yet now, he suddenly acquired a very stern and irritable look across his face.

"Excuse me, Senator, but I seem to think that you are implying that we are going to be forced into financing your campaign and that we are going to make you a senator because of something that makes this firm vulnerable, is that right, sir?" asked Bob Thurston.

"Well, sir, let me say that as a new senator, if I was to be selected to, let's say, the Ways and Means Committee or the Service Arms Committee, then that would be a start in the right direction now, wouldn't it?" asked a smiling Senator Pillow. Now leaning back in his chair as if he was going to relax, light up a cigar, to sip on some whisky.

"Now, Senator, why would I try to make that happen, especially since you're not even an elected senator, nor do I know you or your family? Hell, we don't even have the same friends," said Thurston, with a grin of a Cheshire cat running across his round red face. "If anything, I would be eager to help your opponent. Exactly what it is that makes you think that I would go to such extremes for you?"

H.T. Wetco was one of the richest companies in America, and Bob Thurston was suddenly very angry, speaking loudly, loud enough that the door opened. Sticking her head in to see if all was okay, Gene turned at the nod of Bob's head and immediately closed the door. She smiled, as Gene had seen this particular scenario many times before. She knew that Bob still had some additional tongue-lashing he wanted to give out before she would be called in to escort the senator from the room.

As the senator leaned forward, he raised his hand as if he were a traffic cop stopping a car. "Let's calm down now, shall we? Let me continue on about why we have something in common after all. Allow me to explain."

Now seemingly back in control of the discussion, the Senator asked Bob if he was, in fact, capable of making this decision. He said that he would wait for Mr. Thurston's grandson to arrive, and they could resume the conversation then.

Now even more angered, Bob Thurston recognized that maybe Senator Pillow was hinting that he had evidence of some company wrongdoing. He needed to calm down and let the prey fall into the trap.

"Okay, maybe I did get a little excited in the beginning. Why don't we go back and start over again, shall we? Explain to me exactly why we're going to help you. I'm now very interested. You do have my full attention. So, forgive an old man for getting excited. Seems I have been away too long from the possible excitement of negotiations." Sitting back in his chair and putting both hands together, Bob was waiting for the mysterious reason why this sappy-looking dentist from Pennsylvania was really sitting here in his office.

"Well, sir, even junior senators like I am are being asked to look into certain issues for a committee review or to help write an opinion. In this case, my objective was to find out the reason why, in the late forties, the tobacco industry was destroyed and led to the first American subsidy program. For a product that would only rise in need and sales in the future. A time when advertisement campaigns for tobacco products ruled the airwaves. When the sale of cigarettes, pipe tobacco, chewing tobacco, and cigars ruled the income from sales over all other American goods as smoking was such an integral part of our society.

Because, sir, it would seem a downpour of devastating rains supposedly destroyed a crop not yet in the ground in most states. It, however, set precedence for income subsidies to American companies to a certain senator's constituent farmer friends who had no real need, aside from politics, to receive any government money. Now, I am sure you are aware of the fact that since the crop failure was due to so much rain at the time, the whole industry was supposedly in disrepair and needed help. I could see some help, but millions of dollars went into farmers' pockets with absolutely no oversight from anyone in Congress. It seems as if everyone was rich beyond imagination.

Imagine the alarms that would set off in today's world of policy and oversight committees. Well, I must admit even I initially thought this project was just to keep me quiet. Give the new man on the block something to keep him occupied, say, for the duration of his term, and then good riddance.

But see, something happened in my research. I hope I am getting my point across here, sir, that I'm not being redundant. It seems that the rain may have been planted, or let me say it a little more clearly. It seems certain that a fellow senator who is no longer alive, died, I might add, in a tragic fire, was spouting off about the need to raise the cost of tobacco to the consumers. His reelection campaign would be starting soon, and this would boost his popularity, that's for sure. But the government said no way they would allow the entire industry to raise prices. All from fear, you see, about how the smoking electorate would react if cigarettes became too expensive. Especially given that they shouldn't or couldn't put any more federal taxes on these products. But if a subsidy came, then all bets were off. Then, the federal taxes had to rise to allow the government to recoup some subsidy money. This was called a federal excise tax on tobacco. If right? At the same time, tobacco would go up by twenty percent across the board, making the government and those farmers happy as well. Now, everyone would be happy except the consumers. But this senator was greedy, and he couldn't wait until Congress got around to making up their mind. I was told that he was an impatient man, especially with an election for his senate seat coming up in the next year."

Now sitting back with a smile on his face as if he just ate the bird in the clock, the senator said quite confidently, "As I said, suddenly those unending rains came all over the south, going from state to state. A real freaky storm system, one would have to think. Hell, even the jet stream changed for the occasion, I understand. It was big torrential downpours that almost decimated the entire tobacco industry.

Would you believe that the government intervened and provided the industry with substantial tax breaks and increased subsidies to sustain this industry? Oh, I did say that already, now, didn't I, sir? Well, it was just what that senator needed to win his reelection, it seemed. Lining the farmers' pockets and keeping the tobacco increase in play and the government making a twenty percent profit, ah, everyone was a winner. Too bad his devious ways led to his demise. Burned, as I recall, actually, I had to look that up. I was just a young, innocent man at the time, not even in grammar school. All three were found burned to a crisp. I understand that it took some dentists to identify him through his teeth. That was the first of my findings, by the way. Then, as I had my people looking into more about the rains and weather patterns, I came across some more interesting facts. Seems as if your company is the only one making rain since the forties, rains, imagine that. But no one even knew back then that this was even possible. Imagine a company capable of making it rain and working with the government. The possibilities are endless.

Then, it seems that heavy rains soaked Kansas and the Midwest for months after the big war ended. All those farmers and people who left their homesteads to flee to California, leaving all that property for a tax sale, just how wealthy could people in the know become? Well, crops did boom out there on all that dry, worthless land purchased by some corporate speculators. Or should I say friends of H. T. Wetco and, presto, suddenly they became millionaires overnight.

Then, who would have thought that during the Korean War, every time someone planned a major offensive push into the north or back into the south, it would start to snow so heavily that they stopped right at the snow line, the 38th Parallel? Then, as if it was by a miracle in Vietnam, the rains came every time the Viet Cong planned an offensive. Storms appeared and went almost of their own volition. Amazing.

I would assume that if this were indeed happening, then someone could be manipulating the weather for military purposes. Well, they had to be getting paid an awful lot of money. Wouldn't you agree? But now the best, I like saving the best for last. Imagine if another country had no idea that someone was changing the weather patterns over the Arctic Circle, and all they could get was drought. Year after year after year, and this someday, it was thought would possibly lead to the political destruction of that country. Lo and behold, guess what? It happens exactly that way. Imagine the potential for war if the other country had found out.

But that's not the best part. Imagine if there were other African countries, countries caught up in a high jet stream, and they suffered from a lack of rain, as well. All those dying, starving children would be affected. Lives are lost with the suffering and pain. What company would ever want that on their resume? Even if there was not a single piece of evidence or any proof, imagine the cost of repairing someone's good name. So there now, it's out in the open, and I hope that from this point on, we can start calling each other by our first names, Bob."

Sitting forward once again in his chair, Senator Pillow gave a pompous smile that would have made any man on the receiving end want to end his life.

Now that the cat was out of the bag, Bob found some relief. Sure, his company had been making it rain for years, but so what? The government here and abroad has used his services since 1946. Oh sure, he could make acid rain come and go, but was that really so important? He could also destroy miles and miles of land, making it useless for generations by dumping mercury and potassium chloride from above with no one ever the wiser.

Yes, that other senator did show up here acknowledging the same facts as this idiot was now doing. Yes, he did destroy a lousy tobacco industry, but so what? Look at the subsidies and the profits those companies made doing business with him. Hell, he had nothing to explain. When it snowed in Korea, hell, wear some boots. Same in Vietnam; when it rained, put on a poncho. It's what he was paid for. What the government wanted was not long wars or occupying countries forever. Start the damn war, make the money on the goods and weapons, and start some research, and then get the hell out. Screw the locals. His company wasn't the bad one here. It was the government. Bob knew his company was second only to God. They could make it rain when and where he wanted it. What was the man who said that? Oh yeah, Frank. Frank Benoit. That damn man thought he was God.

Then, sitting back in his chair, he knew what had to be done. Then Bob thought, "Hell, I can't involve Todd in this. I'll need to keep his name clean so he and the company will have nothing staining them should it all go wrong. I'll handle this myself as I did in the old days. This idiot has no idea as to the power I wield." But all the loose ends had to be tied up again as tight as a boiler's knot.

Looking at Senator Pillow, who was now sitting back in his chair as if he had just won a chess match, Bob said, "Well, now, it seems that someone has been doing their homework, haven't they?"

Once again, Bob had that Cheshire cat smile across his face. "Okay, let's do this, Senator. Let me think and confer with some of my 'friends' in the company. We can meet and discuss exactly what committees we have some pull on and where we can find a nice, comfortable seat for you; how's that?"

Now standing and putting out his hand, Pillow said, "Always a pleasure when I get to talk to someone of such authority as you, sir. I do so look forward to our next meeting. Oh, by the way, two of my staff members have all the same information as I do. They might not have all of the pieces to the puzzle connected, but soon, they will hear about this conversation. However, this information will never see the light of day. Even at the request of the committee, for which I was asked to do this research in the first place. So, everything remains secure. I thought you would like to know that."

After shaking hands and turning to see that Gene had already opened the door for him to leave, Pillow thought that maybe the walls had ears. But, so what? He already had this conversation on the tape recorder sewn into his coat. Ah, electronics can be so useful when you need them to be, he thought as the elevator door slid open for him, and he stepped inside, still smiling.

First Visit

"What do you think, Clara? Have you had enough of walking these chambers? Maybe it's time for us to go have lunch in the senators' main dining area. Who knows, maybe today the President could be walking these halls."

Clearly, Clara thought that Luke was going out of his way today, trying to be informative and somehow distinguished in his mannerisms. Although she had to admit he did know a lot of people around here in just seven months, especially the women. Speaking of which, she thought that today, either she was wearing the wrong clothing or, for some reason, an awful lot of young females didn't care for her. Then, it dawned on her that maybe Luke was a player, and she was the new pawn. Well, the last thing she needed was to have this guy trying to get into her pants. Friends were one thing, but what he was possibly contemplating was something else, and she wasn't interested in any of that. Luke would definitely make a great contact, but not that close of a contact. Maybe she should mention Justin real soon, she thought, just to be on the safe side, so she wouldn't have to fight this character off later.

"I forgot to tell Justin where I was going today. I'm sure he would have tried talking his way into this trip," piped up Clara, who was walking slowly beside Luke.

"Who's Justin?" asked Luke.

"Oh, the guy I have been involved with for the last few years. We are really playing it by ear right now. Neither of us knows exactly where it's headed, but that's a good thing for now. We are so busy at work. It seems I've had no free time lately, or perhaps not since I arrived. It's really been hectic and full of a lot of surprises."

Clara finished saying as she turned and went over to a display of the Declaration of Independence and the Bill of Rights, gleaning from a beautiful open-faced cabinet.

"Please don't tell me those are the real articles?" she asked.

"No, but they are as close as one can get to the real thing," said a seemingly indifferent Luke.

"How long have you and Justin been going out? Is this something I should concern myself with? I was thinking that maybe there was an outside chance that we could become really close friends. I'm still hoping about that part, actually."

Clara thought Luke was talking as if he were totally ignoring what she had just said about her and Justin. Now wanting to change the subject, she turned and said, "Hey, what about that lunch you promised me?"

Global Warming

Jeff was a little more than perturbed at the thought that he wasn't being asked to change some statistics. He was just being told to. Neither Jeff nor Tully had ever changed any of their findings from their field assignments. Not one result or the science gathered ever reflected what a paying patron would want it to somehow reflect, and he was not about to start today.

"What's wrong, Jeff?" asked Tully, looking up from a book she was reading. Sitting in their living room at a house they seldom visited, Tully was a little perplexed. Jeff had come home from a meeting with a large corporate sponsor of theirs. This company was the first major corporation they landed. Over the past five years, it has provided them with a very lucrative living. To such an extent that they were able to pick and choose among other companies that sought out their science. Yet, something seemed to be annoying him. However, she knew Jeff was not one to blurt out in anger or show any emotional signs of frustration concerning anything they worked on together. Eventually, he would open up, but right now, he was making the stew until it was boiling over. That's when he would blurt it all out at once. Tully didn't know if he was yet that far into the stew-making process.

"Nothing, Tull. I just need to think about what we have been asked to do," replied Jeff.

Tully looked up from her book and said, "Ah, Jeff, didn't you just say what we have been asked to do? Doesn't that mean that I should also be thinking about whatever seems to be bothering you?"

Now smiling as usual, she started her questioning about something because, for some reason, his wife could not only read his expressions, but she knew him like a book. When anything bothered him, Jeff knew that he might as well go and hide someplace because Tully would wiggle any and all of the information from him, even if it took all night. Yet, she always pretended to be waiting for him to make this "stew" she always said he was making whenever he was deep in thought.

Her grandfather Frank would always say that about everyone. "Don't just sit there and make stew till it boils over. Get it off your chest before it spoils a good kid." So, Tully claimed the same right to invoke his thoughts whenever he wanted some peace and quiet. Jeff liked to take his time to think certain problems out on his own. But now Tully would start her nudging, and she was not going to give him any real chance to work it out.

"Please let it be for now, Tull. We can talk about this later. Right now, let's enjoy being home, okay?" Jeff asked.

"Sure, come here and give this woman a big smooch, then I can squeeze it out of you later," a smiling and now laughing Tully replied.

Their house wasn't as big as most of the homes her cousins owned. All except Cousin Clara, that is. Her thoughts of Clara made her realize that she was off and living now in Washington, DC, working for the FBI. She continued thinking about her and Clara as children. Reflecting back to when they were growing up, how everyone thought them to be sisters, or maybe more like brothers? Thinking and laughing to herself about how much of a tomboy they both were. Tully knew that the next time they had to work for the National Zoo, she would make it a point to have lunch with her. She missed Clara. Even if sometimes the two of them fought like cats and dogs, all over the attention from Grandpa. Each one pulling him in a different direction to work on solving a mystery for Clara. Or looking at some bugs and beetles with Tully. They even had a crush on the same boys in their high school years. Often changing from one to another, as some people changed coats. But a friendship and a bond were formed way beyond just being cousins. By the time Clara acted as maid of honor at Tully and Jeff's wedding, they had, along the way, become sisters. She would definitely make it a point to see her before they left on their next trip.

Jeff wasn't at all sure as to what approach he would use the next time he met with Pete Winslow.

Pete was the scientist in charge of global changes and documentation for H.T. Wetco, just one of the dozen or so companies that now hired him and Tully. But H.T. Wetco was their first and largest contractor, asking them to research climate change and its possible effects on the indigenous animals and their habitat around the globe. So far, all the evidence out there had to point to a certain special moment. According to environmentalists worldwide, something had to be done now and quickly. But this is exactly what was bothering Jeff. According to his information, none of this was really true. Most species of the reptiles and animals he and Tully had captured and studied, well, neither their habitat nor they themselves showed any signs of drastic changes. The only constant existing problems facing most of them were illegal poachers hunting the big game or illegal collectors chasing and capturing everything from exotic snakes to birds.

Another main ingredient was the loss of habitat worldwide. It seems that all over the world, people were clear-cutting habitats for much-needed farmland or living space. With all of his research and their years serving this one community, Winslow now wanted their work to reflect something different than what it was saying in the field, and Jeff wasn't sure he could do that. This led to him and Tully being caught between a rock and a hard place. They either lie about their results or possibly lose work and their reputations. H.T. Wetco was a big part of their annual income. With a sigh, Jeff turned the water off in the shower and climbed back into bed. Bringing Tully next to him and cuddling her head into his arm, whispering, he said, "Okay, you win. The stew pot is boiling over; we need to talk now, okay?"

"Sure, but not right now. I'm sure whatever it is can wait, just a little longer. Right now, I am in the best place in the world." With that, she rolled back onto her side, facing her husband, and started kissing his neck. They had just made love in their usual passionate way, but Jeff could sense that his wife wasn't satisfied for some reason. So, placing both of his hands around her lovely face, he lifted her head and gave her a long and tender kiss.

"Okay, Jeff, let's talk," said Tully, who now sat at the kitchen table with her knees up and touching her chin, as she took her teacup and slowly sipped on the scalding brew it held. Tully was known for making tea that burnt the roof of your mouth, tongue, teeth, lips, or anything it came into contact with. Jeff was standing there with the refrigerator door wide open, bending over and peering in as if something on the very lowest shelf existed there just for him.

"What are you looking for? Close the door, sit down, and tell me what is upsetting you," said Tully.

"Fine, fine, just a minute, please. I know I put that last piece of pie here somewhere," replied Jeff.

"Ah, the blueberry?" asked Tully.

"Yeah, that one. Oh, come on, Tull, you didn't eat it, did you?" asked Jeff with a hurt look on his face as he stared at Tully.

"Yes, you were so long in the shower. My tea was hot, and it was just sitting there. I asked you last night if you wanted it," said Tully, almost looking sorry but not quite.

"Damn, I was really thinking about that pie in the shower. I thought you didn't like blueberry pie?" asked Jeff.

"Well, it was the only good thing in the fridge," replied Tully. "So, I ate it, sorry."

Jeff moved on, saying, "Okay, here's our dilemma. Pete wants us to adjust our data slightly to make it appear that our numbers are leaning more toward the side of global warming problems. Making our findings reflect that the snakes, in particular, are dying off. Unable to lay eggs, find cool places to breed, running out of food sources, make it look as if global warming is affecting life on the planet now, not in the future."

"What! Is he crazy? Doesn't he know that if we get caught, what that could do to our reputation and our lives? We would never work again! Hell, not even a local town zoo would hire us to look in on the birds!" shouted an obviously angry Tully.

"Calm down, Tull, maybe it isn't that bad; maybe we can fudge the information a little, just the stuff that is a little fluffy anyway," said Jeff.

"Fluffy? What in our work is ever 'fluffy'? Why would you even consider any of this? The hell with Pete, let's just walk away from this and continue working for those people who have some integrity!" shouted Tully.

Jeff now thought that maybe sharing this with her wasn't a good idea. Maybe he should have made up a story just to satisfy her curiosity. Then, he alone could have met with Pete and gone along with it concerning just the 'fluff'.

"Listen, Tull, how about we just write up a different accounting about the black water moccasins? After all, we only managed to find four on this last trip. Maybe something is going wrong with them? Just maybe we can go back and find only four again? We'll write it up to show, say, a potential for future eradication of the species due to global warming; how's that?" he pleaded, "After all, what do we care if they put more dollars into funding a study on black water moccasins?"

"No, Jeff, that would be lying, and you know it," said Tully. She was calmer now, seeing how she knew that Jeff was just as torn between this as she was. No one wants to lie or falsify information; after all, it would ruin a person's credentials, and in this trade, the one thing that kept the wolves at bay was holding on to your credentials.

"Look, Tull," said Jeff, "just this once. Just to get him off of our backs until we can find someone else to take his place. I can go back and talk to Adam Eve Pharmaceuticals. They are always looking to hire and don't pay quite as well as Pete's company, but we can afford to take the hit. It really wouldn't set us back that much financially."

"No, I would rather go to them now and just drop Pete right now. Please, Jeff? Something is wrong with this global warming nonsense anyway. We both know that so why not make a clean break now before this lie turns into an even bigger one?" pleaded Tully.

General Margate

Bob Thurston wasn't a man who had gotten as far as he had because he was skittish. Yet it would now seem that a certain stupid and greedy young senator had to be taught a lesson, and it would be his last. "Oh well, so be it," thought Bob. Why should he let this go unpunished? Bob knew that even if these allegations were false, how could his company survive scrutiny and distrust from his stockholders? The stock would plummet to the bowels of the dead. All could be lost in today's open court of public opinion and the need to be politically correct.

"Bullshit," he now thought. "I'll do what I do best. I'll make this all go away, it's at least what I can do before even I'm forced to leave this life."

Bob knew of certain men, and these certain men could make things go away. Bob knew there was a high price to be paid, but that would be fine. After all, he had plenty of money, especially now that he had been widowed. There was no one to spend his money, he thought. Bob knew that Gene had been dedicated to him for more years than he cared to remember, but he also knew that, in his will, he had left Gene more money than she could ever spend. She'll never work again, and besides, why would she work for anyone but me, he thought. Especially after all of these years, we spent together.

Money to fix the problem would be no problem, and he knew exactly who he should contact.

General Margate laughed at the phone call from Bob. Only Bob would call him and ask for a clandestine meeting at his club. Bob's club was no less private than the general's club, so what could Bob be thinking? Everyone there sees the two of them whispering and carrying on as if they had somehow taken control of the whole world. When actually, all they could really see was two old men talking quietly and having a few too many drinks, more often than not. The day would eventually wind down, and off they would stagger their separate ways. Good thing they both had drivers to take them wherever they lived. Yet, most people stopped to talk to both of them on occasion, seeing how they were both major shareholders in the golfing complex.

General Margate was the retired former commander of the Allied forces in the Baltic Arena of Affairs in 1945. During the "big one," they both fondly liked to describe the last and only war they participated in. Legally, that is. The general now reflected on just how much the two of them actually did do. Hell, it was enough that if anyone really knew it all, they'd both be in jail, probably under the jail, more likely, he thought. But what the hell, we've been together for so long that some would think we're joined at the hip, and some have even commented," Margate continued to muse.

"General," said Bob in a tone that indicated they had some serious work to do.

"May I ask what is so important that you want me to drag myself out of the house in the middle of the night?" asked Margate.

"Listen, I have a problem, and before it can infest my company and possibly indict the two of us for past performances, we and I emphasize the *we* part, need to nip this in the bud," finished Bob angrily.

Meeting in the lobby was both robotic and, in a sense, somewhat comic, as they had done this so many times. With their slight nodding acknowledgment of each other, they both turned, walking directly into their private office. A very private office set up for specific purposes. Here, they could take an unsuspecting, yet willing, young lady for a midday rendezvous or to talk about the club or personal business. Many new members were persuaded to join the club in this room. Not many rooms had the luxurious decorations as this one had; from Louis XIV's furniture to paintings that belonged in the Louvre. Some items came to them via the "big one", some from the wealth that they have accumulated over the years. A couple of gifts were from foreign governments to Bob for making it rain and for "playing God," as he was so fond of saying privately. Only to his close group of friends. His special ones, who also made up this club's original membership. However, lately, it seemed as if they were becoming scarcer. Looks as if "old man death" came and took more and more of them each year. That had them both wondering, "Who would be next?"

Standing alone now with the door to their private space closed and locked, General Margate walked away over to the side table close to just one of the large, overstuffed leather chairs in the room. "Okay, apparently, it's important. Let me pour myself a stiff one. How about you, Bob, straight up or frozen?" asked Margate.

Placed on that table next to his favorite chair was a special lamp. By moving it a certain way, a secret panel slid to the side, revealing a cache of some of the best liquor in the world. It was like something right out of the movies. Actually, it was right out of the movies. Bob had brought the movie set from an old mystery movie, *Where the Butler Did It,* the panels already built. Bob had not only the money but also the power to almost get the damn thing free, delivered, and installed. The door to the room got automatically locked when this panel was opened, ensuring confidentiality all of these years. Smiling, Margate turned and said to Bob.

"You know, Bob, some of the best whisky in the world is behind this wall, and no one but you and I really know it exists. What a shame. I really hope you go before me, you old bastard. So, in my sorrowful celebration and, of course, with my misery at the loss of my dearest friend, I'll be forced to come here with some beautiful young lady and drink this whisky all up. All in the memory of you, of course."

"You're too old for that. After three drinks, you'll be lying on the floor sound asleep, waking up to find out you've been robbed. Bring me one straight, and make it the brandy from Napoleon's cask," replied Bob.

Now seemingly somewhat more subdued, at least for now, he spoke. "Listen, General, I had a visitor today. Someone I had no idea that he even existed until today. Some senator that was not even elected he's filling in for that ass they found dead last year, full of dope. Now, this young man comes to me and says that he has found some information about a certain senator who met his death in a fire years ago. A certain senator from a tobacco state, if you remember?"

"Damn, Bob, that was so long ago I would think that the man's own family would have forgotten by now," replied Margate. "What in the blazes could he possibly think he can get out of this from you?" he asked.

"What do you think?" replied Bob, suddenly raising his voice to another octave. "Money, of course, they all want money. Why else does a man walk into your office and make these claims? It's not to wish you well. Not only that, he also wants me to put him on a committee of some real importance and pay for his bid to be reelected by God! What the hell could he be thinking of coming to me, of all people? He must think that I'm some old fart who would gladly give in because I wouldn't want the company hurt. He has no idea as to how I operate, but this bastard is going to find out!" yelled a now very mad and upset Bob Thurston.

"Calm down, Bob, before I drink this liquor in your honor sometime this week. No sense in blowing a gasket over this. Let's just do what we do best and remember what's worked best over the years for us," said Margate. "First, sit down and relax. I just poured you a glass of the best brandy in this known world. Drink the damn thing before you blow apart."

Now sitting and looking at his glass, Bob recognized the most important thing in his relationship with Margate all of these years. The general always had a way of keeping things calm and in perspective. Besides, the brandy was the best in the world; why waste it by not enjoying it? So, Bob leaned back in his big luxurious chair and melted into its softness and comfort, looking at the color of the brandy as he swirled it around in the crystal goblet.

"Here's what we'll do," said the general. "We ask him to show you some proof that he knows something, and it's not just hypothetical. If I remember right, that particular job was done by one of the best in the business. It made it look like the man was a switch hitter occasionally. Why, they never even investigated the fire thing in the first place. No one wants to find out that their husband, a United States senator, was a part-time fag. Besides, what proof can he have? That fire burned for days, as I recall. Unless someone from a séance came and told him something," finished a now-laughing Margate.

"Yeah, ya know, I was so upset at first, I could only think of keeping this quiet and making it all go away when actually I have no idea as to what proof this jackass might have," said Bob. "Nothing but speculation; it means nothing. The man can make all of the claims he wants to. It'll just make me support his opponent all the more, won't it?" Bob was sitting there a lot calmer now that he had time to reflect and get comfort from an old friend.

"Bob, I'll get us a go-between so he's not dealing with you directly anymore. We need to stop that right now so that neither of us is involved if this goes south. Then, if there is something, well, hell, we just make it go away. No big deal. I have just the right man in mind. He recently finished a project for us," finished Margate, now sitting back in his own special chair. He raised his glass into the light from the lamp next to him, and he couldn't help but smile as the clarity of such a great brandy sparkled like diamonds.

Now, taking a more subtle approach to his situation, Bob smiled and said, "Then if things are as he says, why, I just need to find someone who needs some work and can handle this for us. I'll make it a fourth man out party, all by phone, no trace, all money paid in advance in gold."

"That's the idea, Bob, now let's sit back and really enjoy some of this brandy," said Margate. "After all, if we both go at the same time, imagine some lucky bastard taking the wall down and finding our stash. At our age, we might as well start to deplete this nectar of the gods." He finished with a smile as he swirled his drink and held it to the light again just to see the clarity and awaken a smell that only a few men in the world had ever enjoyed.

Justin, Clara, and Work

Meeting with Luke was now becoming easier and more bearable, lately. It would seem that the young and often inquiring Luke, who always inquired about Justin, was often entertaining for Clara. As a matter of fact, to clear up any misunderstandings, the three of them had gone out to lunch on several occasions. At first, it seemed a little awkward for all of them but eventually became somewhat normal. Now that Luke was apprised of Justin, he sort of stopped trying to manipulate their friendship. Not as before, when all he seemed to do was take any advantage of it that he could, smiling and pretending to be this innocent farm boy. It's good that it has started to become more concrete, or she wouldn't meet with him, regardless of what John wanted. But now, Clara thought that they were almost becoming friends. Often, in her line of work, she would use someone like Luke to help gather information on certain aspects of senatorial life. Clara knew this newly forming friendship could also help her learn her FBI agent trade better. Then, she thought that getting things out of Luke shouldn't count because it was the easiest part of her job. Now that her boss, John Bloso, was aware of her new relationship, he insisted she use it to learn the ins and outs of Washington politics. Maybe once in a while, Clara could pick up information that could even be useful to the FBI, he had told her.

So, back and forth, when she could, she would visit Luke to catch up on things that happened in his official capacity. She would often ask for some directions on other issues, and Luke seemed to bask in the delight of being needed by her, and suddenly, their friendship had taken a turn for the better. What she didn't know was that Luke was biding his time until he could convince her that she really needed to sleep with him to become another notch in the gun handle. Then, he could get rid of her and move on to someone else. But for now, Clara still intrigued Luke, and he would continue to play along until the time was right for him to pounce. After all, someday, he could be the senator, and she would need him much more than he would need her.

"What are you thinking about?" inquired a smiling Justin.

"Oh, nothing really," said Clara. "Just about how much has changed since we graduated and came here to Washington."

"Yeah, I know," said Justin. "Just the other day, I was talking to the boss man, and he said that before I knew it, I would have my basic five years in, and I could ask for another assignment area. I asked him why he had been here for so long and had not moved on. He said that his wife and daughter love it in Virginia. They would hang him by his heels before they left. So, he's not going anywhere. Well, we almost feel the same way living in Georgetown, right? It sometimes has its ups and downs, but it is a beautiful area to live in. Speaking about areas to live in, when are you moving in? I have most of your stuff at my place as it is. I really think that we need to start making something happen here, don't you?" said Justin, with a smile on his face that would sink a ship.

Now understanding what he had meant when he said earlier that they needed to talk, Clara just smiled and said, "They still frown on this, Justin, you know that. Yet you insist that we make things harder on ourselves. Why can't we leave it for now and see later what we are about? You know now how I feel about you and my work. I love you both, but I'm not a stay-at-home mom kind of girl, at least not yet." She reached over and made sure that no one was looking as she kissed the top of Justin's head and then walked away before any more of this conversation could continue in the office, of all places.

Walking away from Justin, she heard him give that soft whistle of his as if she couldn't hear it. Clara and Justin were almost living together permanently now. Things had stepped up and have become something special for both of them. It seems Luke suddenly made Justin recognize exactly how much she meant to him. So, Justin finally took the time to make sure she understood his feelings for her. Laughing to herself, she was glad he did as she continued to walk into the corridor.

Clara finally came to realize that she needed him as well. It seems she did grow dependent on him during these past years, and she was now glad of it. But, becoming a stay-at-home mom and giving up her dreams of being an FBI agent now that she had finally become one? Well, things were moving fast, and some of it was okay. But Clara needed to slow that part down a little before it became an issue and would ruin their relationship. This she did know for certain. She did love Justin more than she would ever admit, and the thought of being a mom did excite her a little.

Col. Juan San Louis

General Margate waited in the limo as retired Colonel Juan San Louis, former Special Operational Group/Decoy Unit commander, slowly approached his car. The area for this meeting was in its usual place just outside of Washington, a little place in Fairfax, where the site of a parked limo and car meetings was almost customary. Juan moved to the rear-side passenger door, and when he thought everything was fine, he opened the door and slid in alongside the general. Now, with a big, broad smile on his face, Juan held out a hand and spoke.

"General, it is always a privilege to sit and chat with you. Besides, every time it happens, it would seem my stock and spending money increase a little."

Still looking at the general and with a broad smile on his face, the colonel noticed that the driver was missing. That indicated to him that this meeting had a real purpose. It's not like one of those fact-finding informational needs meetings. The ones called for by the general, every so often, and for whatever company he was working for.

The general liked using his well-known contacts. It seemed to make him wealthy, along with those he hired to do a job for him.

"Well, Colonel, it would seem that that would be the case for our meeting today. I need your help getting a message out to a few people. But before that, though, I need to make clear exactly, and I do mean exactly, what certain individuals might know. Or possibly what future information they might be privy to, knowingly or, hell, even if they're ignorant of it, who cares? I want to know everything, understood?" the general said.

"Sure, sir, I would, of course, need a names list and location addresses, any other personal information that would help, and I need to know exactly how I am to finalize the information I gather. I assume we need to make things somewhat distorted?" replied the colonel.

"No, Colonel, I'll be making all final decisions on the matter," replied Margate.

"Of course, sir," said a now-inquisitive former special forces officer who, on more than one occasion, had quieted the voice of opposition for the general. After all, he added some very good side money to his pension, and if the general needed something done, he would see to it.

"Maybe it was a national security issue, so why not," thought Juan. He fully trusted the general's decisions and demands concerning his responsibilities for this government.

Looking at the colonel and seeing a man he has trusted in the past to get things done for him, Margate was confident it would all turn out just fine. But he also was a man who dotted all of his "i's" and crossed all of his "t's", so he repeated.

"I need you to make sure that when the time comes, I have all the information I would need to make a correct decision. Do we understand each other clearly? I want to be perfectly clear on this, Colonel."

"Yes, sir. I was inquiring whether your need had become, say, expendable. Then I would need to make sure that I have someone in the wings to take flight, am I correct?"

"Yes, Colonel, exactly. If what you find out needs to be left alone, then we go our separate ways. If not, I need someone then to make a flight happen. I know you will have everything in order, I trust. Right, Colonel? Nothing silly-looking, just a straight-up everyday normal departure, got that, Colonel?" asserted Margate, a little sternness now creeping into his voice.

"Yes, sir. Exactly what kind of time frame are we looking at here?" asked Juan, now that he finally had a real understanding of this conversation. Mostly, the general always wanted things in a hurry, so he better ask on this one, he thought.

"Let's say within six weeks, but no later. We'll meet up here again and go over the packet, and I'll make the decision then or possibly a day or two later. I am counting on you, and I have no need to remind you that this is a national security issue. I'm correct in thinking this way, am I not, Colonel?" asked the general.

"Yes, sir. I'll make sure that everything remains secure," said the colonel. With that, they again shook hands, and before he could open the door, a packet was in the hands of the colonel. Not wanting to look because he knew what was inside and not wanting to smile, he simply exited the limo. Colonel Juan San Louis just became slightly richer. He would wait, however, until he got home before he found out exactly just how rich. The colonel knew that the money inside would represent exactly how important this job was going to be. But who cared? The more important the work, the more money he would earn, and by the end of it all, maybe he would spring for a vacation in the Islands. Now, the colonel was smiling.

When he opened the packet in the safety of his home, he was very surprised to find some of the names in it. A Senator Pillow from

Pennsylvania was the main character on the list inside. As well as his top two aides, Ms. Mable Gardner and Mr. Luke Weeks, and someone named Frank Benoit. It seems that everyone on the list lived in Washington, except for this Benoit fellow. He and his wife lived on a farm down on the lower west side of Virginia, almost on the West Virginia border.

"This should be a breeze," Juan thought. He was hired because no matter what else, he was capable of. Juan could make a computer sit up, talk in ten languages, and give change if needed. Juan was one of the best hackers in the world. His sole purpose at the Pentagon was to hack into every computer they deemed a potential hazard for the military and the government. He would hack into those selected computers and not just take information from them, but rewrite the codes so no one else could use them. When they did, it would alert Juan. He was a master at disguises, getting in and out of places, and delivering any type of death warrant if needed.

Juan had, for his government, redirected whole military combat groups of selected countries, deploying them to useless areas. By using different methods of misdirection, he saved a lot of foot soldiers from impending battles, or not. Now, smiling, Juan felt good about this easy job.

He needed to gather the intelligence on how much they knew about former Senator Breems. According to the report he now read, the late senator died in 1949 in Tennessee in a house fire. It would seem the late senator also had a thing for both women and men. The report read that they had found all three dead bodies with both males locked in an embrace. What a way for your wife to find out that you were a swinger. Additionally, Juan was asked to determine what other information was available to them regarding H.T. Wetco. Juan knew that the company was one of the largest DOD contractors in the country. That has to be the pocketbook on this job. Only someone with that kind of money could pay the kind of money Juan found in the envelope earlier. Anyway, he would meet with them once he hacked into their computers and had all the information he needed.

He would show his fake Department of Defense Pentagon credentials, and they would talk, as most people did. No one had to know that he made new ones up every year since his retirement five years earlier. He would comb through their garbage late at night and bug their offices and phones. Everyone's house would soon become nothing more than a big microphone feeding a few tape recorders. Then, a second meeting with the general would be in order, and he would make his final report. Sitting back in his chair and facing his computer, Juan began to get down to business. "Now is just as good a time as any," he thought. Smiling, he wondered how the senator would feel tomorrow when he woke up and had no money.

Information Gathering

"Just a few more questions, please," asked the agent from DOD. "Nice man," thought Mable; he most definitely knew his way around computers. She felt a little bit better now that the Department of Defense was investigating the hacking of their computers. Someone had not only gotten into their system but also changed a lot of the coding and deleted a lot of valuable information. Information that when Senator Pillow finds out who the culprit is, he will have him strung from a pole by his thumbs. She had never seen the senator so angry, shouting and cursing, slamming down his laptop in a fit of rage. He had already sent Luke back into the archives in the basement, groveling for the original documents concerning that tobacco senator. Unfortunately, Luke had burned many bridges there with some of the female employees, and it seemed he wouldn't be out of there any time soon.

"Excuse me, Ms. Gardner, did you say that during the week, someone was also monitoring your e-mail and postings?" asked Agent Millhouse.

"Yes, it seemed as if every time we would add something to the senator's information blog, someone would erase or change some of the material. It's impossible to know how it was being done. Only the senator and I have the password information. Even Luke, Mr. Weeks, never had a way into the blog," she said now with a little awe in her voice. Looking directly at Agent Millhouse so he would understand the importance of what she was about to say, she said, "Whoever it was must be very good at what they do. This is why the senator says that the DOD had to get involved because some of the material we were gathering concerned a potential investigation of a DOD contractor. The senator, of course, needs this to be kept in the utmost privacy. We understand that you report back to the senator under his privileged status and then commit jointly to any statements concerning the investigation. Am I correct on this? If so, then I am making myself at this point perfectly clear when I say that no one is allowed to know any information we gather on this intruder and/or the subject matter that this evil man needed to get his skuzzy little hands on, right?"

"Yes, of course, you are correct. I have no intentions of making any statements even after all the facts are in. That will be left up to Senator Pillow and his staff to decide what you want to say at the end of this. As long as no vital information concerning Homeland Security will be divulged or has been hacked from your computers, am I making myself clear, Ms. Gardner?" said Agent Millhouse, looking a little stern now as he peered down at her.

"Why, yes, of course. Why should we worry about any Homeland Security issues? Nothing was on the system that someone couldn't read on docket papers or any agenda material lying around. Senator Pillow has yet to be put on a sitting committee," she said, with a smile on her face.

Agent Millhouse walked toward the door, turned, and said, "Well, let me get going. I need to make a few more stops, and I will come back to interview Mr. Weeks on Monday. If I need any other information, I will call the main number and ask for you. Is that okay, Ms. Gardner?"

Stepping around her, Juan moved closer to the door, and as he opened it, he pushed a small button on his shirt, a transmitter button to activate the transmitter he had just left behind in her office. He already had access to their outcalls. That is how he handled the call for help last night made to the DOD. Now with the transmitter working from a direct feed from the inside, with the ones now implanted in all three computers, backed up by what he now has hidden inside all the desks. As far as Juan was concerned, this was just another one of his masterpieces. If they typed a word, spoke a word, or used Morse code signals, Juan San Louis would know about it. Then, he had just to return and finish up with this Luke character, which should be easy enough. But for now, he had work to do in two apartments and one house rented by this senator.

The drive down to the Benoit house wasn't bad at all. The scenery in this part of the state always reminded Juan of his home state. Looking at the mountains surrounding the hidden valleys, Juan thought they could pass as giant imaginary waves frozen in time. Just before they would come crashing down on the valleys below, he could almost sense the mountains wanting to burst forward in their final run back to the ocean. Juan always had this melancholy feeling come over him as he drove in the bright sunlight that painted everything one shade greener than the shade of green next to it. He didn't have time to think of this part of the assignment. The ride was taking away any anger he might harbor for the Benoits. Juan thought it was a little strange that someone of their age could be connected to some type of terrorist movement. So, for now, he would sit back in the car and let his senses go to work. This scenery was too beautiful to ignore.

"Good afternoon," Claire said with that smile that put everyone at ease immediately. "Won't you come on in? I hope your drive down wasn't bad." Turning now and moving into the house, she continued talking, knowing that the man was following her.

"This time of year, everyone just raves about the beauty of this part of the country. We love it here. Come this way, Frank is in the parlor. He has done nothing but talk about your visit. We don't get many visitors down here, outside of family, you know, and for Frank to have someone come to talk about his work, well, that is exciting, even for me," finished Claire, as she pointed to a seat nestled in a corner beside the fireplace, not seeing Frank in the room.

"Well, thank you, ma'am, the ride here was just absolutely beautiful. It reminds me of my home sometimes, with the mountains, greenery, and all the little valleys. Beautiful, just really beautiful," said Juan, smiling as if he had known Claire all of his life.

There was something vaguely familiar about her and the house, as if he were visiting his grandmother back home. The house was built probably sometime in the forties and was an old center hall colonial-style home, with pictures stuck to all the walls and resting on every available shelf, proudly displaying her and Frank's family. The years have been very good to both of them, it seemed. Displayed pictures at Disney World, the Virginia shore, and faraway places showed nothing but happy, smiling faces. Faces of their smiling children and grandchildren seemingly wanting to burst out of every frame. Everyone was happy, it seemed, and loved, as well. Both comfort and caution came into his head now, and he shrugged them off as if nothing or no one in this house could want to hurt him. "Grandmothers don't go around hurting people," he thought, chuckling to himself.

"Where is home, if I may ask?" inquired Claire.

"Oh, I'm sorry," said Juan. "I'm originally from Vermont, a small town in the Green Mountains there."

"Miss it?" asked Claire.

"Well, after college, I just never went back. Sort of moved around the country a lot, and by the time you look back, it's too late. I'm afraid my nesting days are over. Now, I sort of like to travel and see a lot of interesting places. Especially historical sites, those that I have never been to, as long as I can afford it? Sometimes it can be expensive, though," Juan said with a slight smile on his face.

Just then, Frank entered the room, and seeing Claire and Juan in discussion, he waited until silence had found its way into the conversation. Then, with an outstretched hand, he said, "Frank, Frank Benoit, as I am sure you already know, and you must be Mr. Starling. We're glad you made it. Sometimes, the drive here is so slow it's almost as if we're waiting for a stagecoach to pull up to the place. Most people driving down here for the first time like to slow down after a while to enjoy the scenery, which I hope you enjoyed. Why, even the grandkids are late getting here sometimes. But you, you're not late. So that means either an early start to your day or you drive fast. Which is it?"

"Well, sir, none of the above, or maybe all of the above, how's that for an honest answer?" replied Juan.

"Absolutely great," said Frank. "I love it when a young man can talk straight. Why, it tells me that we can talk straight, as well. Now, sir, what can I do for you before my wife has you full of her iced tea or lemonade? Which is it? Or would you like to try both?" said Frank, as if he were now talking to one of his children.

"Well, how about the lemonade first? I always have had a thing for lemonade," a smiling Juan replied, now more at ease.

"Me too, Claire, I would love some of that as well," said Frank. As he turned, he gave a small pat to his wife's arm as she was walking away. Turning and facing Juan, Frank said, "Well, sir, what questions can I answer for you concerning my work?"

Frank and Claire had been discussing this visit for days ever since the man from a cable television channel called and said they wanted to do a piece on unsung scientists. Scientists have made great contributions to the world of scientific research. Nonetheless, and especially since his research related to weather. Lately, it seemed as if the weather all around the globe was in disarray. So Frank, after a few minutes of conversation, acquiesced and agreed to this first meeting.

It seemed Frank always knew that his discovery and work were the best. How often did he tell Claire that he was next to God? Jokingly spoken about, of course, because that would upset her. But secretly, sometimes, he meant it. After all, Frank could and did make it rain, from downpours to outright tropical hurricanes. Why, he could do what no other on this planet could do. With his rains, he could deliver both life and death. He could destroy crops and, even at the right time of year, bring on snows that would destroy transportation, close mountain passes, and disrupt the entire system. He could make the jet streams move lower on the planet or even make them circle the Arctic and wreak havoc on unsuspecting countries. After all, he knew why Russia had suffered so many years of droughts, causing their political party to halt due to a lack of rain and causing famine for its people. How many years can anyone put up with all that distortion in the weather without paying a price for it?

Frank was important. "It was about time he got his just due," he thought. Especially since no one was alive from his old company, as far as he knew, it was now a known fact of science that man was capable of making it rain. This interview was about him being the scientist who made it all happen. He also knew that Claire would call all the children to watch the interview, which was good enough.

"So, what kind of program is this exactly, and when is it going to air? I would need some time to let all the kids know the date. Right now, I can't tell you how excited the little ones are about Grandpa. Not every day that their grandpa is going to be on television, you know," said Frank, smiling from ear to ear.

Returning to the room carrying a tray with three glasses filled to the brim and some cookies, Claire said, "Here, have some lemonade, and don't let this old man push you around. Before you know it, he'll have you doing a show only about him and our family." Claire laughed.

"No, that's fine," said Juan, with a smile on his face. "I would like to know everything about this entire project. Who first started to think about it, and how it all came about? How did Frank get involved, and where did the project end up? Even if you think that this is being used now? Could it possibly have anything to do with today's weather we now claim to be out of the ordinary? Whatever you want to add to any of my questions, please feel free to talk about it. This program is about you, Frank, and it's my understanding that you are the man. You finished a project that many in your company couldn't get a grasp on, and you made it all work, isn't that so?" asked Juan.

"Well, it sure is. Right from the beginning. I knew that this project was going to become my path to fame. The company needed the work as well. The war had just ended, and many people went back to farming and making their living off the fields. The problem was that in those days, not many fields could be farmed. No rain, or not enough of it. It always was a problem in the mid-central states. Hell, Kansas was a dust bowl a few years earlier. People moved to California just because they had some rain. When I was asked to look into this new yet ongoing project, it was as if a light bulb went off in my head. I suddenly knew what was not working and what I needed to do to make it work," replied Frank.

For the first time in a long time, he didn't have his often-faraway look on his face when he spoke about his favorite subject, rain. As the afternoon wore on and it became supper, Juan was treated to some of the best pork chops, mashed potatoes, and corn he had in a very long time, including the biscuits with gravy, all washed down with that great lemonade, followed by some local whisky that made the day's end seem as if this day had lasted a week. Wrapping up around nine o'clock that evening, Juan was tired, but he still had to get back to Washington. Tomorrow, he would be finalizing his report and making an appointment with the general now that this had come to an end. Feeling somewhat guilty about the reason why he was there, Juan still had no problem shaking hands and saying goodnight. They had asked him to stay the night several times. He almost acquiesced, but sometimes sleep was a day away in his line of work, which was fine. After all, you didn't do what he did for a living and work nine to five.

Juan now had about two months of work gathered up into a large portfolio consisting of hours of tapes and pictures. Pictures of meetings the senator had with subordinates and other senatorial members. As well as this chipper-looking, young secretary from a local pool, he shared with some other freshman senators. The girl was young enough to be his daughter, but the senator had no problem attaching himself to her, like the leech he was.

"But, oh well," thought Juan. This job was almost over, and he was thinking about returning to the Dominican Republic to take in some rooster fishing. Why not? Right now, he deserved to hang loose for a while, so whatever happened after he submitted the report was something he had no involvement with. How could he be in several places at once? Not if he was fishing in the Atlantic Ocean, taking in the sights with some friends he had down there. They could never place him in Washington, DC, and right now, that is what mattered to him, getting lost as soon as possible after he finished with the general this week, especially if he was asked to make a one-way flight for someone.

"Damn, I hope it will never be those kind old folks. The car looks as if it has sat in the same place as it did two months ago," thought Juan. He had been observing it and the entire area for about an hour. So far, nothing out of the ordinary was going on. It was almost as if he was reliving the whole first meeting all over again, except the weather tonight was a lot warmer, even if a nice breeze was blowing on his back. Juan couldn't wait till he felt the same breeze against his back, but only it would smell of the tropics after a long day of fishing and drinking. "Soon, this will be over completely," thought Juan as he moved toward the car, and he would take that much-needed rest and recuperation known as R&R to most military men.

The limo's door seemed to open automatically for him. Juan stepped to the side as it swung open, revealing two passengers seated in the back, sipping from clear crystal glasses. Closing the door and seating himself opposite the two men, Juan said, "General, always a pleasure to see you again, sir."

With a smile and a slight nod, the general returned the compliment. "Thank you, and likewise on my part. I hope you have gathered enough intelligence for us to make an informed decision after reviewing it. I thought you would be extra thorough. That's why I consented to the extra time," replied the general.

Juan needed and asked for some extra time, finding that the six weeks they had originally agreed upon would not be enough. Things in the senator's office seem to change at the drop of a hat.

"Absolutely, sir, this was one of your more interesting and yet easier assignments. With my need to be thorough for you, the extra time allowed more than enough time to do all of my "i's" and cross all "t's" several times, sir. All the intel is accurate. The recordings will speak for themselves. The videos are conclusive as to who was seeing whom and exactly what has been transpiring with all the people in question."

Juan didn't know the man who accompanied the general and didn't care. However, what he did care about was that this was the first time the general questioned his ability to do the job right, which bothered Juan. He and the general always had a great working relationship with each other. Juan had done a lot of work over the years for him, both while in the service and out of it. The general's questions, for some reason, didn't sit right. Something seemed a little out of place, now thinking that maybe he should know exactly who the other gentleman was. A man who continued to sit and stare at him as if he were trying to bore a hole right through him.

"I don't have any additional information concerning the H. T. Wetco organization. I don't believe you asked me to delve into that. So, everything here is short on that." Now, looking to see if the gentleman sitting next to the general made any move or indication that he was affected by that remark, Juan sat back to see how close he was to this mysterious person's identity.

Laughing, the general said, "Well, son, looks as if you're still one of the best, making that remark to see if the fish rose to the surface. What do you think? This is someone from Wetco?"

"Well, sir, we never have had anyone sitting in on our business, and all I can think is that this gentleman is from H. T. Wetco, seeing how it is the only company we seem to be interested in, in a sort of roundabout way," replied Juan.

"Let me answer that question for you, if I may," said the man sitting next to the general. "H.T. Wetco is not involved with any of this. If they were to be involved, it would be from the perspective that they may have an interest in a certain senator. There is always the possibility of backing him financially in his next election. Or possibly trying to help the senator get selected for a special committee seat. One that would help the people in his district. But that is all, nothing more, nothing less. If the general needs you to delve into H.T. Wetco, then I am sure he would have asked you to from the beginning. Now, as to who I may be, let's just say that the general and I have some common stake in this business. After all, one can never be too sure as to what really is going on behind the scenes, right, Colonel?" He looked at the general, who was now smiling as if he wanted to say, "See, I told you he was smart."

Then, turning now to look into the old man's face to make sure that everyone was on the same page, Juan said, "I meant no disrespect, of course, but every once in a while, it's good to drop the cards and see where they may fall, right? After all, no harm, no foul. But I am handing over some sensitive information here, and I need to be sure that it wasn't all done in vain. That is unless the price of admission has gone up, and if that's the case, then I suggest you toss this stuff right out the window while passing over the next bridge," finished Juan.

"No, sir, I hear nothing but great things about you and just thought I would come along for the ride, just in case someday I may have a need for your services," said the old man.

"Well, sir, I'll be leaving then. Have a great night, gentlemen." Turning to leave, Juan felt a hand go to his arm, and he turned to see the general holding out another envelope for him to take.

"This is for being as thorough with this as I asked you to be," said the general. "Take this and enjoy it, a bonus if you will, and go have some much-needed R&R. I'm sure when we finally finish going through this, I'm gonna feel like I didn't give you enough. Any place in particular you going to?" Turning to face the other man, the general said, "Ah, to be young and travel the world, I can envy that, that's for sure."

"No, sir," replied Juan. "Maybe take a trip to New York, take in a play or something. Then it's back here. I have another offer to take care of, some additional business next month. Never stop working, I say; always make hay when the time is right."

With that, Juan quickly exited the limo. Something was amiss. Why the hell would the general want to know where he might end up this week? That old man with him had to be with Wetco. It suddenly all made sense now—H.T. Wetco, rain, Benoit. But where did the senator and his staff fit in? He should have read the files he made on these people. Hell, he didn't even listen to the tapes. All he saw was the video crap, and that only showed this ass whoring around with as many young chicks as would have him. Next time, though, he would have to become more suspicious of some of the work he was given, especially when it was so little of a job but created the most money he had ever made for such a short period.

The general hadn't really been a fan of Bob's traveling along for the ride. After all, Juan was his man and had been for all these years. It wasn't good to have too many secrets get out into the open, especially when someone wanted to meet one of your wet men. These guys are all special and have to be maintained in that fashion. You just didn't expose some of these people to others. It could lead to a lot of unnecessary problems for everyone involved.

"Why I let you talk me into letting you come along for the ride is beyond me," said Margate. "It was not only stupid, Bob, but it could be dangerous as well. All of these guys become paranoid after so many years, changing themselves to do work that a lot of people would think of as being crazy. Sometimes, I have no idea what you're thinking. Where it's coming from, and by God, you also drag me right into it. How you do that is beyond me."

"Listen to what you're saying, Margate. If I weren't along, that part about the company would have slipped right past you. Of course, he now knows about the company and who paid him so damn much money for even what he called a simple, easy job. We have money, but I don't want to piss it all away. Now, what do we do about this character and his knowing about the company?" asked Bob.

"Nothing! Absolutely nothing. This man has been with me for too many years. He has done so much work for me, it'll be his ass locked away under the jail for life if any of the crap ever got out as to what he has done for us," said a now stern-voiced general. "Do I make myself perfectly clear on this point, Bob?"

"Yes, yes, of course, you do, unless the little bastard goes sneaking around and puts his nose into some place it doesn't belong," replied Bob, with a smug little smile on his face, knowing that no matter what, Margate would go along with whatever he decided had to be done to protect everyone concerned. Besides, he had his contacts working on this already. So, why else would he come along if not to see how Margate was handling his end of the problem? "Call it curiosity, if you will," he thought. Bob was just as confident in his hangman, Pete Winslow. Pete not only handled misinformation for the company, but he handled a certain group of science projects that, every so often, had to be "tweaked", as they say. Bob was confident in Pete's ability to get the job done. No matter what the job, its cost, or outcome. Any task Bob had assigned him over the years, somehow Pete had managed to get the results for him, and that is all that mattered. He reflected now, sitting back in the limo and pouring another brandy, that soon it'll all be over and done with. Then, it dawned on him that his man and Margate were both graduates from West Point. So, what? They probably didn't know each other. After all, there was a big age difference to consider. Then, after meeting him tonight, he was sure of that.

Besides, his man, Pete Winslow, from the very beginning had been called in, and the wheels were already in motion to rid him of this problem. Hopefully, this was the last problem he had to deal with before he left this earth. When he heard the general start to speak, he turned in the seat and just nodded, knowing that's all he had to do in order to get the general to think he was actually listening. But he knew that before this night was over, there would be one less voice to fear.

"That is a fine young man, capable of wiping this slate clean and making it all disappear. If we, and I say we, decide, that is the way we both choose to go. Now we need to visit this Intel and decide what direction we need to take and point him like a dog in that direction," said General Margate as he poured himself another brandy.

Becoming paranoid was the first real sign that one had to get out of this business quickly. Often, it would lead to hurting someone that you loved dearly or someone who may not have deserved to die. Juan couldn't believe that he was becoming paranoid. But what he had just gone through wasn't normal. It wasn't as if the old man there was anything more than someone tied to the general, maybe ex-military, or with H.T.Wetco. Maybe a senior vice president to ensure the general passed along the right amount of money. After all, it wasn't uncommon for everyone to take a little piece of the action when no one was looking. Or, maybe he was just someone from Homeland Security, and they also had a real interest in this senator. But whatever the case may be, he would find out. After all, it is what he did for a living, and he was the best in the world at it, or so it had been said.

Rabbit

Pete Winslow had been asked to do a lot for Mr. Thurston over the years and had done those things without question. He also had been paid a lot more than most in the company and had access to even the private corporate jet whenever he wanted it. Things were absolutely great for him here at H.T. Wetco. He had been a young West Point graduate military man when General Margate recruited him. But Margate dropped out of the picture soon after, and he dealt only with Bob over the ensuing years, to the point that he even avoided the general, whenever possible, at Mr. Thurston's request. Today was no different. He had followed along behind the limo all the way to Fairfax, Virginia.

Then, his instructions were to follow anyone who entered and exited the vehicle and ensure he was not seen or heard. Bob had insisted on that part, saying that the operation depended on not being caught or seen. He was to get as much Intel as possible on the person and bring it back to Bob. But at any cost, maintain a strict code of silence. That meant he was to tail this person to his house, collect all the vital information on what he had left behind, and then today, God would call him home. That was as soon as he had enough to ensure everything was collected and not a second before. Ransack the place and make it look as if the geek was robbed. Following this individual out of the limo and tracking him was easy enough. After exiting the limo, he had walked to a nearby restaurant and, once seated, had ordered a beer and a burger. It all seemed innocent enough, yet he knew this man had to be an ex-Marine or maybe even a Navy SEAL. Something about how he walked confidently and always knew what and who was around him. He had served in Special Forces to climb higher in rank a lot quicker. But life in the private sector paid more, and the perks were a whole lot better than three squares a day if you were lucky.

After the burger was washed down by the last of the beer, the guy got up and proceeded to go to the men's room, only after trying to get some waiters' attention to locate it. Disappearing around the corner, Pete was sure that he only had to continue sipping on his Coke and then could proceed to follow this guy right to his front door. How easy can this be? If this guy liked to walk and the walk was too far away from his car, he would catch a taxi back. But, when all was said and done, Pete thought he would even stop back for a burger and a beer. Apparently, this guy was an amateur at this and not trained other than maybe having some combat training.

So, Pete relaxed and waited until his return. After about ten solid minutes had passed, Pete decided that maybe he better go check and see if his mark had something happen to him in there. It wouldn't be the first time a running rabbit he followed had stepped into a hole. And as sure as God made apples, the man was gone. The back window was left wide open, and a note had been attached to the outside bottom of the window, and it read,

"Gotcha, rabbit, now see if the hole is big enough for the both of us." Just then, Pete knew that he had a big problem. Exactly how big, he wasn't sure, but he knew he had one right now. Turning from the window to leave, Pete was shoved up against the wall with his arm now being twisted around his back with his head shoved hard and held tightly against the wall. His mark whispered in his ear.

"Listen, rabbit, if you make the mistake of following someone, don't make the mistake of it being me. Do I make myself clear? If not, the next time we meet, you will lose something, maybe an ear or a finger, or it could be your life. Think about that."

The next thing Pete felt was a needle going into his neck, and he thought he was dead. But it must have been a simple solution to knock him out so his newfound friend could leave. "Whoever this guy was, he was good," Pete thought. "Really good." This meant maybe he was out of his league for the first time, but that was just too much to think about. No one was going to expose him like that again. "If there is a next time, it'll be on my terms," Pete thought. This would be a good test to keep his senses more awake. But he will find him and make this bastard pay. No one leaves him lying on a crapper's floor. "He also called me 'rabbit', which can only mean one thing. That he's as wet as he was, oh well, damn, this is going to be fun," he thought.

But then, whatever had been injected into his neck was working as his knees crumbled, and he couldn't stop his fall even if he wanted to.

Grandpa Frank's Predicament

It had been three weeks since the interview, and Frank could not understand why no one had called him about his big debut on the Science Channel. He had called them, and no one, at first, even knew what he was talking about. Then, they started passing him around the office as a joke on fellow workers. After all the irritation and calls, they just put him on hold until either his arm fell asleep holding the receiver or he did.

"I'm gonna call Clara. She'll get to the bottom of this," said Frank for the hundredth time this morning. "After all, she's with the FBI, and maybe she can make sense of this nonsense. Why in the world would some young man visit us and make up this story about what science I did and not put it on the air? It is a great story. I should have them knocking down the door to get my autograph.

"I tell you, Claire, something just isn't right," finished an exhausted Frank. It seems as if ever since that interview, Frank has been getting more tired than normal. It was as if he had waited just for this very thing to happen; then he would be "going home to God", as he had been saying too many times lately.

"Frank, listen to me. I am sure that they have a lot more to do than to hurry back and just do your show. Why, there must be hundreds of scientists out there with similar stories. All waiting for an interview, then when it is all said and done, they'll show them all one right after the other. But if you insist on calling them every day, two or three times a day, maybe they'll call the FBI on you for pranking them with your calls," said Claire. "After all, Frank, sometimes you can become annoying," She chuckled and shook her head.

Clara was surprised by the call from her mother. Insisting that she call her grandfather about an interview they had concerning his past job. It seems as if the cable show on Science Discoveries had interviewed her grandfather more than six weeks ago. Now, Grandpa was getting so upset with no one returning his phone calls that he had resorted to calling his daughter three or four times a day. So upset had he become that he was now being belligerent to his own wife. He even called the local sheriff to see if the interviewer had gotten into an accident on his way out of town, and just maybe that was what was holding it all up. The thinking guy lay dead along the roadway, and nobody cared to take notice of it. But whatever it was that prevented this from going on the air, he did need an answer before he passed on, according to him. So maybe, somehow, a call from her office would make them tell the truth. Not that her mom wanted her to say directly that she was calling from the FBI. But to perhaps mention in the conversation that she did work for the FBI.

"Well, it could help," her mom had pleaded. It was worth the try." Not wanting to let her grandfather down, Clara decided to call him and get his side of the story before everyone started calling her.

"Hello, Grandpa. It's Clara. How are you doing? I meant to call earlier, but they have me so busy here that sometimes the days turn into weeks, and I lose all track of time. I know it's not an excuse, but I miss you, and I wanted to call to congratulate you on your acting career."

"Hi, sweetheart. How are you? It's always so great to hear from you. Wait a minute." Frank covered the phone's mouthpiece with his hand, and then Clara heard his muffled shout to her grandmother. "Claire, it's Clara on the phone from Washington!"

He came back to her, "I just had to tell your grandmother you're on the phone. Of course, I have to shout it out, seeing how she can't stand to be around me anymore, or so it seems. Just because some interviewer came here and asked us so many questions, and we had dinner, and off he went. I never heard back from this young man yet, Clara. I even had the sheriff go out and see if he was on the side of the road. Been a couple of months, and every time I call, I practically fall asleep, waiting on hold. I really am aggravated and at my wits' end. I have no clue as to what I should do next," said Grandpa Frank.

"Listen, Grandpa, why not give me the number and the man's name, the day he came out to the house, and what he wanted to talk about? Then I'll call and see if they can give us an answer, okay?" said Clara.

"I knew you would help out. I just knew it. That's why I always say you're the only one in this whole family with any brains. I tell your grandmother all the time, "Call Clara, she'll fix this in a minute!" But no, she calls your mother all of the time, and she won't lift a finger to help me. She says it's all in my head, that I have to be patient, that these things take a long time because of research. I told her that I did all the research, and what the hell did that young man need to do more for?"

"Listen, Grandpa, give me the information, and let me talk to Grandma now. As soon as I can, I'll be there to visit. I promise, okay?" said Clara.

Clara had just hung up the phone after speaking to Mr. Ken Wellington, the chief program director at the Science Discovery Channel in New York. It seems he had no idea as to what she was talking about. They had never sent anyone down to talk to her grandfather about what he claimed to have done. Actually, they had no interest in anyone who could make it rain. Of course, unless they could prove they did make it rain by certain dance steps. But he did complain to her that they would seek a harassment charge against her grandfather if he didn't stop calling them and complaining. It was as if he was becoming obsessed with this, even punching in different extension numbers. Whoever was unfortunate enough to answer received more than an earful. So, after reassuring Mr. Wellington that she would have a long talk with her grandfather, she promised the calls would cease. Once more apologizing for what seemed the hundredth time, she finally hung up the phone.

Clara knew that if her grandmother wasn't present when he made these calls, it was possible that he was hallucinating. But her grandmother was there, and that made it the truth. Oh well, when she had the time, she would look further into it, but right now, her caseload was heavy, and she really didn't have the time to spare.

Günter

After having to walk in the pouring rain down a dark alley in London to get there, Günter was tired of all the shit that he had to put up with when visiting these losers. Why in the world was this woman so annoying? Couldn't she see that he was inches away from cutting her throat? Of all the stupid females he had met in his life, this one took the cake. It wasn't enough to have lured him here under the pretense that she was this sexy female for hire, but she was also someone, in her mind, who said he really needed her. For a lousy hundred Euros, she had no idea that in a minute, she was going to be dead.

"Listen, woman, get me a beer, and then I want you to do what I paid for," said a now unsmiling Günter.

"Screw you, get yourself a beer; who the hell do you think you are, pushing me and smacking me? I could have you killed, you know that, you bastard!" yelled Angie. Angie was a hooker and professed that she was nineteen, but the photo she put on the Internet dating service to find her clients looked nothing like her. As a matter of fact, she had stolen the photo from some other ad, indicating she was willing to do anything for a hundred Euros. Payment for an hour of her time, but tonight, her ad had brought in the wrong client. This one wanted the girl in the picture and a beer. He had hit her with an open hand across her mouth and demanded money for wasting his time. Now, he changed his mind and wanted a beer and for her to go down on him. But Angie stood her ground.

"Frig you, I said, go and get your own friggen' beer, then get the hell out before I call some of my friends, you asshole," she screamed in his face. Turning and not even missing a beat, Günter slashed the knife across her throat and, at the same time, pushed her to his right.

"Hell, no sense and having her blood squirt all over my new jacket," he thought. Then, after he searched the house for any money she may have stashed away, he settled down in a seemingly comfortable chair and finished his beer before he left, not forgetting to turn off the TV.

The loud, constantly ringing phone was the only reason why he woke so early this morning. But Günter was glad that he had taken the call. Seems as if he was going to be paid a little more than usual for doing what he seemed to enjoy the most. Someone in America needed his services. This call was from an old friend of his living in Barcelona. It seems every now and then, those who despise you the most forgive you, or so they say. What he couldn't figure out was why the payment was upfront and in gold, already in a deposited account bearing his name in a bank in Spain.

Leaving England was going to be good for his cough, he thought. The weather here was either cloudy, raining, or it had just stopped raining, or it was going to rain soon. Without that call, he would have been forced to stay for another six months or so, or at least until the heat from Monte Carlo had died.

No one likes it when a whole family of Russian travelers is found in one of the plushest hotels one morning, robbed and murdered. Murdered children always seem to leave people with a bad taste in their mouths. "Oh well, you only get what you pay for," he thought. Günter now realized that he would have to spring for some new clothing. He had to look American, which for him was a bad thing. Günter hated Americans.

Günter also hated Istanbul, but this was the only place he and his kind could safely meet. A place where looking over his shoulder happened only every other hour or so. Not like in some other places where your life wasn't worth much, and often, it felt as if someone was trying to collect a bounty. He was only here in Istanbul because anything he needed to have made was possible here. The best counterfeiters in the world lived here, and now he was dealing with what was considered the best of them all.

Here, Adwadde would find everything he needed to become an American. He would become an American who was finally going home after an extensive stay in Belgium. From his new American passport to receipts showing the cost of this long vacation. Everything he would need to make him as real as any American could be if he got caught sneaking into the country. He couldn't believe his good fortune in having the gold deposited into an account for him.

Although, he was certain Bastian had taken from his payment a little more than he claimed. When this job was done, he thought, what better place to visit than Spain? He would have a nice long conversation with Bastian concerning his money, and he was sure that something would have been "forgotten," and he would suddenly be paid a little more. But what was there was enough for him to retire on, maybe, but good liquor and crazy women can be expensive in Europe, even for a newly made gentleman, as he would become. Life in Istanbul would have to suffice for now. "It sure beats England's weather, that's for sure," he thought as he lay back on the chaise lounge, soaking in the hot sun.

Just when Günter thought the phone call would never come, the phone started to ring. The call that I was waiting for never seemed to come. Reaching over the sleeping, nude body of the young girl lying next to him, he picked up the phone and heard the double click on the end of it as it went silent.

Slapping the girl's bare ass, he said, "Rise, girl, and get the hell out of here, now. I have someplace to be in five minutes, and I'll not have you sleeping in my bed while I'm out." Slow to rise, the girl was backhanded again, now getting up in a hurry from the last slap on her bottom, which stung so much. She backed into the sidewall and scampered across the room to her clothes. Dressed, she wanted to ask for her money but was scared and hesitated.

"But what the hell! No one treated any of Boss Peilar's women like this and lived to talk about it." She lifted her chin high and demanded, "Money; you owe me one hundred Euros in cash as agreed on with Peilar's, or he'll have both of our hides!"

Not being close enough to smack her again and needing to get to a new phone, Günter reluctantly went into his pockets, withdrew the cash, and, throwing it at her, said, "Leave now, dress in the hallway, but get out now, or Peilar's will have to find another girl to fill your place!"

Scared, she snatched up her clothes and opened the door to escape as fast as possible. Everyone had warned her that he was a lunatic, and now she knew that to be true.

Günter took the first flight out to Copenhagen, and from there, he would be connecting with an Air Canada flight to Vancouver. This was the best way to cross the border from the islands. No one ever looked at you twice when you looked like you had been fishing all day, as you pulled into a dock in Washington State, as opposed to someone driving over the border to get into Washington State. Next, Günter would get the van that was set aside for him and drive down into Seattle, where he would hop a train to San Francisco. From there, he would fly to New York and drive down to Washington, DC. He would get several hotel rooms for the project's duration and then take a train to Florida and a cruise boat to Puerto Rico. From there, he would fly back to Canada and disappear into unknown parts. This part of his plan had been set up for weeks now, and everyone had been contacted. Even those who wanted no more to do with him after the Russian incident. But money had a way of making men do things they did not want to do, and his offers were always the best. He also knew that no one was brave enough to make anything too difficult for him.

"Life can be a real bitch," he thought. But for now, he was on his way to America. Günter hated America, all of those whiny people who always complained about everything and never fixed a damn thing. Right now, they seemed to be going broke, and before long, they would become some third-world country. Right now, half the world rejoiced and had waited for this to happen so they could all go out in the streets shouting and dancing.

"No one but Americans were taking America down, and that made it even sweeter," thought Günter. Günter never had any problems crossing into the United States.

Flying into Vancouver and leaving Cold Harbor Quay by boat late at night, they continued running south down past Camano Island, where he was finally dropped off at Golden Garden Park Road, at the Marina, which took up a mile or more in length. Günter departed the boat with a new set of sea legs, which was the one thing he never got used to about long boat rides. It was why he hated being on the water. But he was now safely stateside, and that was all that mattered to him.

Günter didn't care now if anyone noticed him. At this point, he now looked the part of the beleaguered, happy fisherman, finally returning to land after pulling an all-nighter out at sea. His van waited for him with Washington plates, a disguise to match one of his newly made driver's licenses. It was like returning home from a road trip. Nothing out of the ordinary. He was taught to keep it bland. Act as if he had three kids and a wife waiting for him in Seattle. Of course, the van was stolen in Vancouver a year ago, and the plates had come off a car in a small town in Oregon less than forty-eight hours ago. He would abandon the van at one of the many downtown parking garages, and Günter would board the first bus. Who cared where it went so long as he was on it? And when he got off, he could grab a cab to the train station and then make it down to San Francisco to board the plane to New York. He had plenty of time. Actually, he was slightly ahead of schedule.

Günter made his living by ending the life of someone or some group if necessary. He had no qualms about doing his job as long as he got the right amount of money for the right amount of effort. Yet, this was different somehow. An awful lot of money was involved in this particular contract, and he had to wonder if he was a target in the mix. Could it be that the money was to entice him into an area to do, or maybe not do, a job? Maybe he was to become the final piece of mail delivered. He would have to be a little more careful if one could be a little more careful in his business. Especially in the States here, with all of these fat, paranoid people walking around. Damn, he hated this country and its arrogant, sloppy people.

Stepping off the bus, Günter hailed a cab after walking north for a block or two. If he was right, the train station was east of where he now stood, waiting for the cabby to open the door for him. Then he remembered he was in America, and they don't open doors for you here.

Günter liked the long drive south. He was amazed how some areas could remind him of his own country, but he wasn't here to sightsee. He was here to complete his tasks and might as well start with the easiest part of his itinerary.

Günter walked quietly to the house's back door and found it unlocked. Funny, he thought. In America, everyone locked their doors at night. Either from fear of the boogeyman or some intruder, they should have worried about the latter tonight. Creeping into the house, he had not gone more than several steps before hearing snoring from the front living room.

On a chair with a blanket tossed over him was an old man sound asleep, snoring loud enough to beat the band. Günter looked down at him and thought this man was old enough to be his grandfather. Why would anyone think of him as a threat? Pulling out his pistol and placing it against the back of the old man's head, Günter pulled the trigger three times. But the shots made no sound in the night. If anyone else were in the house, they would continue to sleep because silencers had become that good. Now, Günter quietly walked to the front foyer and climbed the stairs to the bedrooms he knew would be located above. Seeing a door open on his left and peering in, he saw someone sleeping on the bed, lying on top of it in a housecoat. Silently, he stalked forward, and again, he fired three silent shots into the back of that head. Backing out of the room, he continued to stalk the hall, and then, just as silently, he went down the stairs. He searched for other signs of life throughout the rest of the house, and finding no one else there, he departed, leaving behind his infamous calling card of a man hanging upside down and nailed to a cross.

More Research

Juan had gone down to the club where the general liked to hang out most of the time. Following the general years ago seemed to have now paid off in locating his place of serenity. After all, every animal has a special hiding place.

Complete in a new disguise, Juan could stand there all day if he wanted to. He had hired a private road repair company and asked them to clean the street areas all along the front surrounding the golf course clubhouse and the road left and right of the complex. Juan had arranged that he would be hired on as a traffic director. This was the only stipulation he had on selecting and hiring this particular company. Right after he showed them his Homeland Security credentials, they readily agreed. That's all they needed: a reason to make money and help the government out at the same time.

He also had called the club and explained to them that Homeland Security was going to pose as a cleaning crew over the next few days out in front of their club. They were told it was because some international VIP was coming to visit someone in that section of town. Some old friends from college were meeting up, and one was the son of the queen, and they needed to secure the area for that visit. So, they would have a cleaning crew out there for the next couple of days, but in reality, it was all security agents doing protection duty. So, they were told. The club, of course, had no problem with the cones and the cleaning, especially since it was being done for free. So, standing there and capturing all of the traffic in and out of the club for two days, Juan felt secure that when he stopped to review all of the tapes, he would find what he had been looking for.

Juan was now staying at a safe house of his, a house that no one knew he owned. It was just one of the many perks of making good money in his business. Anyone in his business needed to have several hiding places. So, Juan made himself comfortable as he loaded the tapes into the VCR. Within minutes, he was astounded at the number of political and business people who made that club a second home for friends and family. In just two days, he had seen every one of any value and importance in Washington at this club, schmoozing and playing around and acting as if this were the main staging area for wealthy and politically connected people.

Then, as he had hoped for, the general was getting out of his limo, followed by the man Juan knew to be the one in the back of the car that night. Now, he needed to capture that image and find out who it was. Then, after checking all of the history, business, and financials of this club, Juan had a growing dossier on his target, and he felt very much at home. Once this information was secured, he would then have to figure out exactly who had put the tail on him that night. One or both of them wanted him removed from the picture, and that bothered him immensely. It had been bothering Juan now for days.

It turned out that he was right. The mystery man was no other than the former head of H.T. Wetco. No wonder he was so upset, he had hit the nail on the head. Now he had to understand, "Why Wetco?" Just how could they be included in the mix of things? This news created a problem, not a big one, but not too small, either. He had to make a decision tonight. To either play tag with the old man, or go to his funeral. But the general would immediately recognize that he was the tagger. Or, possibly take both of them out and go to two funerals. Or, maybe he should just follow the yellow brick road for a while to continue finding out information and then make a decision. Not being one to hesitate about tagging someone, Juan knew that nothing but peace of mind could come from that, but that would stop the game. Juan liked the intrigue. After all, it's in his blood. It's what he has done for a living these past forty years or so, so why stop now?

He knew then that he had already started his game of tag. Right after he became aware of Junior following him, he decided to do a reverse airport flight. One of the oldest and easiest tricks in the book, and because it was so old, maybe they wouldn't be looking out for it. So, Juan had arranged two tickets to two different destinations just to get him and his mark past security. Then, once he and his mark passed security, they waited separately in the passenger gate area before approaching the ticket taker. As several passengers with kids started to approach the counter, the mark quickly cut in front of the line and handed her the boarding pass. Once she had it in her hand, Juan calmly reached inside his coat and pushed a button attached to an inside pocket. This sent a signal out to the cameras, which immediately shut down. It was a fake electrical surge signal used in shutting systems down to prevent frying the cameras. Then Juan simply walked away, went into the bathroom, proceeded to change his facial and hair features, and then left the terminal. So when the cameras came back to life, according to the ticket, he had already boarded that flight to the Dominican Republic. Instead of leaving the airport in a waiting car. Juan knew that someone had an interest in him, and he needed to find that out as soon as possible. Now that he had the video of the old man, he needed to find out exactly who hired Wonder Boy, although why was more important.

Already, two weeks had gone by, and Juan had everything but the old man's underwear bugged, as well as the general's. He had been in and out of that club six times and still couldn't find the lever that opened up that special cellar. Nothing like walking out of there with some two-hundred-year-old brandy, scotch, or some fine wines. "That would surely send a message," he thought. However, right now, that isn't what he wants to do. When he had to, he would send a message, a very special one. What baffled him was that so far, they were both clean; there was nothing on the videos or the tapes that was out of the ordinary. One thing is for sure: these two old men loved to bullshit.

Sometimes, sitting there and watching these two old men in action made him laugh to himself. If he didn't know how dangerous they both were, he could easily want to become their friend. Then, the first sign of something of interest began on this next tape. The old man from H.T. Wetco was bragging about the fact that whatever they had to worry about in Virginia was taken care of by a friend of a friend. Someone called "the fourth man out". It would seem that this individual had come and taken care of the problem, and no longer would they worry about those individuals making any kind of reference to the project. That fourth man out was now being directed to view and start to eliminate all details pertaining to the original problem. But first, he was sending a message of "Tag, you're it" to his second in command. "Make no mistake about it," he said, "He'll get the message and come crawling back to apologize. Then, it would be too late, of course. But definitely, anyone who knew of this would soon forget this ever even existed as a problem." Turning to the general, he said, "Open the gates to heaven, will you. Let's have some brandy, seems as if it's time to celebrate a little."

Hearing this news, Juan didn't know who or what was going on, not yet anyway, but he was sure that if he kept his nose in this, something would come up. Then, doing a little recalling, Juan knew that "Virginia" could be Frank and Claire. Suddenly, he knew. He knew that both Frank and Claire had been eliminated to protect the company. Protect the company from what? What was so damn important that this old harmless couple had to be eliminated? This now angered him because, in his report to the general, he stated specifically that under no circumstances should these people be viewed as a threat to the security of this country and that they should both be held harmless. The guy retired over thirty years ago, for God's sake! They know nothing of what is going on in the world outside of their family. Damn, the old man just suffered a stroke and was barely alive. Let alone a threat to anyone.

Juan just couldn't understand this. And who was this "fourth man out?" Surely, it couldn't be the rabbit. Hell, in a fair fight, maybe that old man could take on the rabbit. Now was not the time for humor, though, Juan thought, as he looked on the Internet to find any news of accidents or some kind of trouble Frank and Claire had gotten themselves into. Juan froze as he read the article in their local paper, *'The Bugler.'*

It read, **Elderly Local Couple Lost to House Fire,**

"Late last night, Officer T. Wells responded to a tragic fire that took the lives of Frank and Claire Benoit. Both Frank and his wife, the former Claire Hinton, were born and raised in Green Springs. They celebrated their sixtieth wedding anniversary here just two years ago. They are past members of Our Lady of Lourdes, and Claire Benoit was the past chairperson of the League of Women Voters. The Benoits moved to Chantilly, Virginia, where Mr. Frank Benoit worked as a scientist for H.T. Wetco and Sons. After retiring thirty years ago, the Benoits moved back to Green Springs."

The author went on to state the names of Benoit's one son and two daughters, grandchildren, and even several great-grandchildren. It seemed, according to the local police, that they had been robbed. The article went on to say how the house was ransacked, and both Frank and Claire Benoit had been physically beaten to death. Possible subjects were a group of marauding teens who had stolen all of the couple's jewelry and had set the back of the house on fire, possibly to cover up any evidence. But it was the fire that had alerted a passing police cruiser, and he phoned it into the local fire station. When Chief Robeson and his men showed up only minutes later, it was only after the arrival of Dr. Sabian that it was discovered that the Benoits had been killed by smoke inhalation. The whole article ended with the details of the funeral and the family asking that all donations be made to the local cancer society.

Juan knew that something had to be done about this. Somehow, he had to find out exactly the general's part in this and his own culpability, as well. Did his interview directly lead to the deaths of these two old-timers? Juan needed answers, and soon, he would demand those answers. Why did he feel this way, he thought. After all, they were just too old people, he never really knew if he stopped to think about it. Yet, he remembered the kindness and the delight in her eyes as she led him into the foyer. Then, later at the table, she almost force-fed him more potatoes, and when she packed him a doggy bag, it was then that he felt once again as if he was leaving his grandmother's house.

Now he knew he was obligated to these two kindly people to find out exactly why this happened, especially after his report said they were harmless. For the first time in his career, he was willing to put everything on hold in order to come up with these answers. After all, wasn't he also a marked man at this point? Maybe to erase all connections to the Benoits?

Maybe this was the reason behind the possible attempt on his life. Then he thought of the rabbit, and if this had anything to do with him, he would make him pay dearly. His thoughts then switched to this Thurston guy and even to the general. Deep down, he knew he should not get any more involved, that maybe now was the time to cash in his chips and just disappear. How many years could these two old men live? Then, the thought of playing tag on Thurston came into his mind, and again it quickly disappeared. No, they had already sent someone out for him. The game was on now, and in his mind, he could only think about how long before more people would have to die or show up looking for him. If he was going to be the sweeper here, then he needed to know all of the participants, and he needed to get this information fast.

Funeral

"Mom is sitting in the corner, and she can't stop crying. She keeps falling against Dad, so I had to come out here for some fresh air. How are your folks holding up?" asked Clara.

"I'm afraid just as bad, Cacky. This just doesn't make any sense at all. Who could have done this to them? They're just harmless, old people," said Tully.

"I know, Tull, I know. I have no idea as to why anyone would kill two defenseless and innocent people. It doesn't make any sense to me at all. But if I have to quit the bureau and spend the rest of my life chasing down the sons of bitches, I'll do it. Oh my god, I miss them so much!" said Clara as she now fell against her cousin Tully's shoulder and started crying.

The caskets were made of hickory with brass-polished ornaments on the sides. One was toned in gold, one in bright white; they were carried to the church and out to the Benoit family plot by family members and a couple of special friends. Jason helped carry Grandpa Frank's casket, and Jeff, Tully's husband, helped carry Grandma Claire's. The caskets were closed because it was told to everyone that the fire had done some extensive damage to already bruised and broken facial bones. The funeral director just said it would be so much easier on the families this way. So, after all was said and done and daylight had started to fade, Clara sat with Tully and talked. But after a while, they still had no answers to their misery.

Jason's folks had made the funeral, and so had most of her team from Washington. John Bloso was there, and as the sun set, he approached Clara and asked her to take a walk with him alone. As they went around the corner, waiting in a chair in the hallway was Dr. Sabian, who had been the family doctor for as long as anyone could remember. John grabbed his arm and helped the doctor to his feet. Once standing, they proceeded to follow John down the hallway to a private little alcove nestled somewhere in the back of the rented hall. The family had used this hall for so many happier occasions than this one, thought Clara.

All of the weddings, graduations, and other reasons to celebrate were done here at McCullough's. But now, here she stood, numb and confused, with her boss and her family's doctor.

"Clara, I brought you here for a reason," declared John. "I want only you to hear what is going to be said, and then I want you to think long and hard on several things. The first one will be if you think there is any need to tell the rest of your family this information. Personally, I wouldn't. But you're all close, so it's hard for me to say or to give you any advice, really. But this I will say, and then I'll let the good doctor here talk. Just know that whatever you decide, I am here now, and I will be until all this comes to a conclusion. I know everything is somewhat unclear yet, but listen to what really happened and why we kept this our secret until now," said John, now looking at the confused expression on Clara's face that almost screamed, "What the hell is going on?"

"What information?" asked Clara.

"Go ahead, Doctor, tell her what you found. And why, up until now, no one knows the truth," nodded John.

"What truth? Damn it, what the hell is going on, John?" Turning now and facing the doctor, she asked, "Doctor Sabian, what really happened to Grandpa Frank and Grandma?"

"Listen to me, Clara, because I cannot say this any clearer, mind you. What Mr. Bloso and I decided on was to benefit this family. It has nothing to do with who has any right to the truth. I thought that it would be best for this family to keep this information quiet. So, what I am going to tell you are the facts of what really happened that god-awful day," said an almost teary-eyed old man who lost more than two patients that day. He lost two of his best friends. He cleared his throat and began again.

"Well, after Tommy Wells got to their place, all he could see was fire. He rushed into the house and immediately saw your grandfather slouched over in his favorite chair. Tommy tried to wake him up, but he was so slumped over and covered in blood. That's when Tommy picked him up and brought him outside. He laid him down and went back inside for your grandmother. Looking around the place and not seeing her, he ran immediately upstairs and found her lying on the top of the bed. Just lying there, and blood covered the back of her head, as well. He knew then that she was also dead and was apparently shot. Tommy said the shell casings were still next to her on the bed. He also found similar casings next to Frank, too. Anyway, I'm getting ahead of myself. So, he lifted Claire, took her outside, placed her next to her husband, and then covered them both with a blanket he had in the trunk of his car. Hell, Tommy was so devastated at this point he said he was crying and wanting to scream his head off. But to the boy's credit, he went right back into that house and began putting out the fire. Seems it was confined to the kitchen. He thought someone must have left something on the stove and forgotten about it. Anyway, the fire boys all showed up at that point, and of course, after I heard it on the radio in my house, I came immediately. That's when I saw that blanket and Tommy standing over it, like a dog over his master's body, with tears running down his face. Then, looking under it, I found both your grandparents lying there. So, when we put both of them into the morgue truck and took them away right away, no one but Tommy and I saw what really happened to them. Clara, your grandparents were killed by being shot to death in an execution style. I found three bullets in the back of both of their heads. I also found this strange card on your grandfather's body. I knew you worked for the FBI, so I called them immediately. I talked to a few people there but was eventually turned over to Mr. Bloso here, and he has been on this since day one. He thought it would be best for the family if we waited to tell you about this until after the funeral. I thought it would be best, as well. That's my job. I have been taking care of this family for nearly sixty years, and that's my job," said a tired old family friend as he leaned against the wall and started to cry.

Now, faced with a new understanding of what had really happened, Clara was stunned. She had no idea what to do next. But she did know that she had to hug and calm down this very special family friend—someone who had brought her into this world.

After calming down the doctor, they proceeded to return to the main hall area, and Clara, now armed with this new information, still had no idea as to what to do next. So, she decided to sleep on it. Tomorrow would give her a fresh new insight as to what she should do and whom, if anyone, she should share this information with. They had been executed in the back of the head as if they were part of a gang, but something had gone wrong. She knew it. This was stuff she ran across in Washington in the dregs of the city. This is what happened to other unfortunate people, not something that should ever have happened to her grandparents. Whoever had done this, and for whatever reason, would pay dearly for it. One thing she knew to be true was that she would not rest until whoever had committed this was in jail or dead.

Being tapped lightly on the shoulder, Clara turned and faced John. "I'm staying in the Chancellor Hotel, you know where that is, right, Clara?" said John.

"Yes, sir, I do," replied Clara.

"Then, in the morning, come by, and I will have the team there, and we can go over what we know about what has taken place here. I want everyone involved, everyone. While we are here, this may not be an isolated incident, and I cannot afford to be taken off guard. I need this perpetrator, or perpetrators, caught before they can strike again if that is the motive here. I can't, and I won't allow that to take place," said John. Turning, he walked over to Jason and said something that had Jason nodding as to confirm what he was saying. Then, after a tap on his shoulder, John and the rest of the agents from Clara's unit left the hall.

Jason looked at Clara and nodded as if he was aware of everything already. Clara was made to wonder exactly what Jason knew and when he knew it. How could he withhold this information from her and not share it with her? He knew she was distraught when she received the news, so much so that she collapsed on their kitchen floor and began sobbing as if she were going to die crying. Everyone knew how much she loved her grandparents, especially Grandpa Frank.

Clara now remembered the last major conversation she had with Grandpa Frank. It was about that interviewer. Now she started to wonder why she didn't take his frustration with that problem seriously. Did that have something to do with his death? Could her neglect have caused this? Could she have prevented this? Was there someone from a television program responsible for this? So many questions now started popping into her head. She shook her head as if to clear her mind. She first needed to sleep some, and then she would be able to think more rationally. Yet, how would that now be possible? How can she possibly find sleep with this on her conscience?

Morning Comes

Clara decided early last night that she would tell Tully and Jeff what she now knew but would ask them to never tell anyone else in the family, no one else. Once this promise was made, she knew Tully would never break her oath. But she had to tell someone else in the family, in case something happened to her, or in case, just maybe, someone had it out for her family. Those thoughts also filled her head last night. Last night had been a long one filled with memories, tears, and pain from the loss of those two people in her life she so loved. But today, the sun was shining, and already she was up and eager to get started on finding the son of a bitch that killed her grandparents.

Justin knew where they were headed, and Clara had decided not to argue with him about when he knew and why he had not told her anything. If he did know beforehand, she reasoned, then probably John had demanded secrecy. As for when would be a proper time to tell her, John would tell him, but would there ever be a proper time for this kind of news? She felt that was probably what happened. Justin wanted not to upset her any more than she was already, and she was more than thankful for that and being there through all of this, but right now was not a time to discuss that.

Then Jason broke his silence in the car, seemingly to know what was going through her mind just then. "Listen, Clara, I know what you're thinking. When did I know, and why didn't I tell you? Well, by now, you also must have reasoned it out that John asked me not to say a word about it until he did. I agreed to that. After seeing you on that floor and holding you in my arms as you cried, I could never have come back home to tell you how they were murdered. Please forgive me if that's what's bothering you. I never meant you any harm by not telling you. I asked if I could be there when you did find out, but John thought it best that I wasn't," said a remorseful-sounding Justin.

Then Clara spoke. "It was on my mind just now as well as last night. But I'm fine with it, really. I understood and thought as much as that's what had happened. Besides, it worked out for the best. Especially with the family, Mom and Dad, Aunt Susan, and especially Uncle Pete, they would have all been just devastated to have found that out. So, I am thankful for that not happening. But this morning, I told Tully. I made her swear she was to talk to no one about the truth, and she swore an oath to me she wouldn't tell anyone, so I'm fine with it, honestly," said Clara, all the while staring out the window as traffic seems to start and stop on its own through this little hamlet, she had grown up in. The ride gave her time to fill her head full of thoughts of the whys and how-comes and if she could have prevented it. These same thoughts crowded her brain all through her restless night. But somehow, lying there in the embrace of Justin just made some of the pain slip away. He truly loved and cared for her, and suddenly, that just meant more now.

Finally arriving at the hotel, they parked the car and walked into the lobby, where they were met by Brad, Sally, and James coming down the hallway. After all the embracing and asking how she was holding up, the small group found its way to the private room being held for them. There, sitting on the side of a table, was John Bloso getting ready to put some information up on a screen just in front of him.

Seeing them enter the room, John said, "Good morning, everyone. Help yourself to the eggs, coffee, and whatever else you want. Then let's sit down and get ready to go over some information that we need to decipher."

So began this morning in earnest to find out the who and the why of Frank and Claire Benoit's murder executioner style and for what reason was a calling card left behind.

"Okay, people, let's get settled. I want to get started. First, I have to ask Clara, are you going to be all right with being in here to go over this? If so, then at any time you need to ask something or you need to leave the room, that's fine. We all understand. Actually, I have you here only as a filler. To what we don't know or what we need to know about the area, people, and a possible local connection, I would ask that you advise us. But I don't think I want you on this case. The protocol would prohibit it anyway, but you will be involved as much as we can make that happen without stepping over any boundaries, you agree, right?" John asked her as he stared directly into her face, waiting for his answer.

Now standing up and facing everyone as well as looking directly at John, Clara replied, "Yes, sir, although I would like to say that I need to be here. I need to find closure on this, not only for myself but for my family. This has, of course, been so hard on everyone. Also, I never had the time to thank everyone for coming. My family deeply appreciates it. Now, someday after these people or this person is found, I'll be able to tell my family the truth, which is so important." Sitting back down and getting a hug from Justin, Clara seemed ready to face what she knew to be forthcoming. With conversation on the murder and brutal pictures and a host of other queries, she wondered to herself if she was really ready.

Then, once again, John began, "So far, all we have is the card, the couple, a location, and a style of murder. What else?"

Jason chimed in, "We have the fact that they were visited by someone approximately eight weeks ago. The individual was a white male in his late fifties and early sixties, of average build and size, with no discernable features that would stand out and say who he was. But after listening to Grandpa Frank describe the man on more than one occasion, I got the picture of what he looked like."

Smiling now, Clara chimed in and said, "As far as everyone in the family who still lives locally and has spoken to a lot of local friends in the last couple of days, no one feels that whoever did this comes from here. No one believes he's a local, but I know that we can't rule that out."

John said, "We know the scene was not tampered with. The officer on the site ruled that out. Then, outside of the firemen walking through the kitchen area and some extensive smoke damage in that same area, for the most part, it doesn't look as if anything was out of place. We know the fire was contained from the quick response from everyone, which was a good thing. We also know that the area was contained and secured immediately. It stayed that way since the bodies were found. We leaked to the local media that this was a home invasion. As we declared it as such, it was said that all of the jewelry was stolen, the house was ransacked, and the perpetrators tried burning it to the ground to hide their passing. This was done right after the initial contact with our office. I immediately dispatched Brad down to make sure that it stayed that way as well. Within five hours, forensics was on-site. They say that all of the bloodstains and splatter were created by what we will now classify as a professional hit. It has all of those ear markings. The bullets used were a .22 long rifle, three direct shots to the back of the head, with a silencer, seeing how the wife never heard any of the shots ring out. The project was done while both victims slept. He got in because the doors were left open, and there was no sign of forced entry anywhere.

My personal take on this is it actually looks as if one guy walked right in the front door, found them asleep, and shot both of them in the back of the head. Three bullets of the same caliber were extracted from both bodies, and the shell casings for all six shots were found in place at the location of the shooting. The only thing out of the ordinary was the fact that this shooter left a card behind. This card has so far turned up nothing in our database. Currently, our own FBI headquarters has nothing on file. They do, however, now have the bullets and the shell casings. We have contacted Interpol, the CIA, and all military branches, including Homeland Security, on the method and that damn card. They are going through their databases to find any information they may have squirreled away on this character. Then, a question needs to be asked. Was this a mistake? Did this idiot go to the wrong house? However, as of now, no one else has turned up dead in this area with the same MO. One other thought to process; just maybe he thought they knew something about him, or they could have possibly seen something this character was involved in. It would also have to be something local. Because, as of two years ago, following a stroke suffered by the male victim, they have not traveled around in or out of the country. Is that right, Clara?"

Waiting for an answer but only receiving a nod of affirmation, John began again. "So, if they did see something they were not supposed to see, it had to have been local. We also can't rule out our own. This could be something of retribution. First against Clara, then others in this agency and its agents. So, we need to pore over everything that could possibly be suspect in all of our ongoing investigations. Maybe this is just a dumb way to send a message or one helluva roundabout way of sending it. So are someone else's grandparents or elderly aunt or uncle the next target."

Now pausing for just a moment for his last statement to sink in, John began again speaking but in a much louder voice. "I cannot, and I will not stand by and not cover every base there is concerning this. This, people, is a direct attack on this agency and its agents. Make no mistake about that. I will not tolerate anything on this that is put aside because you may have thought it has no bearing. Everything has a reason, and I want to find this guy, and I want to know that reason. Have I made this perfectly clear?"

As if in a planned orchestrated chorus, everyone said, "Yes, sir."

Once again, John, who had been walking around the room as he spoke, took to the front of the room and, looking at everyone, he pointed at Sally Romano and said, "I also asked Sally to go over the area with a fine-tooth comb on the funeral days. I wanted pictures of every person within a mile of the activity. So, in a minute, we will begin to look at the footage from this. So go to the head or get some more coffee. Take out the notebooks, and let's get started in, say, ten minutes, so be back here and ready, people."

With that, John walked over to Clara and said, "I'll stop the movie from rolling if you see anything or anyone out of the ordinary. I'll let everyone know that if they can identify anyone and know them not to be local, then we have to develop these leads as fast as we can, and that is the job I am willing to give you. You'll have to stay out of the field and concentrate on running down these leads. Clara, you know the people around here better than anyone, of course. So, keep that in mind as you get bored and want to complain to me about sitting so long at your desk."

With that, John left the hall, all the while knowing that soon, if not even sooner, she'd be itching to get more involved, and he couldn't have that.

Now ready to view the footage, John said, "Okay, people, let's start the slide show, and speak up if you see anyone you know who doesn't belong here."

With that said John quietly sat down to watch the footage crawling across the white screen in front of the group. He now hoped that someone would recognize someone, and the hunt would begin. So often, the killers are known to come back to watch the mourning of lost ones. They come back to take part in the drama and to show sympathy. John knew that somewhere out there and very close was the killer. Just how close, he didn't know, but he had a gut feeling that this was all a part of a bigger plan, and he was just at the tip of it. But wherever he was in the scheme of things, one thing John knew to be true. That in ten years on this job, he had never once given up or come home empty-handed, and he wasn't about ready to start now.

But what he didn't know was that Günter hated Americans, and as far as he was concerned, he would never hang around watching a funeral to share in the drama. He made the drama. He didn't need to live in it, and he was on the verge of creating a lot more of it.

The day after the funeral, John and his team would all be heading back to Washington. There was work to do, and coordinating with the local sheriff's office would be easy enough as Clara would remain behind for at least two weeks.

After a week of mourning had passed, it was time to leave. Tully was meeting with Clara one more time, and after a long hug, she decided that what Clara was saying was for the best. She and Jeff had to go back home and live life. Not to live this nightmare any longer. To go do what they knew had to be done, and Clara would continue to give them updates on the investigation as long as it wouldn't hinder the outcome when the bastard was caught. Tully agreed, and again, after many hugs, she promised Clara that she would be in Washington to spend time with her this coming month.

"No matter what has to be done, I promise you I'm coming there to spend some time and to catch up. Also, I want to know more about this Jason fellow you have been hanging around with. It'll give us a chance to see the city and to do happier things together, okay?" asked Tully.

"Yes," said Clara, "I can't wait. I'll even take a week off, and we can explore the city and find out what's been going on that I haven't been privy to. I can't even tell you where a museum is located, let alone the zoo." She laughed.

With that, they parted, and Clara went back to the house to say goodbye to her mom and dad. They had taken it very hard, and Clara kept insisting that they come and stay with her and Justin, but her dad wanted no part in that. He would be content staying at home, and he also had a lot to do concerning the cleanup of the fire damage at the "main" house.

"Things will get better," he said, "they always do. Somehow, God blesses us with the ability to remember only the good times and to forget the bad. Because of some act of cowardice by some strangers, I will not allow that to make me become hateful and only have vengeance on my mind. When I can fill up my mind with the best memories, I can think about my mother and father-in-law."

Her dad had tears in his eyes once again, and her mom went to him immediately to help comfort him and to have it help comfort her. Her mom was on medication at first. She couldn't even walk without help. But the doctor came through, and by the end of the funeral, she was almost her old self again. Aunt Susan was not far behind as well, but Uncle Pete swore vengeance on every teenager that he knew. He was the opposite of the girls. Pete loved trouble, and he loved his parents, and to think that they were killed by kids made him as angry as anyone had ever seen him.

But her mom had made sure that everyone at the funeral was comfortable, and later in the hall, everyone had something to eat, making sure they all weren't just sitting there sad and crying. Especially the kids, so often it is so hard on them. The little ones wanted to know why we were having a party and Grandpa and Grandma weren't there. They just couldn't figure it out. So, her mom came to the rescue, and Reverend Wiley as well.

Clara noted that everyone from Our Lady of Lourdes was great. During mass, however, no one had a chance to recover from the singing of Ave Maria. It seems as if everyone tried to dissipate into thin air. The song sung by the church's boys' choir made the hair on the back of everyone's neck stand up as tears soaked so many faces.

Mass always holds a special place for this family. It was always a time-shared tradition to go with the entire family every Sunday. How sad it would be, Clara thought, for her mom and dad now to go alone. Life was harsh, and often, she was looking in from the outside. Now she felt as if her family was on the inside, trapped in a predicament, not of their making, and only two of them in the family knew the truth. With neither of them knowing the why, nor did they even have any idea as to the who. The glass is thick from the inside; it's dark, and it hurts to become a statistic, not to ever know if you'll ever see the light of day again.

Justin started back to Washington three days after the funeral was over. The team had already left. Clara and Justin, beforehand, had gone by the police station to see Tommy Wells and thank him personally once again for all he had done for her family.

Clara said that she would be following up on some pictures of people she didn't know and that she would like him to go through them as well. She knew that she wouldn't know everyone who showed up. It was why she was hoping that Tommy could possibly identify all of them for her. Of course, he agreed and said once again just how sorry he was. Tommy thought that he had been too late in getting there; that had he somehow gotten there faster, maybe one of them or both of them would be alive today. Clara hugged him and said no, they were gone long before the fire had started, and that if one of them had lived, soon that survivor would have passed on from a broken heart. They loved each other that much.

The days had gone by quickly, and it was now time to leave. Leaving her hometown was always a little hard, but somewhat harder this time. It seemed as if somehow a chasm or void had grown over the area like a hard shell. Clara knew that she would, of course, come to see her mom and dad. She would return for parties, weddings, and anniversaries, but something would always be missing. Clara lost a part of her this week, that part that only she can remember. It is a part of her that is only a memory now living inside of her forever, no longer the part that was always so blatantly alive inside of her. She knew that she would never see those smiles again, hear Grandpa Frank's roaring laugh or get his special wink when no one was looking. No more encouragement to do what she wanted to do, and "he'll take care of the Indians," no more extra ice cream, and a special hug when Tully wasn't looking. Someone took her grandpa and her grandmother from her, and she swore now that she would hunt them down till she had the satisfaction of knowing that they had paid for their sin.

Second Attempt / Missing Pieces

Juan decided that maybe it wasn't such a great idea to go to the funeral after all. Maybe someone could identify him, so why take the chance? Turning the car around and heading back home, he knew it was the smartest idea he had had about this emotional swing he was feeling lately. He would now follow the local paper and see exactly what was going on. Maybe some news about the deaths would become more visible in that local newspaper, the Bugler, but it seems as if, for some reason, it wasn't making any headlines. Only the local advertisement paper, their *Town Crier,* carried any information about the murder. Juan had some idea as to the reason, like maybe what had happened to them was actually too gruesome to print. If that was the case, then he had to figure out what the motive had to be. Something was wrong here. He had met with them, spoken to them, and knew and reported that they were no threat and couldn't possibly be a threat to anyone, let alone the country. Hell, Claire's lemonade spoke volumes about her character; she was all grandma and grandma only.

Lately, though, it was quiet in the workings of those other two bastards. Juan couldn't believe that the general actually was a part of this, that he could possibly condone the outright killing of these two innocent people. Juan had killed people, and he knew what it was like to hold someone's life in your open hands and then make a fist. Life was precious, yet it was also precarious, especially when you involved yourself with something wrong. Sometimes, a price had to be paid, and no one really liked to come up with the fare when it was due that he knew oh so well.

Then it hit him. There is the contact! Frank Benoit did work for H.T. Wetco. Somewhere in their lives, Frank knew Thurston. They knew each other more than in a boss-worker relationship. Maybe the general was in on it as well. The three of them could have been involved in something of ill will, and these two wanted no survivors. No one left alive besides these two to have a recollection of what had transpired. This had to be why they made him a target. So, no link to them would exist now that the old man was dead. He knew now that Benoit was an integral part of who they were or what they did, maybe from the war with the general or maybe from the business where Thurston was the boss.

Frank Benoit was murdered for what he knew about these two bastards. Now Juan once again smelled the trail, and it was a fresh, clean smell. One that only someone in his business can appreciate, so with that idea ringing in his head, he decided that he would know everything about Frank Benoit that there was to know about him.

Frank was more interesting than Juan would have ever thought. He had gone down there to interview him. They sat quietly and spoke about his discovery and what Frank thought it would mean to the world. But Juan had no idea as to the volume of relief and/or devastation making rain could have on the planet. Frank talked, and he had listened but thought most of what was said was self-influenced like Frank had a sort of overindulgence in his own importance. Was he some old man discussing what he thought sounded important? Now Juan, after the last three days of investigation, found out that Frank Benoit was indeed important.

Frank could make it rain, and his rain could be cold, wet, and wonderful, or it could be full of enough toxins to kill the land for decades. It could be rain that would seemingly never stop or rain that was never coming. It only looked as if it would rain. Thurston owned this company, this company had influence, and exactly how much influence did it have with the military? This discovery has had to have played a very significant part in the military's way of doing business around the globe. But why now would it matter? Why now, after all these years, would there be a reason to murder two old people? It didn't make any sense. The guy had been retired for over thirty years now. What was the hook here? Juan knew he would not stop until he had all of the information needed to piece together that part of the puzzle. What was the hook?

Picking up the material and pressing it against his chest was one way Juan used to see if there would be some kind of anything to jump out to him as he continued to ponder on the reasons why these two old men would have those two murdered, especially since their operational mode seemed to always be in high gear. But now, with hiring someone to kill those two old people, something had to be up. He will have to be very careful now, very careful. Maybe they were on to him, and maybe he'll once again be on the menu and possibly its main course.

Juan left the car where he always parked it on Thursday nights. He religiously, without fault, changed parking spaces nightly, and he had several secured spots just in this location. He even changed locations with never the same location two nights in a row. That's what probably saved his life as the bullet passed over his head and slammed into the side of the wall. Immediately, he went down and became invisible. To find him now was a game of cat and mouse that he lived to play. Now, it was anyone's chance. The deal was even, and there was no bluffing or making a call. All cards were dealt, and before the clock ticked away another hour, someone tonight would be dead. Slowing his breathing down and opening up all of his senses, Juan could now relax and delve into the noise of the night. Someone was out there, and someone wanted him dead, and he knew it was not the rabbit. So, he would have to survive this night and then deal with the other problem later, but right now, close the mind and open the mind's eye. Listen to every sound, don't move a muscle, yet relax, take it all in, and become one with his surroundings as he had been taught. Then he heard it, even if it was ever so slightly made. Someone was crawling toward his position.

Taking off his shoes and his belt, he emptied his pockets as well. Nothing was going to make as much as a scrap of noise. Then, reaching up, he tied the belt to the door handle of the car he now leaned against. With that done, Juan took both shoelaces off and made the knot to extend his now-longer rope, leaving his shoes pointed outward by the side of the back tires, just enough to be seen by this mysterious crawler. Then, sliding under the car next to him, he pulled slightly on the rope ever so lightly to give away his position, and then he let go. The movement from the belt rope hanging down along the side of the car and the placement of his shoes brought his unknown attacker, who jumped over the back of the car as he continuously fired his pistol into nothing but concrete. Juan returned fire from his hiding spot, placing two shots into this mystery man's ankles, who now collapsed onto the concrete and stared in disbelief with an empty gun now pointed at Juan. Juan had no clue as to who he was, and he didn't care as he pulled the trigger and watched his wide-eyed assailant, who knew that death was knocking on his door. Juan watched as his assailant was now jerked backward from the shots, and he seemed to dance as he died.

Rising up as quickly as he could and taking his belt and shoes, he quickly made for the exit. But not before he took the assailant's gun, and upon emptying his pockets, Juan found nothing to identify him as to who and why he was there to have died on that very night. But he now knew several things. They knew where he was, and he was now a marked man, and lying dead behind him wasn't the rabbit.

After arriving back to his original home, Juan knew it had to be the general or Thurston, which meant that he was no longer safe even at home. Apparently, someone made him and marked him. How the hell was he so stupid? How could he have believed that he was above this and out of suspicion with everyone, thinking he had gone to the Islands for a rest? It had to be from the fact that he had that interview with the old couple. And now he had to be erased so that nothing would lead back to his handler, the general. So, it was the general that wanted him dead, maybe. But for now, he had to assume that because who else could have possibly known one of his hidden locations?

He knew he needed to use another one of his secured locations. Then, if he was once again marked, he would know that only the general may have set a tag on him. He was too trustworthy of the general in the past. He must have followed him constantly just to see where his nests were and then use that against him if ever the need arises, like now. For now, the general was the leading player in this, and he would make a house call soon. Then he would have a long-needed talk with him. Leaning over the bed and beneath it in the wall, he located a wall switch that opened a circuit to another switch in his closet. There, he switched that one open, and the wall slid aside, revealing a small armory. Selecting several pistols with silencers already mounted, ammunition, and special ops clothing and hurriedly packing his belongings, Juan headed out to his other car. That's when the thought occurred to him that they could easily have someone waiting at that location for him as well. So, he caught the local bus to Harpers Terrace and, from there, took the subway over to Dixon

Street, where he kept a locked storage bin. Slipping inside, he started up his Volkswagen van and slowly departed. Finding his way over to another safe house of his that he hadn't used in years, he thought it was a good thing he was the owner. The young neighbor tenants on the other side of the house never heard him come in. It didn't matter. After a few hours of sleep, he would be gone anyway.

Several days had passed, and so far, so good. Things were now quiet again, and no local news spoke about a body being found shot in a garage downtown. This told Juan more important news. The people behind the attack were good, maybe even having a cleanup crew of their own. Or they apparently had some major influence with the local law enforcement officers and the local rags as well. So, Juan found himself now with a new dilemma as he had spent the last two days tracking down information on the Benoits. After all of his research on the Benoits' immediate family history, he decided to also delve deeper into the past archives from their local church and newspapers, where they reported about the graduation of Clara Beach, granddaughter of Frank and Claire Benoit. Then, of course, he continued his research on his granddaughter Clara, and it seemed that she was assigned to the local Washington, DC bureau. Now, he had even a greater problem, especially if it was found out that he was the one who interviewed the Benoits about the fake television show. This would immediately make him the prime suspect in a murder case.

He knew that this information wouldn't come from the general, seeing how the general must know that he did retain some proof that he was hired to do research on Frank Benoit. In case something did go wrong. The general must know that everyone kept something back. That was a part of the trade. Then, yet again, how much more can go wrong? he thought. What else was there of any importance? He had pored over the entire interview several times now and hadn't found anything new to add to his discoveries. Yet he knew he was missing something, and he had to find that piece and find it soon.

Maybe it was in with the senator's material, yet he also had spent hours going over the remaining material on Pillow as well, and nothing was jumping out at him. But something nagging at him said the senator could be the key to this. Somehow, he had a much larger role in this than he had uncovered. What he now needed to do was to work on finding out exactly why he felt this way about this senator. He needed to know what this senator was about and how he fit into this equation. Exactly where was he now, and could the senator be capable of hiring the person who tried to kill him? Hell, how did he even find out that it was he who pretended to be from the DOD? Was he now aware of the fact that he was the one who had hacked into his computer and made his life miserable? Then again, the finger went right back to the general. He may have provided him with that information. After all, who else knew about the second meeting when he was followed but the general and this Thurston character?

Could Thurston be behind the making of all of this? If so, why? What is his part in this besides the fact that Frank Benoit worked for him? Or is he just caught up in some kind of conspiracy as well, and the general would make him disappear next? If the military needed something horrific, not seeing any daylight, then this was a great possibility. If so, then Thurston would be a target soon. Juan wouldn't get much sleep tonight. Somehow, this was growing larger by the hour and more complicated by the day. Maybe he should just play tag with those two idiots and tag the senator as well. That way, everything would disappear, including him. But right now, he needed more to go on before that decision could be made. Now, he needed to find out how important this senator was to his whole problem. Was he even aware of the Benoits? Juan needed to find out exactly how he was connected to the general and Thurston. It just doesn't get easier, thought Juan. Smiling to himself, he understood how important this had become. This was what made him tick, and this was what the big game was all about. Someone's life and someone's death, and he decided then that it would not be his death.

Mable Gardner

As she walked along the crowded street, Mable was excited. It had to have been years since she found someone really attractive, and this same someone also found her just as attractive. This was not someone who was really into her job and what he could get out of her. Then she thought to herself. Wait a minute, it's not like I'm bad-looking, and I should be happy a man is paying me some attention.

Mable was shapely, and she was what men called energetic and petite. The way she dressed may have sometimes implied she was sexy. It was just that in her line of work, she really didn't have time for frivolities. Oh, she managed her rolls in the hay, no doubt about that. But as soon as they got either that piece of love or what potential information from her they needed, they were gone. Mable knew that when she chose this career, that was exactly what she was in for. How many years did she sit behind Loretta and watch her and how her life went? But finally, one day, love did find Loretta. Even if the candidate was married and lost his reelection bid, so what? Now, they live quietly in another state, and she's finally happy taking care of their two children.

Then she thought to herself, those infamous words her mother always said about her and this job. "Mable, you'll always be the bridesmaid, never the bride." So what, she thought, at my age, so what?

But this day could change that. She was on her way to meet this handsome fellow from the German embassy, Luther Rudman, who was a dashing, sophisticated attorney working at their embassy. The problem was that he said he was not allowed to fraternize and that they had to meet for the first few times privately to make sure that there would be no trouble with his superiors in his job. This would only be until he could talk to his superiors about how he had met this beautiful woman and how he wanted so much to get to know her. But, and there always is that 'but,' it was because she worked for a U.S. senator seated, and that was where the rub came in. It was okay to be with anyone anywhere as far as the German embassy protocol was concerned. Unless, of course, the individual man or woman you fell for was employed by an elected official in that country. Or he or she just happened to be the elected official. Now, that was definitely a no-no.

Mable's feet just didn't seem to go fast enough anymore. Then, a thought crossed her mind that maybe she should think about working out a little. Maybe she was getting a little older, and she was tiring quicker; not much, mind you, but she was slowing down, it seemed. Yet she did walk those endless corridors in the capital as if she had been raised there, back and forth, up and down those steps seemingly a thousand times a day. After all, now that the senator was the lowest of them all, they surely didn't give him the office his predecessor had occupied. They couldn't move him to the attic fast enough. It was as if they had a closet all picked out before he even knew he was coming. But that's all right. She had known the senator for a long time. Actually, he was her dentist whenever she was in town, not out working on a campaign somewhere.

It was Mable who actually said to him, "Why don't you run for the open seat? You know, that's what I do for a living. I'm a campaign manager. I have worked campaigns from one end of this country to the other, and I can help you win when you come up for reelection. Let the committee select you to fill the seat. The governor will go along with it. After all, he is your cousin, and by the way, how long did I work on his campaign to get him elected? Think about it. Besides, once in Washington, you can easily make your way back there for a long time. Of course, I'll miss you as my dentist. But I'm sure we can find someone down there that'll take care of that."

Not that she was surprised by his reaction to her suggestion, and that he took her up on it and was actually sent down here. She was more surprised by his changed demeanor since he had been here. Mable was even more surprised when he started patting her on her ass every chance he got or trying to rest his hand there for as long as he could. She corrected him of that just as quickly as it had started. His whole persona has changed, she thought. Then suddenly, the bimbos started showing up. They seemed to clutter the office as if they were campaign contributions. She had to admit to herself that she didn't really like what she was seeing lately out of the senator. Washington was taking its toll on him, and even his wife and kids had now moved back to Pennsylvania just to be away from his stupid antics and not to be embarrassed by his constant gloating. But if he was working on something big, as he claimed, something that'll "keep us here till the chickens come home to roost," who knows? With him anymore now, all she could hope for was maybe he'd give up his senate seat when this all died down. That way, next year, she could move on with her life. The quicker, the better, she thought.

Finding herself in front of Maxine's, out of habit, she started fixing her hair as she shuffled down her top and made sure that she was standing upright. Then, as she entered, she quickly looked around for Luther. There, seated by himself in a corner booth, sat what she thought was the most handsome man in Washington. Luther waved her over, and he stood as she seated herself. Ah, she thought, the real sign of a gentleman. They hadn't done much in their relationship. So far, it consisted of visiting some museums, walking in the parks, and going out for dinners and lunches.

They had actually met for the first time at the National Museum of Art. Mable happened to pick that Sunday afternoon to go there. As she was walking around, she couldn't help but notice this tall, attractive man with blond hair who was taking in the gallery just as she was. He would stop and view the artwork at the same time she did. At first, it bothered her, but then, when he moved on, she thought nothing about it. Except she did miss sneaking a glance in his direction whenever she thought she could without being caught.

When out of the blue, he said to her, "What do you think of this artist, may I ask?"

Coming out of her thoughts and surprised by the sudden voice behind her, she looked around and saw that it was him. The very same person moments ago she was craning her neck around corners to see where he had disappeared to. Only now to find him standing right behind her and asking her for her opinion on a painting they now shared.

"Great," she said. "I like the control of the colors and the flow of them. It's as if he found a wave and caught it in bright colors, and the end result is flowers seemingly never to end. It's as if you were to look behind the painting. They would continue on the wall and beyond. That's why I came today. I really like Mujo and his style. Is that why you came here? Or is this place somewhere you used to meet women at?" Mable finished with a smile on her face as she was now staring into the bluest of eyes she had ever seen. Tall, blond, and definitely in shape, and when he spoke with that accent, it seemed to go through her skin right to the tickle-me part.

"I, too," he said with a smile. I like the artist, and of course, it is always a pleasure to meet a beautiful woman who enjoys art as well."

"Touché," she said. Then he immediately said, "I have a feeling that you also like fine food. Am I right on this?" he asked her.

"Is this a prerequisite?" she asked, smiling, still smiling as if it was glued to her face now. "Do you often ask so many questions about a woman's habits before you even know her name?"

"Forgive me, please. I found that speaking with you was as if I had known you for a lifetime. I am Luther, Luther Rudman. I am from

Bamberg, Germany. Not to influence any decision you may be asked to make about having lunch with me, but I am with the German consulate here in Washington. And no, I am not a spy. Nor do I work on secret computers. I am just a simple attorney, as you would say here, a lawyer for the embassy and its employees. Actually, I do marriages, or who may want to get married or who wants to buy a home or a car, insurance's boring, very boring work. But I live in America, and I can go to so many places here and see so much, and I got to meet you today. So, what more can a simple man ask for? With all of that said, will you accept an offer from me to have lunch someplace nice?"

Luther was charming her right out of her shoes, and right now, he could have them, actually. She'd give them up with a smile and walk right out into a snowstorm barefooted and collect eggs.

Waking up from her minute relapse, she replied, "Well said, well said. For a minute there, I had you mixed up for a felon. Someone who came here to maybe make a pencil sketch of what he's looking at. Then you start talking, and I think I ran into a gentleman. How surprising is that? Yes, lunch of course, yes, lunch, shall we go now? Oh, before I forget, Mable is my name, my first name. Mable ah Gardner, and not to impress as well, but I am the right hand of a senator right here in Washington. Senator Pillow from Pennsylvania, actually I am his chief of staff," Mable finished speaking before she could turn her head away from his eyes. Those damn blue eyes were way too bright, she thought, and he was way too handsome to be a lawyer. Most lawyers she met from foreign countries usually were geeks and looked like geeks.

"Ah, we have a slight problem," he said, looking at her. "We are not allowed to date or see outside of work anyone who works for an elected official in a democratic country. Germany wants no problems, you see."

Thinking fast on her feet, Mable was confident she had the answer. After all, she was known for her fast thinking and her quick wit. "Well, how about this: as the senator's chief of staff, I ask you to lunch. This way, we can talk about how Germany can help Pennsylvania when it comes to ah making better bratwurst. Pennsylvania has a lot of Germany's finest cooks and bratwurst makers as residents, so will that do?" she said, now smiling up at her new best friend.

"Bratwurst, you say good German bratwurst. As an attorney, I have to ask, did they take a patent from our country illegally? I see that we do have this need to sit down at a fine restaurant and, over lunch, discuss how we are to settle our dispute." Luther was smiling now as well, waiting for her reply.

"Yes, I think so," replied a smiling and invigorated Mable Gardner as she took his outstretched arm and was led out of the museum as a willing participant in whatever the gods would make happen on this day for her.

Now, several weeks into their relationship, she was very comfortable around him, and he felt the same. For the first time in her life, she wanted to call home and say, "Mom, I think you may have been wrong about the bridesmaid only," but that was just wishful thinking on her part.

As usual, Maxine's was a little crowded. There was the normal hustle and bustle of the waiters coupled with the noise of everyone who laughed, laughter that needed to be heard and noticed, so shrill laughter seemed to be always in vogue. Even those "loud" whispered remarks that were heard were, in a way, comforting. It was always nice to be in a place that had some life in it. Lately, with the economy in such a slump, with a lot of people out of work, it's good some things did remain normal.

Luther was in a good mood. Mable could tell by his smile as she finally got situated at the table they shared. She was still very much intrigued about her new romance. She sometimes felt that maybe someone would pinch her, and she would awaken at her desk. It would be one in the morning on a snowy night in Washington. It was as if a dream was taking place or maybe a movie, only in this one she was seeing herself on the screen, acting this all out. But those thoughts were short-lived when Luther reached for her hand and kissed it lightly and remarked on how radiant she looked today.

Blushing in front of the waiter, who was now standing at her side, she simply ordered her usual iced tea and a salad with some sort of chicken on the top. Was she being a little flighty right now? Had it been that long since someone paid her some real attention? Has she been so involved in someone else's life that she can't remember when she last thought of herself? Shame on me, Mable thought, shame on me, as she could still feel where his lips had touched the back of her hand. No matter how long they have been together now or what lies in their future, she was happy.

"What are you working on right now?" asked Luther, startling a surprised Mable from her personal evaluation in that short-lived minute she took for herself.

"What was that, Luther?" she asked.

Looking at her now and with a smile on his face, he leaned across the table and said, "Working. I asked what are you working on. I saw your eyes glaze over, and I knew you were in some kind of deep thought or maybe a trance." He laughed.

"No, actually, I was thinking that maybe I should pinch myself to see if all of this is real," she replied.

Luther turned his head sideways, and with the biggest grin he could muster, he said, "Yes, I know also that feeling. I was thinking about that as I was on my way here this afternoon. I couldn't help but think that my mother was wrong. She always said that I was not destined to be with a woman ever, and I would say, 'Why not?' and she would always say. 'Because you think too much of your business and not enough about you.' Maybe that was true then, but now, since I have met you, I can only think of you, and then I wonder if something is wrong with me," as he took her hand again and asked her if she understood what he was saying to her.

"No, what are you saying?" she replied. Looking into those deep blue eyes of his always had a way of making her go squiggly in her stomach.

"More than just lunch or a dinner, something more concrete. Maybe even making love to you. I have certainly had that on my mind lately. As a matter of fact, it's what's always on my mind." He laughed.

"Oh, so that's it, huh? After three weeks of feeding me, it's time to sack me, huh," she said with a smile now.

"No, no! I did not mean to imply that we leave the table now and go to my place, but to at least think about it, yes maybe," he asked her as if he was somewhat now embarrassed to have mentioned it at all.

"Yes," she clamored and looked away. "I mean," she continued now, looking directly into those eyes, "I mean, yes, I have had that on my mind as well, actually. Thinking that maybe you thought something was the matter with me and you really didn't find me attractive enough, as if someone told you I had a wart somewhere, and you didn't care to see it." She laughed.

"You are teasing me, right? I would love to see and visit all of your warts one by one," he said with a look of astonishment on his face. How could she think that he wouldn't want to make love to her?

He couldn't imagine any real man in the restaurant not wanting to make love to her.

"Quit thinking about it. Apparently, it is something we both want, so when it happens, it will; now, how's that for taking off any pressure that we leave the table now and go? Besides, I am hungry, and you did invite me to lunch," she said with a mischievous smile on her face. Now laughing together, it seemed as if a weight had been taken off both of their shoulders.

Still Guessing

Juan was busy, really busy; he was following so many people in so many different disguises that, after a while, it started to become a blur. The only thing he had found out so far was that Clara was indeed the granddaughter of Frank and Claire Benoit, that Senator Pillow indeed had goings-on right now with H. T. Wetco, and that the FBI was looking for a mysterious man in the city. A hard hunt was being activated to find out the location of this guy and the identity of this individual. But Juan knew that a dusty trail was always just that, dusty. One had to narrow down the objective to the point that there would be no mistake about the identity of the one that finally gets selected as the "he's it" in this game of tag. He also knew that there was a real potential that it would be easy in this game to find more than one person needing to be tagged out. He also knew that the larger the game and the more players involved, the more of a chance that someone would discover that he was rifling through volumes of private information via the computer. Although he was considered one of the best hackers in the business, he still had to be very careful now that the FBI was involved in this. So, every day, he also consumed his time by personally visiting some of the players.

He had now followed Agent Clara Beach and her boyfriend Justin several times. He knew where John Bloso lived and the other agents in that office who now worked on this project. After all, if someone was stalking agents and their families, as was one of the scenarios they once had mentioned and he had picked up on, then you couldn't rule that out. He didn't have much to go on yet, and he knew that there was probably not much time left before someone would strike a target. What target was to get hit? Right now, he was lost to that fact, as if he was dropped into the woods at night someplace on the planet. But if there was another target, he would have to find out before they did. That could be the ace card he would need to play should they tag him for the hit at the Benoits because of that interview. He would drop a dime in the FBI and alert them to the hit and clear his name at the same time, somehow.

But for now, Juan was following Pillow's chief of staff and her pet, Luke. It seemed Luke and the senator should trade lists of the female groupies that chased after them, and they bedded, even though he was impressed. But what he couldn't figure out was the connection between Luke and Clara. Was she playing him? He couldn't have been bedding her. There was Justin, but in today's world, it happens. So, what was the unknown connection? Perhaps she was unaware of the connection between the senator and Wetco, where her grandfather had worked and retired.

He was certain that she knew nothing of the general and Thurston's role in all of this, as the thought of dropping a dime on their potential involvement crossed his mind. But that wouldn't be of any real value, not yet anyway. Yet he knew that he would have to get all this down and mail it to his FBI contact. It could also be good if he took a picture of a local paper to capture the date. He would then show in the background some of the information he had collected so far. That way, if the general or Thurston somehow died rather suddenly, it wouldn't leave him holding another empty bag. He would need to have proof that he was following leads concerning those deaths while working on orders from his employer. He was now getting to believe that it would turn out to be Bob Thurston and H. T. Wetco, which he knew had a lot to do with this, but for now, that was just a feeling, and feelings never got a job done.

Juan was going to be a little busy this weekend. He had to follow and finish bugging several more homes and private phones. But by Sunday afternoon, maybe there would be time to watch a little baseball, he thought.

Günter's Second Hit

Günter had been following his next target for some three weeks now, and it was time to make that move concerning her and his job. He never liked America, and now he had to be in its capital. How much anguish must he be put through, he thought. If only he had a bomb large enough with him, he thought. No one in this city would be thinking about it as it exploded because they are so busy running from place to place just to buy and have more. Greed makes it seem as if this country is run on greed. They have such a need to have more, to have it bigger and faster, and to have only the best. Forget the rest of the world and its problems. As long as they can suck the lifeblood from everyone else for their own good, they will continue to make his world angry.

How he wished he had been hired to make a larger spectacle instead of sending a message to someone by killing this woman. Günter followed her through most of her day and sometimes at night to see if she still met up with this German. Germany shall miss one of its sons soon. This one is going to be on the house, he thought. For some reason, he had decided very early on that he did not like this man, this large blond German man.

Following them as they walked arm in arm down the Germans' street, Günter knew that he would be having fun tonight. He thought about how they would both look at him in fear when they knew death was but minutes away. Günter liked those looks. He thrived on them. They make it easier for him to do what he so likes doing. He would keep some of them alive a little longer just to see how they contorted their bodies trying to escape. Then, with a smile on his face, he would listen as they pleaded for their miserable lives. While some actually defecate on themselves, as others would beg or cry, even clawing at their own skin as if coming off, it would be a different person there instead of the one who is to die. He remembered several of them he had to wake up after passing out from the fear. Laughing, he thought back to those times, waking someone up to kill them so they could sleep forever; now, how funny is that?

Then there are the women who plead for their lives, offering up their bodies to him forever as if that would change his mind. Never would that happen. But they had no idea that he couldn't care less. He took them when he thought he wanted them, and why not? Within minutes, they would not remember it anyway. He now almost laughed aloud at that thought. So, would his thinking about sex make him want to take her tonight, maybe? Now that he thought about it, why not make the German watch as he takes her?

Yes, tonight I will take her and make him watch, that big blond German moron. Then I will let him watch as I cut her throat and have the blood drip over him like a bath.

Now getting excited, his pace quickened a little, and the distance between him and his victims grew closer. Almost finding his pace in step with his quarry, Günter's breathing became heavier and his focus more purposeful. Günter was on the hunt, and his prey was just in front of him, and this made his manhood start to harden as he drew closer, quicker.

Unknowingly as to what was about to happen, Juan had picked this very night to follow Mable Gardner and her new boyfriend. If she even had one before this guy. It would make anyone wonder because she burned the midnight candle. Almost seven days a week for that lowlife senator she worked for. Juan was truly impressed by her work effort, that was for sure. Lately, however, she has been stepping out with someone from the German embassy, a lawyer, as he told her. When actually, he was the liaison in charge of their International Affairs, more known to others as the chief spy for the German embassy.

Who knows what they were spying on concerning Senator Pillow? But he came across several taps concerning this senator, and it was confusing at the moment. This guy is a none-sitting senator, not on any working committee. This non-functioning freshman senator from Pennsylvania. You can't really get much lower on any pole than that. The German embassy looked into him to secure more information on Mable than the senator, but who knew for sure? It would seem that way on the exterior. Juan began to think that these emotions were just maybe real. He was seeing emotions from both of them. That's why he decided tonight he would follow them just in case he was wrong. He would become very annoyed if that wasn't the German's intent. Could the only reason why he needed her in his apartment was to make love to her and then drug her and question her until he found whatever it was that they needed to learn? Was a decision concerning her fate already made? Could she be the next target? If she was the next target, then was he the killer all along?

Perhaps someone hired him to make these hits on the side, considering that bringing in an unknown from out of the country would be a little more expensive. How easy was this for him if he was the hired gun living right under everyone's noses? Could it have been the Benoits first and then Mable? Is this all done to send a message to Pillow to back off something involving H.T.Wetco? This is still a nagging question that continues to fill his mind. Why Pillow? Why did a message need to be sent to him now? He knew that soon, and very soon, he would have to solve this problem.

Then, out of the corner of his eye, he could see that a man had suddenly appeared behind the strolling couple. Grabbing Luther's arm, he then shoved him forward. Then, grabbing Mable, he wrapped his left arm around Mable's neck and held her tightly against his body. He could see that some words were now being exchanged as the big German charged forward. Just as quickly, he could see that Luther was jerking his right shoulder as if something invisible had punched him hard there. Juan knew that Luther had just been shot. This has now changed the game. Juan, of course, was carrying both his fighting knives and his gun, encased with a silencer.

Moving along rapidly, he crossed the street a half block or more from Luther's house. Juan then stopped to wait under one of the many trees that lined the street. As he looked back at where the confrontation was still on, he thought they might not make it this far. There was this possibility that this mysterious man would kill them both as he waited in the safety of the trees. Juan made up his mind that he would have to get somewhat closer to them. He had to make something happen. He needed to quickly take control of the chaotic reactions that would take place immediately following his intrusion.

Günter was surprised at the reaction to his initial contact with his quarry. He had not expected this German to have any sense of manhood. Then, to have now attacked him as he held a gun was ludicrous. He expected this man to fold and to fold immediately. The woman he now held close to his body, he had already cut her in the neck to get her attention, as she began to bleed. It was a nice steady flow of dark red blood, he thought. Apparently, the German did not see the knife come into his hand after he shot him, then he said. "Another move, and I will cut her throat right through, on the spot."

Now, it seemed that shooting this idiot didn't seem to make a difference either. For some reason, he still could feel the anger gushing from this German. Günter had to decide if he wanted some enjoyment now or try to get them into the Germans' apartment that was just several houses away.

Luther was sure that he was going to make love to Mable tonight. They had decided earlier in the day that they would meet at a local Italian restaurant near his flat and then take a leisurely stroll to his place. As they had agreed last week, if something happened, then it did. No pressure, no rush. He was sure she would accept it if he told her his true feelings about falling in love with her. She would probably admit to him that she felt the same way, in a way. Or maybe she really felt this way, which would have made him the happiest man alive. As he turned to say how beautiful the night was, how the walk was too slow, and that maybe they should run to his house, this is when he felt the push on his back, sending him forward. But because of his training, he managed to keep from falling on his face right there on the sidewalk. He stopped himself from going any further and managed to make a turn to see what the hell had just happened.

That's when Luther sees the knife being held tightly against Mable's throat. As if in slow motion, and to his horror, he sees the man bringing the knife back across her throat. The blood was mesmerizing as it began to run down her neck onto her blue dress. The pain in her eyes made his nostrils flare from the anger now welling up inside of him. This man had no clue as to who he was, but he was certainly now going to find out. This was a mistake, a big mistake, one that was beyond the man's comprehension. This mistake would cost this man his life tonight. Now, for Luther, all the years of training and dealing with tough, deadly people have come into focus. He knew what he had to do. Luther decided to move forward quickly before this man could take control of the situation. That's when he felt the initial impact of being shot. Luther thought that was the thud you hear as the bullet enters the body. Then comes a shock that follows. It is unbelievable; it is unthinkable. It is something that should not have happened so easily, especially to him. He is forced to stagger backward from the bullet's impact. Luther realizes that his attacker is talking to him now, telling him to move forward and not make a sound or any other stupid move, and everything will be all right. What bothered him was that the voice was in German. His mind began to race as he tried to search for it. Somewhere in there, it would give him a name for the face that he looked at. Who was this man, and how are they connected? But right now, do what he says. Go along with it until he can make a change and attack. But if he simply went along with him all the way into the house, they were both dead, and Luther knew that.

Juan was looking at this from a different angle now that he had crossed the street. He could see that Mable was almost in shock and that she was bleeding from under her chin. He had cut her throat. Juan didn't know how deep the cut was, but apparently, it was deep enough to have put her into shock. As blood now covered her front as if she had been doused with a can of red paint. He knew that he could not allow this to continue any longer. Pulling out his pistol and still being hidden by the back of this tree, Juan placed the first shot into the man's shoulder on the hand that held the knife. He then fired once again and placed this shot into the side that had turned away. Now, the assailant dropped his knife and began to run down the street.

Suddenly, he stopped, placed his arm against a tree, and fired one shot that took Mable in the back. She found herself falling forward into the arms of Luther. Luther then turned her, placing his back into the line of fire. Now falling to the ground, Luther covered her with his own body. But the unknown assailant turned and vanished into the night, leaving Mable bleeding in the arms of Luther, who was calling 911. While screaming for an ambulance to come to save the girl he was in love with.

Holding her as tightly as he could, he called his embassy and told them he had been shot and was lying in the street several doors down from his home. Now, turning his full attention to Mable, he could see and knew that her life was rapidly slipping away. Taking off his tie and making a tourniquet, he placed it around her neck. He then found the place where the bullet had entered her back, just above the left shoulder blade. Luther began to press hard on the open wound to help stem the flow of blood as he waited for the ambulance to arrive. He knew that somehow, somehow, he would not let the first person he truly loved die tonight. He also knew that she was not safe, and he would have to take care of her from here on out. For the rest of his life, he would protect this innocent woman who was possibly targeted by someone who wanted him dead. But then he remembered that someone else had come to their rescue. Someone else had saved their lives tonight, and he had no clue who that person was.

But he'll find that out. He'll find out if that someone was supposed to be there or if it was just a gift from God for a chance meeting like this. Luther scanned the area as he heard the sirens approaching from a distance. Because he knew he was also now vulnerable, lying there on the sidewalk, holding back Mable's life force as it wanted to slip away on her that night.

Juan now was also able to disappear from the immediate scene. He would try to follow this unknown assailant into the darkness beyond the lights of this influential neighborhood. All the while, he was thinking about what the hell had just happened. One minute, he was following them to see if this boyfriend of hers was actually a paid assassin when all hell broke loose. Juan had been involved in many of these tag games, but this one came too quickly. This one was too professional to have made it look like a holdup for cash. This was not a mugging. This was a professional hit, missed by a professional, which means he'll be back. Now was the time to concentrate on who the hell that was that came in as a blur and exited with two of his bullets.

Günter slid under the truck he had parked there earlier in the day. Quickly, he detached the hinge pin, lowered the bottom door, and slid quietly inside the truck. Not wanting to make any noise, he just lay there catching his breath. The heat from the vest, the bullet shock, and some pain only added to his heightened senses. What the hell happened? He asked himself in disgust. He just missed for the first time in his illustrious career. Had he just missed his first kill? He had the bitch in his grasp. He had his knife in her soft, white skin. She was bleeding, and he could smell the blood and feel the warmth of it and how nice and sticky it felt as it touched your own fingers. He missed, son of bitch, he missed. Calm down became his mantra, for he now understood that he needed to breathe in nice, long, easy breaths, bring in the breaths slowly, fill the stomach, relax, relax.

After waiting almost an hour, he sat up in the truck and started to pull off from the curb when an officer stopped him and asked him for identification. Smiling at the officer and producing his embassy credentials and his international driver's license, he said in perfect German that he needed to return to the embassy right away, then acted as if he had made a mistake and said in English, "Excuse me, Officer, you don't speak German, sorry, I need to get back to the embassy."

"Okay, have a safe trip," he replied, stepping aside and watching the unmarked truck leave the area.

As the ambulance arrived, so did the local police and the men from the embassy unit assigned to him. Suddenly, the air was thrumming with different background noises made by so many people who were now gathering around him and Mable as the police and his men continued to lock down the area. The responding medics were hovered over her as she lay there on the sidewalk. Everyone is doing their job right now to keep her alive. And all he could do was to continue to pray. As a medic stopped the flow of blood coming from Luther's shoulder wound and wrapped it in bandages, a young police officer approached.

"Sir, can you tell us what happened here tonight?" he asked, as he was now leaning down, trying to help Luther to his feet. "Come over here, sit down, and give me an account of what happened. Did you get a look at the assailant? Do you possibly know the person who assaulted you? I need to see some form of identification, please, and do you know that woman lying over there? Was she with you tonight?" The young officer continued his questioning, and Luther never responded. He just kept looking at the medics, raising her up and putting her into the ambulance.

He felt a hand go to his shoulder, squeezing him as if to say, "It's okay now; I'm here." he turned to face a friend. He lifted his head and looked into the face of Ulmmer. He was the number 2 station chief concerning International Affairs. As this undoubtedly would now turn into an International Affairs problem, he thought.

Just then, another medic approached him and said, "Sir, if you can walk, I need you to come to the ambulance. I need to take you to the hospital. Can you walk? If not, I can get a stretcher for you."

"No, I can walk," Luther replied, somewhat still in a daze.

"I need to lift that shoulder a little. I need to get a sling around that shoulder. There may be some pain. Just bear with me if you can," the medic asked him. After that was accomplished, he walked Luther over to another waiting ambulance. After he and Ulmmer were situated, they sped off into the night. Not far behind Mable, he thought. All Luther could think of was why, who was this man, and why, why tonight, why right in front of his house. He needed answers, and he would not stop until he had them. But first, get to the hospital, get this shoulder taken care of, and get right over to Mable. He then realized that Ulmmer was in the ambulance, staring at him as he looked up and saw a worried look that made up his friend's face.

Then Luther said, "Ulmmer, my friend, what a night, huh? I'm sorry for dragging you out of the comfort of your home for this."

"Not to worry, Luther. I was only getting ready for dinner as it was a long day, and I just got in the door when they called me and told me about your dilemma. So, I put the entire first protocol into effect, sir. The ambassador is under guard. The embassy is in total lockdown. Everyone is accounted for, and I have guards in place at the homes of everyone on the list. Now that I am riding with you and our team is following us, everyone is covered. Now, tell me exactly what happened tonight. Last we spoke, you had a dinner planned, a nice personal night out, and maybe a day off tomorrow. So, is this how you celebrate, Luther?" Ulmmer asked with a smile on his face, trying to lighten a sudden heavy load. One that, by the look on his friend's face, seemed to be weighing the ambulance down.

Luther told him exactly what had transpired that evening, even the thought in his head about teasing her to run to the house. It had made no sense to either of them.

"Maybe it was just your usual mugging taking place," Ulmmer said. But no, Luther kept insisting that this man was a pro. Someone had sent this man specifically to kill him on this very night. The man had waited to perform the task when he knew Luther would be the most vulnerable when he was with Mable. This could only mean that someone has been following him, possibly for weeks now.

He then said, "Ulmmer, I want you to have the offices swept, also my house and car. I need to know if we have someone in the works. Find out who is new to the embassy and who may have had any questions asked about his or her activity in the last two months. See if there is any unusual activity concerning any staff member. From the embassy cleaners to the cooks, look at everyone. Also, place guards in Mable's room. I know that she is probably safe, but I won't take that chance. Tell the locals that she is under German protection as a witness to what happened here tonight. If that doesn't work, tell them, for the sake of international peace, let our men stand there with theirs. Say anything but make that happen for me." Luther was now reacting as he was supposed to. He was the man in charge, and shot or not, he would step up and do his job. Mable would be fine, and if she wasn't, if she should die this night, then he would tear the world apart to get his revenge.

Emergency Room

The hospital emergency room was crowded with people milling about in the halls. No one knew exactly what was taking place when the excitement began. The first ambulance pulled up to the back doors when suddenly the place was busting at the seams with police officers. People were speaking German with badges and guns being waved as if they were flags, and you needed both to be here. The requisite is a need to hold one in each hand as if you're in some sort of parade going on in the hallway.

When they first wheeled Mable in, the doctors were all over her, climbing on the gurney as if they were ants and she was a hill of sugar. The woman who lay on that gurney had blood-soaked towels on her neck, and she was moaning and trying to talk, but couldn't. Mable sounded as if she had a root canal done as she was whisked away before anyone really could fix their eyes on her for any length of time. Immediately, she was placed in the trauma room attached to the emergency area. Once in, the doors were closed to prevent any intrusion on what was happening there. The men standing outside those doors said it was none of your business. Then came the second ambulance, and again, the activity in the room was overwhelming for those seeking relief from a summer's cold. Everyone moved out of the way as this man was shuffled into another room where he was given needles and drips, and someone took a pair of scissors to a seemingly expensive shirt. Being asked to lie down as they worked on a shoulder wound, he apparently received somewhere out there in a city that managed to have this happen to someone almost every night. Then, after settling him down, they took him into the elevator and up to another waiting operating room to sew up that shoulder after they had removed a bullet.

A bullet that would continue in its travels this very night to the German embassy. By morning, it would have given away all of its secrets, including the pistol that fired it. Then, just as suddenly as the whirlwind of activity that had so recently entered the foyer downstairs had come, it was now gone, as everyone settled back and took their sigh of relief, just to continue arguing with a desk nurse over who had health care and who was on welfare.

First Lead

Justin was sitting on the couch, getting ready to watch television, when he took the call. He was asked to be the lead on a shooting that took place that night in the Heights section of Washington. It would seem that the FBI had a need to be there because it was a shooting that involved both an American woman and the liaison of International Affairs from the German embassy. So, it now becomes a matter for the FBI to investigate, he was told over the phone. So, not really wanting to leave Clara alone, he asked her if she would like to work with his team to help investigate the incident. Clara, who had not done anything in the field lately, couldn't have been happier that Justin had asked her to help. Well, finally, she would have something to sink her teeth into. And at least tonight, she wouldn't be alone either. Then she smiled, thinking to herself that she liked to work under Justin, but this time it would actually work.

Walking into the hospital, Justin flashed his badge, followed by Clara doing the same. However, he wondered if Clara ever felt as he did now. When he flashes that badge of authority to Justin, it's as if he holds a winning lottery ticket in his hand and is showing the world. That badge meant a lot to him, and he was proud of it. So, every time he could flash it in someone's face, he did as it said, "Move aside, I'm allowed in here, I'm FBI." Geez, he thought, how much of a kid could he still be, as he held back a slight giggle. After all, he was the lead here, and it wouldn't be right if people saw that he was smirking to himself as he walked around looking for someone who could actually help him, trying to pretend he wasn't lost. Looking over the area, he could see a captain in the local police force talking to several of his men.

Justin approached the captain somewhat wearily, knowing full well that the man would tell him it was his case and the FBI had no real jurisdiction here, but he would advise him of any real information should it appear, and when it did, and that would be after his men worked on it. Justin had been through this same scenario on several occasions, especially here in Washington. For years since the Jack Ruby case in Dallas, it has always been *us* versus *them* in a lot of local problems. After Justin had introduced himself and Clara as his second, he was greeted as cordially as he thought he would be. The captain told him that two people were shot tonight in the Heights section of town.

The Heights was where a lot of embassy people lived, and one of them happened to be with the German embassy. It's when he asked, "So that's what makes it international?" Then, without waiting for a response, he continued telling Justin that the woman who was in the operating room when they spoke was American. Her name was Mable Gardner, and she was the chief of staff for Senator Pillow from Pennsylvania. This individual and what had happened to her tonight would be put under his jurisdiction. It did not matter who she worked for. She was a Washington resident. So, this made her his problem and a problem for the Washington police department, which was more than capable of handling it. However, he then told the two of them that if they felt that they needed any help, he would ask for it personally. But I don't really count on his needing any help. With that, he turned his attention to another officer who had approached him to ask him about some mundane problem he needed help finding an answer to.

Upon hearing who the female victim was, Clara was immediately taken aback. She knew and had met Mable on several occasions when visiting Luke, and so had Justin. Wow, she thought, what a coincidence this was. How could this have happened? She thought. Isn't anyone safe anymore? It was as if these people were out partying in the city's slums. They were shot right in the Heights.

The police captain then finished talking with the officer, turned back to Justin, pointed at a man standing in the corner, and spoke.

"See that big fellow over there, well, he's with the German embassy. You might as well introduce yourself to him and ask him if he needs your help. No sense in your standing around here. As I said, I'll call you if I need any help. Oh, by the way, those fellows also want in on this and are providing a guard around the clock for the woman." He then turned and walked toward the nurses' station, where his men were standing.

Justin thought to himself. No doubt he had to get there to put in his donut order before they left, and just brought him back a coffee.

Justin tapped Clara on the shoulder and said, "We might as well go introduce ourselves to that guy as well. Before the evening turns into a long, boring night where no one wants to deal with us, and we have to leave empty-handed."

So, turning, they walked over and introduced themselves to this fellow named Ulmmer, who then told them that the German embassy had requested that their officers be allowed to be included in the investigation as well. That had confirmed what the captain had just said. Apparently, the woman, Mable, who was injured, was with the liaison of International Affairs for the German embassy, who was shot as well. So, they feel that now they have a stake in this. They needed to find out if she had been unknowingly used as a means or a decoy of sorts to help this assailant get to their liaison officer. This was their current line of thinking, and until proven otherwise, they would remain assuming that she knew their attacker. Then he asked Justin why the FBI was investigating this. "Was it because he was with the German embassy, and she works for an American senator? Somehow, this equates to the FBI getting involved. I need to tell you this: for at least several weeks now, they have been seeing each other personally."

Looking at Clara, Justin turned to Ulmmer and said, "Tell me exactly what had transpired tonight. Understand as well that we are going to investigate this incident fully. Seeing how it falls within the parameters of what we do and what we are required to do by law, both internationally and nationally. The law here is that any foreign employee injured in any way on U.S. soil is covered. The FBI has full investigative powers. So, we might as well both come to a conclusion right now that whatever comes from any of this, we share, so that we can both come to the same conclusions concerning this. If someone set up your man or if this was just a freak accident, whatever happened here, we both find out. I have the local police who are going to conduct their investigation around Miss Gardner only. They, however, will not be conducting any investigation on your man outside of maybe some inquiries. But we will. So, if there is any need to think that she was somehow more involved in this, other than just as a victim, then you will need to share that with us. Also, we will need to know all about your man. I'm sure that what he does there for the embassy is confidential and can be held that way for his own safety. I say this because this whole incident may have been caused by his job at the embassy. Then, unknowingly, she was used to getting to your man, and it may have cost her life if she doesn't come through this tonight."

Now that Justin had said what needed to be said by him, he stood there as the big German looked him over to size him up for some reason. In the hesitation that now existed between the two men, Clara spoke up.

Saying, "Let's go over to the cafeteria, sit, and talk about exactly what you know as to what took place tonight. I'm sure you have enough men stationed here guarding not only your man but apparently her as well. At least, that's what the captain complained about. Besides, it'll give us someplace where we cannot look so official. We can relax and come to a working agreement on the protocol from your end. Ours is fixed with a little leeway. But for the most part, unless we have something concrete against the woman, then we have to suspect that this all came about from your man."

Looking at her with appraising eyes, Ulmmer had found that, for some reason, this woman was not a second to anyone. She knew what she was doing, separating him from his authority. Getting him to someplace where they can become equals, and if relaxed enough, he would come clean with what had really happened tonight. What they felt was the direction they needed to go in to find out who this man was.

He thought, was he to share this information with them before his people found him and executed him? Surely, that is exactly what Luther had on his mind tonight. Find him and kill him. Or should I have the Americans come in and save this bastard? Well, Ulmmer thought, at least I can use a cup of coffee right now until Luther is able to talk some more.

Turning, he called over to Helmut and said, "These two are with the FBI, and we are going to the cafeteria to talk about the protocol for this case. Should Luther become available and need to talk, come get me immediately, understood?"

"Yes, sir," replied Helmut, who had just recently been assigned to this division. He thought if things like this happened often, he would have to go back to statistics. This was too much like work.

Justin, Clara, and Ulmmer sat in the corner of the cafeteria and sipped on what was to have passed as coffee. They were sure that someplace it might have been, but right here and now, this was like bad acid rain turned black with age.

"Wow, it actually burns the roof of your mouth. I just hope that someday it comes off. This is horrible coffee," quipped Clara.

"I have had worse," said Ulmmer, "but right now, it is hard to remember when."

"Ulmmer, what can you tell us about what happened out there tonight?" asked Justin. That's when Ulmmer decided that maybe he should tell the truth as closely as he could, without stepping over any boundaries, of course. That is exactly what Luther would want to do after he caught this man; he could do it. Personally, he could care less. After all, if it were him, he would not hesitate to do the same as Luther.

After about an hour had passed, and after listening to Ulmmer talk, he made it sound as if there was a love story being told, that Mable and Luther were just these two victims of a mugging gone wrong. Although Luther never said that this assailant had ever asked for jewelry or money. It went down as if he were only after one thing, and that was both of their lives. He had seemed bent on getting them into Luther's house, where he would have them alone and under control. What he didn't count on was that Luther would attack. Then, somehow, some outsider would come to their rescue?

Now Justin and Clara had another thing to cope with. Who exactly was this benefactor, and why did he not turn himself in? Was he a neighbor who carried a pistol with him when he walked the dog at night? They would have to share this with the captain so the police could canvas door to door to try and find out who the benefactor was. They had to find out exactly who he was. After all, he did shoot at the man and supposedly shot him. Maybe this guy could identify him in mug shots or photos. Or maybe he had been following this man for some other reason and intervened when he had to. Something here wasn't right. How often does this take place? How often, thought Clara, maybe never? Especially with someone from an embassy who was with someone who worked for a U.S. senator.

They were obligated now to tell the captain what they had just found out, seeing how it wasn't told to him at the request of Ulmmer's boss, Luther. Maybe because he already knew who had made this attempt on his life and would find this individual on his own. Then what, and make him disappear?

That's when Clara spoke up and said, "If you know this man or if you have any idea as to his identity, you have to tell us. I'm sure that you're aware of the fact that should he be found dead somewhere here in the U.S. after we have him identified as the man for this, we will have to investigate it, and should we find out it was you or your boss that made that happen, we would have to prosecute. Or revoke your diplomatic privileges and deport you, asking the German Government to prosecute."

"Just as in Germany, we would have to if it were against one of you. Yes, of that, I know, but if we have no clue, as we have no clue right now, why worry about that, right?" said Ulmmer. Fully well aware that if they knew who this guy was. If the Germans found him first, he would disappear, and so would the shooter. Both were never to be seen again in the U.S., Ulmmer laughed to himself.

Just then, Helmut showed up and said, "Luther was requesting that Ulmmer come to his room as soon as he could."

Getting up from his chair and thanking them both for the wonderful coffee, Ulmmer was about to leave when Justin said, "We'll be right behind you, Ulmmer. If Luther can talk with you, tell him to save some of it for us. We need to talk to him tonight, okay? It's protocol, so he'll understand, given that we're all on the same team. Everyone wants to move on this while it's still hot. Please tell him I only have a few questions tonight, okay, thanks."

Leaving the table together and following Ulmmer and Helmut to the elevator, Clara quickly said to Justin, "Listen, go handle this part alone; I'll meet you in the emergency room area. I want to check to see if Mable is going to make it and tell the wonderful captain about the Samaritan. Also, I should call Luke and tell him to contact and inform the senator tonight if that hasn't already been done."

"Okay, I'll see you there," replied Justin, lightly touching her shoulder, a gesture that Ulmmer hadn't missed. Clara turned down the hall, going in the opposite direction, and she brought out her phone and called Luke.

"Luke, hi, it's Clara. How are you?" she asked him.

"Fine," he replied. What's wrong, Clara? I would never have expected you to call me late in the evening unless something was wrong. Justin and you are okay, or are you squabbling about something? If so, yes, you can come over. I have been expecting this call for a while," he said.

"No, Luke, that's not the reason why I'm calling you. I just spoke to the metro police captain in charge of the problem I'm having. It seems that he didn't want to notify anyone concerning Mable Gardner outside of her family in Pennsylvania first. However, I think it differently. Luke, Mable was hurt tonight in a possible mugging. She's at St. Anthony's Hospital in the Heights. Maybe you should come down, and I can explain what happened to her. Luke, maybe you should be the one to call the senator and tell him as well. It seems the captain wanted to wait till the morning. So that's up to you if you call the senator tonight, but my advice would be to make the call. Anyway, I'm here in the emergency room. I'll tell you why we're involved because we are definitely involved, Luke." Clara finished speaking and waited for a response.

When Luke said, "Oh my god, Clara, is she going to be okay? I'll be right down there, and I'll call the senator. I think he needs to know tonight. If he found out that I knew and never called him, he'd fire me on the spot. Let me get this done, and maybe I'll come down with him if he'll come and get me. If not, I'll be down on my own later."

After that, she hung up the phone and walked to the captain to tell him that she had solved a potential problem for him and to find out exactly how Mable was doing.

Mable was on her second blood transfusion. It would seem that the supply of blood that was available to her on the shelf was quickly being depleted, so this one needed to stay in her body. But unfortunately, she had no way of knowing that. Right now, Mable might be in the physical realm, fighting for her life. But in the world, she was now occupied and talking to her grandmother. Funny, she didn't remember her grandmother that well. She had passed on when she was a little girl. Grandpa had been around, and he was a busy old man. Often too busy sometimes to even come and see her. But her mom said that was because he was some kind of engineer for an oil company, and he just liked being away. Now that her grandma was gone. Yet now, thinking about this, Mable needed to figure out why, if she was gone, what was she doing here trying to talk to her?

Then she remembered that she was being held tightly, and she felt wet under her chin. That someone had grabbed her from behind and shoved Luther forward toward the ground. He had caught his balance and came forward to grab her. But then he fell backward once again, and she ended up here talking to her grandma for some reason. Could she be dead? Her grandma was dead. Is that why she can see and talk to her grandma?

But I can't understand what she's saying to me. I can see her lips moving, and I know she is talking, but I can't hear a word of what she's saying. I can feel something heavy on my chest. I feel as if I'm floating. I'm so tired, I need to sleep. I need to rest to catch up on my sleep, she thought. Then, I could go see if Grandma was still around.

Luther knew he had to talk to the FBI about what had happened tonight. The sad thing was that, aside from what he went through, he had no idea what really happened. One minute, his thoughts were on taking Mable, the girl he had fallen in love with, to bed. The next thing he could only remember was watching as a man was cutting her throat. Why? Of all the things to do to him, why would someone hurt Mable? Unless they had been following him for weeks and seen how he had started to care for her, they wanted to use this emotion against him. But why would someone from his past hurt him now? Luther was more than halfway to retirement from the spy business. He hadn't been in the field in what had to be fifteen years now. Then, if Mable said yes to marrying him, he would get out altogether immediately. He had no real enemies that he could bring to mind. Oh, he had hurt people and had destroyed a few lives. But these were other spies. They were people of his trade, and most of them at this age were retired as well or dead. So, could this have been someone's child looking for revenge?

Then he thought, I looked right into his face, saw this man's face, and didn't recognize him at all. The more I think about it, the more he looks like no one I have ever seen. Could he have been a hired gun? Hired to come looking for me, find me, and kill me? But who would have paid an outsider? Or was it someone working in the embassy itself? Someone who possibly waited until now, until I finally found happiness, just to take it away from me. If that were true, then he would start looking in the embassy. He would also find out who wasn't capable any longer of going into the field and handling his own business, someone incapacitated. That would be the reason he hired someone to take care of his business. He would then find the answer to who had a motive for revenge.

Lying there, closing his eyes, he thought about the fact that he still couldn't think of anyone. Everyone at his age has retired, Luther thought. Some of those men he would still go have a beer with them if he were asked, just for old times' sake. He knew that spies from the Cold War were not old; they had just started early. The Cold War had ended for years, and those who were really great, those of the East German spies, were already working for them. They have had more than enough time to have done him in. No, this was more than that, and he needed to rethink exactly what was going on. He also needed to find that Good Samaritan. He wanted and needed to know why he was there. Right at that moment, to have saved their lives. He also needed information on Mable. He needed to make sure that she was going to be fine. Right now, he had no idea as to what he'd do without her. He wanted so badly to bring her home to his mother.

He badly wanted to say, "Look, Mother, you were wrong! Someone loves me, and I love her." With that, he started to cry and was wiping away the tears when Justin entered the room.

"Is now a good time to talk?" Justin asked. "Should I call a doctor? Are you in pain, sir?"

"No, please come in. I was just filling myself up with self-pity when I recognized that sometimes things work out, and with a little prayer from me, maybe this time I will get my way. So, you are Agent Justin Beach from the Washington Bureau, I assume," inquired Luther as he continued to speak, telling him, "Ulmmer said you needed to stop by and ask some questions."

"Yes, sir, I am from our Washington bureau. Here's my card. I'll just place it here on the table," replied Justin.

"That'll be fine. You know, of course, by now, all that has transpired. I assume that Ulmmer brought you up to speed. I believe someone is missing, a Clara Beach, your wife or sister?" asked Luther with a smile, then said, "If she is your wife, I didn't know that field agents in the FBI worked together. That would seem to be somewhat stressful to me."

"No, sir, not my wife or sister. Oddly enough, we have the same last name," he replied.

"Ah, it's nice to have someone you care for with your last name already in place; it's quite convenient," said Luther.

Wanting to change the subject, Justin smiled and said.

"Clara went down to check in on Miss Gardner. She actually knows Miss Gardner on a personal level. She has had some dealings with her office and has met her on several occasions, so she feels a need to make sure everything is okay. So, she went down to check on her," said Justin, leaving behind the comment he made about caring for her. There was no sense in even addressing that issue because it would become a rub, A rub between them, and he didn't want that. Not yet, anyway.

"Can I ask if you're up to explaining everything to me tonight? Or I can come back in the morning, and we can go over everything then. I just thought it would be the right thing to do, introducing myself to you tonight, sir. That way, you understand that we are treating this with urgency and with care. I understand that the two of you were romantically involved. Rest assured, that has no bearing on how our office will proceed on this, seeing that there is a need for confidentiality and privacy. As far as what happened tonight, we are going to find out exactly what happened and find whoever did this and make sure that they are put away for a long time," said Justin with the best FBI imitation he could bring forth.

"Thank you, Agent, if I may, Justin. But rest assured that we are going to be looking into this as well. I already have agents at my disposal looking for leads. Perhaps we can exchange some information that will, of course, help both ends to be met," said Luther, looking at Justin as if he were the canary and he was the cat.

"Understand, sir, that we can both look, and when found, he falls under the laws of the United States. I would hate to see any kind of justice handed out that was not, to say, correctly administered. I'm sure that if this were a mutual undertaking in Germany. We both would be concerned about not breaking German law," replied Justin. As he seemed to increase his height by breathing in and looking down on Luther. Justin didn't need any German dictating to him that he was going to do whatever he wanted to do on this and have it justified under his watch. No way. This man will have his day in court, and if found guilty, he will spend a long time in jail. That he knew to be true, it had to be.

Then Luther turned over and said, "When you go out, would you be kind enough to ask how Mable is for me and have one of my men bring me some news, please."

Justin replied, "Of course, maybe Clara has heard something by now, and I'll bring the news to you. Thank you for your time, Luther. Oh, and I'll be back tomorrow if I have any new information for you."

With that, Justin closed the door, nodded to Ulmmer, who was standing outside, and said, "Tough guy in there. Me, I'd be drugged up and sleeping this off."

"No drugs for him, and I doubt if he will get any sleep tonight. He has enough people in the field right now that there will be no rock that will be safe from not being turned over," said Ulmmer with a smile.

Clara was talking to Luke and some other man near the nurses' station when Justin approached them. Justin looked at Luke, nodded to the other man, and said, "Hi, Luke." Turning to face Clara, he then asked, "How's she doing, Clara? Any news yet? I told Luther that if I heard anything, I would have one of his men bring it up to him. Tough bird, that Luther, and he definitely is concerned about Mable, so anyway, any word yet?"

"Right now, she is stable. It seems as if it happened at just the right time. Finally, she stopped bleeding, and she's all stitched. The bullet fragments we have are already on the way to the lab for analysis. This is Senator Pillow. Senator Pillow, this is the FBI agent in charge of Justin Beach. If you're wondering, he is no relation. We do get that asked of us almost all of the time we're introduced. Just thought I would clarify it before it became an issue or made into a question," said Clara, facing the senator. She really had no use for the guy, but he was a senator and had to be respected. He could make trouble for them after all; however, in this case, she was sure he would stay in line and not become an ass of sorts.

"What can you tell me, Agent?" he asked Justin.

"So far, all I have is that she was attacked while walking to a friend's house. The two of them were jumped by a man, and he cut her throat, then while running away, he actually took the time to turn around and shoot her," said Justin.

"Apparently, he must have wanted her dead. To go to all of that trouble, wouldn't you agree?" he asked Justin.

Before he waited for an answer, he began again by saying, "Then I heard that some guy walking his dog turned and shot that other man. Is that why he ran off? Tell me if I'm wrong, but in Washington, DC, guns are illegal. If so, then answer me this. Why would someone living in the Heights of all places would be out walking his dog with a loaded gun? It all makes no sense to me, none at all. Unless the guy he really wanted to shoot was this person she was seeing. I understand that he is with the German embassy. An attorney. If so, then who wouldn't want to shoot attorneys, right? Ah no, I didn't say that, did I? Well, it was only meant as a joke to sort of lighten up the somber mood here.

Anyway, what was she thinking of, dating a German from the embassy? I need to find out what conflicts of interest or laws may have been broken. After all, she works for me, and I am a U.S. Senator. So, who knows how many? Anyway, I came here as soon as I could. I brought Luke along, and in the car, he told me that the three of you somehow know each other, That you and Clara know Mable. If so, it would seem I am left out of what is happening in my office with my staff." Now, he looked directly at Luke and shook his head as if to say they would be discussing this later.

Justin stepped toward the senator, who took a step backward as if he didn't want to get trampled on. But that was just Justin's way of taking over the space and sending a message to the senator that he was in control.

Then, looking directly into the senator's eyes, he said, "Well, let me say this, sir. Right now, we have no clue as to who shot and knifed Mable or Luther, her friend. We don't know if it was an attack designed to get to Luther or Mable."

Justin felt no need to tell the senator that Luther was also the Liaison of International Affairs Commander for the German embassy in Washington.

"Apparently, Mable and Luther have some attachment to each other. So, if any laws were broken, neither one of them knew it. I am sure that both of them did a lot of research concerning any possible laws that could have been in their way, and we all know that he is an attorney. With Luther being shot as well, but realizes that it was in the defense of Mable. Then, right before he was to continue walking to take this confrontation into Luther's home. Out of the view of the public, as we have it now, a lone gunman shot the attacker. Not once, but twice. At that time of night, he hit him out of the sight range of Luther. Which indicates he had to be a very good shot. Whoever he was, we have no idea. As to why he was there, we only have speculation. First, he was walking a dog. I don't believe anyone has ever seen a dog. So, someone was watching and possibly waiting for this to happen. Maybe someone intercepted this man's itinerary, and he was there to prevent anything from happening to either Mable or Luther. Or maybe even to both. As Mable could have been the target all along. Which is why he turned and fired on her? But right now, all it is. It's just more speculation. Until we get further into this, I can only say that you have now been brought up to speed on everything as we know it. As well as what speculations all the parties looking into this have made. One question that remains in my mind for now is how he knew where Luther lived. So maybe he was after Luther only. Right now, however, there are the Washington, DC police who will be investigating Mable's part. The FBI is on both her and Luther's case, and, of course, Luther will be asking his men to investigate this as well. So, hopefully, we can close this out very soon. As soon as I have any other real information and not speculative, I will personally see to it that you receive it all," finished Justin.

He was at his best that Clara had ever seen him at, and she was very proud of the way he just handled himself. She thought to herself, there, take that, you swine.

"Agreed, and I can say that you are definitely on top of this, and it makes me very happy that you are assigned to this, Agent. If I can bring my office to bear any weight to help your investigation, contact me directly. If I am not available, you can certainly contact Luke. I understand that Agent Beach and Clara phoned him this evening. Otherwise, we would not have known of this until tomorrow. This is something I will address with the captain's superiors. Who the hell does he think he is to keep me out of this, and why would he?"

With that, the senator hit Luke on the arm and said, "Let's go, I have a busy schedule set for tomorrow, and Mable will not be pulling my ass out of the fire, not in here, she won't be."

After that statement and Luke's shrug as they left, Clara was glad they did because she was on the verge of calling a dirtbag exactly that: a miserable dirtbag.

As they left the hospital, Clara thought that somehow, they would find out information about this person who tried to kill those two tonight much sooner than later. She also had to ask Justin why he gave away so much information to the senator. Information he had not shared even with her. Oh well, it's a long night yet, and before sleep would come, they had to go to the office and make out their initial report. To see if anyone else was going to be assigned to this. Then, how, in the scheme of things, did this weigh in as important?

With so many things happening to so many people of importance in this city, it's a wonder they didn't work twenty-four hours a day, seven days a week. It certainly was bad that these two had been attacked, more so this time than she may have liked it to be, because they knew Mable. Right now, though, her grandfather and grandmother's murderer was still out there on the loose. Who could possibly be looking into making someone else in the department lose a loved one? Then there are the two missing children of Congressman Fallty. God only knows who may have kidnapped them.

She was also involved in the murder of three girls, all tied to a rolled-up carpet left in a van with a tag left on it that read, "Three makes nine and one to go." A serial killer may be stalking the DC metro area, and there just weren't enough men or time to work on it all. So, if the police said they would be on top of this and the German embassy said they would be investigating, then maybe she shouldn't be on this case. Maybe it would be up to Justin all alone to solve this one, she thought.

Yawning, she put her hand to her mouth and said, "Justin, would you mind dropping me off at the house? You can go to the office, do the report, and then come home. I'm really tired, and for some reason, I can't keep my eyes open."

Recently, they moved into a brownstone on Benton Court in the city, so no one had the upper hand to make a comment about, "It was my place first."

"No, of course not. I'll swing down Firth Street and let you off at the corner. Is that okay? I want to get in myself, you know. No sense in your keeping me company as I type out this report. So, I'll just have to type out this report alone and by myself," Justin said with a frown on his face as if he were to start crying at any minute.

"You're a bum," she said. "Go ahead, don't drop me off. I'll wait there with you. Hopefully, Brad will be there, and he and I can talk all the while you type."

New Information

Grant Fisher was the man in charge of ballistics, and he found it interesting that the same gun that killed those two people in Virginia, the grandparents of the new agent, was now used in the shooting of a secretary of sorts in Washington, DC. The lead agent on that case, John Bloso, had said that anything that anyone finds concerning that case had to be brought to his "attention immediately and I mean immediately."

"Well, I wonder if this is immediate." Grant thought to himself. It was one o'clock in the morning, and he didn't know if now was the right time to call anyone at home, especially the lead agent's home.

"Wait, let's see, he thought, the agent that is in charge of this new case is Justin Beach. Wow, same last name as the agent whose grandparents were killed. I think I'll go upstairs and see if this agent is hanging around finishing up a report on what happened tonight. I can give him the information and have him decide if he should make that phone call." Simple how things sometimes work out for the best if someone gives a lot of thought to the problem.

Grant chuckled to himself and entered the elevator to go see if Agent Beach was indeed upstairs. Stepping from the elevator and seeing a young girl standing in the hallway, he approached her, saying.

"Good evening, madam. I see you're burning the midnight oil as well. Where may I find an agent named Justin Beach?" Grant asked the young lady and then said, "I understand that he is the agent in charge of an incident that took place tonight. So, I am assuming that by now, he is back in the house, filling out his reports."

"Yes, he is, and I'm actually on my way to see him now. Hopefully, he is done with those reports, and we can finally leave this place," replied a tired-looking Clara.

"Are you and he married? And has he dragged you along in this long process to keep him company?" asked Grant.

"No, actually, I'm an agent as well. Seeing how there was no one else alive in this corridor, I left my badge in my purse in the office. Next to Agent Justin's desk is my own. I'm Agent Clara Beach, and you are?" Clara asked with a slightly upwardly turned eyebrow, now trying to assess who this distinguished old gentleman was.

"Actually, I work in the bowels of the building," he said with a smile. "Very seldom do I trek into the upper floors. Unless the occasion really necessitates that I must. I'm in the ballistics department. I'm the one who tells you if someone has used the same weapon more than once or at what speed a projectile has hit someone or something. And I can even tell you the name of most projectiles once they have smashed themselves to bits. So, how's that for importance?" he asked her. Now showing off his very white teeth from smiling so much.

"Actually, I am in a little dilemma this evening, and hopefully, Agent Beach will get me some much-needed freedom from it. I'm not much for confrontations. Especially early in the work evening for me. Late shift, you see, and I love the peace and serenity it offers me. So, Agent Beach can handle the potential excitement for this evening. Wouldn't you agree?" he said.

"I would have to say so right now, although I hope whatever it is you have to say to him doesn't keep us here for too much longer. I would like to get him home and get to my bed," Clara said with a little hint of tiredness in her voice.

"Oh, so you two are married," he inquired, looking somewhat surprised.

"No, we just room together. But tonight, he put me on as the worker bee, so to speak, on the case he was assigned to, and it's his duty to fill out the report tonight, and I'm sure he is at his usual best, crossing all of his t's and dotting all of the i's. As usual, I might add. Which is okay, and it has to be done, but sometimes I can get a little tired and irritable." She laughed and then added, "A woman's prerogative, you know."

"Yes, for sure, and how well I do know," replied Grant.

"Justin, this is Agent." Clara hesitated because she really didn't know his last name.

"Grant Fisher," he replied, "Or just Grant to everyone I know here. In charge of the ballistics department, downstairs, lower floor, 3 B. Third door down with the large glass front, my name is actually on the door. It's a good thing, it is. See, sometimes I can get lost in my work, you see, and it can lead me to God only knows where down there. So, once in a while, I do get turned around. Anyway, I have a little dilemma this evening. I was hoping that, seeing how it is slow tonight, I would come up here and ask a favor of you if I may."

"Sure," replied a smiling Justin, "What can I help you with?"

"Well, it applies to the bullet I was sent tonight. I will now assume you're the AIC?" Now, looking at Clara, he said. "We are very slow. So, I thought I wouldn't wait until later to run the test. Maybe this little fellow had some importance, seeing how some ambassador was shot and a young woman with him. Anyway, I ran all of the testing myself, and I have found a match for this particular article." Grant finished the statement as if he were announcing a surprise birth as he held up the bullet, now rattling in the glass vial that held it. Then he said to them. "It comes from the same gun that was used to murder those two older people in Virginia last month. I do believe the names of those victims were Benoit, Frank, and Claire Benoit. This bullet, well, it comes from the same gun. Seeing as I was requested by Mr. Bloso, "That if anything comes in with a link to that investigation, I was to call him immediately. So, this is an immediate phone call."

He again shook the vial, then put it back into his pocket. "But I fear calling him at this hour of the night, and I thought that maybe I would leave that decision with the agent in charge of tonight's melee. That I fear is you. Agent. After all, we are slow tonight, and I really haven't met you yet, and a trip upstairs is always good for introductions, making new friends and all," he finished with a smile and looked at Clara and Justin, whose faces suddenly went blank, and had a startled look on them that he couldn't understand. Was calling the boss that bad for everyone? He thought maybe he shouldn't have come.

"You're saying that the bullet used in tonight's shooting came from the same gun of the murderer of the Benoits? Are you certain of that?" asked Justin. After all, he had to be perfectly clear about this because this was a break in the case of who killed Clara's grandparents.

"Sure, I am sure, Agent. I have been doing this for over forty years now," replied a startled Grant.

Someone would actually question his ability, how disturbing a thought that was to him. He definitely had to get upstairs more often. It would seem that some people didn't know just how good he was at his job, this agent being one of them.

"I am absolutely positive about this match, Agent," he replied with a degree of self-righteousness directed toward Justin. Then suddenly, it dawned on him about the possible connection between one of these agents and the Benoits. What was he thinking? How could he have missed that? Oh well, he was a little slow tonight down there, and he did need to come up here more often. He already admitted that to himself.

"I am sorry, but one of you is related to the Benoits, correct?" he asked them, now with a different tone in his voice.

"I am," said Clara. "They are, or were, my grandparents. It is inconceivable how this same man is now in Washington, in my city, and he is shooting people here with this gun. That tells us a lot of information, it clears up a lot of questions we have had concerning that case, and it adds some confusion to this one," said Clara to no one in particular.

"You're right," said Justin. "I'll call John, however, in the morning. Right now, if it is at all possible, we need to leave and come back fresh in the morning. Thank you, Grant, for being so astute."

Saying that, he turned to Clara and spoke. "With this new information, we can possibly now suggest that it was a planned hit. One of the two victims was the target, or both; we now know that. However, the question remains: why? Why was the same gun used in one double murder in Virginia and now in an attempt on another two victims? In Washington. Did they even know of each other? How are your grandparents connected to either of these two people? Both are in the hospital, and both have been shot by the same gun tonight."

But now, with this new information, hopefully, tomorrow will bring us some new information when we can talk to Luther or Mable if she is awake, which is why we need to leave and go home and get some rest. Tomorrow will be a big day around here."

"Of course, I will now go back down and finish my report and go over everything that I have there pertaining to this case, and I will leave everything with my daytime counterpart, Clyde Wriggle," said Grant as he turned to leave. He stopped, then placed a hand on Clara's shoulder and said, "Don't be sad, young lady, we always get our man. Sooner or later, this person will make a mistake, and we'll get him. Go home, go to sleep, and get that much-needed rest you told me in the hallway earlier that you needed. In the morning, everything will work out for the best. If I can be of any additional help, always feel free to stop by door 3 B. Even if just to say hello. Good night, agents."

With that, he turned and sauntered down the hallway, glad that he had met two lovely people and happy that he was quick to have recognized the need to bring this to everyone's attention so quickly. After all of these years working here, it was just another incident. However, he did like those two, especially her; she reminded him of his own granddaughter.

Juan's and Günter's Visits

Juan had just returned from the emergency room, where he could get a place to view the ongoing activity there. The place was crawling with local police and German intelligence, with the FBI now stepping in. As the two FBI agents came through the emergency room doors, one began flashing his badge and was immediately directed to a captain in the local police force. Juan waited around and watched as if he was waiting to see a doctor, as the rest of the evening's sick sat there and gawked at the whole ordeal. When he initially came to the hospital, the place was in lockdown. Immediately, he was asked to show his identification, and his new ID showed him as a colonel in the U.S. Army. When asked what he was doing there, he simply stated that he had come down with a horrific migraine and needed some relief. Ever since his two tours in Iraq, he had been getting these migraines. This gave him immediate access to the emergency room, as he was then escorted by a police officer inside the building.

This would give Juan a chance to sit in the waiting room and watch everything that was unfolding around him. He learned from the woman sitting next to him that, apparently, a shot woman was still in the operating room next door to the emergency room. The man who was also shot had been taken elsewhere to be treated. The one person he was glad he hadn't seen so far was the shooter, though it was another one of the reasons why he was there. He knew that he had definitely hit the man twice. It was possible that he had on a vest to protect himself. That vest spoke volumes to Juan. It said this guy was the pro he thought him to be and not just a stickup man in the wrong spot at the wrong time. Juan knew that the next time one of his bullets hit the mark, it had to be right between his eyes. Sitting there, Juan felt more vulnerable, especially if the shooter did show up and recognized him first.

But he needed information, and the more he had, the easier it would be for him to make a decision on ending his involvement. His thoughts continued to go back to just silencing the general and Thurston, and now adding the senator to that list. He would then go away for a while until things settled down. Then, he would come back and look for a new employer or retire. This job had paid him exceptionally well, but if he was to spend any of it, he had to make his decision soon as to what he should be doing. It was beginning to sound good to him while he sat there waiting for his turn to come up. He was glad that in any emergency room across this country, one could possibly wait until the cows came back to the barn long before someone would call out his name. This allowed him the time he needed to keep perusing the area and to learn as much as he could while there.

That's when he looked to his far right and noticed that the senator was now walking into the room, followed by one of his aides. The senator seemed very upset and was now shouting at the police captain as if he worked directly for the senator. Then he turned and called a nurse over, and they began a long, loud discussion. When a young lady approached them, and upon flashing her badge, they all began to speak in normal decibels as the aide and the agent shook hands, acknowledging each other. She then started talking to the senator and he seemed to be listening intently as a look of concern seemed to creep across his face. Juan had to now evaluate this in a possibly different light. Maybe the senator had no idea as to why Mable was now in the operating room fighting for her life. Either that, or he was a great actor. But Juan doubted that because the same look of concern was on the face of his aide Luke, wasn't that the young man's name, Luke. So, if both of them are upset, maybe this had something to do with a miss-hit. This guy just picked the wrong people to make a mistake on. Then he rethought that. After all, he wore a vest and made a departing shot at her. Therefore, it had to be Mable that he had come for. If the senator was somehow involved in this, then it was just another message being sent and delivered to that moron of a man.

He had something on those other two, and it included Frank. Frank is the reason why Claire is dead. She was just an extra. If she hadn't been in the house that night, she would probably still be alive, he thought. Frank's death made sure that he was not around to disclose something important, something he shared with the senator, maybe? Or something he had on one of those other two idiots, he thought. He would go over that interview once again. One more time to try and find out what Frank said that could mark him as a hit. Juan didn't understand why Frank was quiet after all of these years since retiring from that company. Then, instigating something from its past, did he need money, and was he going to blackmail them?

Perhaps you could inform the new senator about it? Could what he knew be used against both men? Could the Senator use it to become important enough to possibly use it in his upcoming election? Or maybe it was that the senator had something important on those two and Frank. Something he had found out or what he was told by someone else. He approached someone about it, maybe Frank, and it scared him enough that he contacted Thurston to let him know they had been found out and discovered, and he was scared. Was it then that the wheels started to turn against everyone in the know? However, it had started. Something made those two decide to send the senator a message by killing Frank and his wife.

Can't be, he thought. The killing of Frank had to be from what he worked on or from what he knew about H.T. Wetco, his former employer. The general is involved because their friends and the general offered this Thurston character my services. Once I completed my interviews, I was now a liability to Thurston. Who had hired the rabbit to eliminate me? Maybe it was the rabbit that hired this shooter because he failed to get me? Now, this shooter is loose, and one of his targets was the senator's chief of staff, Mable. They were boldly sending him a message to shut up before he disappeared next.

Now somewhat a little satisfied that he had a possible motive and some reasoning for this, Juan decided that he no longer had to wait around. He doubted the shooter would appear there tonight. The man had balls, but they weren't that large. But one thing remained loose, and that was exactly what the senator had on those three men. Why was he not killed tonight instead of the shooter going after Mable? Still a mystery, he thought, as he left with a smile on his face. Yes, Juan did love these mysteries, and he was getting closer to winning this game as well.

Juan was now putting the pieces in place. Someone was hired for murder, and he was brought in from the outside, contracted to eliminate everyone he had met and worked with the general and H.T. Wetco. Of that, Juan was now sure. Well, that was one down, and how many other pieces to go in this puzzle, he thought.

Now, what did Luther and Mable Gardner share in common? Could he have set her up for one of his own men to make the hit? Juan thought about that for only a second. No, he knew love when he saw it, and this was love or the beginning of it. So, this hitman had only been after Mable. That had to be the only reason why, after being shot, he would turn and fire at her on the way out. Mable was the next target in line to be eliminated. But again, why?

This shooter had to be going right down the same list he had worked on for the general, and Juan now knew why he was targeted, because he had seen the list, which now put him on it.

Günter's anger wouldn't subside. He had no idea who the hell that shooter was. He only knew that he escaped with his life because of his specially-made undergarment. How many times has that piece of clothing saved his life, he thought, and tonight, well, it had to be added to that number. Günter knew that it could be dangerous to go by the hospital. But he did have all of the needed credentials if he were to be stopped, and his German was both fluent and impeccable. After all, he was German, East German, but nonetheless German. He knew enough about the embassy and its employees, right down to knowing the ambassador himself. So, his mind was made up, and he knew which direction he had to go as he headed for St. Anthony's Hospital.

"Can I help you?" asked a police officer sitting astride a motorcycle that was parked, blocking the entrance to the emergency room.

In perfect German, Günter said, "I need to go inside," then changed it immediately to English.

"I need to see some form of identification," replied the officer, who now walked forward and held out his hand. Günter looked down at it and immediately looked up and waved to someone behind the officer, making it look as if he truly belonged there tonight. Not looking around, the officer repeated, "I need to see some identification, sir."

"Sure," replied Günter, "Sure, how is this?" as he handed the officer his German credentials.

Now, looking at the credentials and, of course, being out there not thinking that he had to stop the actual guy who did the shooting earlier, he simply said, "Looks fine, sir. Park the truck in the lot over to the right and walk down the walk there. You have to use those doors on the left. These doors are closed off now until we get things under control. I'm sure you understand." With that, he turned his back and walked away from the truck, feeling as if he had just talked to the devil himself.

Günter was, of course, in the mindset to have killed this man right then and there, but he didn't want the new problems created by that, not right now anyway. Maybe on the way out, he would take care of that, and for free. He didn't like doing things for free. But he was, after all, in America, and what better place to kill people than here?

`Günter walked into the hospital and then moved off to his right because, located down a hall, was the emergency room, as the sign had said. But tonight, he did not need signs. The activity down there was full of excitement. Günter knew that in all of the excitement going on down in the emergency room, maybe now would be the perfect time to go there and finish his work. The question was, though, does he go down there, guns blazing like an American cowboy, or does he slip into the rooms? Finds her and executes her then and there, leaves, and kills that cop out front on the way home for the night?

He walked down the hallway toward the commotion. He could see that farther down on the right was perhaps a waiting room for people to see a doctor. Günter thought maybe a diversion would be nice. He could shoot a lot of these people just sitting around. In the confusion, he would slip into the rooms, find her, and kill her. His head ached. He sometimes had this problem when he was excited and angry at the same time.

Like in Helsinki, when he had to wait behind the draperies for almost an hour. Just to kill her and him for what they owed his boss. How that had made his head hurt so much. Later, he killed the whore who had waited in his room several floors up. That kill was just to help settle his nerves back to normal.

"Can I help you?" asked the police officer who stood next to a man in a gray suit with blue eyes and blond hair—the perfect German, he thought. Not answering the officer, Günter turned and spoke in German to the suited man, asking him if he was working for the Americans or the German embassy. The man said in English that he was working for his boss and then asked him who he was and what he was doing there.

Günter looked at him and said in German, "Of all the nights I have to find myself looking for my wife, she had to pick this one to get me lost on. This place is a madhouse. I have no idea how to get to the maternity ward. Can you show me the direction it is in?"

"This man needs to get to the maternity ward," he said in English to the officer who accompanied him on these rounds. "Can we show him or point him in the right direction?"

The officer looked at Günter and then at the German guard from the embassy who had been assigned to walk the halls with him and said, "Actually, I'm lost as well. Let me go and ask the nurse. Why don't you stay here with him, and I'll be right back?"

Knowing it would be impossible tonight to get within five feet of her, he decided to leave while he still had the chance, given that the place was crawling with local police and guards from the German embassy. So, Günter turned and said in German, "Damn it, I left some flowers in the car. I was so excited to come in here. Please wait here, and I'll be right back. Please wait. I need to get the flowers in case she gives me a son tonight."

That said, it was a way to give him a chance to leave, so Günter merely turned and hurried away. He would have to wait, and waiting always cost him, and that also made him angry, very angry. He needed to find a working girl tonight, have his way with her, and then watch her bleed.

Tully's Visit

The next day, as the light came through the windows of the bedroom, Clara lay there snuggled under the covers as she continued her tossing and turning, not quite ready yet to get out of bed. Justin, however, was already up, and she could smell the coffee now brewing downstairs. She also knew that he was in the shower. Today, as every day, he was performing his usual routine in the morning. As if he were one of those tall pink birds she saw on television that performed a dance to be noticed. First, it's go down, put on the coffee, open the front door to grab the papers, close the door gently so that the squeaky hinges won't wake the dead, walk up and kiss her hello, then get in the bathroom first, and use up all of the hot water.

But today is going to be different. No sleepy eyes this morning. Not allowed, seeing how last night they had finally gotten a clue on Grandpa Frank's murder. It turned out that the same gun was used in another crime they had investigated last night. Today was going to be a very interesting day, she thought. Now, if only I could get out of bed and into the bathroom. But first, I need to have some of that coffee I smell.

"Is that the doorbell?" yelled Justin from the bathroom.

"Doorbell, she thought, "I didn't hear any doorbell." Just then, she heard the bell ringing. "I can't believe I need to get out of bed for the doorbell," she thought. My teeth aren't even brushed yet. My hair is a mess. Who could this be so early in the morning?

"Clara, you are going to answer the door and see who it is," yelled Justin from the bathroom.

"Yes, yes, hold your pants on, Justin. I look like a mess. At least let me comb my hair a little," she replied.

Walking down the stairs, it dawned on her who it could possibly be. Today was the day that she and Tully had planned to get together. Today was her day off. She had forgotten all about it with all of yesterday's excitement. Now what, she thought? She certainly couldn't ask Tully to come back on another day.

Opening the door, she stared directly into the face of her best friend, her sister, and her cousin Tully, who stood there smiling at her. Then, just as fast, they both embraced each other, and Tully said, "Oh, how I really miss you, Cacky." A name she had given to Clara ever since she could remember. Because *Clara* was just too close a name to their grandmother's name, *Claire.* Not that Tully was jealous, but there was always competition between the two of them for their grandparents' affection, that's for sure.

"Come on in, Tull," said Clara, who was now smiling from ear to ear as she yelled out, "Justin, Tull is here, and I have the day off. Do you remember that? So don't you dare come down those stairs half-dressed?" Turning to Tully, she grabbed her hand and led her into the kitchen, all the while looking up the stairs to make sure that Justin had heard her. "I can't believe that I forgot," she said to her cousin. "Sit down and let me pour you a cup of this coffee. Are you hungry, Tull, or can you wait, and we'll eat out this morning?" she asked her.

"No, just the coffee for now, and we can eat out. I have all day and I am so excited. I told Jeff not to call me, no matter what. I don't care if a herd of buffalo escapes and runs down Pennsylvania Avenue today, don't call me," she said with that wonderful laugh that was her trademark.

"I had forgotten all about today, Tull. We had a late night last night. So, I was going to work today because of yesterday, but I know they'll only assign me to more desk work. So, I'd rather spend my day off with my best friend," Clara said, hugging Tully once again.

Just then, Justin walked down the stairs and walked directly over to Tully and hugged her. They had spent a week together, and he had gotten to know both Jeff and Tully very well. By its ending, it was as if they had all been friends all of their lives. He was asked a lot of questions, of course. Always in a teasing manner, his reply was that as soon as Clara said yes to marrying him, he would be a much happier man.

"How's Jeff, and how did you manage to get away from him today? Oh, I remember now; you're both doing some work for the Washington Zoo for a month or two, right?" he said as he reached for the coffee mug now being offered to him by Clara.

"Yes, but today is my day to spend with Cacky, so I told Jeff not to bother me. No matter what happens there today. I think we have to just go over some additional changes they want to make in two areas. It's some climatic changes with some habitat changes. We haven't even started yet. It is typical zoo planning. They plan at the same time you work; that way, they always have that 'I told you so' attitude. Something that is common with your typical zoo people. Why Jeff and I tried to stay away from the zoos, but we ran into some trouble with one of our major clients. So now we need to make up for the loss in income. That is the only reason why we are now doing the hated zoo work," she said, looking at Cacky now.

"Is everything okay, Tull? We can definitely loan you guys some money, right, Justin?" Clara asked.

"Of course," he replied, "Whatever you need within limits, of course, but we have a lot saved up, and until she marries me, we have nothing to spend it on."

"No, we're fine," said Tully as she grabbed Clara's hand and held it as if to say, "Thank you for being so kind." "It was that one of our better clients, or so we thought, decided that he needed us to make changes in a lot of our reports to reflect global changes and the effects it was having on our studies. At first, Jeff said no big deal. But when we discussed it, I felt it was a big deal. In no way would I have this man jeopardize our credentials. We worked too hard all of these years to lie and lose what we worked for. The only thing we have is our professionalism, integrity, and honesty. After all, in this recall for truth, so much doubt is now being cast on all those bad global reports. Why would we change things to make his company look great if it wasn't? In fact, the more you examine this company, the worse it appears, and it has been this way for years now. So, I just told Jeff to tell this guy to go to hell and walk out of his office. So, he did. Well, maybe not in those words, but we dropped him as a client and picked up some zoo work. Besides, with zoo work, guess where I am today, instead of off in some South American jungle being bitten by a snake," she laughed as she sat back in her chair and sipped on the hot coffee.

"Good for you, Tull, the nerve of that guy. Is there a reason why the company I work for would want to investigate this bum?" asked Clara.

Laughing out loud now and turning to place a hand on Clara's shoulder, Justin said, "You know, Clara. Every time someone does something wrong, we can't automatically start an investigation, even if they think so. She would have the bureau investigating everyone that she disagreed with."

Clara simply looked at Justin, pointed to the door, and said, "With that said, I think you're late for work, Justin. Take your coffee with you and remind everyone that I am off today. But call me and let me know about any new information concerning that gun. Or if they have any idea as to who the shooter is. With that information, you have to keep me in the loop, okay?"

"Yes, dear," he replied and once more said a hello and a goodbye to Tully with a hug. "I hope you and Jeff come by for dinner today or sometime this week now that you're both here in Washington working. Tell her, Clara, we will not take no for an answer."

With that, he left, and finally, she was alone with Tully when she said, "Yesterday was a fiasco, and I have some disturbing news for you about yesterday as well."

"Really, what happened yesterday?" asked Tully.

"Justin got a call saying that they had assigned him as the lead to investigate a shooting that took place in the Heights. So as not to leave me alone, he decided that I tag along as his second. We often do that to keep each other company on things that we think might be bland. However, this turns out to be a shooting that involves a woman we both know who works for Senator Pillow. The senator from Pennsylvania, anyway, got the job because his cousin was the governor there, and they had to appoint someone to fill a vacancy. Anyway, we go there, and it turns out that the shooter, whom we have not yet caught, used the same gun to kill our grandparents. Last night, as I kept Justin company, he had to write a report of the incident. The ballistics guru from downstairs came up and asked Justin to call our boss. He didn't want to do it because it was so late. It was because the gun was the same one, the same gun used in both crimes. I would go in today to find out more, but they won't let me work on the investigation. Since this gun was used in both crimes, I'll have to leave this case as well. I can go back to work to push papers tomorrow, so phewy to them. Anyway, I would much rather be with you today."

"I don't understand, Cacky. How could it be the same gun? Did he buy it from someone, or did he use it to shoot them and throw it away, and this guy found it and used it to shoot this girl? I'm confused. Why would it be the same gun?"

"Well, let me say that sometimes these criminals all move in the same circles and trade guns. Or they sell it to someone who moves it from a local area into another area, and some idiot does another crime with it. There are many reasons, and we are not ruling out that it was the same shooter, but I can't imagine it was," said Clara, looking at Tully and hoping that it was an okay explanation.

Sometimes, explaining to people who didn't know much about these types of convicts was hard, and she had to hope that Tully would understand. Tully asked her for a full disclosure of what had occurred last night and how it truly involved the family.

Clara said, "I can't really tell you everything because most of the investigation so far is based on speculation, Tull, but let me say this. We are probably close to solving this, and as soon as I can get some real information, I promise I will tell you everything, even if it costs me my job."

"Okay, Cacky, let's go get some breakfast, but I think you need to get dressed first," Tully said with a smile.

Confrontation / Tides Turn

It was the front page of every morning paper in Washington, DC.

"Shooting in the Heights." A German embassy worker named Luther Rudman was shot after a botched holdup attempt on his way home last night. He was with the chief of staff of Senator Pillow of Pennsylvania. Mable Gardner was also shot, and rumors have it she underwent an operation for a knife wound she also had received from the mugger. Currently, her condition is listed as critical and guarded.

It was enough to know that Thurston was having it all his way as if it were his own death mantra being played out in real-time, and he was the conductor. But this is ridiculous, thought the general. Now, we have stooped so low as to have innocent women knifed and shot on the streets in one of Washington's better districts. Just who in the hell did he hire for this job, a blind, stupid idiot? Someone who didn't know one end from the other concerning guns and knives.

It seemed the more he read, the angrier he was becoming. How the hell does anyone justify such stupidity? Especially when he was a concerned participant? He had enough professional people looking for this type of work sitting around and not doing a damn thing. Any one of them would have been more than capable of making these problems disappear. But no, this ass had to hire some fourth man out, as he called it. What exactly did that mean anyway? Too many damn movies for that old man. He needed something more concrete to do with his time. This guy, in his old age, wasn't right in the head anymore, or so it seemed to him now. How the hell did he let this go this far without stepping in? Oh, that's right, because he already had two old senior citizens who were near death anyway, killed. So, what was he thinking that he was ahead in the game? Bullshit, and then he lost another would-be assassin trying to kill his own man.

My own man, I can't believe that I sat there and listened to him complain that my man had gotten away and was still missing, that he actually tried to kill the guy who tried to kill him, and now this mess. It involved an innocent woman.

When is this going to stop? When half of the people he knew turned up dead, wounded, or missing? Eventually, this had to get back to him. Eventually, he would be named a coconspirator, and what then? Hell, if he were alive, he would wish he were dead himself at that point. If dead, what kind of a legacy would this leave for his family and name? For God's sake, he was a West Point graduate. You kill the enemy; he had been taught, not civilians, because someone made a comment about the past and wanted money.

For God's sake, give the man the money. You have more than God does anyway, and you'll never live to spend it all. But not you; you thought you had to teach someone a lesson, and now it's all backfiring on your ass, and damn it, you got me involved. Where the hell is that jackass now? He thought I had to stop this before it goes any further than it has already.

General Margate's blood pressure was anything but low right now. He had had enough of the shenanigans of Bob Thurston. He knew that the only way to put a stop to this madness before it got further out of hand was to do this with his men. He had to make contact with Thurston's people, who were involved in this, and then eliminate them immediately. Two could play this game, he thought, and he was a much better player than this asshole friend of his who had seemed to have gone mad.

Bob Thurston had just put down the paper. It was the fourth one he had read this morning. He knew damn well that this whole incident was of his making. Then the phone rang. This was the fourth time this morning that the phone was ringing itself off the hook.

What the hell did Margate want? What was he thinking about now? He must know that I read the damn paper just as he does. Or does he think I've gone blind? How the hell did I know that the bastard would miss the kill? Not my fault, not my fault, and what's to say it was our man anyway? It could have been anyone, even an ordinary street thug, who actually was the person who botched this up. Hell, the guy is from the German embassy, and there are lots of people who still hate the Germans. It could have been some Muslim extremist or a Jew who is still angry and trying to send them all a message. I need to get someone inside that embassy to feed me some information. That way, I can tell that old geezer to knock off all the damn phone calls; he's got to be trying to drive me crazy, and he doesn't know he's probably five minutes from succeeding.

Pete Winslow had just gotten off the phone with Mr. Thurston and was now in charge of recovery. "Take charge, Peter, make it all go away for me, and add to that your pal, the general. Any problem concerning that one?" he asked.

"No, sir," Pete said, "not a problem. I'll make him last. Just in case you have a change of heart. Other than that, I'll make arrangements tomorrow for things to start taking place. Is that soon enough for you, sir?"

"Yes, that's fine. And yes, make him the last on our list. I may have a change of heart unless he keeps ringing my phone, then I may make him first," said a tired-sounding Thurston. Maybe he was getting too old for this; maybe he should have just paid the damn man and had been done with it.

"Okay, sir, if there are any changes in the plans, just make sure I know, please. Is there any word as to the location of the original rabbit, sir? I would like to start at that location." Pete knew that Juan had gone underground and was in hiding, but he knew a lot of people, and someone for the right amount of money would help locate him.

"No, nothing. However, I may ask our mutual friend if he could possibly make contact with him again and use that to help your position on this," replied a somber Thurston.

"Fine, sir, just keep me in the loop, and I'll begin taking care of things. Good-bye, sir." And with that, Pete knew what he now had to do.

Pete Winslow

Pete knew that to ensure things were done correctly, he sometimes had to do them himself. Imagine reading in this morning's papers that someone had made an attempt on the life of a German embassy officer and the senior staffer on a senator's staff. Not just anyone, his chief of staff.

Ridiculous, he thought. I know damn well exactly what the old man is paying for. Well, enough to know this man had missed his mark. He should have just turned the whole thing over to him from the beginning. Right from the beginning, he could have settled this, and no one would have been the wiser. All of them would have met with just plain accidents. All were made to look as if it were a part of life, their deaths, as he would have made them die. Now, he would have to go out and locate this Juan character and take care of that. Along the way, making sure the senator and his woman were gone. No sense in having her around to identify anyone or pick up on what the senator was killed for. Then, if he could make the arrangements, he would meet and kill this so-called fourth man. Which was a bunch of crap, the man missed his mark, and he was supposed to be the best out there. I can't wait to surprise that genius. Then, I have to make sure the general disappears as well. Not too hard to do, but it won't be a job I'm gonna like, nor do I have to like it. I guess Mr. Thurston is right, though. The son of a bitch could be on his deathbed and decide that was the best time to confess and clear his soul for the afterlife. Well, it looks as if I have to do all the heavy lifting and clearing of the mind myself. If he had only given me the go-ahead right from the beginning, I wouldn't have to gear up now to make all of this happen. Oh well, I might as well enjoy it. It'll be all over soon enough.

Pete has walked in the halls of the Senate building several thousand times, he thought to himself, and still it impressed him.

Maybe someday that'll be exactly what he will ask of the old man, to make him a senator.

"Pick a state, he'll say. Go there and buy yourself a house and run for any office. If I have to buy the state for you, boy, you're in."

He had always envisioned in his mind that that was how the conversation would go. The old man wouldn't hesitate. He had been like a father to him since they first met. That's why it was so important for Pete to solve this problem. To make it all go away. He couldn't care less who the person was that had to disappear. For the old man, consider it done. After all, thought Pete, what better job could he have ever worked at? Pete was nearing the senators' lounge and quickly looked inside, seeing that it was empty. These blowhards could scream about Americans needing to stop smoking and raise the taxes on cigarettes enough to force poor people from buying the damn things. Yet because they got them for free, they actually had a smoking lounge just for their usage, but right now, no one was in it.

Pete went into the lounge and sat waiting for his contact when the senator's staffer, Luke Weeks, showed up and introduced himself to Pete. Pete was pretending to be looking for information on the girl who had been hurt two nights ago and was willing to pay heavily for that information because his company needed to make headlines, and the company was willing to pay for that.

"Just get me some material, he said. Anything that we can use to help us make this not go away for a while. Maybe it'll make the police and everyone work a little harder to catch the guy. That's why I need it, Mr. Weeks, to keep this out there every day under scrutiny for everyone to see. It's the best way to make sure the guy gets caught quickly, I assure you of that," said Pete over the phone.

When Luke showed up empty-handed, he just felt that it wasn't right and that he really wasn't sure he could trust this guy. With whom he had never met, with certain selective information he had asked for after his third phone call to him.

"Why did you ask to meet me?" said Pete. "If you have nothing to give to me, why waste my time with your nonsense? You should have called me. I can't run down here to meet you and shake your hand as if you're somehow important." Pete was mad, very mad, and he wanted to get that point across to Luke, who now stood there as if the tongue-lashing he just received had come from his father.

"Slow down, man. Who are you talking to like that? Here's how it's gonna work," said Luke. "The last thing I need to do is to have a meeting with the guy who actually did the shooting. And how do I not know that it wasn't you? To gain access to the building and reach my location, you had to pass several detectors and present your credentials. So, I can now assume that you're safe to deal with.

You want to know when the senator will visit Mable, and I'm going to give you his itinerary for the week. I get you some photos and information, and in return for this, I get the cash. By the way, you will need to give me half of it upfront, trust, right? That shows trust, ya see," said a cool and collected Luke.

Who was nervously looking around, but this guy managed to get this far, so he must have some pretty good contacts, Luke thought. How else could he have just waltzed in here alone? So maybe he was glad that he was on the up and up here, giving him this information.

"Okay," said Pete, "how about I give you half now and the rest on delivery this afternoon of everything I want. Is that fair?"

"Look," said Luke, more confident now, "I have everything that you need already made up. It's back in the safe in my office. I can get it and bring some of it back here unless you have all of the money. If so, then I'll bring it all back with me."

"Do it now," said Pete, "that way, I can make one trip and not have to come back here this afternoon. I would appreciate that, and I do have all of the money we talked about on me. I really need this material. It will up my worth at the paper. Especially when they nab that bastard."

Pete wanted to sound as if he were some working reporter who needed this to make a break in the case so he could become famous for his efforts, and Luke was falling right into it as if he were a fish on a hook.

Luke had made sure that in the packet, there was absolutely nothing that could come back to him, even though the paper was not from the office. Cool, thought Luke, he was really cool at the moment.

"Here's the cash in this envelope as asked," said Pete. Then he emphasized, "Remember this face and forget it as soon as possible. I've a recording of everything we just discussed, and I also have the packet now. So, relax and have some fun with the money. When I need some more information, I'll be in touch." With that said, Pete brushed past Luke and said, "Remember, be a good boy, go have some fun."

Luke wondered what the hell he had gotten himself into now. The packet contained the senator's itinerary, nothing else, and then it hit him. What happens if something now happens to the senator? No, the man was all over the place. Anyone who wanted to do him harm could easily do so. Unless this guy really wanted to embarrass the man, then he should have told Luke that. If Luke felt about the senator as he did, he wouldn't have had to pay so much. If there was any way to put that bastard in his place, Luke was willing to participate.

Luke then thought back about someone hacking into the senator's computers and making his life difficult, and thought maybe this was the guy. What had he done, he thought. Then he realized that if things got too bad, he could always cry stupidly and contact Clara and Justin to beg them to help him out. And he hoped like hell that they would. Maybe, just maybe, he should call them and cry wolf now beforehand. To cover his ass before something did happen to the senator. He has to really think about this. Yet as he walked away, his emotions were dwindling down as he touched the envelope now tucked in the corner of his jacket pocket.

Pete knew that the boy was an idiot and had no idea that soon he wouldn't be able to spend that money. After all, how could anyone who was pronounced dead spend money? He actually had to chuckle to himself; the young man just sold out his boss. No one seemed to have any loyalty anymore; no one, and that's such a shame. Pete knew, though, that he would have to follow and watch Luke's actions for the first few days of this week. If he were to run to the cops or those FBI friends of his, then this would be the time to do it when he felt guilty right after this meeting. It always happens in the first contact, seeing how it's the heaviest guilt time. Guilt had a way of running its course. Heavy in the beginning and lighter in the end, as time seemed to always diminish the importance of the act. Eventually, the price of the deed seems lower when taking over as a long-term benefit. You always thought that as time moved on, you were not paid enough. So, Pete would watch, and if he did go to someone to rat himself out, he would also take care of that.

But right now, he had dropped a dime in what he hoped was the right place to set up a meeting with the so-called fourth man out. He didn't think that Mr. Thurston would have forgotten how to convince the man to put a stop to anything, and so far, the other two calls had worked, and the same message was out there. He would now have to see if there was a response.

Waiting in the coffee shop in Alexandria, Pete thought that the man approaching the counter could very well be the one he was looking for. He did fit the description that was given to him on a public message board he had logged into. This was the same board used for the original two contacts to be made. He thought, thank God for computers, rather than leaving it to the daily paper or a secret drop area. Hell, in some of these boards, one could deal with life and death just as he was now, and no one was the wiser for it.

The man turned and looked his way, and Pete saw the missing button on the shirt. The fourth one down left opened, and the signal that Pete was to follow him to the lot where he had a van parked. It was left in a place where they could hold a private conversation. Following him to the lot, Pete was a little leery at first, but had to come to recognize that the other guy must have been a little leery as well. So, he had to act a little loose but not too loose. Or his own life could be forfeited on this day. He was in no way going to get into that van with the shooter. If this guy were an anonymous hire, then even now, Pete stood a good chance of having a battle on his hands, and he didn't need to add that to his plate. Not right now, that's for sure. Pete watched as the guy entered the van and sat behind the driver's side. Pete walked around the front of the van to get to the passenger's side. But Pete stopped. Looking into the van, he said, "Open the hood." Complying with the demand, Günter unlocked the van's hood and got out. Now, the conversation began with both men standing next to the van and looking into the motor area.

"I understand that you are the man who represents the person who was so willing to pay in advance for my services. And now he may have no more need of them," said Günter.

"Yes, as a matter of fact, I do. But your thinking is wrong. I am now running the program, and I may have other needs for you to fulfill. That is the only reason why we broke protocol, as I said in the message. As well as we are willing to pay a higher premium for your talent. Is that at all possible for you to handle this trip? I will assume that it is, seeing how we are having this meeting," said Pete.

Looking at Pete and sizing him up, Günter knew that sometimes, in the middle of his work, some things could change. He never liked changes and was about to say something about it, but what the hell, more money and from an American. He decided then he'd take the money now, and should things change later, he could kill this man in his sleep. Staring at Pete, Günter replied, "First, the money is to appear in my account in less than twenty-four hours. I will stay somewhere and will watch the television. Am I to finish the task or wait at this point?" inquired Günter.

"Wait," said Pete, "I have a possible new target to contact. I'm going to leave now, and I don't expect us to ever meet again. Am I going to have a problem with that in the future?" Pete looked at the man he was now standing next to and felt the raw negative energy flowing from him like a stench coming from a sewer that was overflowing. No doubt about it, thought Pete, this man is a killer, so how did he miss his mark?

"No, there are some people that I have dealings with that know me, and now I will count you as another. But rest assured, should your name ever be used as the one that spoke of me in any way, we will meet again. If you're thinking I made a mistake, think again. I missed. Because I wanted to send a message of fear first, then take her and use her in front of the German. I got carried away as it sometimes may happen, but it has never happened twice," finished Günter.

With that, Pete turned his back on the man and slowly walked away, knowing that if the shooter raised a hand toward him, he would be shot dead in his tracks by his protection. Sitting in a cold storage truck now, twenty feet away. Günter had wanted to shoot the man and make it all go away, finish his jobs, and go somewhere and relax. But if he did, he was certain that someone would end his own life. This was the only reason why this coffee shop was selected. He had to park in the only open lot in the entire area.

The man was smart, but we shall see if we meet again. If necessary, we will know exactly how smart.

Luke thought it would be wise if he didn't mention the money and concocted a different story about why he needed to talk to Justin and Clara. He had to tell someone about what had transpired yesterday in the smoking room. He would make it sound as if something was a little suspicious concerning his conversation, and have them check it all out. After all, if the guy was legitimate, well, no harm, no foul, right? So, Luke called the bureau and asked for Clara. When he found out she was off that day, he asked for Jason. After all, he said he was the lead in this, right?

"Hi, Justin. Luke Weeks from Senator Pillows' office, how are you?" Luke asked.

"Fine, Luke, what can I do for you?" asked Justin.

"Well, I was asked to provide this individual with some information on Mable and on the senator and his whereabouts over this week. I was offered a lot of money to do this to aid a reporter in keeping the story ongoing in his paper. He said that it would put some pressure on the local police, and it'll make things happen a lot faster concerning the arrest of that shooter," ended Luke, who was now waiting for a reply. Silence only seemed to be speaking at the moment.

"Luke, do me a favor, would you? Is it at all possible for you to come down here this afternoon and talk about exactly what happened and possibly go over some of the finer points in that discussion?" asked Justin.

"Sure, Justin, I'll just tell the staff that I'll be out for, what, two hours, would you say, or do you think more?" asked Luke.

"Well, let's say, with traffic and all, maybe by closing time at your place, you'll be able to get back there. You know what it's like getting around here during rush hour," said Justin.

"Okay, see you in a few minutes," finished Luke. With that done, Luke put out the sign that the senator had insisted upon, saying he would be gone for a few hours but would return later. That way, it looked as if they had some idea as to what they were doing. Actually, the staff thought of it as something left over from his dental days.

Justin now had to wonder if Luke had possibly seen the killer or if the guy who went there was a real reporter. It was better, he thought that Luke would come into the office and go over everything to make sure everyone was on the same page with this visit. Jason was, however, sure that he would eventually find out that the reporter had, in fact, paid for the information. Or claim that he had paid for it. But whatever happened, he wanted to at least make sure that Luke had, in fact, not had a visit from the shooter.

Wow, what a great day for Clara to tour the city with Tully. He had spoken to her by cell only minutes ago. Oh well, when he gets back home, he'll tell them about his visit with Luke, the great one, and how it all ended. Someone played Luke, possibly to keep ahead of the pact, and was willing to pay Luke for information.

The information they obtained from Luke was interesting, now seeing how the reporter didn't appear to work for anyone they had contacted. Justin had assigned Brad Burke to keep this part of the investigation open and running until they had an answer as to who this reporter fellow really was.

Brad had been second on this since they had to replace Clara because those bullets matched. Brad was a confident agent, and although he may have been a slight pain in the academy, he turned into a great friend and agent on the job. As they all were, it seemed. Probably from the immediate submersion into crime and the problems taking place here in Washington almost every day, it would seem. It seemed everyone needed an agent to handle their case or problems if they were high up in the political pecking order. But Jason thought Brad was good, and he was smart enough to find an answer to this just as fast as anyone could.

Death Finds Us All

Luke was coming out of Sherry's house, and he was glad that she was the wife of a junior legal aid to the vice president. They kept him hopping from one thing to the next. His life sucked, and Luke was glad that he was a little more stable in his line of work. Not by much, but a little more than this guy Bruce. But without his job, Sherry wouldn't be alone as much. Nor would she have that special need that had to be filled at least once a month, laughed Luke.

The first shot took him in the left arm just above the elbow. That's when the second one took away his voice because it had entered his neck to prevent him from crying out. The third one, almost put there for fun, took Luke in the chest and hurled him backward against the front door. No sound was heard other than his banging solidly against the front door and dropping to the first stoop. When Sherry opened the door to see why Luke was now knocking on it, she had no idea that the thing that hit her solidly in her head was why she seemed to suddenly float and not know where she was.

The police arrived at the house not because someone had heard the shots that rang out silently in the early evening. Taking two lives. They responded because it was an eerie scene to see one person lying on top of another, and the door to the house was left wide open. Several people had gathered out in front of the house. The police were questioning some gawkers and several others in front of the home. The callers had stopped their cars. Seeing what appeared to be something highly strange as they were driving by. I saw it long enough to be frightened and called 911. No one could believe that it was Sherry in her open housecoat, showing her bare buttocks for the world to see. No one wanted to believe that there was also someone else there under her, and this someone was not her husband and was just as dead. As the front door was left open, the police could walk over both bodies. The light from a hallway fixture overhead now spilled out of it, and every officer there thought the husband did it. But an autopsy would be needed to see if she indeed had had sex with her dead partner and if it was around their time of death. But the first person they would ask what had happened would be her husband. He was the first to be a suspect if, indeed, she had been caught in an affair. Not that in Washington, having an affair was taboo. Of that, everyone here knew that was a long-standing joke. But for some young men, it was just too hard to handle, and every so often, someone snapped as this husband must have done.

Pete was glad he had insisted at their range that he become more than proficient in using his Ruger Mini-14. It shot a 223 round, and from his parked car with a silencer on, it made no sound whatsoever. It was nice to know you can count on some things staying the same. Now, he just had to change the directions the working authorities would look at with a fine-tooth comb. Was it possible to connect all the dots back to his boss? He had to revisit that thought later. So, a subterfuge was now coming into play, one that did require the services of his newly hired shooter.

The call had come into the FBI headquarters about eight o'clock that evening. By the time the message reached Justin, he, Clara, Jeff, and Tully were just getting served their dinners.

"Would you mind repeating that, please?" he said over the phone. "Can't believe what I'm hearing. Okay, sure, okay, okay, when you get the results back in, let me know immediately if you would. Thanks, of course I will. We're having dinner with her relatives, so I'll tell her when I get off. Yes, good night to you as well."

He finished the conversation, hung up the phone, looked at Clara, and said, "Captain Black sends his regards. He called from the precinct to tell us that Luke was just shot tonight. Right outside of some woman's house during broad daylight. Can you imagine that?

He thinks the husband found out about her carousing around and took matters into his own hands. What a shame; two people died for nothing more than two people not facing up to the truth. Besides, this is the second person this week hurt from the senator's office, it is why the phone calls to me. Glad I don't work for him. This guy even tried to put the move on my girl as well, right, Clara?"

Clara simply nodded, looking at him with a blank face that had been present since Justin had started talking to her.

"Clara, are you all right?" asked Tully. Grabbing her hand, she asked her. "Do you want to go into the ladies' room? Is everything okay? You don't look so well. Maybe we should go?"

"No," Clara responded, "I'm fine, just a little shocked is all. Something just popped into my head suddenly. Yes, we both knew Luke, and I know he was definitely a player. How could a single man living in Washington not be? But Luke was smart and above average in the sneaky department. So, I find it hard that the husband did this. I certainly don't know the man, and he certainly may have, but something tells me he didn't do this. Did he tell you who the husband is?" she asked, now looking at Justin.

"Yes, some third-rate lawyer assigned to the VP's office, always away, and they can't find him right now. But he is supposed to be in California with his boss. If that's so, it'll be hard to prove he returned here, did the deed, and flew back to California. It doesn't sound logical to me. If that is where they find him tonight in California, and out to dinner with the vice president's staff. Which is why Captain Black phoned me, seeing how Luke is from the senator's office and he has another employee fighting for her life in the hospital as we speak, just sounded strange to him and now to me as well," finished Justin.

"Wow, is it always this exciting?" asked Jeff.

"No," said Clara, "most of the time, I'm running to find out information on something someone else is working on. With the family problem, I'm only involved in this new case because Justin asked me to tag along. Then, when it was found out the same gun had been used, well, bon voyage to me," said Clara.

"Stop, Clara. You're always working on something that intrigues me," said a smiling Justin.

"Yeah, like, who takes milk and who only gets one sugar?" she laughingly replied.

Just then, their meal had come out, and as the serving girl was placing the plates in front of everyone, Justin raised his glass and said, "Toast, a toast, to our best friends, our family who have come home to roost, at least for a month or two."

Contact / Renewed Faith

The general picked up the morning papers, and once again, the headlines glared back at him, announcing:

"A Double Murder in Broad Daylight." Late yesterday afternoon, the body of Mr. Luke Weeks, who worked for Senator Pillows, was found shot along the side of Mrs. Sherry Billings. Both were shot in front of Mrs. Billings' home on Eastlake Terrace. Robbery was the original thought held by police who arrived early at the scene. However, they did not discover any evidence of an apparent robbery. Of course, they will not know if anything is missing until the husband, a Mr. Bruce Billings, returns from California. Mr. Billings, an attorney, is currently working on Vice President Currie's staff. He was in Howard County, California, late yesterday afternoon. Washington, DC Metro Police, who had originally thought he might be the lead suspect in this shooting, have now cleared him. Making him no longer a suspect.

Then, it went on to talk about her father being a retired admiral in the U.S. Navy. The general had had enough of this nonsense. He had not been able to raise a phone conversation with Thurston since the first incident, now this.

Son of a bitch, he thought, I need to get to this guy now. I need to put an end to this. I have to see if the sign still works for contacting Juan. I need to bring him home and have him become a part of my search for this maniac and put an end to all of this stupid killing. Besides, if this serves me right, he also can get to Thurston before he gets to me. By now, I am sure that I am on someone's list. I can't believe how this has traveled so far down the wrong road when it only seemed like yesterday we were in the club, drinking only the best liquor in the world.

Getting up from his chair, the general went to the bar and poured himself a strong one straight up. He'll need that to explain to Juan he had nothing to do with the hit placed on him, and he could only pray that he would believe him.

Juan had been checking the normal channel to contact him for the last month or so to see if there was a chance that he could have been wrong in his assumptions. But as of yet, nothing had appeared to have told him otherwise. When, right before his eyes, was a message from the general. It read, "Missing you, TT, please come home; all is not right, and I do need you right now. Love you, Momamia." Then, in the next few spaces down was another one: "Thinking about you and I miss you, the house is a wreck, and I have nothing to wear, come and take me shopping please, signed T T." Three more spaces down were another one; it read, "Hi TT missing you, and I need to tell you how I care, can we meet at the market, I have had such a terrible time home alone lately, mom." Then the last one posted read, "T. T. I can be at the movie by six am on Thursday; I hope you can make it, Dad."

Now, Juan was startled. He knew that the general was out on a limb and things had gone wrong. But was it of his own accord? Or from Hammond's stupidity? Just yesterday, the junior in Pillows' office was shot and murdered along with his innocent wife who was having an affair with the kid. That's what lonely wives do. They have affairs, and when caught, the husband is normally to blame. Here, the guy is off on the other side of the country, working for the vice president of the United States, no less. How damn stupid can these guys be? Someone had to be leading this band of idiots, and maybe it was the rabbit, he thought. But what to do with the general? Should he make the appointment or skip it? Then he thought that maybe he should have a meeting. Tonight. A great time to meet, and why not? He could easily close down the alarm. Enter the house, wake him up, and if he doesn't get satisfying answers, then what better time to send him on his way to God?

As the Story Goes

Luther sat next to Mable, who had remained unconscious since the shooting. Doctors told him that with the sudden loss of so much blood and the trauma she suffered. It could remain this way for a long time. So, every day, Luther made sure that some time was spent holding her hand and asking God to forgive him of all of his sins and to please find some way to let her know he was there and that he loved her very much. Often, Ulmmer would stop by, and they would quietly talk about things happening around town and in the world. That way, if she could hear, she would know that he cared enough to try to keep her informed, as he would say. "Mable, my dear, Ulmmer is here, and we are going to update you on the day's news. This way, you hear more than the conversation I have with your doctors and nurses. As well as more than my constant praying and whining about how I love you, and when this is finally over, we shall be married, and I will not take no for an answer unless you want to live with me happily, forever.

That I shall leave up to you, but know this: my mother wants me to marry, and she is a very tough woman, so I do not think that we shall live together to make her mad. So, the only alternative is that you must marry me." He would chuckle to himself as he finished this almost ritual part of his conversation with her.

Luther had every known avenue of intelligence his agency could provide in helping to track down the man who shot them. So far, the only information they had come up with centered on a known expatriate German named Lars Günter Mallern, whose last known address was in Russia's St. Petersburg area, who was a world-renowned assassin for hire. Lars had been eluding the German authorities and Interpol for over ten years. He had become somewhat of a recluse with the dawn of the computer age. Very few people knew his whereabouts and/or how to contact him. But Luther felt that if he was in the States, it was a very opportune time to put an end to this madman.

His dossier read like a horror story. He had been linked to killing not only his male targets but also women and children, along with innocent bystanders as well. Anyone he could torture or rape, Lars would, and his card was an upside-down cross, like the one that was found in Virginia.

There, however, was only one catch to this, and it was a big one. Lars was pronounced dead three years ago in a shooting in Morocco. His body was flown back to Germany for burial, and it was attended by a lot of people, including Germany's head of Interpol, who identified the body on its arrival in Germany. Now, the question remained. Was that Lars who was buried in Bremerhaven, or was someone else made to look like Lars? Two days ago, when the information was given to them, they had petitioned the government to exhume Lars's body and to check his dental records to see if, in fact, it was him buried in that grave. So far, the German government was having some difficulty convincing the only known relative, a sister of his, to let them exhume that body. But he was positive it would be done with or without her consent. This was too important an endeavor for the German government not to have it done. After all, if Lars were still alive and operating, he would be a ghost, and no agency could accept that in his world. Luther found it hard to imagine a killer like Lars who could come and go at will. All at the expense of a lot of people. But tonight was story night. Luther had decided to read Mable a story once a week to see if something would stimulate her and awaken the girl he was to marry.

FBI

John Bloso had called a meeting of agents under his command to go over their reports concerning activities that were currently under his scrutiny. The main investigation of his group was, of course, the Benoit murders in Virginia. He started with Jason and Brad's report on the activity concerning the shooting deaths of Frank and Claire Benoit to see if it fit in any way into the shooting of the German liaison, Luther Rudman, and Mable Gardner, the chief of staff for Senator Pillow. Other than the gun being the same. Now, maybe add to that the killing most recently of Luke Weeks and Sherry Billings. It was now time to let them know that German intelligence had just informed him this morning about a possible suspect in the shootings whose method of operation met the criteria of the Benoit shootings.

"Listen up, people, I have some good and yet disturbing new information pertaining to the shooting deaths of the Benoits. We now have a potential suspect in this case," said John.

You could hear several murmurs along the table and some shuffling in the chairs as well. As things quieted, John continued, "This was shared with us by German intelligence yesterday. However, it does come with a potential problem. The suspected individual, Mr. Lars Günter Mallern, is now our prime suspect in this murder. However, as I just said, there is a problem." John coughed slightly as if he needed to add some emphasis to what he was about to say. Continuing, he told them.

"He's been dead for three years now. Known to be buried in the Bremerhaven cemetery in Germany." John waited for several people, including both Justin and Brad, to finish their mumbling, something he didn't want to hear.

"Listen up, guys, his last-known address was in St. Petersburg, Russia. However, he was supposed to have met his demise in

Morocco. Apparently shot dead in the process of carrying out a hit there. He was identified by the German liaison to Interpol prior to being buried. However, the body is due to be exhumed this week. Should Mr. Lars turn out to be an unknown buried there, then Mr. Lars will be considered armed and dangerous in the United States. However, we will not put this out for public information," said John.

Again, there were, of course, some more murmurs. As John began speaking again, he looked directly at Justin to say this would interest him. "No need in the man fleeing and no one having a chance to capture him, dead or alive. So, until we do find out that he is not in that grave, consider him here in our city and still capable of killing. Any questions on this?" asked John.

"I have one, sir. When will we know whether he is or isn't in the grave?" Justin asked.

"It is supposed to happen on Thursday, and whatever the outcome, Interpol will be calling us from the morgue. That's how important this has become," said John. "What is going on with the investigation concerning Mable Gardner and Luther?" asked John. "Is there any more information pertaining to the shooter?" he asked Justin.

"No, sir, we have canvassed the area for a month now. No one has come forward to admit seeing the incident or admitting that they shot the attacker. As far as all the evidence we have, it still remains that the same gun was used in both crimes, but nothing to say it was the same shooter," finished Justin.

"Brad, how's the case coming from your perspective?" asked John.

"Well, sir, as Justin said, we have no evidence that the same man committed the two shootings. However, I did find a reason to bring in a new avenue to look at. I spoke to Justin about this last week, and we both came to the same conclusion. To see what, if anything, the people at H.T. Wetco would know about Frank Benoit and why he could have possibly been targeted. As a scientist working there, was there something in his past that would make him this target? After all, it wasn't but several weeks before the shooting that he had a visit by someone who passed himself off as a reporter for a scientific discovery show. This was someone who was very interested in what Frank did for H.T. Wetco.

Mr. Benoit, it turns out, was extremely upset over the fact that the show never aired. So much so that Clara's mother called asking for relief and asked if she would call the show's New York headquarters. Clara made that call, and they were tired of Mr. Benoit calling them to threaten a harassment suit against him if he didn't stop the calls. So, I paid a visit to the firm H.T. Wetco. There, I met with Mr. Todd Thurston, grandson of its founder, Mr. Bob Thurston, who, by the way, is still active occupying a corner office upstairs.

He is, however, no longer directly involved in the company's daily business. As Todd told me, it's more of an ambassador's position or a room to hang out in. So, I asked for and was granted a meeting with Mr. Thurston Sr., and he did acknowledge knowing Frank and said that what he worked on was privileged information at one time, but for all intents and purposes, it wasn't that big of a deal lately. He felt that the Internet could probably tell me more, but he would try to answer any questions I would ask if his failing memory held on. He said Frank Benoit made it rain, not just rain, but it seems as if he could make it rain acid or several other types of rain, including some sort of heavy metal rain. After a while, the company learned to interpret the upper atmospheric winds and could influence the jet streams. The more I listened, the more he talked as if his company worked directly for God. He had a real air about himself. I don't know if that stems from not having daily conversations with people or if he just wanted to get this out to impress me. But as far as Mr. Benoit was concerned, he thought the man was a genius. Especially back in those times, it had to be somewhat an exciting time; the big one had just ended. We had nuclear bombs, the atom being split, rockets, jets, television, radio, transistors, and making it rain. Science was in vogue then. But he had no idea that Frank was dead, or at least he pretended not to. As I told Justin later, something didn't seem right for some reason.

He had another man in the room with us during the whole interview. A Mr. Pete Winslow. I found out that he was a graduate of the Point, served his country honorably, got out, and went to work directly for Mr. Thurston. When I mentioned his name to Justin in my report, he remembered a conversation he had where this name may have been mentioned. It turns out his hunch was right. We discovered that Mr. Winslow also takes care of other company business. It seems as if Justin's future wife," as a slight giggle was heard," Clara has a cousin, Tully. She and her husband, Jeff, actually worked for Pete Winslow and H. T. Wetco. They no longer do it because it seems that Pete Winslow asked them to fudge some information pertaining to climate change and its effect on certain animals, and they refused. Speaking with the Osbornes, they said the man could often be somewhat abrasive and demanding on certain issues.

I also checked into the possibility that Senator Pillow might have had some dealings with H. T. Wetco. It seems that Clara now remembers having a conversation with Mr. Weeks about his function when they first met. He said that right then, he was more concerned with getting information about a dead senator from 1950 and a company called H.T. Wetco to keep his boss happy and off his back. Clara remembered that her grandfather worked there, and at that time, Frank Benoit was still alive, so Clara absently volunteered her grandfather's time to answer any questions he may have difficulty answering if that could help him. Mr. Weeks responded by saying no and that everything he needed was in the archives, just that the time element in getting that information was sometimes very slow.

I checked his travel logs and sign-out sheets concerning travel, and it seems the senator is a stickler for that. Now, I began to think that maybe Luke Weeks was the reporter who interviewed Mr. Benoit. But that turned into nothing. I don't think he's ever been south of Washington in his life. So that's what I have so far concerning this," finished Brad.

Just then, Justin chimed in and said, "The more I think about this, the more I'm thinking of some kind of a conspiracy." This was definitely followed by laughter. Even John laughed at that one. "No," said a smiling Justin, even he had to smile at this, "no, listen, what if, for some reason, H. T. Wetco and Clara's grandfather did make it rain? Imagine if they could, when and where they wanted to. What would stop, say, the army or any of the military from getting their hands on this and using it as a weapon? What if they could somehow control what was happening in the sky? What if they have used this technology to make it difficult for certain countries to support farming or transportation avenues, making everything just vast mud holes? Imagine if they did this. Imagine if this senator found out about something that had happened in the fifties concerning this. Then, he decided to cash in on it. What better reason than to kill everyone who had knowledge of that? Then, start to go after everyone in the senator's office one by one. All conjunctive theory, of course, but it fits into what has been happening. It's the only explanation I can find that makes any sense of this mess," finished Justin.

After a few sidebar conversations started to take over the meeting, John said, "Hold on, everyone, Justin, great theory and points well made. I want you, Susan, to follow up on his thinking. Just maybe this theoretical assumption has some real merit. Imagine that, and if it turns out to be half correct, then we have motive enough to go after H.T. Wetco. I can also say this, ladies and gentlemen, this stays in this room. No one, and I repeat no one, is to talk about this until after Susan reports back to me and I call a meeting to discuss this further. I am clear on this, people. I would hate for someone to talk out of school and lose their job over speculation such as this one," said John with that look of "Keep it tight, people" in his eyes.

"A very thorough report, gentlemen. I'm glad to see that both of you are going back and forth with each other and rehashing all avenues. Continue to meet weekly and update each other's progress. Something has to crack it open soon.

The next meeting on this will be scheduled for the fifteenth of this month at 1:00 p.m., with lunch served at 12:00 p.m. Susan, have a report ready on that theory. Okay, people, let's get back to work. God only knows we have enough of it," said John.

Open Discussion / The Confession

Juan entered the house as if he lived there, going through the alarm system and the back door locks as if he had done the installation himself. The time was around two in the morning, and he was sure that the general would be fast asleep. Or at least he hoped so. Walking down the hall and pressed somewhat against the wall, Juan knew this had to be done as quietly as possible. Reaching the door, he peered into the bedroom and found the general sitting up in his chair and lying across his lap, resting his old 1911A1 pistol from the war.

"Good evening, Juan. I was expecting you. Sit down, rest a while, and let's talk about what the hell's been going on," said a smiling General Margate. "I really didn't know if you were coming in tonight or tomorrow night. But I figured, at my age, how much sleep do I really need? So, I decided to wait for you. Besides, old men sleep better during the day anyway. But before we get started, let me say two things. One, I really don't appreciate when and how you like to conduct meetings. Second I need to clear some things up. The first one is. I had absolutely nothing to do with someone trying to make a hit on you. My god, I was crazy and angry at that. But what can I say? Some people think just too much of themselves anymore. Second of all, these murders that have taken place around you, let's say, for lack of a better word, interviews. Well, I have had nothing to do with those, either. The maniac who was in the car with me that day was Bob Thurston. He's the founder of H.T. Wetco. So, after all of this fiasco going on, I needed to talk to you. I really need to tell you everything. Just in case, I've made the same list you're now on. So, do I trust you that we can both put away our toys and sit like men and talk? Or should I say at the count of three? What's it to be, Juan?"

Said a tired-looking old man sitting in a chair with a pistol in his lap.

Looking at him now, Juan could see the strain this had on the general. His face looked as if he had aged more than a few years. Now Juan had no reason but to listen. Quickly saying.

"No, aside from standing here in your bedroom, I have no problem with finding out the truth tonight. It's why I came in the first place. If I were going to shoot you, it would not have been here. I would have done it by now in your good ole boys' room at the club. Then I would have taken the pleasure of adding that jackass to accompany you so you could take him along for the ride down," finished Juan, who was now leaning against the wall, showing a sign of trust.

"Okay, fair enough," said Margate. Let's go into the living room and have a seat. I'll get out some Scotch, and we can talk."

Juan waited until Margate went past him before moving. A just-in-case move, right now, would be a hell of a time to get shot dead than have the general say he was an old man protecting himself from an intruder.

Sitting comfortably in the chair across from the general with all guns holstered, Juan began, "Right from our second meeting, I was tailed from your car. I was being followed, no doubt, right back to my home. But before, I would take him back there. I made a stop at the hamburger place down the street. I went in and waited for this guy to enter, and when he did, I was sure he had come for me. What I couldn't discern was whether he was from you or from the old man who was with you. The why of it also threw me for a loss. Then I figured you could contact me anytime the old man couldn't, so it had to be his. Just so you know, I waylaid him in the men's room and gave him a departing needle. I left him in there to let him sleep it off."

Then Juan admitted to the general about how it was he who shot the shooter of the German and Mable Gardner, why he had been tailing Mable that night, thinking that maybe the German was the shooter and was using love to make killing her that much easier, especially if she lay naked under his covers.

But as sure as God made apples, a shooter showed up when all hell broke loose, something I hadn't planned on for sure. I thought then that a systematic killing of everyone I interviewed was beginning. But I couldn't figure out the why of it. Even now, I'm not entirely sure why.

Then, saving for last the Benoit murders, Juan told him how he felt over their deaths. He tried to explain how he felt so ill at the news of Frank and Claire being murdered. It was the first time that someone's hit made him feel slightly nauseated. These two were nothing but two old people, and it made no sense to him at all. He told him of staying for dinner and how it was like a part of him had come home to his grandma's house. It wasn't right, and now, with Luke dead, he had to step in and find out the truth and what the hell was going on and try to put a stop to it. That was the only reason why he was in the general's house tonight. He had to find out the answers to these useless killings, and he did not intend to leave until he did, regardless of the outcome.

Then General Margate spoke. "I went ballistic at first as well. When, almost every week, I woke up to the news that someone from the senator's office was shot dead or an attempt was made on the life of someone who worked there. If that type of news wasn't in the papers sometime during the week, I felt that maybe someone missed a shot during the night," yelled the general.

His voice had gone up several octaves as he was complaining about the news lately. Juan began to wonder if the old man had gone mad as well. But he quietly sat there and continued listening as the general began to speak again.

"Juan, it makes no sense to me anymore. All of this useless killing, and for what, to make some old man feel like a king? I know of his reasoning, of course, and that's what has me so damn angry. That old coot has all the money in the world, and he will not part with a penny of it to buy someone off. Unless it's his own damn idea to do it, but he'll spend a bundle on bringing in some hired gun and then have his own man do the running of the hitter. I am assuming that it's his man, Pete Winslow, who is now doing some of the hits. I believe he's the one that you have already met. See, his specialty is that Mini Ruger-14 with a silencer. It was what killed the boy and that young woman on her front step. My god, he had done it in broad daylight nonetheless. What if some passing child had seen the murders? Would he decide that the child had to go as well? Both of them seem to have gone mad, I tell ya. Besides, maybe I'm the next in line of the 'in-the-know people' that need to die.

Bob's gone off the edge, and that's why I asked for a meeting, Juan. To tell you everything in case I'm gone soon. I don't want the damn man to get away with anything on this. I want him to pay for every life, including mine, if he takes it."

Juan now knew that he had to convince the general that maybe now was the time to just take a long vacation until he could settle this all down.

"Well, let's start from the beginning and tell me it all. I want to know why in the hell this is going on, and, General, please don't tell me for Homeland Security. Because right now, screw Homeland. I want the truth," said Juan, who was now looking at the general as a cat looking at a canary.

The general served him a fine old Scotch, then sat down across from him and started explaining to Juan why he was hired in the first place. Then he told him the why of what he thought had gone wrong in the process. Then he finished by saying, "I really think that the old man has gone crazy with his last grab at power to protect his company. Juan, as ruthless as he had been in his past, well, he is more dangerous now because he knows that life is not forever and so do I; it's why I said I would work with him originally. So, no matter what it cost to protect his company right down to the end, I knew he would.

He somehow had perceived that Frank Benoit could become a danger to him and the company; that the senator would get to him. Then Frank would admit to something he didn't know a damn thing about just to enhance his lot in life. Then he came up with this fourth man out crap. That had him hire this killer from Istanbul or someplace. Just so no one would trace the mess back to him. He thought he needed to kill the senator's closest people just to make sure that the senator got the message. More than likely, by the time it all stopped, he would have killed the senator as well, because I have been calling so much and complaining to him about stopping this. I feel that somewhere along the timeline, I may now be at the top of this list as well. He knows I hate this stuff. More now than ever! Listen, you and I both know we have had our share of targets. But this is crazy. No rhyme or reason to it. He wanted you killed because that was cleaning up just another loose end. The man is seemingly now drunk with power, and nothing matters except to wake up one day and once again sit in his office without a care in the world."

The general finished talking and sat back in his chair, pouring down the Scotch like a glass of cold water on a hot day.

"Okay, so let's say you and I make a pact and a plan," suggested Juan.

"Hold on, Juan, I may have a lot of faults, and so does Bob, and there's no doubt about that statement. But I am not going to decoy a meeting so you can ambush my best friend. Hell, I'm into this up to my ass, and so are you in a sense," finished Margate. "But here is what I will do: I'll just lie back and see what information I can get to you. All clean and accurate, and let you take it from there," he said with a smile.

"No, I have a better idea," said Juan, "you're getting the hell out of here, and I am now going to trace out, follow, and eliminate his pet. Before I do that, I need to find out exactly how to contact his shooter and make sure that before I leave town, he is out of the way as well. So, I think before you leave, you should say goodbye to your friend. I suggest you return from out of the country for his funeral. That is the only way I can play this game. Too much has gone by, and I need to put a stopper in it," said Juan.

"I really don't think you can, Juan," said Margate to his old friend, "listen, I know you're good. Hell, probably the best I know of. But this shooter who did the Benoits, from what I understand, cost the old man a pretty penny for him. Say, almost a million in gold upfront to come out of hiding to do this job. As I understand it, you have to go through half the world's population of misfits to get to talk to the bastard."

"Don't worry, General," said Juan, "I know half the misfits in this world already."

Turning away from Juan and walking over to the liquor table, the general poured himself another stiff one, and then turning in place, Margate said, "Well, let's say we start with finding and stopping this Winslow character. You know, the guy you met in the bar that day," chuckled Margate, "then we can take it from there. Because once he's gone, I may be able to stop the ole man from continuing with this nonsense."

"No, I have to get to the shooter, or he'll come for one of us one day, or both of us. Guys like him, even if the contract is stopped, they don't care. They finish what they started unless you pay them to stop and then pay them to begin on something else. That's the only way to get him to stop," said Juan.

Moving to the Scotch bottle on the table, he poured himself another one, then reached out with the bottle and again filled the general's glass.

"Okay then, it's settled. We first take care of Winslow and then go after the shooter. If the ole man doesn't get the picture by then, I will go to his funeral, agreed?" Said Margate to Juan while holding out his hand.

"Agreed," said Juan as he took the general's hand, and for the first time in a long time, he felt at least he was back in the game with one partner.

"Oh, one more thing, Juan, I may have failed to mention this somewhere along the line," said Margate, whose head was now down as he looked to the side of the room. "This isn't just about the ole coot wanting to protect his company. See, it's a little more complicated than that, sort of," said the general.

"Okay, let's start from the beginning. Exactly what do you mean when you say, 'it's a little more complicated than that'?" quipped Juan, who was now becoming more disappointed in this as everything seemed to be growing out of proportion.

"Well, there may be another reason why all of this is happening now. See, right at the time of these last Olympics. The Chinese hired Wetco to make it rain in Beijing. Just to clear up the smog that had gridlocked the city. This would be too big of a show to have the world see that they had more smog than LA's on their worst day. It's so bad over there that you need a seeing-eye dog to go to the corner store. Well, anyway, let's say it's possible the Chi-Coms may have purchased this knowledge on how to disperse it evenly. To make it work correctly. See, now that the science is out there on it, everyone knows how it works. What they really are in the dark on is how to make it work, dispersion. That's why Wetco is so damn rich, they hold that secret. It's the dispersal of those gases in the right pattern.

Over the right area. Using the correct correlation between gases, volume, weight, and energy. All needed to be correctly released in the distance to make it effective, and what charges to use and how they are placed. This is highly confidential material here. It is for the eyes only, even in that company, and is very top secret.

Well, it goes without saying that since the Chinese have 'purchased' this sensitive information, they may be using it more than they should. Why does America suddenly have more snow all over the country? There are more torrential rains around the world than ever before. As I understand it, the CIA may be investigating this matter as we speak.

See, all those Chi-Coms have to do is head north on their own border, watch the jet streams come and go, and then start changing that stream to the right amount of liquid in the air. Next thing ya know, on the other side of the world, in America. Our entire south and east coast is up to its ass in snow and rain. Even Georgia had snow. Hell, the weather patterns have been freaky lately. Why is the CIA so interested in finding out if the old man and his grandson sold out to the Chi-Coms?

See, the real culprit behind this is the Bildburg group, who are demanding that they 'share' in this knowledge. It appears that a leak may have occurred, revealing that this technology was possibly used to cause a drought in Russia for ten years.

So, Todd, the old man's grandson, knew that it would be only a matter of time before he had to share the knowledge and the wealth. But if it looked as if the Chi-Coms were the bad boys here. He could use that as an argument to ensure that no one else gains this knowledge. So right now, we may have a lot of different players already involved with this, or they soon will be," said Margate, who was now sitting down and looking up at Juan.

Juan's head just shook back and forth as he was about to burst.

No sense in killing this stupid old man, he thought. He would probably need him for later to help him possibly get himself untangled from all of this. Right now, he needed to leave and rethink this.

"I'm out of here. I'll be in touch," said Juan as he left the general sitting in that overstuffed chair with a bottle of empty Scotch next to him.

Surprise / The Hits Keep Coming

Justin had just come home from the office, and he was as tired as a dog. It had been one of those days. It seemed as if nothing was getting done today. Except maybe he was completing the circle he traveled on faster than a moment ago. He knew that Clara would not be home when he opened the door. She had called Justin earlier and said that there was a pre-holiday shoe sale, and she just had to go before everything was sold out. Laughingly, he said, "Sure, why not? Go, and if you want, I can come down to the mall to meet you, or I'll just go home and make some supper. How's that?"

"Great, I'll meet you at the house. I promise I won't be long." Then there was silence on her end, and then she responded, "No, I won't be long. I promise it's just that I need some shoes, and with this sale going on, well, I might find what I'm looking for," she replied, holding the phone to her head as she walked to the car.

Just then, the doorbell rang out, and Justin said, "Doorbell, sweetheart, let me go." Now yelling into the phone, Justin said, "Sweetheart, call me when you're on your way home so I can start the dinner."

Clara just loved it when he called her sweetheart. "Okay, my big man." A name that brought Justin a smile every time she said it. "I'll call just as soon as I get back to the car, and call me if I'm running late so I don't get lost in shopping," she screamed into the phone before he hung up on her.

Answering the door, Justin was taken aback by the man standing there with a pointed gun in his face. However, he did hear the shot even if it was silenced. It seemed to Justin that his face exploded as he fell to the front step. Even before he would pass out, a scream filled his ears. It came from his brain, for his voice was never to be heard again. Floating gently to the stoop was a card of a man nailed to a cross, hanging upside down.

Less than an hour earlier, Luther and Ulmmer were parking their car in the hospital's private lot. They would then make their way up to visit with Mable this evening. Today was their special reading day. It turned out that even Ulmmer liked to read to Mable, and Luther found that funny. Although Luther definitely enjoyed the company, it was often a long night. Especially when he didn't know if she had heard him or not when he read. What did it matter, he thought to himself? He had not fallen out of love with her.

Putting his arm around his friend's shoulder, Luther said, "Ulmmer, what am I to do with you? Please don't tell me that you're falling for Mable as well. I have to say she's all mine, and you're married, my friend. But to have your company is a pleasure nonetheless, especially since Marta and the kids are back in Germany. Shopping and spending an early holiday with her parents. I look at it this way, my friend. You stay out of trouble, and I don't get any reports that you have drunk all the beer down at the canteen," laughed Luther.

Walking between the parked cars on their way to the side entrance, there was movement from behind, and before either could act, it was already over. As the man stepped out from between two cars, he shot Luther in the back twice. Ulmmer then turned to face the shooter. He shot Ulmmer twice in his chest. Ulmmer fell back to lie across his boss as if he could protect him a little longer, only to receive one more bullet to his head. For the shooter's insurance, it was a job well done.

It had happened so fast. It was so methodical. That only one person could have done it, Luther thought. As Ulmmer lay dying in a parking lot in America, suddenly, he wanted to be back home to Germany, to be with his wife and two daughters. The shooter turned and walked away into a silent night, but not before he flipped his infamous card out onto the bleeding holes in Ulmmer's overcoat.

Clara got that call. The one that she and John had always feared might come someday. Clara fell immediately to the ground, landing on her knees. The scream of NO came from a voice she did not recognize. Her own. Now, putting her hands out to help her not fall completely horizontal, she felt the concrete cut her palms. Her hands were still shaking uncontrollably, and then suddenly, she had to throw up. It all came in a rush, and she could do nothing but wipe her mouth with her sleeve. Now sitting up and before the tears would wash away any semblance of a voice, she said into the phone.

"He's been shot! Where are they taking him, Brad, where?" She cried.

"To St. Anthony's Hospital. I'm in the ambulance with him now, and I have already notified John. Clara, he's on his way to the hospital as well. As a matter of fact, the whole office is probably on its way there. We have no idea who else may be targeted. You have to take cover. Find your way to the hospital. But do not come in. Call me or John, and one of us will come out to get you, do you hear me? Clara? Do not expose yourself. God forbid someone is waiting for you to show up to finish what they have started. Is that understood, Clara? Call me or John first." Brad was excited and had no idea about her frame of mind right now, and/or even if she had the phone to her ear. So once again, he said, "Clara, I need you to acknowledge what I have just said to you."

Clara was in shock. She was crying and listening to Brad, praying that Justin would yell from the background, "Listen to him, Clara," but that shout never came. All she could hear in the background was the siren. Then she could only whisper.

"Brad, thank you for being with him. Please tell him I am on my way, and yes, I heard you."

Brad then said, "Clara, it may be exactly where they or he intends to make a hit on you."

Then, almost in pure frustration, he yelled into the phone, "Oh my god, we're FBI! For Christ's sake, how in the hell can they think they can get away with this?"

Then suddenly, he knew that he was way off base, shouting into the phone in anger. With a calmer and reserved voice now, Brad immediately apologized to Cara, saying, "Clara, please forgive me for showing my frustration just then. I'm just so frustrated and angry right now. I am so sorry."

Through a choked voice and with tears flowing down her eyes, Clara said, "I'm on my way there right now, Brad. Not to worry, I'll call you as soon as I get to the front door."

St. Anthony's Hospital was busy as usual, but occasionally, there may be some significant accidents with multiple injuries taking place somewhere else in the city. That's when they are asked to take on the overload of patients involved. Since they are not an enormous trauma center, they usually receive minor-injured patients. However, several months ago, there was a shooting in a local neighborhood, and their ambulances had to respond. It turned out that the response was for the best, especially for a particular young lady. One who still lay in a bed tucked away at the end of a private room area. But she is alive today, thanks to their surgeons. This day, however, is turning toward one of the worst days in this hospital's history. It had started out with very few requests from people in the emergency waiting room.

Now, this day, with its sudden turn of events, is putting a very large strain on everyone who worked there, seeing how right now, being wheeled into their version of a trauma operating room were two men. Both happened to be shot, no less than right in their own hospital parking lot, not five minutes ago. However, the good news, if it was possible to have any good news in a shooting, was that because of the proximity to their emergency room, one might yet live. The other had already been pronounced DOA before they placed him on the gurney to wheel him into the building. It would seem that one of the bullets had torn through his heart, and he bled to death in minutes, aside from a small hole that was made in the front of his head. Ulmmer had passed on. The hospital staff all remembered seeing him from the previous shooting. Standing at six feet five and weighing about two hundred and fifty pounds on a light day, he was definitely someone hard to forget. Why, it was so sad. Now, this large man lay on the gurney, covered by a sheet that concealed his broad frame.

Twenty minutes after the shooting happened, word had gone out to their embassy, and once again, the emergency room was crowded with badges and guns. Some coworkers of his stood about, looking at the draped body as if Ulmmer would rise, laughing at them, at any minute now. Some probably were hoping that this would somehow turn into a joke on them. But he did not move, and now his wife would have to be called and arrangements made to send his remains back to Germany so that he could be called a hero and mourned by those who love him. But right now, his body was taken to the morgue until the German embassy could make arrangements to pick up his body.

All the while, Luther lay on a flat table in a cold operating room in the hands of God, as several surgeons were fighting to save his life. But God had somehow known that he would be shot today. On this day, Major Frank De Paolo, U.S. Army (ret), had just returned from Iraq. A place where wounds such as these were unfortunately too common. It would take several long and tense hours for the major to make sure that Luther would see the light of day. As the major was working on Luther, he was told that an FBI agent was now en route to this very hospital, also, with gunshot wounds. His thoughts were in his head. The major then decided to have someone else close Luther up as he cleaned and went into the operating room next to the one he had just left. Looking out the small window in the door to the operating room, he saw his patient being wheeled into the hospital.

The doors to the entrance were suddenly slammed against the interior walls from the force of the attendants ushering in the gurney. If to say they were too slow in their job, make way, a man in need. Lying on the gurney in front of him was what once must have been a handsome man. Now, however, his face was shattered, with the back of his head containing an exit wound, one that couldn't hold a quarterback from falling out if that was its sole purpose in this man's life. The gray matter that was on the side of the bandage said this fellow was just hours from seeing his God. The major looked down, and all he could see were so many young kids, five thousand miles away. He hung his head down and said a prayer for the young man as his own tears started to flow.

Once again, the front doors to the hospital and all entrances were blocked off. The halls and the emergency room were standing-room-only. From local police and the FBI agents, along with German officials, there was no room for anyone else to move about.

Faces strained to stop the crying that wanted to burst forward from grown men and women, crying from the loss of a dear friend to them. A young and vibrant Ulmmer had been pronounced dead on arrival. No one could figure out the why of it. But every man there swore that whoever had shot and killed him would one day regret such a bad decision. But they couldn't leave where they stood or sat, as their boss, Luther Rudman, now lay in the operating room fighting for his life as well. The doctors from this hospital, God, and their prayers were all trying to keep him alive on a flat table in a cold operating room.

Now, moving among them were others who also may yet mourn the passing of a young man too young to have given his life for a job he so loved. But everyone there knew that life and death were a part of the struggle that came with his job.

Clara called Brad and said she was in front of the hospital, that the police had every exit cordoned off, and that she could get a police escort. Brad immediately said no, that he was already on his way out to get her. When she asked how he knew her to be there, he said, "They now had eyes on the roof covering this whole area, and they had to make sure that John or I knew when you pulled in."

Clara then asked him, "Why so much security, Brad? Has someone else from the office been targeted?"

"No, Clara," Brad said. Then, he said to her, "That German attorney, he and his second, well, they also were shot today." Then he went on to say that the second in command now lay dead in the morgue. His boss, Luther, whom she knew, who had also been shot before with Mable, was now in the operating room being worked on to keep him alive.

Brad exited the sliding doors and approached Clara, whose makeup had made its way down to her chin. On the way over, she had called her mom and dad and told them what had happened, that the FBI would call Justin's folks to let them know that he had been shot and was now in St. Anthony's Hospital emergency room. "And just as soon as I know something, Mom, I'll call you back," said Clara.

"Don't bother unless it's to call my cell. Your father and I are on our way there. I'll also call Tully and let her know what's happened. Tully will go there immediately, and she will keep you company. Besides, she'll need to know right now that you're ok, Clara. Then, when you hang up, I want you to call Justin's folks as well. To hell with your protocol, he's your future husband, you will call them. Or they will never forgive you should something go wrong, Clara. They would want to hear it from you first. So, call them when we hang up, understand?" said Clara's mom, Marian Beach.

"Yes, I'm sorry. I do know better." Sobbing once again as if it would never stop, Clara, through a choked voice, pleaded like the little girl she was to her mom.

"Mom, please come as soon as you can," said Clara before she hung up and dialed number 6 on her speed dial for Justin's folks.

"Mrs. Beach," said a now-somber Clara.

"When are you going to call me Mom, Clara?" asked Debra Beach, who is the mother of Justin and soon-to-be mother-in-law of Clara.

"Please sit down and listen to me. Are you sitting?" asked Clara. "Oh my god," yelled Debra, "please don't tell me bad news, Clara."

"Listen to me, please. Said Clara. Justin has been shot. They have him on the way to St. Anthony's Hospital in Washington. I'm on my way to him as we speak. A woman in a car parked on our street had seen the whole thing as it happened. She immediately called 911. And they got there in minutes. One of our agents, Brad Burke, was on his way to our house at the time, and he arrived before the ambulance arrived. He has been helping Justin since then. He went to the hospital in the ambulance with him. So, Justin isn't alone. Brad has been with Justin ever since. They're at the hospital now, and I'm on my way to see him. I was shopping for shoes, and he asked me if he should come along. I told him he didn't have to, then he said he would cook supper for us. I said I would call him as soon as I got done, and then I got the call."

Clara was crying once more as she continued to talk to Debra, saying, "Please come now, please. Mom and Dad are on their way as well."

"Listen to me, Clara. I know it's hard, but you must concentrate on driving. God forbid that you get hurt now as well, Clara. You have to drive safely, and we're on the way. If I need help getting into the hospital, I'll call your cell. Tell Justin we're coming. But please stop crying and concentrate on the road before both of you are in the damn hospital," said Debra Beach.

"Yes, Mom, I will," answered Clara. It was the first time she had ever called another woman's mom, but she knew that they were connected, and now they would be for life.

"Clara, come on, get inside," said Brad. Grabbing her arm and stepping between her and the road that led to the hospital's front door, he walked her into the building. Brad wanted to make sure that his body protected her from any harm that could come from behind them.

Looking back at Brad, she asked, "Brad, how is he? Is he okay? When did you get here? Is he in the OR right now? Who's in there with him? Did he say anything? Did he tell you who shot him? Did he lose a lot of blood? Can I see him now? Take me to him, Brad, please," asked Clara as she rapidly spoke and asked Brad every question that came into her head. She was full of questions, and Brad could only hold back the information by biting his lower lip till it hurt. He knew that today was going to be a very sad day for her. It would be known forever as one of regret and one to start her life of loneliness, until he hoped that someday she would be ready to live life once again. He had known the two of them since they all mustered that first day at FBI school. Brad thought she was hot and wondered how he might attract her to him. Like a moth to a candle, only this candle was too hot. She wanted nothing to do with him. Saying it was his arrogance. Well, why not? After all, he was a third-generation FBI agent and felt he could help her "learn the ropes," as he said to her one day. Her reply to him almost shocked him when she said that getting into her pants and wearing them was a lot different than letting him into her pants and not having any on at the time.

Wow, what a girl, he thought. Since then, they added Justin to the madness of the FBI school. Only to make wanting her more important when Justin joined them, but time often seems to heal all wounds. Even ones of the heart, he thought quietly. So, rather than be enemies, once assignments came down for them and placed them in the same Washington offices, they had all kissed and made up. A start of a new friendship than he thought, and now, with her and Justin living together and with their planned marriage, he only wanted the best for his two best friends. Now, he had to escort her into a private conference room and listen to John Bloso tell her that the love of her life was dead.

Walking into the room and seeing John there, Clara thought Justin must still be in the operating room. It was the place set aside for family, a secure and private place until they could all be with Justin.

"Clara," said John as he took her hand and led her to a chair for her to sit in. John moved in front of her and looked down. He saw her whole body shaking as if she were standing in ice water.

Now feeling the tension, Clara looked up and said, "John, please tell me he's okay. Please. Listen, even if he isn't perfect, I don't care. I'll quit the department. I'll take care of him no matter what. So, please just tell me! I can't wait any longer to find out how he is! This is killing me to wait! I called his mom already, and she is on the way. So are my mother and father. Can I go to see him now? Where is he? Is he still in the operating room? Let me go to him, please, John." She was now begging and pleading. She felt she had to beg now. It was as if everyone wanted to keep her away from him. He must still be in the operating room, she thought.

Fine, when he is out of there, she didn't care when, she would go to him and tell him that she loved him. She would quit the bureau, and they would marry or not. She didn't care. All she wanted now was to go to him and tell him she loved him, and that she would never leave him, and always take good care of him.

"Please!" she screamed at the top of her lungs, "Take me to him," as she fell to the floor. Kneeling there and crying, that uncontrollable sobbing of tears that made her say she was so scared of what she didn't know. Where was he? Was he still alive? It's the one question she could not ask. Because if she did, she thought he wouldn't be. So, she cannot ask that question. As long as she doesn't ask that question, Justin will still be alive. Looking up from her kneeling position with tears streaming down her face and her body racked with her sobs, she once again cried out, "Please, please, John, where is he? Please take me to him."

Brad started to cry as he bent down and hugged her to his chest, and there they stayed. Each locked into the other's embrace, crying, and Clara knew then that she had lost her Justin.

As John looked at the two of them sitting there hugging and crying, he now knew that Clara understood Justin was gone. He also knew that love was the most significant and important bond in humans. It did not matter if two people worked together. It didn't matter what station in life they held. What mattered was that they loved each other, and John knew that the bond that held them once would remain with her for as long as she lived. It was something that only those who were fortunate enough to find true love could ever experience. Unfortunately, the one who remained would carry the bond with them for an eternity. John knew that they had found that bond. It was hard not to turn and run home to Beth all of a sudden. One of the hardest parts of this job was telling someone that a loved one was no longer here. When it was one of your own people who had to be told, it became the hardest thing anyone had to do. He then thought about how he now understood why the bureau didn't want inter-departmental marriages and dating. It was now going to be hard on everyone, and by the looks of things, he may have lost two agents instead of one. A hard thought, but nonetheless, it was maybe the truth. John could no longer suppress his emotions, and he started to cry as he was very saddened by her loss and the loss of a colleague and friend, Justin Beach. To be forever known as another young man killed in the line of duty on this day, a day he would never forget. One that would be as a tattoo placed on his mind and heart, a wound that would never heal. John was now going to become the one man he did not want to become. John was going to become vengeful. Someone would pay for this crime. Someone had to pay. No one kills one of his agents in cold blood at his home and then disappears.

No, wherever you are, whoever you are, I am going to make you pay for this heinous crime against my friend.

Clara's mom and dad, Justin's mother and father, along with Tully and Jeff, now stood outside the hospital's morgue and consoled each other. Clara had no more tears left in her body. She was dry. She now had only one thought on her mind, and that was to find the man who shot and killed her future husband. Her best friend, her colleague, the man that she had come to love more than herself. She had intent, clarity, and purpose now. She found herself moving away from the sadness as she searched deep within herself. Clara needed to find that spark of barbaric thinking. She needed that place now more than ever. It would be the one place that would protect her from this madness. The one place she needed to find herself in as she now became the hunter and no longer the hunted.

If whoever had done this had hoped that she was in the house as well, maybe even hoping that it was she who had opened that door today, then so be it. For no longer would she search for any logical answers to riddles? Right now, she knew only the facts. Mable had been shot along with her boyfriend, Luther. Today, Ulmmer was dead, and now so was Justin, and with him, he took her life. He took her reason to live every day, he was the reason why she wanted to wake in the mornings before Justin did. Then she could lie there and stare at him before he awoke, almost in disbelief at the happiness they shared together. She thought, whoever he is, he may know who she

is, but soon he will have to face her, which will cost him his life. Clara
had no plans to see him in court.

A Change of Mind / Stop the Madness

The call that came to Juan's phone only confirmed what he had already known. Two people lay dead in St. Anthony's Hospital. One was an FBI agent, a young man named Justin Beach. The other was a German embassy worker. A second embassy worker was left fighting for his life in that same hospital. Just rooms down from where his girlfriend lay in a coma for nearly four months now, from an earlier attempt on her life. Add to that. The loss of her coworker, who was found shot to death in front of a lover's house, where she had died in the same incident.

Juan knew that no matter what the thinking was on Winslow's part, these shootings and deaths would not throw the hounds from the scent. Especially now that they have committed and done the unthinkable, with the brutal killing of an FBI agent on the man's front doorstep, no less. What the hell could they be thinking? He wondered. Exactly how far was this to go? Now, maybe he should join the general and just leave town altogether until the smoke cleared and the guns ran out of bullets. This, he knew, was not good for anybody. These two actually thought that this would change their thinking on this. Absolutely not. It would now serve to only enhance and increase the number of agents assigned to this fiasco. He had to take care of this now, today. Somehow, he would leak some information to the FBI and have them finish his work. But should something go wrong and he was caught, then he would have to testify, potentially, and that would not serve any purpose for him for sure. So, he had to manage this in a different way. In a way, he thought that would not implicate him, or should it? Just then, the phone rang, and Juan knew who it was before he lifted the receiver.

"Juan," said General Margate, whose voice seemed to be on the edge of shouting. "I have to tell you that, as far as I am concerned, do whatever you need to do to stop this madness. I can no longer be involved in the screwing up of these two blundering idiots. What the hell could they be thinking? For God's sake, the young man was an FBI agent. You just don't go and kill any police officer, but to shoot an FBI agent on his front doorstep, you have to be crazy." The general was angry, and Juan knew that right now, the entire world was probably just as angry.

"Listen, General," said Juan, "I have had my share of stupidity in life, but this borders on craziness. I'm thinking of coming down to you and keeping you company until this is over. Or I have to make it happen soon, extremely soon, if I'm to do this at all. As far as I'm concerned, I will handle all three of them. This has to end now."

"If I am implicated in this from the beginning," yelled the general into the phone. "Then I have to hold some of this baggage now. Because I didn't turn this around or turn him in or, hell, even try to stop them if I could. No, I don't want any more involvement in this. Juan, end it all with my blessings. Make it three, and I promise I will take care of you. You'll never work again, I swear. I need this to go away, and now. Have I made myself clear on this, Juan?"

"Yes, sir, and I can say that once I am done, I will take a long-needed vacation from this mess if that's at all possible. I'll be in touch, sir." With that, Juan hung up the phone.

He had no idea if he could get the right plan in place within such a short time frame to work with. Juan was good, but to kill three men and walk away, hop a bus or plane, and go sit in the sun? Well, he would certainly try, he thought once again, smiling to himself.

Manipulator

Pete Winslow looked at Clara through the emergency room glass doors. Pete had sent Günter to wait around until one of them showed up. Then he was to walk to the front door and, as it opened, shoot whoever answered it in the face. Apparently, it was her lover who opened the door today. He had told Günter that death was not to be instantaneous, but he was to make sure he would not be identified later and that his target was definitely going to die.

"Can you handle that, Günter?" he asked him.

"Yes, little man, now go away before my boredom here leaves me insane enough to have you for lunch," said an aggravated and bored Günter. One who had no idea that the man in front of him had recently exposed his identification to a friend of his working for Interpol. They had now placed him in the United States. The body recently dug up in Germany has not been identified. However, they now know it is not Lars Günter Mallern in that grave.

"When you get the job done, I want you to go to Baltimore. There, check into the Baltimore Hilton. Ask for the room set aside for Dr. Ingle. Dr. Jonathan Ingle. Wait there until I send for you, and don't become visible. Stay off the room service, and don't hit on any of the cleaning staff. Go out for your fun and use only cash. I'm sure you know the drill. After all, you're the big gun, aren't you?" said Pete with a shit-eating grin on his face, one that Günter was sure that he would one day erase, free of charge.

He now had a clear view of her as she and her family huddled and shed tears for their loss. Well, maybe they should have kept their noses out of his business, he thought to himself, with a slight chuckle. Pete had come into the hospital through the main doors right after he shot both of those Europeans. What easy targets. One day, they're all sophisticated and secure. Next, their guard is down, and they become such easy targets.

Hell, all he did after he left that card was to walk around to the front and walk right in the main doors. He then walked down to the main offices located on the right side of the building. Here, he was greeted by Monsignor Hays, the operations manager of the hospital, with a handshake followed by a back-slapping hug from a golfing buddy of his. After all, it was a Catholic hospital. His company, H. T. Wetco, was one of the main contributors to the hospital, which allowed him entrance no matter who or what was going on there. Bob Thurston always ensured that the hospital never had any unmet needs. His company gave millions to the hospital. So much so that a wing for cancer patients is named after his wife. It was here that she passed from that disease. The chapel downstairs, as little as it was, still held her picture done in stained glass. So, getting in with or without security was easy enough for him, that was for sure.

As he continued to stare at her, he began thinking about how lucky she had not been home earlier. Looking at her and eyeing her up, he thought to himself. Go ahead, pull the trigger on her right now. In the melee that would ensue, he would get away cleanly. Everyone here was on such an edge right now and probably a little trigger finger-happy. There's no telling who could get shot. They would be willing to shoot anything or anyone at the drop of a hat right now, he thought, smiling to himself.

Idiots, I could kill them all, and what would they know? I could walk right up to any of them and make them just as dead as they would ever be, and again, a smile came to his face. This is fun, he thought. Here I am, standing not more than twenty feet from them, and they don't even know I'm here. How stupid are they?

For some reason, this was funny to him, and he kept smiling and wondering what would happen if he just shot her right now. That's when the thought left his mind as he couldn't believe his eyes.

How lucky is this? he said to himself. Jeff Osborne and his pain-in-the-ass wife, Tully, just walked into the spider's lair, and they have no idea. Here they are, hugging and crying with the Beach girl. They know her. Now, what an easy mark she had just become. She has no clue how this just became so much easier to rid himself of, possibly not only those two ingrates but her as well. Once she's gone, the investigation will turn toward his shooter. The Germans would love to get their hands on him. So would the FBI if they found out he killed those two old farts in Virginia. He thinks he's so tough, so smart. I'll show him tough and smart. But for now, I need the FBI looking left when I'm going right. Just as soon as I can get rid of this damn female agent, I'll make my final move on him, this Lars, yeah, Lars, my ass. Then, right after she's dead, they can find him and prove that Lars killed the old people, the FBI agent, and finished with her. By then, they'll forget all about Wetco, case closed, move on to other business.

The last piece of the puzzle will be the general and his dog. He may have gotten away once when I sent that inapt idiot Pierson, but next time, it'll be me he'll deal with, and I don't make mistakes. When I'm done sending these last messages, I can finally take a nice little vacation with the company's jet and some female companions. They all love the jet.

With his newly found information and feeling great about the situation so far, Pete left the hospital with a spring in his step and a whistle. Right now, things are looking up.

The old man will be proud of me, he thought. Probably make me a member of the club he's so damn fond of.

Another Funeral

Juan moved to the back of the church. It was crowded. The streets were full of FBI, Secret Service personnel, police in uniform, German embassy officials, and even the mayor would be talking here today. Washington was all abuzz about the Mass now being held today for the slain FBI agent.

A young man was murdered in cold blood by an unidentified person just four days ago. Senator Pillow himself was here, and so were many who wanted to see this young man off. At the church's altar, there stood a tall, frail-looking bishop, who began to speak to the crowd of people who had been lucky enough to find a seat in a church that was small in comparison to the Cathedral that he normally spoke at, but Clara had insisted that the Mass be held here. After all, it was the church that they had planned to marry.

Rising from his seat and walking to the altar, the bishop began. "He is now in the hands of God. I'm sure that there is a lot of comfort in knowing that," said the bishop. "He may have walked among you and loved and lived with you as well. But when one hears the voice of God beckoning, we answer that call as Justin had heard a call to duty when he searched his soul for what he wanted in life. So, he has now answered the call from God. Justin is not alone, and neither are we, for we carry him in our prayers and in our hearts. We close our eyes, and we can still see him, as we remember his voice and his laughter. And it is this gift to us from God that we all cherish. Memory, for our memories of those we lose here while on earth, helps to keep us in balance. As our faith does in the Lord, that one day, we shall all be together again. For our memories. Those that are fond and warm. Far outweigh those that we want to forget, and with God's blessing, we do forget. We should remember Justin as he was full of life, love, and beauty. Not bound to this earth for long, but long enough to have touched so many in so short a time. It is always a tragedy when some ruthless individual, for no reason, takes a young life. But we have something far greater that we hold in each of us who knew Justin. Something no one can take from us, our memories. So, take those that you have of Justin and wrap yourself in them, become comforted, and come to believe that when God calls us, we shall also hear his voice. And we all shall return to God. For we are all born to die, and that Justin now rests with his God, our God. May God have mercy on his soul, may he bless and keep safe all those who find comfort in him.”

The Mass went on, and eventually, they all found themselves walking out of the graveyard. Most people looked back where they could see Clara standing there with her parents and Justin’s parents, saying their last goodbyes.

Juan did not want to get too close to the site. He knew it was probably being recorded. He would wait for a while before leaving the graveyard. But he had to look himself to see if Winslow had the balls to show up. If so, he would follow him to hell and back to end this part of it now. Shaking off the sudden cold air that flowed around the graveyard, at last, he could leave. No one was left in the area outside of the fellows who, now with the aid of a backhoe, were filling in the gravesite. What an ending to such a fine young life, he thought.

Discovery / Finding Out the Truth

In the weeks that followed Justin's death, Clara had a constant visitor, her cousin Tully. Right now, it seemed as if the two were inseparable. First, it was Justin's and Clara's folks who stayed and helped her clean out the closets. Then, before she was alone to contemplate when she would go back to work, Tully came unannounced and has been with her ever since. Clara's own department put her on administrative leave "until she was ready to come back," they said. However, she had to now go through some psychiatric evaluations to make sure that she would be ready to come back when she decided it was time to. "No rush, Clara; just make sure that it's the right time," John had told her. He also wanted her to know that Grant Fischer had come upstairs almost every day to inquire about her health and that he said, "Hello." Brad would stop by once a week and catch her up to date on the activity at headquarters and on the investigation into Justin's murder.

Because of the death of the German Ulmmer and the second shooting of Luther, it was now an international problem. A massive search was now being conducted to find the missing Lars Günter Mallern. It would seem that someone else lay in that grave in Bremerhaven, Germany, not Lars as once thought. However, work still needed to be done to find the common link between Justin and Luther. It seemed as if the investigation was starting to move away from the senator, especially since Luther had been shot once again, and with the death of Luke Weeks at his married girlfriend's house, nothing seemed to fit anymore.

Jeff, Tully, and Clara had made the decision about a week ago that Friday evenings would be pizza and movie night in her living room. Now that the pizza had been delivered and with most of it having been eaten, they all moved into the living room to begin the night. It was Tully who had heard the knocking at the front door as she left the kitchen to answer it. Upon opening the door, a masked man stood there, and he had a gun pointed at her face. His one finger on his left hand held upright against his lips to tell her to be quiet. He moved quickly inside and harshly turned her in front of him as a shield. Moved her into the living room, where a startled and upset Jeff stood and tried to grab Tully. But the man holding her jerked Tully back into him, bringing her that much closer.

Clara stood and faced the masked man, and she flared in agony and anger. She knew that this could be the bastard who killed Justin. This masked man was now standing right in front of her, holding Tully close to him for protection. He needed to die.

"Listen," said the masked man, "all of you sit down right now. If I see movement out of anyone, someone dies right here, right now! Not as much as an unneeded blink of the eye, or I can shoot my way out." Looking now directly at Clara, He said, "Understood, Agent? Do I make myself perfectly clear on this?"

"Yes," said Clara, "Leave them alone. If you need to shoot someone, make that me. They have nothing to do with anything. They're my guests, and we're in for the night. But, of course, you would know that already, wouldn't you?"

Releasing Tully with a shove forward, the masked man pointed the gun at Clara, waving the gun for her to sit on the couch. So now Clara was sitting next to a very scared Tully, with Jeff on the far side of her. Now, all three are afraid to move, or it could cause this intruder to harm one of them. They all knew that they were in a dangerous position, so for now, they would do as asked. Clara knew that her backup gun was under the very seat cushion that she sat on right at this very moment. How to get it out and kill this bastard was the only thought now streaming through her mind.

"Listen once again, I'll say this. Only once to prevent some unnecessary bloodshed here. I'm here to only tell you a story, Clara, one that you may find very interesting. One that you'll need to believe is the truth or you may never live to see this thing through to the end. I'm going to give you information on why Justin was killed, as well as your grandparents, why Mable was shot and Luke murdered. Everything right now is for free. You just need to let me finish this so that whatever steps need to be taken, you can and will. But know this. I have gotten to you once, and I can get to you again in the future. Don't make this any more difficult tonight through your stupidity. Understand this right now! I am not the one who killed anyone that you know. I'm strictly here to set the record straight. Do I have your attention now?" the masked man asked them.

Shocked by it all at the moment, Clara said, "On my word, as long as you live up to your end. That no one is going to be hurt tonight, or so help me, kill me now, because I'll spend the rest of my life hunting you down like a dog on a bone. Am I clear as well?" she asked, now standing and looking directly into his eyes.

"Fine, I have no problem with that," he said. "Sit and listen to a story you'll only hear from me once. I wear the mask because I do not want to be identified. In the future, I want no reason to go to court as a witness to what I am about to tell you. Nor do I want to be hunted down by you and your fellow agents. One time and one time only, you may ask questions. But for now. Understand that you are still my captives, and I will shoot you or all of you if you press me. Don't think this is anything about you. Any of you. It's all about me and my getting away from this and not looking back." Finished the masked man.

Clara definitely knew he was a professional, and maybe if this was going to clear things up, she would be better off staying in her seat and listening.

"Okay," she said, "you have the floor."

Then he said, "What I'm about to tell you now may seem impossible for a reason to kill anyone, but believe me, it isn't. This message is from the person who initially hired me. He wanted you to have this information."

Making sure they were all seated on the couch and facing forward, he then walked to the back of the couch and told them to continue facing forward and to just listen.

The masked man began, "Right from the beginning, I have been involved in some way. Originally, I was hired to investigate Senator Pillow, his staff, the Benoits, and your grandparents. For a private, well-paying party, never was there any talk of killing anyone. I was just to find out what they knew about a certain subject. It was what Frank Benoit did when he worked for H.T. Wetco. I was to make a report and deliver it in two months. Take my money and go on a now much-needed vacation.

However, when I turned over the information that I had collected to my contact, another man was present. I now knew exactly whom he worked for, and that's when I also became a target. But I unknowingly, at the time, that everyone on this list was to become a target. When I left that vehicle, a man followed me. He tried to kill me."

Not telling them where it was because that was of no real consequence at this juncture. He then continued, "This was something that set off my own warning bells immediately. My first and only conversation with the Benoits was as a reporter doing a story for television. I was the interviewer who talked to your grandparents. I needed to know what he did for H. T. Wetco and everything about them as I could drag out. Although Frank talked enough that he had no problem doing it, I was finding myself way off base there. I was coming to recognize that they both were of no threat to Homeland Security. As I had been led to believe was my purpose for the visit, or

I may have presumed it. I stated that in my report as well. Besides, at their age and sitting there enjoying their company, they were not even a threat to the local mosquito population. I felt as if I was with my own family visiting before my drive back home. Then, when I found out they had been murdered, I immediately began my own investigation.

Right before I entered my house one evening, a second attempt on my life happened in my parking garage. I managed to kill that man in self-defense. These people must have great contacts because that body I had left behind was never even mentioned in any paper or newscast.

So now I figured that because I had done these interviews, it was the reason why I was now a target. I decided then to pick one of the interviewees. I chose Mable and followed her. Seeing how she had just met a new man, and he was now in her life. So, I followed Mable and this guy, Luther. Now I'm thinking that Luther was the killer of the Benoits, and he was making a move to eliminate Mable. But he wasn't. Turns out she was just in love with the guy. However, it was a good thing I followed them that night. I'm the armed neighbor the police are looking for. Only I was a tail for Mable's sake, and it turned out for the better.

I'll give you a description of the shooter later. Currently, I have the best source: the man who hired me to conduct the original investigation. You need to know that he had no idea this would lead to so many senseless murders.

But he knows for certain that the shooter is a gun for hire out of Russia. They named him the fourth man out or some bullshit like that. But this shooter was hired to apparently kill everyone involved in my original investigation. And that included him and his contact, which happens to be me. They want no one around who could implicate them."

The masked man paused, and tapping Clara on the back, he said, "I know you think I may have set up your family, but neither of us had any idea that this would be carried to such dire extremes. Believe me, no one in their right mind could do this. And no one could have foreseen any of this."

He then continued his storytelling. "They have a need to make this all happen to save their own asses, and until everyone is dead, they'll continue to kill. I know why Luke was murdered. He had done some research on H.T. Wetco, the company responsible for all of this. It was about some incident that took place sixty years ago. It seems this senator named Pillow stumbled across a potential carrot to hang in front of these characters. It was damaging enough to have him think they would pay him a lot of money to shut up. He also wanted this firm to put him on a sitting senatorial committee and pay for his reelection campaign. The man has balls, for sure.

It all happened when he was asked by a committee to get information on subsidies, but this ass found out about how this senator and Wetco conspired to make it rain for forty days and nights. This destroyed the tobacco industry at the time. It started with American subsidies for farmers.

So, they murdered this senator from Tennessee. Now, the original founder, who is old enough to die any minute, decides to take things into his own hands and make it all go away. Sort of like a departing present to his unknowing children, who are left holding the fortunes of this company in their hands. Clean and clear of any damage he had done when they started this company.

It now appears that your investigation may have been closing in on some truths as it progressed towards this particular company. The very company that your grandfather worked for and what he managed to do for them. So, they needed a diversion to lead the investigation away from them, which led to the killing of Justin. They needed to hide the fact that your investigation of this company could turn up some ugly truths. Much more than just the murder of this senator sixty years ago.

Because it would involve the U.S. military and this very government as well. This company has perpetrated some outlandish horrors against humanity around the world for decades, hidden by this government. So, by your coming close, too close, it would seem that they needed this diversion taken even a step farther away. So, killing Luther now became the play to throw people off track. But instead, they shot and killed Ulmmer by accident. However, they had meant to kill Luther to make it look as if an old enemy had shown up, and maybe Justin had found out about it. They needed it to look that way. As if someone was here to settle an old score, and Justin may have known who it was, so he needed to be silenced. It was easier to make it look like it was an international problem. But instead, it was to hide the truth."

A pause followed for a few seconds, and then he began once again to talk. "Now," said the masked man, "that was a little summation of what has been going on lately."

Clara sat back, and she had her hands over her face. The whole time that he had been talking, she wanted nothing more than to get her gun and shoot this son of a bitch. Then, figure out if he was telling the truth later. But for now, screw him and his theories.

As she listened more to what he was saying, she came to recognize that there were too many things that ran true. She knew that he had to have been in some of those places and seen what had happened. He pieced everything together so finely. He had to have been in all of this right from the beginning if he was the shooter. Then why confess now and try to implicate someone else? It made no sense to her.

"What if I say that I believe you? Then what? Where do you expect me to go from here? My life is ruined. I have just lost the love of my life, and you're telling me it's because someone was murdered sixty years ago. Are you kidding me? We lost our grandparents because someone thought they could be a problem for Homeland Security. However, it turns out they used your interview as a pretext to find another reason to kill them. Even after you said that they're harmless? Fuck you, you bastard. How do I really know that you didn't kill them all, and when you're done here, you'll just shoot and kill us?"

Now she was almost screaming as tears came down her face, and she began to sob. "How do we know you're telling us the truth?" she once again demanded from him.

"Because I'm going to give you the names of those who have ordered these killings. And the name of the man who carried them out. As far as the shooter goes, I'll handle that bastard myself," the masked man said, as if he, too, was tired and angry at what had transpired over these last few months. Actually, he was because he could see and hear in her voice the reasons why this had to come to an end.

"Clara," he said in a tone that would ask her for his forgiveness. "I can make you only one promise that the names I'm going to give to you are the ones that need to be stopped. They have paid for this hired killer. They have lied to me and to my contacts about the purpose of gathering information for them. I believe that all of the shootings and the senseless loss of yours came from one man besides the hired killer. His name is Pete Winslow, and the company he works for."

Before he could say another word, both Jeff and Tully said out loud, "H.T. Wetco."

"We used to work for them. Pete has asked us to falsify the results of some research we did for them. We said no and walked away from doing business with them any longer," said Tully.

Now Clara came back into focus when she heard Tully and Jeff speak up.

Then Jeff said, "That's why he called two days ago and asked for a meeting with us. He said he had some important business to discuss and asked if we would mind meeting him for dinner."

"What?" said Tully. "You never told me about that?"

"Well, I knew your answer would be no, so I just forgot about it," answered Jeff.

"Listen, what would be the chance that we make that meeting?" said the masked man. "I don't want either of you there. I can handle this alone. But what I need is for him to come out of the hole he's been hiding in. I can't find him anywhere, and I have certainly been searching. If you two could set up that meeting for me, I can go there and pay him a personal visit. I need to ask him politely about the whereabouts of the shooter. When I'm done with him, I swear you can have him, Clara. But right now, I need that name. Otherwise, this guy will continue doing what he does best. So. Until I can take him off the streets, no one is safe."

"What are you implying that H.T. Wetco killed Justin and our grandparents?" asked Clara.

"Exactly," replied the masked man.

"But why? Our grandfather retired from that company years ago; he doesn't know anything. Why would they have them killed? What did your investigation have to do with this?" Clara asked, and again, you could feel her tension rising.

"Look, Clara, as I said before, I was under the impression that they had in some way compromised Homeland Security. That's all I knew then. I was to ask him questions concerning his work at H.T. Wetco. I thought by telling him that a science channel producer wanted to put his story on television, he would be easier to talk to. When I left, I knew then that they couldn't possibly be a threat to national security. Damn it, I thought to myself, he could only make it rain. Then, after all of the information I have been able to get and see for myself, it's for that very reason that they killed him. So that no one could come to him and have him reveal anything he would be willing to say for the sake of a conversation about who he once was.

Clara, your grandfather reinvented life. For God's sake, he could make it rain. Not just rain, but he could control when and where he wanted it to. From acid rain to cold, wet water, he was a genius, and that's why he is dead. To them, he was a liability. Think of what, in the wrong hands, making it rain could do. Wipe away crops, flood certain areas, kill millions of people, make droughts, and starve millions of people. Then, if the company he worked for was crooked, which they are. He instantly becomes a liability to them, and I'm sorry about that, but at least you now have an answer as to the why of it all," finished the masked man, who was now sounding more sympathetic to their cause than any of the three of them had expected since he still wore the mask and held a gun pointed at them.

"Listen to this one more time," he said. "There is a certain group of men out there who lead the world. Make no mistake about it. One of the people in that group has said that it is better to kill off the many that are of no use to them. As they only take up needed space, they eat too much, and they provide nothing to society. So, killing them is nothing more than thinning the herd. What better way of thinning the herd than to drown them in these suddenly trying, desperate times, with the imbalance on the planet? The right to claim Global Warming for doing this. Taking away those things we all use daily. Just to hurray along the need for us to follow."

"You're right," chimed in an excited Jeff, "there is no imbalance. But as scientists ourselves, we have been asked to hedge the readings to show that global warming is happening now. That is one of the reasons that so many floods are happening, because of global warming. But what you are saying is a certain group of individuals who have control over the weather may be making life-and-death decisions by making the world think that it's the planet doing it," finished Jeff, who suddenly had a light go off in his head. It was as if he had just come to an agreement with this masked man.

He finally had an answer to something that had been bothering him for years. "Man could create and change the weather patterns on the planet, and this could easily be used for the purpose of thinning the herd. After all, look where most of the people who die from disasters such as floods live. Mostly in countries that produced nothing and are forever at war with one another. People that were just that, people. They produced nothing they could share with the world. Yet they seemed to need the most care, which came from dollars—hard-earned dollars from others. On the flip side, make it snow and have the price of oil so high that it would make them millions from demand. Huge snowstorms would occur in areas such as the middle and eastern coasts of America. Could this be the real truth behind global warming? They needed to use it as something to hide behind to keep control. To hide the truth. That is what this is about. Money and control?"

Then Clara asked him, "Who else is involved in this from Wetco?"

"Their original founder, a man named Bob Thurston. He is the guy who had me hired through a mutual contact. He's the man who paid for and recruited the original shooter. Their former CEO, COO, hell, your grandfather worked directly for him," said the masked man.

"Bob Thurston's hired henchman is Pete Winslow. According to my source, who has been right all along, Pete can be tied directly to the killing of Luke Weeks. He did it with his Ruger Mini-14, silenced."

Now Clara knew that he was for real. As no one knew the rifle or the caliber, or that the kill was silenced.

"Okay," said Jeff, "enough of this. Why doesn't Clara just call her office and have them pick these asses up and lock them away for good right now? Hell, let's just go shoot the bastards now on our own!" He was angry for a lot of reasons, but none of them knew what the main reason was. This company had been lying to the world for years about global warming. Exploiting the fears of those who had no real idea as to how this was taking place. Creating new industries that were found to bilk the government out of billions of dollars. He had seen enough and now had heard enough to make him want to explode.

"No. Not yet." said the masked man. "I need you to set up that meeting so I can get him to tell me where the shooter is. Without that information, all of us still remain a target. Either one of them could be next to knock on that door out front and make another kill. Do you want to be scared every time the doorbell rings? I can make him talk. I just need to get my hands on him."

"Listen to me," said Clara, now in full focus, "I can't be a part of or have knowledge of your killing someone, not by accident, or on purpose. I'm an FBI agent, and I worked too damn hard for that to be thrown away. I would need a guarantee that we take him in alive once your information is obtained, and I want a guarantee that when you go after that son of a bitch that killed Justin, I want in on it. I want to be there. I need to look him in the eyes. Right now, he is as good as dead according to the records, even if it wasn't his body in that grave."

"Okay, here's the play," said the masked man. "You are to contact me through Craigslist under Missed Connections. It has to read, tall, blond, and handsome at the corner drugstore yesterday. Then, go into the events section and list a party for two. Give me the date, the time, and the location, nothing more. Just that way, and it has to be on the same day, understood?"

"Consider it done," Jeff said. "Maybe tomorrow I can contact him and set this up. He usually gets right back to me."

"Great," said Juan, "now I need all three of you to get up and walk into the bathroom. I'm going to lock that door from the outside and leave. I need to make sure that I can trust you not to follow. Because I have no clue as to what you're all thinking right now, emotions could still get someone killed tonight. I don't want that. Believe me. I don't. I want the shooter, and after that, I'm on vacation."

With that, they peacefully walked into the bathroom, but before he could lock the door, he said to Clara, "It was hard sitting on your piece all night without shooting me, wasn't it?"

"At first, maybe." Clara told him, "But, now I need to trust someone, and right now, you are as good a person as anyone. However, if this is a charade to throw us off the track because it really was you who killed Justin, we'll meet again. I will come looking for you."

Turning, all three walked into the bathroom. Then she heard something being dragged and placed against the bathroom door. Now that they were locked in. That was good enough to convince her that maybe he was for real. Just maybe by the end of this week, she would dance on the grave of the person who killed her: Justin.

Multiple Deceptions

It was often said quietly, of course, that Pete Winslow never trusted his own mother, so why would he trust someone like you? However, Pete's men were known as the Blue Brigade. They were dedicated and loyal to the end, trustworthy, but most of all, intelligent. He only selected former AIA officers, couriers, and retired Army Rangers. His people, once given orders, understood the chain of command. They followed orders explicitly right to the end. Always dressed in jeans unless someone was told otherwise. On a stakeout, the rotation was always four up and off. No one was to be seen more than once in any given seventy-two-hour span.

That day, they, of course, were at Clara's house when the intruder knocked on the door, and her cousin's face was stuck with fear as she backed into the house. That's why, when the call came late on that Monday to say that the Osbornes wanted a meeting, Pete knew then that a rat was under the covers. His rat had made that house call. It was the one that got away once, but it wouldn't happen again, not this time. This time, the rat would pay with his life, along with the other two, and hopefully, he could convince them to bring a guest. Pete also knew that it was over as well. Someone had made him, and even if in hiding, no one had been able to find him. They now knew of him. That he was sure of, but he was smarter than any trap that could be laid for him, especially by these idiots.

Pete often dreamed about having a shootout, killing as many as he could before that lucky bullet with his name on it found him. And until then, just how many could he kill? he wondered. He knew that in making this last stand, it had to be perfect, absolutely perfect, for him to take the corporate jet and go to a place he had, a place that not even Bob knew existed.

Juan had been casing out Clara's place for about a week and had easily picked up on the surveillance taking place on her house. At first, he thought it was the FBI. This group too often used an old signaling form of communication with each other. One that he had learned a long time ago, almost in another lifetime. The only alternative was to follow one back to the nest and see where it led him. Of course, it came as no surprise when it led back to a safe house, a building owned by no other than Wetco. They would give someone a report on the activity that had taken place during their shift. Now, no matter what Juan did, someone would have a set of eyes on him, which made this all the better, he thought. It would play right into his hands. Set up a fake meeting and get the rabbit out of the hole. Even if he surrounded himself with a hundred men, Juan wouldn't miss his mark. He had one other play he had to make. He needed to bring someone else into the game to make it that much more interesting. Then, when he made his grab and go, the confusion in the area would allow him a quick escape, and Winslow would finally be his.

Luther was asleep once again; it seemed that all he ever did anymore was sleep. The funeral for Ulmmer was horrific. His best friend and confidant was no longer alive. There was no one around to cheer him up. His wife and the girls had gone back to Germany for good to be near the grave of her husband and the children's father.

Mable was becoming slightly coherent now of her surroundings. The doctors say, "It's only a matter of time before she comes around. It seems that she is stuck on fear right now, and she is suffering from such massive anxiety about the shooting that she is confused, but she's mending." Luther couldn't even remember the diagnostic name for the damn symptom. He began to wonder if she would ever be the same lively, beautiful, educated woman he had fallen in love with or just a vegetable. He could live with lively, beautiful, smart, just not a vegetable, and that's another reason why he stayed in his bed so much.

Just as he was drifting into the place of his security, where he was free once again and safe from his business, he felt the hand go over his mouth. It tightened like a vice. Luther knew that today he wouldn't get any sleep but the long sleep of death unless he made an attempt to get free.

"Don't try it, Luther. Move a muscle, and I'll cut you open like a mackerel, understood? If so, just nod your head. After all, I've come here to bring you the best news of your life. I'm gonna give you the shooter. You know, the one that I put two slugs into on that first night you two met," said the masked man.

Luther suddenly relaxed his whole body, lying on the bed as if it were a part of him. But Juan knew that a man of his caliber could strike out from any position and make this harder than it needed to be. So, Juan took his knife and placed it gently across Luther's chest, the slicing edge facing just an inch from his neck. Then, with his left hand, he showed Luther his pistol and spoke.

"Okay, we play nice in the pen this evening, Luther, and everything you wanted to know about Lars is my gift to you. When I'm done, I leave, and you'll be on your own. Are we clear on this? If so, just nod, not too vigorously, no sense in slicing your own throat now, is there? If I wanted you dead, Luther, we wouldn't be having this conversation now, would we?" Now finished speaking, the masked man moved to the foot of the bed, looking down on Luther with a gun pointed right at his chest.

"It seems a man can't get any needed sleep anymore. Even in his own bed," replied Luther, sitting up now. "You do know that I have a nine-millimeter pointed right at you, don't you?" he said, smiling now at the masked man. "Why the mask, may I ask?"

"Just for precautions, if I had to kill you tonight, no sense in letting everyone see who it was now, is there?" replied Juan.

"If you truly bear me good news, then no one would be shot. I would think," Luther said, smiling, "especially if you have news that I am really interested in. For that, my newly found friend, I would pay you handsomely."

"Seems as if lately everyone wants to make me rich when all I really want now is a vacation," said the masked man. "But let's say this: you sit up in bed like a nice boy and put that gun away. I'll take off my mask and formally introduce myself to you, and of course, put my gun away as well. I'm going to tell you a long but extremely interesting story—especially the end. There is no need to clap or cheer at the end, although the smacking of the lips will be perfectly fine. So, deal or no deal, do we shoot it out right here and now, and may the quickest finger win? Oh, by the way, when it all goes down, I need you and a lot of your men to be there, on my side, to help me settle my own score, deal?"

Luther now had no reason not to trust the man. Hell, he had so many new bullet holes in him now that one or two more at the end of his story wouldn't matter anyway. "Deal," he said.

Taking off the mask and sitting down in a chair placed across from the bed, Juan began to tell his tale. At the end of it when he said that he could bring Lars Günter Mallern out of hiding and that he had the names of the men involved in the hiring of him, and one would be there, Luther was beside himself.

"Friend, if what you have told me is true, may the light of God shine down on you forever. If I wasn't in this damn bed, I'd give you a hug," he shouted.

"Well, let's just settle with making my plan come true so we can all get some sleep. Me? All I want now is to go on a nice, long, warm vacation," said Juan.

Disclosure

Clara had some doubts about what they had just heard, even after they got out of the bathroom alive. She expressed this to Tully and Jeff.

"It all sounds great, and it even sounds as if he told us the truth; how do we really know that we can trust him?" she asked them.

"Clara," said Jeff, "Look, it wasn't my grandparents, nor was it my future husband, but somehow, someone had to come forward and confess. If not to confess, then I really believe that it all would have been found out eventually, and maybe just as he told it to us tonight. So, do we turn our backs on this new information, or do we act on it? Me? I say act on it. What do you think, Tull?"

"I agree with Jeff, Cacky. This guy made a lot of sense, and he even knows that Pete Winslow is involved in all of this. I can't imagine ever tying him to the deaths of Grandma and Grandpa. How could we ever have done that without his help? So, I have to say yes, make the call, and let's get this guy and everyone else involved. If we can help make it come true, then let's go for it, please, Cacky."

"Okay," said Clara, "I'm in. But I have to ask Brad what he thinks, and whatever it is, we go by that. There is no way that the two of you can become involved in this. If something were to happen to either one of you, it would devastate this family. Not to mention that I wouldn't be right in the head from something happening to one of you because of me. Are we clear on that, and please say yes."

After that initial conversation, they called Brad, and hearing that Clara needed him to come over as soon as he could, he couldn't get there fast enough.

"What!" Brad yelled. "Someone just came to the door, then held a gun to Tully's head and threatened all of you. Then he told you this cockamamie story, and now you all believe him. You what now, want to help him catch the killers, and you don't want to tell John about this? Am I really hearing you right, Clara? Forget coming back to a unit that has put in tons of man-hours searching for leads to this. Forget the additional men now here, men I keep stepping over who are in the office, trying to find Justin's killer. Fine, fine, forget all of that, but you forget ever coming back to that office. Geez, Clara, please try to make some sense out of this.

How can I go along with putting you and these two in harm's way just so you can get some kind of revenge? Don't even look at me and pretend it isn't for that because I know it is. You've changed. And I can't be a part of your revenge. I want the bastards to all fry. Hell, I'll even pull the damn lever, but I cannot see you pissing away everything you worked so hard for. Clara, this was Justin's life. He absolutely reveled in his being an agent, and you're willing to throw that all away because you want revenge? Sorry, you have to count me out on this one. I'll wait a day or two until all your secret arrangements are made on this. But then I have to go to John. God forbid it's all a ruse. Then what? I'm going to tell John I knew this was going to happen. I told you so, but you wouldn't listen. Shit, I might as well join the foreign legion right there and then, but I don't think that they would even want me." He was standing with his hands on his hips, with a scowl on his face.

Clara now had her head down, ashamed for even thinking about besmirching what Justin had indeed come to love so much. Brad was right, of course. What right did she have to not have the very thing Justin was a part of? His beloved FBI. If this was not finished in the way it should have been. Her not asking for their help wasn't very smart on her part.

"Brad," she said, "listen, I am truly sorry. It was just that this night started out with having a pizza and settling down to watch a movie, then all hell broke loose, and I got carried away. Monday morning, I'll call John before we contact this Pete Winslow. You can come with Jeff, Tully, and me to his office, and we can tell him everything. I'm sorry, you're right. Revenge is my motive right now, and I can't tell you that it'll ever go away. Because if I do get this guy alone, I will accidentally, on purpose, probably shoot the bastard. I know that in the bottom of my heart, and I can't let go of it."

Tully moved to give her best friend and cousin a hug. This night had been hard on all of them, but she had even seen the glossy look that came over Clara's eyes when the masked man said he could produce Justin's killer for them. The whole purpose behind all of this was getting Justin's killer to come out and pay for his sin.

"Okay," said Brad. Now that he had accomplished what he wanted, suddenly, there wasn't as much tension in the room. Looking around, he said, "Any more of that pizza around? I'm hungry now, and is there any time for that movie left on this crazy night?"

John was beside himself. What the hell was going on under his command? No agent in their right mind would keep this kind of information from him over the weekend because they thought he needed the weekend to rest.

"For God's sake, what in the hell were you people thinking about!" he yelled. "I'm your group commander, aren't I, or have I been unknowingly replaced by stupidity? I told you two, ANYTHING AT ALL concerning this case was to be reported to me immediately! I don't care if you make that call at three in the morning and I'm having a great time with Beth, I don't care," he yelled once again so that the whole building seemed to shake.

"The last time you and Justin held back information until after the weekend bullshit, I thought I made myself perfectly clear then that I didn't want it to happen again!" Going behind his desk, he placed his head in both hands and just silently sat there, shaking his head back and forth. Then, in a twenty-octave lower voice, he said, "Clara, we could have gotten information from this guy, we could have gone for footage from any cameras in place, we could have possibly found out who this masked marvel was. Clara, you know our protocol. How could you have slipped up so badly? How?" he asked her.

"John, please, I was upset; it was all my fault. Every decision was made by me. If we needed as a family to bring this to a close, then I felt that the way it was handled and done was going to be acceptable to you, again, my fault. I just haven't been the same lately. But I really think that this will all come to fruition. The man was real, and his story is believable, really convincing. That's why it turned out this way."

John then stood up and said to Clara as he pointed toward the two people sitting and waiting outside his door, "Okay, bring in the other two who, by now, have had to hear me yell, but at this point, so what? I want them here to add or change things as they heard it as we go over everything."

Going to the door, Clara tapped lightly on the window with her knuckle, and when Tully turned around and looked at her, she waved to them to come inside. Not that either one of them wanted to after hearing John yell so much.

Jeez, Tully was thinking, I'm glad I don't have to work for that guy.

"Hello, Tully, hello, Jeff. Is there ever going to be better circumstances for us to meet? After all of this is over, I'll have everyone over for my favorite dish, spaghetti and Beth's meatballs. Until then, sit, and I want to hear everything just as you've seen it and heard it. I'm going to tape all of it as well. You guys have any problems with that?" he asked them. After all of the yelling that just ended, neither one wanted to get into any heated discussions concerning a tape recorder, that was for sure.

"No, I think we're both fine, right, Tull?" Jeff asked her.

"Sure, that's fine by me. Maybe we can get a copy, and later, we can listen to it and see if we missed something or overstated something," she asked.

Now smiling, John said to her, "Jeff was right. You do have a knack for making sure that all your i's are dotted. Okay, so why don't you begin, seeing how when you answered the door, it was a gun pointed in your face that started all of this?"

After all, three had a chance to recall everything they could and then fell to answering some questions by John, and by then, the day was almost over at that point. The only thing left to do was make the call to Pete Winslow and have him take it from there. If, in fact, Pete was involved, and so was H.T. Wetco, then this would all play out. If Pete had no idea or inkling of any of this, then the masked marvel would have to be found. That was now something that irked John to have been so close, and now they were back to square one.

John had been given a team of twenty agents who had now been assigned to the task of ending this hunt for the killer. A killer who had shot and killed the FBI agent in charge, Justin Beach. With evidence, this same shooter killed Agent Clara Beach's grandparents. He also then shot and wounded a senator's top aide, who remains in the hospital to this day. He is also responsible for killing a German agent at the same time as shooting a German embassy official in Washington, DC. Finally, killing an innocent woman who was with a worker of Senator Pillow. Well, this made the hunt for this shooter an even more important case. To be solved than any they had in their current books. This was not only personal but also a slap in their face, and a hard one at that. The only evidence that they had to date was bullets pried from the wounded or dead and a now-known grave site that did not hold a killer. Wanted for years by Interpol, who may now be illegally in the United States, killing FBI agents. Yes, he had been assigned twenty agents, but he often left the office late at night, thinking that maybe he didn't have enough.

"Everyone, settle down, settle down," called out Brad, who was now the lead on this case since Justin had passed on.

"Listen up. I would like all of you to take notes and write down your questions so that we can have a question-and-answer period at the end of this session. I have with us here, as some of you may know her, Agent Clara Beach. What you are about to hear is her explanation of a visit she had on Friday evening. The sixteenth of this month at approximately six-thirty at her home address. Present with her was Mrs. Tully Osborne and her husband, Jeff. They are also cousins to Clara, or our Agent Beach. Now that you know that, please do not ask me who is also talking on the tape."

A few laughs could be heard, which he used to settle down the agents around the table. While overhead speakers played, the session began. "FYI, people, this is the voice of Mrs. Osborne, known as Tull or Tully," said Brad. Hearing that the recording had stopped, he said, "Okay, please continue the recording." Then, after everyone had listened to what had transpired on that evening, some sat back in amazement.

To think there was a possibility that one of the largest DOD contractors in the nation could be involved in double murders as well as outright clandestine activity that could have resulted in the deaths of millions of innocent people around the world. The Chinese government was now privy to this as well and was actually using it. It had been used in the Vietnam War, which was called Operation Popeye, as well as during the Korean War. How it was used to clean up the Dust Bowl states, and with certain people having such privileged information and significant investment money, they brought up large parcels of land in those states, making them all wealthy beyond belief. That a group that the FBI had known about since its beginning, the Bilderberg group, may have ties to this as well. It was unbelievable that certain presidents of the United States, from Curter to Omama, had supposedly met with these people.

Imagine making the weather change to suit your corporate needs. For some, this was just too Orwellian, to say the least. Is this how they made global warming seem real? Hiding behind snows unheard of or rains unprecedented? Using both to destroy crops and people's lives. Now, are they making the cost of oil skyrocket out of control as our government sits back, not uttering a word about this? It was wholly unimaginable to some.

But the killings had started, and for some reason, the main person behind all of this was a scientist who made this all happen. His granddaughter was FBI agent Clara Beach. Her Grandfather, Frank Beach, was murdered by a man who was thought to have been dead and buried in Bremerhaven, Germany. It just made this whole thing incredible, to say the least. But their job as a whole had nothing to do with the whys of it all. It had to do with the end results of some of the actions taken by the people involved in this. They knew that murder was still against the laws of this country. For those who murder in cold blood an officer of their special community, well, it was something that someone had to pay for. Police killers are always the number one priority of any department that loses an officer that way. This is and will always be an unwritten code that they want to live by. If global warming is influenced by politics, then so be it. If Justin was murdered to keep that ongoing, then they will enjoy closing this down.

The Ending Is Always Near

Juan read the message on Craigslist three days ago. Today was that scheduled meeting. It was to take place at a restaurant he was familiar with, named The Upper Room. It was located on the second floor of a building in downtown Alexandria. The restaurant had no real exposure. Not as much as he would have wanted. He would have preferred a nice, open-air dining experience. He laughed to himself. But nonetheless, this was also accessible to him for what he needed to do tonight. Relaxing into the chair, he lifted his cup of coffee off the side table and sat back to examine his play so far. He had already contacted Luther and given him all the pertinent information regarding tonight's scheduled dinner. Yet again, the man couldn't stop talking about how he was going to make him wealthy and/or pay for his much-needed vacation when this was over. Right now, he also had in motion Clara and her cousins, and as suspected, she also brought in the FBI contingent working on this case. Juan knew all along that was exactly what he needed to have happen. With a smile on his face and seemingly still a little tired, he slumped into his favorite chair to get a few more minutes of relaxation when the motion sensor alarm went off. Now, who in the hell could that be? He asked himself. Going into the standing cupboard, he moved a lever on the side, and the little back wall opened, allowing him access to his office.

There, he looked into the video monitor where he could view the two men who were now approaching his back door. Great blue jeans, he thought. He had to be slipping a little. He knew they were there, yet he didn't avoid them. That's okay. He would open a lowering door, placing him into a private section of the basement, where he would take care of business and be done with these two. Or just let them search and not find him at home. But they had to know he was still there. They must know that he hadn't left yet if they had staked out his place all night. Juan then thought, let them become nervous and leave. And when they went out to keep a watch on his home, he would just come up from behind them and finish it all outside. Great idea, he thought. That way, he wouldn't have to clean up the mess it was sure to make. They were good, he had to admit.

They came into his home quickly, quietly, and ready, but when they found nothing, that's when they both knew they could possibly lose this battle. They knew he was here, now at home, which meant that he must have been forewarned of their coming. It meant they had just become the prey. Damn it, thought Reynold Brice. Brice, who was the lead and a former Ranger, retired, knew he had to vacate the house immediately. He now remembered that Pete had said to be careful. He said this mark was good. Now, he may pay for his stupidity for not paying that statement more attention. Motioning quickly to his partner, they both went to the back door and exited the house. They would go to the car and make it known that he was hiding. Holed up somewhere in the home. When asking what to do next, they would probably be told to just maintain vigilance in the home. Take him on exiting if possible, and if not, follow discreetly behind, and at the first available chance, take the markdown.

What they didn't know was that Juan owned the home next door as well. A connection existed between both cellars. From one private room to another, making any emergency exit was very easy. As a matter of fact, Juan was already outside behind the car and was waiting for them to enter it. There, he would eliminate them both and leave them sleeping in the car. As both men approached the auto, Juan had a lead to an invisible dog leash in his hand while standing behind a large Dutch elm tree that blocked their view of not only the invisible dog but also of him. Right after they entered and sat down, the driver of the car opened a flip phone and was at the beginning of dialing. When the first bullet took him behind the head, exiting out his front right eye. The next bullet took the passenger directly in the throat, exiting into the seat. Firing one more shot into the both of them, Juan continued to whistle as he walked down the street.

He knew they would come looking for these men sooner or later, so going back to his home was out of the question. Juan called his cleaning crew to make this all disappear.

"Larry, it's me. I need you. I was hoping you could make that pickup at the dealership as soon as possible. Lois and I are going out tonight, and I'm sure that it would cause commotion if her sister goes by there and sees her Buick LeSabre just sitting there. It's her red one. The hard top convertible. The damn thing is brand new. So, enjoy it, will you? Thanks, Larry."

"Thanks, pal. I'll be around to settle my bill with you," came from a voice on the other end of the phone. With that done, he sat back in his favorite chair and waited. Not fifteen minutes had elapsed when a wrecker pulled up to the car—covering it so it wouldn't be damaged on the ride back to the barn. After carefully hitching it to his hook, off they went, with the now-attached red taillights blinking as he pulled away from the curb to tell people that a vehicle was being towed to try not to run into it. What a way to start this day, he thought. Juan hadn't even finished his second cup of coffee yet. But now things had changed slightly. It would now seem that Winslow knew that he was behind this meeting. Why else would he pick this very day to have him marked and eliminated? If he didn't know?

If Winslow had the location of his final hiding place since he had left Clara's house, why wait to use that information? Why wait unless it was to send a message that said, "I'm sorry you're missing the action tonight. They'll meet you in heaven or hell, but tonight, you'll not be alone."

So, the game's ending was finally on, and Juan was suddenly glad that, in one way or another, it would finally be over very soon. With that in mind, he made a phone call to General Margate to let him know that the end game was in play, finally.

Clara was not allowed to go near the restaurant, no matter what.

John declared now more than once to her. "I don't care what you do, Clara, but tonight you're in the wagon. Not outside, definitely not in the restaurant, and you'll not have a weapon on you. You're not cleared yet for return, so at the office or in the wagon. Those are your only two choices."

Clara desperately needed to convince him that she should accommodate Jeff and Tully. "My God," she said, "what if something dangerous should happen to them? I could never forgive myself. Never, please, John. I'll go as a cook or a waiter in the back room," she again pleaded to no avail.

"No," said John, "and that's the end of it. In fact, they'll both be wired. Since it's a meeting just to talk business, he shouldn't suspect them of anything. Except for playing hardball about changing information on snakes or whatever, he'll ask them to do. So, you can monitor their entire conversation from the wagon. But that's it. You'll be secured in the wagon, and you'll know everything going on in there. That's the best I can do, Clara. Take it or go back to the office."

Clara knew that John had said his last words on this subject, so she would let it rest until later, perhaps when she could possibly plead a little more to be a part of the team working in there tonight. No one from the restaurant's actual working staff would be in there working tonight. As they showed up for work, each would be escorted into waiting limos parked outside of public view. From there, they would all be escorted, minus their cell phones, to a nice little private area where contacting anyone about what was going on in there tonight would become impossible for them. Aside from Mr. Winslow's private table for four, the rest of tonight's diners would be FBI agents.

Anyone coming or going into that restaurant tonight was not coming away with a happy meal, that was for sure.

Luther knew that unless Lars had made severe changes to his face, everyone on the street had his face imprinted into their brain. There was no way that anyone who even matched his last-known height and weight was going to go unnoticed tonight. Luther had maintained the strictest control on the information concerning tonight. After all, he still wasn't sure that this man, Juan, had told him everything. It could also be someone in his own embassy who could be tipping off this maniac for who knows how much blood money. Money, Luther realized, was the color green, even if blood stained it red for some, so what? Many a person took and spent red money. So, he only trusted his own team with the information at first. But his need for more men forced him to bring in some specialists, and they had to know what they were looking for. So, right now, he was just a little on edge.

Sitting in the van and seeing all of the FBI action going on, he wondered if Lars had already picked up on this and decided to make a move on some other night. He could only hope that the man was still a braggart and still a little psychotic. If so, he would see him tonight, no matter how many stood in his way. Due to local protocol, he had notified the FBI that he and his men would be on-site tonight. As he was told to stand down, his reply became a little insolent, well, maybe, especially when he said, "If they grabbed Lars first, he would be taken to the German embassy for questioning, good old-fashioned German questioning. Besides, isn't he supposed to be dead already?" before hanging up the phone.

No matter what happened or how it happened, Luther needed this to happen tonight. He needed to put an end to this horrific feeling that Mable may be slipping away from him before he had his chance to show her off to his mom.

Juan had to smile to himself, standing outside the Wetco safe house, watching the blue jeans crew, as he now referred to them, as coming and going. However, in the last hour or so, they began filling up the building as if they were planning a raid on Somalia. Juan had been thinking that these couldn't all be mercenaries. Hell, they just couldn't be. Some had to be outright hired Americans or even ex-servicemen. He didn't think they had any idea of what people they were preparing for tonight. He wondered if they knew about the killing of an American FBI agent. Possibly, tonight, they could be smart enough to see what was in front of them and walk away. The FBI only wanted their boss tonight. Not the possible death and destruction on the scale of what they seemed to be gearing up for.

Juan's plan from the beginning was to make sure that everyone knew of the meeting. There was hope after he had first discovered that these "blue jeans" characters actually had a staging place. This is the place that Pete Winslow would leave from tonight to make that meeting. Juan also knew that Pete was smart. Smart enough not to take a meeting in such a place where anything was possible. If he had been marked as a shooter in any of this, then he wasn't safe there, public restaurant or not, now that he knew.

So, if it were me, Juan thought, I'd take a limo, pick up my quarry, and take them somewhere else. I'd give myself some time and set up a diversion along the way to ensure my privacy wasn't disturbed.

Just as he finished that thought, his dream seemed to appear right in front of him as it pulled up and sat idling by the back of the building. Juan then walked out along the front side of the staging building. There, he continued to walk directly up to the limo and tapped on the driver's side window. Then, as the window was lowered, Juan spoke, "Open the door on the other side and let me in," just with enough force to make it sound as if he had the authority to make that happen. As Juan walked to the other side of the limo, expecting it to happen, he could hear the lock being released as it clicked up into place. Juan slid into the limo and leaned forward to distract the driver's attention away from the gun that now poked him in his side.

"Listen to me and listen carefully. I need to know who you are right now. I want your bio in ten seconds, or tonight is your final night on this planet," Juan said in an almost hypnotic whisper loud enough for the man to start talking immediately.

"Please, I'm a retired cop. I have eight grandchildren and a wife. Listen, I was hired because I make my living as a limo driver now. I want no trouble, mister. I was told this job involved working for a company that performed sensitive operations for Homeland Security. With my background, they could use me. All I had to do was drive Mr. Winslow around or some other officials. That's all, and should anyone ever try to stop us, I would drive over them no matter what, or we all could be dead. So, I agreed, and the money has been great. But I'm out of here right now. Just say the word, and I'll walk away right now. Hell, take the car, do what you want with it."

"I'm gonna say this once, understand? I am going to kill you tonight in that very seat if you so much as make one mistake. Did I say that clearly enough for you? I am with the Department of Defense. I work for the real Homeland Security agency. I'm reaching into my coat pocket to show you my credentials. So, make any move except to read it, and I shoot," finished Juan, as he reached into his jacket and showed this man his credentials.

"Am I breaking the law? Has all of this just been a ruse? Listen, I served for 20 years in the army and I defended my country in three actions. I don't need to be involved in any bullshit against my own friggen' country," he said almost in anger and in the hopes that the man holding a gun at his side would believe him. He desperately needed that. Shit, tomorrow was his granddaughter Megan's seventh birthday, and he had a pony coming to take her friends for rides.

"What do you want from me? Whatever it is, I'm in. Want me to walk? Just say so, and I'm out of here right now. Want the car? Just tell me, and I'll catch a cab home. If you need me to stick around, I will. But tell me, what the hell is going on?" he pleaded.

"I need to know who your passenger is tonight. Who are you here for?" Juan asked.

"Why, Mr. Winslow, of course," he replied. "I wait here until his car shows up, he gets out, and then gets directly in here. From then on, I'm told where to go. If we need to stop to pick up any other passengers, he tells me where to go. Once in a while, he picks up some hookers or the same old man. Lately, he just rides around talking to himself. My job is to ensure we never have to stop for gas, to keep my eyes forward and my ears closed, and to keep the liquor cabinet in the back stocked with brandy. So, I do, and for that, I make a lot of extra money, and I ask no questions. I'm also an ex-police officer from the Washington Metro. Sort of double dipping on the retirement. But with four boys to raise, I needed the work and food money, school money."

"Quiet," said Juan, "I've heard enough; now listen up. Right now, you are to work for me. Let's say you're back on a real government payroll now. I need to know that you're being honest with me. I need to know that I can trust you, can I?" asked Juan.

"Yes, yes, definitely, one thing I'm not is a traitor to my country!" Now aggravated, the driver, staring very hard at Juan, said, "Listen, man, it's no problem."

"Good, then sit up for a second, will you?" asked Juan. As the driver sat up, looking at what was now in Juan's hands, he jumped in his seat, thinking that maybe Juan was going to hurt him somehow.

But Juan simply placed what looked to be an envelope under the man and sternly said. "Sit."

"Now look at this ring on my right hand. Kind of funny looking. Well, it's not a ring; it's a frequency detonator. See, within twenty-five yards, all I need to do is hit this button on the top, this one here." Juan pointed to what now looked like a small shirt button." See, that's the one I'm talking about. Then, boom, your ass gets torn into several new pieces. By the way, you're sitting on a nice slice of C4. You know what that is, right? Now let's see, I have your word that you're going to help me, and a promise from you to be on my side. And now I'm betting your ass that you do mean what you say," said Juan. Looking at the man with a big grin on his face.

"Oh, by the way, I'm going to get out of the car right now and place several more under the backseats. If you as much as move a muscle, I will put a bullet into the back of your head. Call it a night and come up with another plan to stop your boss. So, open the back door and be a good boy, will you?"

Juan stepped out of the limo and placed two charges under the seats in the back, making sure that a little tape made them unnoticeable to anyone getting into the car. Returning back to his front seat, Juan said, "By the way, what's your name?"

"Jake, Jake Cartucia," Jake said.

"Okay, Jake, here's how it's going to go. You introduce me as your brother-in-law when Winslow gets into the car. You have had bad diarrhea all day long, and just now, it seems to be coming under control, but you didn't want to take any chances tonight. You didn't want any problems for him, understand? So, you decided that you would bring me along because no matter what, I could be trusted. I wasn't always, let's say, a good old boy. I've had some troubled spots in my life, but nothing bad. So, you do use me when and only when it is necessary. Got that, Jake?" Juan asked him.

"Then tell him that if this isn't okay with him, then you'll drop me off right down the street, and I can drive home. See, all I need is five minutes with him. You're going to buy me five minutes, Jake. Winslow knows me and has met me. Except this time, I'm different. I have a new face on, he'll never know it's me. One of the reasons why it'll be so easy to kill you right now and walk away from all of this is that if someone sees me walking away laughing, they'll give the police a bad description, Jake. So, you're in a bad spot, I'd say. So, you need to trust me on this."

Pete Winslow was running a little late tonight. He had not heard back from those two misfits he had sent out to take care of the pain in the ass. By now, they should have had the job done and returned to the "nest," as he liked to refer to his meeting place. Pete liked the fact that all of his Blue Birds left and came back to his nest. Instead of carrying food back for the chicks, they carried information back to him. Information that he was missing right now, and that pissed him off. He knew that both of them were more than capable enough of doing the job quickly and quietly. Now he had to wonder if something happened to them, as if they were caught in the act or after it. Or maybe he had a girlfriend there with him, and right now, those two idiots were having too much fun to leave. Whatever the problem, he'll settle it later.

Earlier he had called Günter to tell him that tonight it was over. "Go back to whatever place it is that people like you go to and have a great life. What makes it over is that tonight, at precisely eight o'clock in the evening, go into a restaurant called The Upper Room in Alexandria, find me, and place a bullet into my left upper arm. Make sure it's my left; I'm right-handed. Then, shoot and kill the people at my table. Walk out and go home. Just make sure that it is in my upper left arm. Should something go wrong and you can't shoot straight, I have a backup plan in place. So, unless you want to shoot everyone in the restaurant, aim straight."

With that, he hung up the phone and laughed quietly to himself, seeing how the only people there tonight more than likely, would be the Germans and the FBI. After all, he had leaked information weeks earlier that this was the killer that they all had been looking for. This ghost seemingly arose from the dead, all the while living in Russia. Now, all he had to do was get to his nest, get into his limo, and take off. Call these two and tell them that he will be picking them up. Then, without saying a word, make the change in the itinerary. Once he had them, he would then let them know instead of going to Alexandria. He would be driving to another "better" restaurant, more local. Besides, some of the best food can be found in Washington, DC. After all, it is the nation's capital.

Of course, someone would be following them, but as smart as he is, he already had the tail covered. He would take a route that some of his men were stationed on all day, and they would block anyone's path who followed. They had been in place repairing a gas leak in the front of one of the H. T. Wetco office buildings. Ah, it's so nice to plan ahead, he thought.

Günter's Revenge

Günter had been bored out of his mind at first. The edge only started to come off in the last two weeks, seeing how he was meeting so many hookers. He had no idea that this area was loaded with working girls. He found himself becoming very fond of the big black women. He was always up for games and toys, even a little pain, and he liked that. Günter may have found one, and he would consider giving her the title of the best in the world. She gave great pain, and she loved taking it. The nastier he was, the more she found a way to become so much more, and that was what he liked the most about her.

But the phone call had come to him about four weeks ago. Telling him that they were digging up his grave. He knew this would be very bad for his private side of life. Now, the world would know he wasn't buried there. However, it was okay because he would return to Istanbul and, from there, go to Argentina, where there were lots of Germans living. But what still bothered him was someone had sold him out. That person would curse his own mother for birthing him.

Günter wasn't surprised when he read in the paper two weeks later that, once again, two German officials had been shot. One was dead, and one was still alive. Both were found at the same hospital he had visited. The lucky one had been the one he wounded the night he knifed the girl. After calling his contact in the Russian embassy, he wasn't startled to find out that his calling card was left behind to convince someone that it was he who had been the shooter. Not only was it left, but also when he shot the FBI agent on his doorstep that very day. When he tossed one down on the man, that meant it could only be one person who was trying to frame him. Tonight, his shot would not be in that man's upper left arm.

Trust was something Günter never gave out, not at all. He had picked up the tails on him right from the beginning. These men were like amateurs, he thought. Why did they all dress alike in blue jeans, idiots? At first, he thought of killing one or two, and then they would get the message. But instead, he decided that it was time he took the offense and brought the fight home to them.

It meant that Günter would have to leave his beloved crazy chick's house early one night. He would exit through her back window, slide down a ledge onto a roof to make his way around to the side. The far side of the house. There, he would wait all night, if necessary, to follow one or both of these men back to where they went. It would be only a matter of time before he would find the location of the rest of these people. His handler had to be a micromanager, he thought. The guy had no imagination. It all had to be by the book, including his trying to set himself up. Only an idiot would put someone up in a hotel after he was paid such a large sum of contract money.

Just to wait for more names? Hell, let me kill those on my list now, and I can come back for the others. In his business, unless a contract is canceled by having all parties completely agree on it, the first one stands in place until the job is completed.

Günter had been told it was what now happened. Okay, but where was his money? Only his original monies were placed in his bank account months ago. It now became evident that he was the man to be tagged. But before that, he would find their location and put a stop to all of this. Günter knew a place had to exist. This guy was ex-military, and he needed his chain of command so he could always be in charge. Just more stupidity, he thought. Günter was glad of that, actually. Seeing how it was that fact, he depended on these guys to lead him right back to their mother hen. A place Günter would need to be to make it all go away. Then, he could finish out the original contract and go south. So, when the call came, he was a very happy man.

Killing the girl wasn't fun, as she had this bright smile on her face until she realized that it would be her last. But she was a great whore, one of the best. However, Günter did not need to leave someone behind who could talk about him later with all the play now set. Günter went hunting.

The restaurant was teeming with people coming in and out, just as any night. So tonight could not look any different, and it didn't. Luther and his men covered every outside avenue. And not so much as a mouse would go undetected on this night. Everyone wanted a piece of this action. That's why Clara thought that this was a little over the top in the anxiety and stress level everyone was rising to. But death waited for no one, and it never seemed to step aside to wait for those it followed. She knew that tonight, she and everyone here had to be on top of their game, or death could come knocking.

Excitement and nervousness filled her stomach tonight. But it seemed that another part had been added. Time. It was going slow more slowly than she had ever imagined it could. It was all she could think of. Sitting there in that wagon was when—when—when is this finally going to happen? Clara knew that if she texted John one more time, he would probably burst into the van and fire her on the spot. It was just that this was taking so long to happen from her perspective while sitting here in this damn van.

Luther was becoming annoyed at the fact that there happened to be a lot of movement on the streets tonight, but no Lars and he was fast becoming frustrated as all hell. He was sure that Lars would at least stake out everything before he would act. Luther himself had been here almost as much as the street signpost, every day casing the place and making sure that he and his men would have every inch covered. Nothing could get in or out of his circle tonight. Not without his knowing about it.

John waited with the phone in his hand. Sure, Clara would call him one more time about the possibility of her coming into the restaurant tonight. But when it didn't ring, John thought that maybe, just maybe, she had finally accepted his answer from his last conversation with her. Finally, he thought.

Then, turning and looking at the sitting and milling around agents, he said, "Listen up, people, we are now going to have the Osbornes place that call. So go through it all once again and make this place sound as if they're making some money tonight. Jeff, Tully, let's go make that call now." Turning and walking down the stairs and into a back office, John closed the door and asked, "Everything up and ready, I assume?"

"Yes, sir," said a smiling female tech wearing headphones. The room was wired to record the entire conversation and it would be used as evidence in the case against this Pete Winslow, their leading suspect right now. "Great, okay, people, listen up, we're about to begin, need to sneeze, pass gas, giggle, go outside right now. Otherwise, go ahead, Jeff, place the call." As Jeff dialed the number on his cell phone, John asked, "Is this coming through, Penny?"

"Yes, sir," she replied, stating the date and time of the call for the record as she continued to listen to the ringing.

"Hello," was the answer. "Jeff?" "Hi, Jeff. I am so glad you called. I was getting a little worried there. I thought that maybe you had forgotten about our meeting tonight?" Pete said into the phone.

"No, not at all, Mr. Winslow," replied Jeff.

"Good, good," said Pete on the other end of the phone. Then he said, "Listen, Jeff, I have had to make a slight change in plans, unfortunately. I have to fly out to England tonight. I need to make an afternoon appointment there for the company. It seems as if some discussions on global warming have led to this emergent meeting of the minds, so to speak. Why, I was so glad that you are reconsidering your position on our last conversation."

Jeff could almost see the man smiling now as if he had something to do with the Washington National Zoo having to let them go due to a lack of funding. This, of all times, came right after the San Diego Zoo had called and cited the same reasons.

"Well, we're already here in Alexandria. We just decided at the last minute to drive down and take in the town, have a light lunch, and meet you here this evening," said Jeff, who was now looking up at John. Raising his hand toward John as if to say, "What now, help?"

John just rolled both hands, indicating that he should continue to speak to Pete and make him come here.

"Mr. Winslow," said Jeff, "it would be so much easier for us if you came here tonight. I know it's out of your way right now because of the change in your circumstances, but Tully is sitting here with a lime margarita in her hand." There was a slight extended silence on the other end of the phone as if he was silently cursing both of them.

"How about this, Jeff, I drive down to pick both of you up. We can go to dinner, have our conversation, and then my limo driver can bring me to the plane. From there on, the limo is yours. You can have him drive you back to your car or to wherever you both care to go. I would like to cancel this, but I urgently need to discuss some matters concerning tomorrow's meeting in London. Certain things have come up and I need you and Tully to really set me on the right track. You know the company has always valued your opinions, Jeff, as well as we do pay a lot more than zoos," he finished.

"Okay, sir, fine, come down here, and we'll be upstairs at the bar waiting for you. That way, we're not outside standing around waiting. If you don't mind, of course," said Jeff, now looking once again to John for some advice. However, none was forthcoming.

"No, not at all, then it's set. I'll be there within the half-hour," said Pete as the phone went dead.

"Damn it," yelled John. "Great! All of this work for the guy to have changed his mind. Unless, of course, this is all just a ruse, just to get you out of our hands? That somehow, he has this all figured out, and right from the beginning, this was a setup by him. What does he want with you two if that's the case? To send some message?

Unless this is real, and his going to England right after dinner is as well. Maybe our masked man has us all fooled. Maybe he is the shooter and is playing us all for his own enjoyment. Son of a bitch, get Luther on the phone, bring him in here now, and if he doesn't want to come inside because he's afraid of missing something, drag him in here," said John. Whose voice, for some reason, seemed to be rising in crescendo the more he spoke. With Luther's arrival and his being now fully informed of the new proceedings, Luther thought that maybe just Lars would show up. Walking around the office and holding his hand under his chin, Luther turned to John and said, "I think Lars is on his way here, right now. I think that this Winslow character is setting Lars up to be eliminated. Two reasons why I think this. First, it is to rid himself of the connection to the killings. Second, it is to have us either capture Lars or have a shootout with him. If we kill Lars, and I think that is what he is planning on, he is ahead. There is no way that Lars is going to be captured alive. Not here in America. That's for sure. The man could never languish for life in an American prison. He hates America. I think the meetings got mixed up on purpose. Had they been in Washington and been picked up, they still wouldn't have ended up in Alexandria. I don't know if they are targets or not, but I do have to think that Lars is on his way here. Do what you need to do here. I suppose you do have at least a small window of opportunity with him coming here. My group will take in Lars when he shows up, not to worry, we will not be shooting up this city."

John turned and looked at Luther after he had said that and replied, "Don't, Luther. I would hate to have to send someone to jail for the murder of an innocent passerby. After all, my people are just as eager to have him one way or the other as you are. But not to the tune of killing someone by accident. I can't have Günter shooting up Alexandria. I know we both understand that, and so do your men, right, Luther?"

"Yes, yes, of course, they have their orders and will follow them precisely. Now I have to go outside and be with my men. Thank you, John, for bringing us in on this, and as you say, no one wants to see anyone hurt today," said Luther as he extended his hand out to John.

John, seeing the gesture, just smiled and said, "No need to shake on it, Luther. We both know what you want, and good luck with that."

Juan watched as the black Mercedes pulled up next to the building and stopped. Coming out of the driver's door was a very large man, and of course, he had on his blue jeans, wearing a brown corduroy sports coat over the top. The coat looked large enough to house a couple of small people under it. Juan hoped like hell he wouldn't have to confront that guy. This giant of a man had to bend down in order to reach the door handle. Maybe the car was lowered for some reason, thought Juan. As the door opened, Pete Winslow exited from the car's back passenger door and began walking toward the front of the building. Instead of coming directly to the limo as he was told that was how it was done each time.

Juan turned and said, "Talk to me, Jake, why isn't the man walking to us? Was there some sort of signal you failed to give?"

"No, no signal! I have no idea as to why he walked into the building right now, believe me I don't," said Jake.

"Okay, here's the deal, this I press from twenty yards out and you're dead, Jake. So, I'm going to get out of the limo and go to the side of the building and wait in case you're lying to me. If you're not, when your boss walks out, don't pull away from the curb. I'll come and tap on the window and you just open the door. If you don't, Jake, then the both of you can rot in hell tonight."

With that, Juan opened the door and got out low against the limo, making sure that no one looking from that side of the building would get a clear shot at him. Walking quickly to the building's corner, he turned and waved at Jake, who sat looking at him as a guppy in a fishbowl. Hoping against all that, nothing was going to go wrong tonight. He wanted to be home tonight, he thought to himself.

Pete needed to stop inside to make sure that nothing was wrong. That one inside, he would find those two meatheads were there, and they could quickly explain themselves to him. But when he found out that they had not called or shown up, he became concerned that maybe his tag didn't happen. Or his men no longer would play the game.

"Darby," he said, looking at the man sitting behind the desk. "I need you to find out what the hell happened to those two. Find out and call me on the cell immediately when you do. Also, I want to begin the distraction in Alexandria, get our men inside, and at the tables. When I walk down those stairs, make it look good. No one is to get hurt in the restaurant except the shooter. Then just shake up the place a little. As soon as I walk down those steps, make it all happen. I'll be long gone when the smoke clears. Take the plaster off the ceiling with enough rounds to make it hard for anyone in there to hear for days.

Right now, I'll drive down there and get those two. By the time the third gets the message that she needs to come and collect them, it'll be too late. Tonight, all of them will be on a long ride to hell. Darby, only you know what the shooter looks like. When he shows up, kill the bastard. End this nightmare right there and then. I'm sure he'll think some kind of trap is inside for him, so he'll hesitate before he comes in. But just as soon as he hears shooting, he'll make a move. Instead of me being in there, I'll be gone. You just make sure he doesn't leave the place alive.

I'll call you and Big Tommy later. Pick me up and we'll all fly out to Mexico and lie on the beach for a couple of days and relax a bit. On the company, which always sounds nice, right?" With that, he turned and hit Big Tommy on the shoulders, and pulling him aside out of range for anyone to overhear him, he said, "Hold down the fort, Tommy, make sure that these guys get it right. This mission is too important to this company for it to all go down the crapper tonight."

"No problem, boss, by the time we get on that plane, no one will be alive to tell anyone about anything. I'll make sure of that," Big Tommy said with a smile. Big Tommy's job tonight was to make sure that none of them would see the light of day when they all came back to finalize the evening's antics. This mission was over. Ended. As no one other than he, the boss, and Darby had any clue about the happy ending he had in store for tonight's survivors. What they couldn't afford was someone who needed more money at the end of the project to possibly talk to be alive. No one would be alive to make that request, thought Big Tommy. He liked how mass killing made it more enjoyable for him, rather than just one kill and going home. He remembered his last really great day in Bosnia. Oh, if only he could find a genocide war like that one again.

Turning away from Tommy, Pete walked down the stairs and opened the front door. It was there that he died instantly. If he had any thoughts considering who had done this, they came as his soul rose to meet its maker. The shot took him in the head and blew it apart. It dangled from his neck, cut almost in half. The bullet that hit him came from a rooftop fifteen hundred feet away, and it was a fifty-caliber rifle that sent the message of "tag, you're it."

The bullet lifted his body backward, slamming him backward into the hallway, his body crashing against the steps. It was astonishing to Jake that the whole place wasn't emptying right now. But for Jake, he had no idea as to what to do now. Seeing how he in no way could move while sitting on C4. Rolling down the window and pointing to the doorway, he yelled,

"Holy shit, did you see that! The man is dead, half his friggen head is lying in the hallway. I watched it explode!"

"Get out of the car now, Jake," yelled Juan. For Juan knew who it was that had made that shot. He also knew that one bird was now gone, and the other one was coming home to roost. But from where? From what direction was the shooter? The shot had taken Winslow directly in the frontal skull area right above the eyes. Juan had enough time to see the door open as Winslow's head disappeared before it could move through the entire door frame. Thus, he caught a glance of the jerking reaction to being slammed by such a force. Turning now to face the car once again, Juan yelled at Jake. "Jake, get out of the car now! Crawl over to me. Use the limo as a shield."

The second shot Günter took was on a full run. Having just slid down the fire escape of the building, he used to target and kill the little man who bored him. The next shot took Jake in the side of his head as if he were threading a big needle with a rope. Jake's head exploded from the impact, and Juan wanted for the first time in his life to suddenly become invisible. However, his years of training allowed him to make it behind some dumpsters, not more than ten yards off to his left. Juan dropped to the ground to discover which way the set of feet would be moving toward him. But instead of looking for him, they simply went to the front door as all hell broke loose.

Günter threw the two smoke grenades into the room at the top of the stairs. Then he opened fire as he ran up the stairs. Racking the M4 back and forth as it threw out enough death to keep everyone upset and moving. At the top of the stairs, he threw three grenades, one for each wall as he continued firing from a prone position, lying at the side of the stairwell. Making sure that everyone in there would be too occupied now with trying to find him. Trying very hard right now with staying alive to have noticed the grenades before they could go off. The grenades did their job. Making everyone in there, to start screaming from shrapnel cuts. When the floor began collapsing to fall below. Leaning against the right side of the room.

Günter then changed weapons as he threw a flash grenade into what was left of the room. This time, he had his favorite two pistols. His twin Thirty-Eight Super's with the extended magazines taped back-to-back. This he used to provide himself with thirty beautiful rounds in each magazine. Giving him sixty rounds to end the commotion that he so enjoyed bringing to those he wanted to talk to in such a harsh way. As the second magazine was finished, he looked around the room, and to his satisfaction, no one moved; hell, no one was even moaning, which said to him, job well done.

Günter turned, and the first bullet took him square in the chest. Followed by three more, not centimeters apart. The impact drove him back against the far wall. Falling now on the floor, Günter reached down for the strength he had to find. Desperately, he threw his last grenade forward, followed by his patented flash grenade. Juan saw the black grenade and the flash can coming at him as he turned and dove backward and found the stairs to start his slide down. The impact of the grenade, however, had other plans for Juan as it lifted him up and threw him into the wall at the side of the stairwell. Crashing into the wall and feeling the searing pain that the grenade had left behind, Juan could only crawl now to safety. He knew he had to set up a position to return the fire. Fire, he was sure to come. But when he heard nothing but silence, it was quickly followed by more silence. He crawled out from his hiding position, ever so weary as to make sure that he didn't give himself away in this cat-and-mouse wait. But when there was no response, he got up and limped around the room, looking to see where the shooter lay. Nothing, no one was to be found. The damn man was a ghost. With all the carnage and destruction, the shooter had vanished. The man was in and out, creating enough damage to last anyone a lifetime. Juan knew he had to vacate as immediately as sirens filled the night air.

When Hell Freezes Over

Luther got the call and sat down in the front of his car, holding his head for a second, he then lifted it and screamed as loud as he could. Walking back into the restaurant, he found John and motioned for him to come to him. Then, sitting down as John approached him, he asked a passing agent if he would pour him a very large glass of brandy. Waiting for some explanation, John sat down across from Luther, and when none was forthcoming, he said, "Luther, what happened, don't tell me if it's bad, you have Lars, I didn't hear any shots, thank God, what exactly is happening out there?"

"I have just received a call from my contact, and I need you to contact the DC Metro. Apparently, our shooter showed up there at a Wetco building on Third Street and Bellaire. Where all hell has broken loose. Our man, Lars, killed Pete Winslow, shot him right in the head, about a thousand plus out, one shot. One shot, and then he killed the limo driver on the way in. Ran up the stairs, and between grenades and bullets, he murdered everyone."

Yelling now, he said, "Shot them all! The son of a bitch got away. Our man shot him four times in the chest. He threw a grenade back at him, and after the smoke cleared, the bastard had gone missing. How the hell has this happened?"

Turning and shouting out, John called out, "Penny, wrap it up and get me on the DC Metro line right now. I need to find out if they're responding to an incident at Third and Bellaire." Now excited and still shouting, he continued, "Everyone, clean up and let's move out. I'll meet everyone back at the barn. Brad, go and get Clara and meet me at the car. Susan, make sure that this is all cleaned and cleared, I'll see you at the barn. Jeff, you and Tully stay with Susan and wait for us back at the office. Do not go anywhere else, do not leave until I get there, understood?"

"Sure, fine, John. Go do what needs to be done, and we'll wait for you there," said Jeff. Turning now, he walked over to Tully and said, "I wonder if we can find any food here or maybe a piece of pie. I'm a little hungry right now."

"All you ever think about is food, especially pie, but ya know, I'm hungry now as well. So, let's go and look." With that, they walked into the back to find someone who could make them something to eat.

Clara was beside herself when she found out that tonight. Pete Winslow was dead. With the shooter, this Lars Günter Mellon, gone, gone into the night as if he was invincible and invisible, that made her want his life in her hands now even more. He had killed her grandparents, her future husband, and others who should still be alive. Tired and still angry when she got to the car with Brad, she couldn't hold back the tears of anger as she said, "That bastard was shot four times by the masked man, and he walked away? What the hell do we have to do to kill the bastard!"

"Calm down, Clara," said Brad as he put his arms around her shoulders. "We'll find the man he's been shot, and there is nowhere he can go. He needs aid, but has nowhere to get it. He'll show up someplace half dead, and we'll nail his ass to the cross."

Luther walked over to the car and asked if they had room for one more. John looked at the man and had to wonder if he would ever be the same after tonight. Everything that he had planned on seemed to have fallen apart tonight, and you could almost sense the disappointment in his stance.

"Sure, we have plenty of room. We're going over to the crime scene now. Metro police said that your man was right. There are bodies all over the place, and one of them just happens to be Winslow. Shot in the head as proclaimed, half the upper floor, as I understand it, is now lying on the first floor. The guy came in throwing grenades with guns blazing. I don't think he really cared who he hit. One guy is alive, slightly wounded, and scared out of his wits. The lucky bastard was in the crapper when all hell broke loose. Thank God he had enough sense to hide in the closet. Unfortunately for him, though, when the ceiling fell in, so did the closet. Right to the bottom of the first floor.

He's in protective custody, with a few broken ribs. When we get there, I'll tell Metro that we'll take him and find out as much as we can. But I have to ask once again, is there anything now that you're willing to say about our masked man? Maybe a name, description, something that can put him on our side, and if I need to hunt the man down, I have something to go on?"

"Let me say, this is when I hear from him again, I will ask him if it is okay," said Luther. Now grinning, he asked, "I hope this does not affect my chances of a ride there with you."

"No, not at all, get in and we can discuss this a little better as we go along," replied John.

Juan searched the entire area and found no clue as to how the man got away. All he knew was that now he had a better look at the shooter and would recognize him if and when they met again. Thankfully, he had on a disguise that night. If the shooter went looking for him, he could only hope that he looked like no one in the DC area. Then, as the sirens grew louder, he decided it was time to leave and make his own way back to his vehicle, where he would place a call to Luther to let him know what had happened that night.

Günter was angry. He should have first taken care of the guy hiding behind the trashcan before going upstairs. He was wrong to think that he was just another scared soldier in hiding. It must have been that very guy who had shot him before. Now. Again, possibly when he had just finished taking care of his business. But he got a good look at him, he thought, and he would hunt him down before he went home. But right now, he ached from those shots being right on top of the other. Even with his vest, it now felt as if he had some ribs cracked. They would be scouring the land for him, and he knew it would be soon, so right now, the most important thing for him was to contact the Russian embassy.

He had to see when he could catch the plane he was promised to New York. There, he could rest and recuperate for as long as he needed to. As he walked along the street going to his van, Günter placed the call and was told to meet his contact at the Thirtieth Street lot. With that completed, Günter was already feeling much better. Soon, he would be free from anyone suspecting that he had something to do with tonight. In New York, he would rest until he decided what to do next.

Juan called the general and was surprised to find out that he was back in Washington tonight. "What are you doing here?" he asked. Then, in a slightly harsher tone, he said, "I told you to stay away until this was cleared out and secured."

"Don't you worry about me? What has happened tonight? Is everything somewhat normal, or should I go and hide behind the Scotch bottle?" he laughed.

"No," said Juan, "don't hide, just be very careful. Right now, the shooter just killed fifteen men, including your pal's best friend. Took him down over a thousand out and, on the run, took down his limo driver. Then the damn bastard blew the hell out of the Wetco building on Third Street. Some place used for storage. Nothing left of the building or the people. His pet mustered up in it tonight. It was a clean slate; I had never seen one man create so much havoc and do so much damage in such a short period of time. That's why I'm saying I have no idea as to who is next on his list. It could very well be you. The only good news is I had four close-range hits millimeters apart. If he isn't lying dead someplace, then his ribs are broken and he hurts really badly. So, he may seek public aid, or maybe he has other contacts around here that can help him, so lie low and I'll be in touch."

With that said, Juan hung up the phone and placed another call to Luther.

The general heard the phone click dead and knew it was time for him to make a call he had dreaded to make. But he couldn't lounge around a villa in Mexico and play dumb as to what has taken place in Washington. Especially since he felt so damn bad about it starting on his watch.

The first thing yesterday, the general flew to Washington because, one way or the other, this had to stop. So, he placed a call to his friend Bob Thurston to maybe have a meeting with him and get this all to stop once and for all.

"Bob, how the hell are you?" he had asked Margate.

"I'll be damned, thought you disappeared with some young girl down to Mexico for a while. What has brought you back in the middle of the week? Don't tell me she left with a younger man?" he asked.

Then, with a slight chuckle in his voice, the general replied, "No, no, nothing like that. I just thought I would come up and have some of that brandy before it's all gone, or I'm dead and buried. One never knows just how long you'll live, right, Bob?"

"Beats the hell out of me anymore, say, why don't you come with me tonight? I have the plane ready to go to England. I have some guests coming, and we can go someplace, talk old times, and maybe get laid if we hold out long enough," he said, laughing into the phone.

But the general wasn't buying any of it. The humor was a way the old man often hid his anger, and Margate thought this was one of those times. But he had come back to put an end to things and to straighten out what part of this mess he could. So, he said, "Sure, exactly where are we to meet, Bob? Hell, my bags are still packed, and I can come right over. We can go where the sun is always shining when we're not there."

"I'll send over a limo for you. No sense in taking a cab there. That's why I have the damn limo. To use it," chimed in Bob, who was now thinking that maybe tonight he should just end this friendship. But then he thought, after fifty years or better, how could it have come down to this? No, he had said that if the man stopped his harassing daily calls and they could become friends again, then let the buzzard live. Hell, just how many years did he have left in him anyway? So, Bob said, "No, don't worry about the limo. Look for Hank to be there in about another half hour or so. See you at the airport."

Margate hung up the phone and placed the envelope on the table. In it were the instructions he'd leave behind for his attorney, on matters of the mind and heart. Tonight, he wasn't coming back home. He felt it deep in his bones. Like those days in the big war when he would sit up for hours the night before any big battle and seek an answer from God. When he asked him if he could please live just one more day, but tonight, he wouldn't be asking his God for anything. Except maybe to let him in for a few minutes to just see the place before he had to leave.

Now, he would call Juan and tell him of his departure. The man had been loyal and almost like the son he never had. So at least he can call and say goodbye, he thought. He could hear the cell ringing but there was no answer. After the second attempt, he decided to leave a message.

"Juan, it's Margate, Bob's limo driver is picking me up in about thirty minutes or so. I am supposed to meet the man at the airport, and we're flying off to England, supposedly. Who knows? Anyway, the reason why I am calling is that first, there is an envelope on the Scotch table alongside my favorite chair. Take it to the addressee for me and hang around. He has something to talk to you about. Then do me a personal favor, will you? The only table lamp in the private office at the club. Well, go in there some night late by yourself. You do know how to do that, right?"

A slight laugh would now be heard in the message.

"Lift the lamp up and turn it upside down. It'll open a private door. I believe the one you may have been searching for already, and enjoy some of the finest brandy left in the world. So, you know my intentions for tonight. I intend to kill Bob Thurston. He is the one who has set up and financed this entire charade and mess. He is a good man, Juan, but somewhere along the line, he left reality behind to become this horrific man. One that I never knew existed. He has brought in a specialist to kill those who have gotten in his way this time around, and I have to believe that I am on that list. Along with you, my friend. So, I will end it all tonight. It has been my pleasure to have served with you, and I leave this in your hands, my dear friend."

Margate hung up the phone and felt at peace. It had been a long time in coming. But finally, he no longer needed to ask the Lord to take care of him one more time. No, right now, as far as he was concerned, he wanted to shout out as loud as he could, "I'm coming home, Lord, finally."

When the limo pulled up in front of his house, Margate put down the finished glass of Scotch. Damn, he'll miss that, he thought, but his mind was made up, and he could see no other way out of this situation. Then to stop the man who started it, the driver walked around the limo and said, "Good evening, General. How are you tonight, sir?" Looking at Hank as if he was looking at a very old friend, and he was, he replied, "Hank, how long have I known you?"

"Well, sir, it's been about fifty years now, I guess. Why do you ask, if I may ask?" replied Hank with a now curious look on his face. Then he said, as he opened the door for Margate to enter the back of the vehicle, "What's the matter, General? Not feeling well tonight? By the time you get to England, whatever is upsetting you, sir, I'm sure will be gone."

"Let's hope so, Hank," he replied. "Let's hope so."

The ride to the airport was uneventful as General Thomas Margate, the last surviving four-star general from the Second World War, exited the limo with a very sad feeling.

Juan had heard the message and decided that he needed to take matters into his own hands before he lost a friend. Bob Thurston wasn't worth losing a friend over. He decided to take action to prevent that loss from occurring. Hopefully, it would also bear the truth and clear him in all of these doings. "Luther, it's me. Can we talk safely?" he asked.

"Yes, I'm in the car with the FBI now; we're leaving the scene as we talk. What can I do for you?" he asked.

"I have a situation about ready to start. Bob Thurston is about to meet my contact, who did the hiring of the shooter, and that's the rub. Right now, in about half an hour or so, it'll go down."

"Where and how do I say to our friends how I know this?" Luther asked.

Juan had a throwaway, and there was no way the call could be traced, so he said. "Tell them that I called just now, and when I hang up the phone, it can't be traced. Explain to them that the shooter could be boarding a Wetco plane in about twenty minutes with Bob Thurston on board. Luther could possibly be taking him out of the country. Maybe Europe, who knows for sure, but I need to get there to protect my man. This is why I called you. It is all going down right now as we speak," he finished.

"What airport is he leaving from?" he asked Juan.

"On the opposite side of Dulles is a private runway set aside for private commercial jets. They have a hangar there, so I'm sure that's where they intend to leave from. Have your new friends call the tower, have them stop the plane from taking off, and of course, do not have them alert anyone. But damn it, hold up that plane. You have to do it now, Luther. I'm on my way there as we speak," said Juan as he then hung up the phone and turned on his phony siren. Sounding as if he were an unmarked metro cop chasing down the highway.

Luther couldn't get the words out fast enough to explain to everyone about the phone call that he had just received.

"Are you certain of this guy's credibility?" asked John. "We both spent a lot of time, effort, and money on making sure that we got our marks tonight, yet it all went to crap. It turns out he shows up at a warehouse, killing everyone he can find, and now he's on his way out of town in a company jet, an H.T. Wetco company jet. Oh, did I mention that your masked marvel just happened to be there when it went down at the warehouse?"

This time, in a much higher voice, somewhat strained, John asked Luther, "What makes you think we can trust this information?"

"Because he also wants to protect a friend of his, the man who gave him all of the information," said Luther in a voice that reeked of desperation. "The one that had him research everyone. He's going there as well to meet up with Bob Thurston. Their destination is England from this attached private runway at Dulles. Can we get there now, please? Just bear this one out; we can't keep coming up empty," pleaded Luther, who desperately wanted to be there if Lars was getting on a plane, any plane. This could become the last time he had a shot at the man, and he wanted it.

As if reading his mind, Clara said, "John, if this is our last chance or not, we need to take it now. Especially, we know that this Thurston was in fact the man who hired Günter. It's just too important to turn away from."

"Turn the car north, get to Dulles as fast as you can, Brad," John said to Brad, who was now driving."

Picking up his phone, he called Dulles and had them connect him to the tower that was dispatching private planes from there. "This is FBI Agent John Bloso. This is emergency ID number fifteen. I say again, fifteen. Do you understand?" he asked the person on the other end of the phone.

"Yes, sir, I do," was the reply.

"Okay, then, there is a plane owned by H.T. Wetco about to depart from your area. Are you aware of this? If so, I need you to contact them and hold them up. Tell them the departure avenue is loaded, and they will have to wait for clearance. Do you understand this?" he asked.

Again, the reply was, "Yes, sir, I do. However, I have to say that they have already requested this tower for clearance, and we gave it to them. But they are still parked on the macadam at this juncture. I'll make that call now and tell them that there is a holdup. Can I ask, sir, what your ETA is?" he asked.

"We're about ten minutes out, but I will need to assess the situation upon arrival, so keep them there for at least half an hour, do you have that?"

"Yes, sir, thirty minutes or more to departure, and how will I know it was enough time for you to get here and assess the situation?" he asked.

"If I am not on-site in ten minutes, I'll call you back. Now hold up that plane," said John. Now driving as fast as he could, Brad made for the airport. It was a good thing he was driving because he knew how to get there. His dad used the airport often to take him and his family away on vacations in the Wetco company plane.

Juan raced to the gate and turned off his siren miles back to not alert anyone to his coming. Suppose the old man thought that he was getting out of this that easily, well, no way. He had become fond of the general and didn't want to see him end up a number in what had become a numbers game. Parking the car along the side of a hangar, Juan crept around until he could see the jet with its lights flashing into the night. He had done what he thought he could do, and that was to beat the limo to the airport. Sliding into a position that would allow him the view of the open plane's door, he then turned to make sure that he would not be taken from behind. Moving slightly to his left and taking a new position behind some empty crates, he sat and waited for the limo.

Prior to the limo pulling up, the jet's engines shut down. From out the front door but not coming down the stairs was the old man that Juan had seen on so many other occasions, Mr. Bob Thurston. The entire misery that so many families have gone through lay at the feet of this individual, standing there as if he ruled the world. The more that Juan wanted to shoot and to just end it all, the more he knew that the man was the only key to his and the general's salvation. Juan got the thought of killing the bastard quickly out of his head as the limo pulled up and stopped. The driver got out, walked around the car, and opened the door for his passenger to exit. Exiting from the car and standing as tall as Juan had ever seen was General Margate, his friend.

"I'd take your bags to the plane if you had any," Hank said to the general with a smile.

"Not to worry, Hank, tonight I won't be needing any," he replied.

Just then, Thurston waved to the general and said, "No bags. Why? Are you going to buy all new clothes in London, General?"

"No, I don't know if I'll ever see that place again, Bob," he said as he looked his old friend in the face.

Taken somewhat aback, Bob said, "What the hell are you talking about? Why, we're headed there tonight."

"Maybe so, but I don't think I'm going anywhere," was his reply.

"So that's it, huh? You came all the way here to say it's over? After all we have been through. You come here tonight to say goodbye! You son of a bitch. Why, because I protected what was mine, what I worked so damn hard for. Is that it? You honestly don't think that I would have you waltz in here like some marshal and stop me from doing what I want. Hell, no, you old coot, hell no. Shit, I'm liable to kill your dumb ass tonight myself, you make me so damn mad. Do you know I have made you! What you are I made you, damn it! Not someone else! It was me that made sure that you got those last two stars, me! I had them give them to you because I could. That's how much power I have. And now you want me just to stop this. As if my company's not worthy of me. To hell with you, I say, shoot the bastard, Hank, and let's go to England."

Before anyone shot anyone, the general had his beloved 1911A1 out and in his hands, but before he could shoot and blow them all to hell, Juan shot Hank twice in the chest, dropping him to the ground like a sack of rocks falling from the sky. As the general turned to see who had done the shooting, he took a slug to his left shoulder, knocking him back against the limo. Juan fired two shots into the plane's doorframe. The last thing he wanted was to hit the fuselage and cause any potential eruptions or fuel leaks that could burn them all to hell. Yet it was enough to make Thurston jump back into the plane for cover. This allowed Juan to rush over to the general's aid.

Smiling down at him, he lifted him off the ground and then said, "Let's get the hell out of here. I think the cavalry is coming right about now."

Juan could hear the sirens fill the air as the black Lincoln pulled into the yard and slammed on its brakes enough to turn it sideways to the front of the jet. Jumping out of the car were three FBI agents and Luther. All with weapons being drawn. Surrounding the plane, they ordered the pilots to leave the cockpit and to come out of the plane. That's when Bob Thurston came to the door and opened fire on the agents. His surprise attack allowed him to shoot Brad in the right shoulder, knocking him to the ground. John returned fire at the attacker and forced him back into the plane. As seconds passed, suddenly, a gun was thrown from the plane, and the first of two pilots came forward, yelling.

"Don't shoot, don't shoot, we have him down, and there's the gun."

"Walk backward down the stairs, both of you, with your hands held high in the air, now!" yelled John.

As the pilots walked down the stairs backward, they left behind an unconscious old man lying on the floor of a fifteen-million-dollar plane. Rushing into the plane to see if a passenger was hiding, Luther found no one aboard. Lying there was Bob Thurston. Outside were two pilots and one dead limo driver named Hank.

In the commotion of stopping the plane and Thurston's shooting spree, it allowed Juan to take the general by the arm and lead him to the side of the building. Shimming a side door open, he walked the general into the area, sat him down in a corner, and said, "Stay put this time, will you, please? I'll be back to get you later." With that, he departed, found his way back to his car, and sped off into the night. The general had no idea as to why there was a need now for secrecy. He ached, and the wound was still bleeding a little. Even if it was just a minor flesh wound, hell, he didn't even think that Bob had a gun. He couldn't remember Bob ever firing one in his presence. It's no wonder the old man couldn't shoot him dead. He had no idea as to how to shoot. Laughing to himself now, he heard the door to the hangar he was hidden in open. He watched silently as a figure walked over to where he lay hidden and said,

"Come with me. You're safe now. My name is Luther. I think we need to talk."

The only way Juan knew it would now work out for him was to have Luther take the old man in. That way, he and Thurston could yell at each other and contradict one another or just come clean. He had faith in the general to do the right thing now. He also knew that he was still alive, and that counted for a lot. The two of them would each hire the best attorneys out there and argue in court the merits of trying to find the right reason to kill people. But for now, he was sure that the general would more than clear his name and help them enough that all charges against him would be dropped for turning state evidence.

He had asked Luther to make sure of that for him. He also made a promise to Luther that he would track down the shooter if it took the rest of his life.

The End.